Praise for #1 *New York Times* bestselling author

NORA ROBERTS

"Nora Roberts is among the best."
—*The Washington Post*

"Roberts has a warm feel for her characters and an eye for the evocative detail."
—*Chicago Tribune*

"Roberts' bestselling novels are some of the best in the romance genre. They are thoughtfully plotted, well-written stories featuring fascinating characters."
—*USA TODAY*

"When Roberts puts her expert fingers on the pulse of romance, legions of fans feel the heartbeat."
—*Publishers Weekly*

"With clear-eyed, concise vision and a sure pen, Roberts nails her characters and settings with awesome precision, drawing readers into a vividly rendered world of family-centered warmth and unquestionable magic."
—*Library Journal*

"Her stories have fueled the dreams of twenty-five million readers."
—*Entertainment Weekly*

Also available from Silhouette Books
and Harlequin Books by

NORA ROBERTS

THE MacGREGOR GROOMS: Three Passionate Proposals
The meddling, matchmaking MacGregor patriarch
is at it again!

SOMEDAY WITH YOU
A second chance to embrace life and discover love

A PLACE TO CALL HOME
A solid foundation makes for a lasting love story

MacGREGOR EVER AFTER
When it's meant to be, love always finds a way

SECRET GETAWAY
Diamonds can be a girl's best friend—or her worst enemy...

WRITTEN IN THE STARS
Fairytale magic can charm the most stubborn heart

For the full list of titles by Nora Roberts,
please visit www.noraroberts.com.

NORA ROBERTS

WEATHER THE STORM

Includes *The Welcoming* & *Without a Trace*

 Silhouette Books

SILHOUETTE™

Recycling programs
for this product may
not exist in your area.

Weather the Storm

ISBN-13: 978-1-335-45280-1

Copyright © 2023 by Harlequin Enterprises ULC

The Welcoming
First published in 1989. This edition published in 2023.
Copyright © 1989 by Nora Roberts

Without a Trace
First published in 1990. This edition published in 2023.
Copyright © 1990 by Nora Roberts

For questions and comments about the quality of this book, please contact us
at CustomerService@Harlequin.com.

Silhouette
22 Adelaide St. West, 41st Floor
Toronto, Ontario M5H 4E3, Canada
www.Harlequin.com

Printed in U.S.A.

CONTENTS

THE WELCOMING

For my friend Catherine Coulter,
because she's always good for a laugh.

Chapter 1

Everything he needed was in the backpack slung over his shoulders. Including his .38. If things went well he would have no use for it.

Roman drew a cigarette out of the crumpled pack in his breast pocket and turned away from the wind to light it. A boy of about eight raced along the rail of the ferry, cheerfully ignoring his mother's calls. Roman felt a tug of empathy for the kid. It was cold, certainly. The biting wind off Puget Sound was anything but spring-like. But it was one hell of a view. Sitting in the glass-walled lounge would be cozier, but it was bound to take something away from the experience.

The kid was snatched by a blonde woman with pink cheeks and a rapidly reddening nose. Roman listened to them grumble at each other as she dragged the boy back inside. Families, he thought, rarely agreed on anything.

Turning away, he leaned over the rail, lazily smoking as the ferry steamed by clumpy islands.

They had left the Seattle skyline behind, though the mountains of mainland Washington still rose up to amaze and impress the viewer. There was an aloneness here, despite the smattering of hardy passengers walking the slanting deck or bundling up in the patches of sunlight along wooden benches. He preferred the city, with its pace, its crowds, its energy. Its anonymity. He always had. For the life of him, he couldn't understand where this restless discontent he felt had come from, or why it was weighing so heavily on him.

The job. For the past year he'd been blaming it on the job. The pressure was something he'd always accepted, even courted. He'd always thought life without it would be bland and pointless. But just lately it hadn't been enough. He moved from place to place, taking little away, leaving less behind.

Time to get out, he thought as he watched a fishing boat chug by. Time to move on. And do what? he wondered in disgust, blowing out a stream of smoke. He could go into business for himself. He'd toyed with that notion a time or two. He could travel. He'd already been around the world, but it might be different to do it as a tourist.

Some brave soul came out on deck with a video camera. Roman turned, shifted, eased out of range. It was in all likelihood an unnecessary precaution; the move was instinctive. So was the watchfulness, and so was the casual stance, which hid a wiry readiness.

No one paid much attention to him, though a few of the women looked twice.

He was just over average height, with the taut, solid

build of a lightweight boxer. The slouchy jacket and worn jeans hid well-toned muscles. He wore no hat and his thick black hair flew freely away from his tanned, hollow-cheeked face. It was unshaven, tough-featured. The eyes, a pale, clear green, might have softened the go-to-hell appearance, but they were intense, direct and, at the moment, bored.

It promised to be a slow, routine assignment.

Roman heard the docking call and shifted his pack. Routine or not, the job was his. He would get it done, file his report, then take a few weeks to figure out what he wanted to do with the rest of his life.

He disembarked with the smattering of other walking passengers. There was a wild, sweet scent of flowers now that competed with the darker scent of the water. The flowers grew in free, romantic splendor, many with blossoms as big as his fist. Some part of him appreciated their color and their charm, but he rarely took the time to stop and smell the roses.

Cars rolled off the ramp and cruised toward home or a day of sightseeing. Once the car decks were unloaded, the new passengers would board and set off for one of the other islands or for the longer, colder trip to British Columbia.

Roman pulled out another cigarette, lit it and took a casual look around—at the pretty, colorful gardens, the charming white hotel and restaurant, the signs that gave information on ferries and parking. It was all a matter of timing now. He ignored the patio café, though he would have dearly loved a cup of coffee, and wound his way to the parking area.

He spotted the van easily enough, the white-and-blue American model with Whale Watch Inn painted on the

side. It was his job to talk himself onto the van and into
the inn. If the details had been taken care of on this end,
it would be routine. If not, he would find another way.

Stalling, he bent down to tie his shoe. The waiting
cars were being loaded, and the foot passengers were
already on deck. There were no more than a dozen ve-
hicles in the parking area now, including the van. He
was taking another moment to unbutton his jacket when
he saw the woman.

Her hair was pulled back in a braid, not loose as it
had been in the file picture. It seemed to be a deeper,
richer blond in the sunlight. She wore tinted glasses,
big-framed amber lenses that obscured half of her face,
but he knew he wasn't mistaken. He could see the delicate line of her jaw, the small, straight nose, the full,
shapely mouth.

His information was accurate. She was five-five, a
hundred and ten pounds, with a small, athletic build.
Her dress was casual—jeans, a chunky cream-colored
cable-knit sweater over a blue shirt. The shirt would
match her eyes. The jeans were tucked into suede ankle
boots, and a pair of slim crystal earrings dangled at
her ears.

She walked with a sense of purpose, keys jingling in
one hand, a big canvas bag slung over her other shoulder. There was nothing flirtatious about the walk, but
a man would notice it. Long, limber strides, a subtle
swing at the hips, head up, eyes ahead.

Yeah, a man would notice, Roman thought as he
flicked the cigarette away. He figured she knew it.

He waited until she reached the van before he started
toward her.

Charity stopped humming the finale of Beethoven's

Ninth, looked down at her right front tire and swore. Because she didn't think anyone was watching, she kicked it, then moved around to the back of the van to get the jack.

"Got a problem?"

She jolted, nearly dropped the jack on her foot, then whirled around.

A tough customer. That was Charity's first thought as she stared at Roman. His eyes were narrowed against the sun. He had one hand hooked around the strap of his backpack and the other tucked in his pocket. She put her own hand on her heart, made certain it was still beating, then smiled.

"Yes. I have a flat. I just dropped a family of four off for the ferry, two of whom were under six and candidates for reform school. My nerves are shot, the plumbing's on the fritz in unit 6, and my handyman just won the lottery. How are you?"

The file hadn't mentioned that she had a voice like café au lait, the rich, dark kind you drank in New Orleans. He noted that, filed it away, then nodded toward the flat. "Want me to change it?"

Charity could have done it herself, but she wasn't one to refuse help when it was offered. Besides, he could probably do it faster, and he looked as though he could use the five dollars she would give him.

"Thanks." She handed him the jack, then dug a lemon drop out of her bag. The flat was bound to eat up the time she'd scheduled for lunch. "Did you just come in on the ferry?"

"Yeah." He didn't care for small talk, but he used it, and her friendliness, as handily as he used the jack. "I've been doing some traveling. Thought I'd spend some time on Orcas, see if I can spot some whales."

"You've come to the right place. I saw a pod yesterday from my window." She leaned against the van, enjoying the sunlight. As he worked, she watched his hands. Strong, competent, quick. She appreciated someone who could do a simple job well. "Are you on vacation?"

"Just traveling. I pick up odd jobs here and there. Know anyone looking for help?"

"Maybe." Lips pursed, she studied him as he pulled off the flat. He straightened, keeping one hand on the tire. "What kind of work?"

"This and that. Where's the spare?"

"Spare?" Looking into his eyes for more than ten seconds was like being hypnotized.

"Tire." The corner of his mouth quirked slightly in a reluctant smile. "You need one that isn't flat."

"Right. The spare." Shaking her head at her own foolishness, she went to get it. "It's in the back." She turned and bumped into him. "Sorry."

He put one hand on her arm to steady her. They stood for a moment in the sunlight, frowning at each other. "It's all right. I'll get it."

When he climbed into the van, Charity blew out a long, steadying breath. Her nerves were more ragged than she'd have believed possible. "Oh, watch out for the—" She grimaced as Roman sat back on his heels and peeled the remains of a cherry lollipop from his knee. Her laugh was spontaneous and as rich as her voice. "Sorry. A souvenir of Orcas Island from Jimmy 'The Destroyer' MacCarthy, a five-year-old delinquent."

"I'd rather have a T-shirt."

"Yes, well, who wouldn't?" Charity took the sticky mess from him, wrapped it in a tattered tissue and dropped it into her bag. "We're a family establishment," she explained as he climbed out with the spare. "Mostly everyone enjoys having children around, but once in a while you get a pair like Jimmy and Judy, the twin ghouls from Walla Walla, and you think about turning the place into a service station. Do you like children?"

He glanced up as he slipped the tire into place. "From a safe distance."

She laughed appreciatively at his answer. "Where are you from?"

"St. Louis." He could have chosen a dozen places. He couldn't have said why he'd chosen to tell the truth. "But I don't get back much."

"Family?"

"No."

The way he said it made her stifle her innate curiosity. She wouldn't invade anyone's privacy any more than she would drop the lint-covered lollipop on the ground. "I was born right here on Orcas. Every year I tell myself I'm going to take six months and travel. Anywhere." She shrugged as he tightened the last of the lug nuts. "I never seem to manage it. Anyway, it's beautiful here. If you don't have a deadline, you may find yourself staying longer than you planned."

"Maybe." He stood up to replace the jack. "If I can find some work, and a place to stay."

Charity didn't consider it an impulse. She had studied, measured and considered him for nearly fifteen minutes. Most job interviews took little more. He had a strong back and intelligent—if disconcerting—eyes, and if the state of his pack and his shoes was any indication he was down on his luck. As her name implied, she had been taught to offer people a helping hand. And if she could solve one of her more immediate and pressing problems at the same time...

"You any good with your hands?" she asked him.

He looked at her unable to prevent his mind from taking a slight detour. "Yeah. Pretty good."

Her brow—and her blood pressure—rose a little when she saw his quick survey. "I mean with tools. Hammer, saw, screwdriver. Can you do any carpentry, household repairs?"

"Sure." It was going to be easy, almost too easy. He wondered why he felt the small, unaccustomed tug of guilt.

"Like I said, my handyman won the lottery, a big one. He's gone to Hawaii to study bikinis and eat poi. I'd wish him well, except we were in the middle of renovating the west wing. Of the inn," she added, pointing to the logo on the van. "If you know your way around two-by-fours and drywall I can give you room and board and five an hour."

"Sounds like we've solved both our problems."

"Great." She offered a hand. "I'm Charity Ford."

"DeWinter." He clasped her hand. "Roman DeWinter."

"Okay, Roman." She swung her door open. "Climb aboard."

She didn't look gullible, Roman thought as he settled into the seat beside her. But then, he knew—better than most—that looks were deceiving. He was exactly where he wanted to be, and he hadn't had to resort to a song and dance. He lit a cigarette as she pulled out of the parking lot.

"My grandfather built the inn in 1938," she said,

rolling down her window. "He added on to it a couple of times over the years, but it's still really an inn. We can't bring ourselves to call it a resort, even in the brochures. I hope you're looking for remote."

"That suits me."

"Me too. Most of the time." Talkative guy, she mused with a half smile. But that was all right. She could talk enough for both of them. "It's early in the season yet, so we're a long way from full." She cocked her elbow on the opened window and cheerfully took over the bulk of the conversation. The sunlight played on her earrings and refracted into brilliant colors. "You should have plenty of free time to knock around. The view from Mount Constitution's really spectacular. Or, if you're into it, the hiking trails are great."

"I thought I might spend some time in B.C."

"That's easy enough. Take the ferry to Sidney. We do pretty well with tour groups going back and forth."

"We?"

"The inn. Pop—my grandfather—built a half-dozen cabins in the sixties. We give a special package rate to tour groups. They can rent the cabins and have breakfast and dinner included. They're a little rustic, but the tourists really go for them. We get a group about once a week. During the season we can triple that."

She turned onto a narrow, winding road and kept the speed at fifty.

Roman already knew the answers, but he knew it might seem odd if he didn't ask the questions. "Do you run the inn?"

"Yeah. I've worked there on and off for as long as I can remember. When my grandfather died a couple of years ago I took over." She paused a moment. It still hurt; she supposed it always would. "He loved it. Not just the place, but the whole idea of meeting new people every day, making them comfortable, finding out about them."

"I guess it does pretty well."

She shrugged. "We get by." They rounded a bend where the forest gave way to a wide expanse of blue water. The curve of the island was clear, jutting out and tucking back in contrasting shades of deep green and brown. A few houses were tucked high in the cliffs beyond. A boat with billowing white sails ran with the wind, rippling the glassy water. "There are views like this all around the island. Even when you live here they dazzle you."

"And scenery's good for business."

She frowned a little. "It doesn't hurt," she said, and glanced back at him. "Are you really interested in seeing whales?"

"It seemed like a good idea since I was here."

She stopped the van and pointed to the cliffs. "If you've got patience and a good set of binoculars, up there's a good bet. We've spotted them from the inn, as I said. Still, if you want a close look, your best bet's out on a boat." When he didn't comment, she started the van again. He was making her jittery, she realized. He seemed to be looking not at the water or the forest but at her.

Roman glanced at her hands. Strong, competent, no-nonsense hands, he decided, though the fingers were beginning to tap a bit nervously on the wheel. She continued to drive fast, steering the van easily through the switchbacks. Another car approached. Without slackening speed, Charity lifted a hand in a salute.

"That was Lori, one of our waitresses. She works an early shift so she can be home when her kids get back from school. We usually run with a staff of ten, then add on five or six part-time during the summer."

They rounded the next curve, and the inn came into view. It was exactly what he'd expected, and yet it was more charming than the pictures he'd been shown. It was white clapboard, with weathered blue trim around arched and oval windows. There were fanciful turrets, narrow walkways and a wide skirting porch. A sweep of lawn led directly to the water, where a narrow, rickety dock jutted out. Tied to it was a small motorboat that swung lazily in the current.

A mill wheel turned in a shallow pond at the side of the inn, slapping the water musically. To the west, where the trees began to thicken, he could make out one of the cabins she had spoken of. Flowers were everywhere.

"There's a bigger pond out back." Charity drove around the side and pulled into a small graveled lot that was already half full. "We keep the trout there. The trail takes you to cabins 1, 2 and 3. Then it forks off to 4, 5 and 6." She stepped out and waited for him to join her. "Most everyone uses the back entrance. I can show you around the grounds later, if you like, but we'll get you settled in first."

"It's a nice place." He said it almost without thinking, and he meant it. There were two rockers on the square back porch, and an adirondack chair that needed its white paint freshened. Roman turned to study the view a guest would overlook from the empty seat. Part forest, part water, and very appealing. Restful. Welcoming. He thought of the pistol in his backpack. Appearances, he thought again, were deceiving.

With a slight frown, Charity watched him. He didn't seem to be looking so much as absorbing. It was an odd thought, but she would have sworn if anyone were to ask him to describe the inn six months later he would be able to, right down to the last pinecone.

Then he turned to her, and the feeling remained, more personal now, more intense. The breeze picked up, jingling the wind chimes that hung from the eaves.

"Are you an artist?" she asked abruptly.

"No." He smiled, and the change in his face was quick and charming. "Why?"

"Just wondering." You'd have to be careful of that smile, Charity decided. It made you relax, and she doubted he was a man it was wise to relax around.

The double glass doors opened up into a large, airy room that smelled of lavender and woodsmoke. There were two long, cushiony sofas and a pair of overstuffed chairs near a huge stone fireplace where logs crackled. Antiques were scattered throughout the room—a desk and chair with a trio of old inkwells, an oak hatrack, a buffet with glossy carved doors. Tucked into a corner was a spinet with yellowing keys and the pair of wide arched windows that dominated the far wall made the water seem part of the room's decor. At a table near them, two women were playing a leisurely game of Scrabble.

"Who's winning today?" Charity asked.

Both looked up. And beamed. "It's neck and neck." The woman on the right fluffed her hair when she spotted Roman. She was old enough to be his grandmother, but she slipped her glasses off and straightened her thin shoulders. "I didn't realize you were bringing back another guest, dear."

"Neither did I." Charity moved over to add another log to the fire. "Roman DeWinter, Miss Lucy and Miss Millie."

His smile came again, smoothly. "Ladies."

"DeWinter." Miss Lucy put on her glasses to get a better look. "Didn't we know a DeWinter once, Millie?"

"Not that I recall." Millie, always ready to flirt, continued to beam at Roman, though he was hardly more than a myopic blur. "Have you been to the inn before, Mr. DeWinter?"

"No, ma'am. This is my first time in the San Juans."

"You're in for a treat." Millie let out a little sigh. It was really too bad what the years did. It seemed only yesterday that handsome young men had kissed her hand and asked her to go for a walk. Today they called her ma'am. She went wistfully back to her game.

"The ladies have been coming to the inn longer than I can remember," Charity told Roman as she led the way down a hall. "They're lovely, but I should warn you about Miss Millie. I'm told she had quite a reputation in her day, and she still has an eye for an attractive man."

"I'll watch my step."

"I get the impression you usually do." She took out a set of keys and unlocked the door. "This leads to the west wing." She started down another hall, brisk, businesslike. "As you can see, renovations were well under way before George hit the jackpot. The trim's been stripped." She gestured to the neat piles of wood along the freshly painted wall. "The doors need to be refinished yet, and the original hardware's in that box."

After taking off her sunglasses, she dropped them into her bag. He'd been right. The collar of her shirt matched her eyes almost exactly. He looked into them as she examined George's handiwork.

"How many rooms?"

"There are two singles, a double and a family suite in this wing, all in varying stages of disorder." She skirted a door that was propped against a wall, then walked into a room. "You can take this one. It's as close to being finished as I have in this section."

It was a small, bright room. Its window was bordered with stained glass and looked out over the mill wheel. The bed was stripped, and the floors were bare and in need of sanding. Wallpaper that was obviously new covered the walls from the ceiling down to a white chair rail. Below that was bare drywall.

"It doesn't look like much now," Charity commented.

"It's fine." He'd spent time in places that made the little room look like a suite at the Waldorf.

Automatically she checked the closet and the adjoining bath, making a mental list of what was needed. "You can start in here, if it'll make you more comfortable. I'm not particular. George had his own system. I never understood it, but he usually managed to get things done."

He hooked his thumbs in the front pockets of his jeans. "You got a game plan?"

"Absolutely."

Charity spent the next thirty minutes taking him through the wing and explaining exactly what she wanted. Roman listened, commenting little, and studied the setup. He knew from the blueprints he'd studied that the floor plan of this section mirrored that of the east wing. His position in it would give him easy access to the main floor and the rest of the inn.

He'd have to work, he mused as he looked at the

half-finished walls and the paint tarps. He considered it a small bonus. Working with his hands was something he enjoyed and something he'd had little time for in the past.

She was very precise in her instructions. A woman who knew what she wanted and intended to have it. He appreciated that. He had no doubt that she was very good at what she did, whether it was running an inn… or something else.

"What's up there?" He pointed to a set of stairs at the end of the hallway.

"My rooms. We'll worry about them after the guest quarters are done." She jingled the keys as her thoughts went off in a dozen directions. "So, what do you think?"

"About what?"

"About the work."

"Do you have tools?"

"In the shed, the other side of the parking area."

"I can handle it."

"Yes." Charity tossed the keys to him. She was certain he could. They were standing in the octagonal parlor of the family suite. It was empty but for stacks of material and tarps. And it was quiet. She noticed all at once that they were standing quite close together and that she couldn't hear a sound. Feeling foolish, she took a key off her ring.

"You'll need this."

"Thanks." He tucked it in his pocket.

She drew a deep breath, wondering why she felt as though she'd just taken a long step with her eyes closed. "Have you had lunch?"

"No."

"I'll show you down to the kitchen. Mae'll fix you

up." She started out, a little too quickly. She wanted to escape from the sensation that she was completely alone with him. And helpless. Charity moved her shoulders restlessly. A stupid thought, she told herself. She'd never been helpless. Still, she felt a breath of relief when she closed the door behind them.

She took him downstairs, through the empty lobby and into a large dining room decorated in pastels. There were small milk-glass vases on each table, with a handful of fresh flowers in each. Big windows opened onto a view of the water, and as if carrying through the theme, an aquarium was built into the south wall.

She stopped there for a moment, hardly breaking stride, scanning the room until she was satisfied that the tables were properly set for dinner. Then she pushed through a swinging door into the kitchen.

"And I say it needs more basil."

"I say it don't."

"Whatever you do," Charity murmured under her breath, "don't agree with either of them. Ladies," she said, using her best smile. "I brought you a hungry man."

The woman guarding the pot held up a dripping spoon. The best way to describe her was wide—face, hips, hands. She gave Roman a quick, squint-eyed survey. "Sit down, then," she told him, jerking a thumb in the direction of a long wooden table.

"Mae Jenkins, Roman DeWinter."

"Ma'am."

"And Dolores Rumsey." The other woman was holding a jar of herbs. She was as narrow as Mae was wide. After giving Roman a nod, she began to ease her way toward the pot.

"Keep away from that," Mae ordered, "and get the man some fried chicken."

Muttering, Dolores stalked off to find a plate.

"Roman's going to pick up where George left off," Charity explained. "He'll be staying in the west wing."

"Not from around here." Mae looked at him again, the way he imagined a nanny would look at a small, grubby child.

"No."

With a sniff, she poured him some coffee. "Looks like you could use a couple of decent meals."

"You'll get them here," Charity put in, playing peacemaker. She winced only a little when Dolores slapped a plate of cold chicken and potato salad in front of Roman.

"Needed more dill." Dolores glared at him, as if she were daring him to disagree. "She wouldn't listen."

Roman figured the best option was to grin at her and keep his mouth full. Before Mae could respond, the door swung open again.

"Can a guy get a cup of coffee in here?" The man stopped and sent Roman a curious look.

"Bob Mullins, Roman DeWinter. I hired him to finish the west wing. Bob's one of my many right hands."

"Welcome aboard." He moved to the stove to pour himself a cup of coffee, adding three lumps of sugar as Mae clucked her tongue at him. The sweet tooth didn't seem to have an effect on him. He was tall, perhaps six-two, and he couldn't weigh more than 160. His light brown hair was cut short around his ears and swept back from his high forehead.

"You from back east?" Bob asked between sips of coffee.

"East of here."

"Easy to do." He grinned when Mae flapped a hand to move him away from her stove.

"Did you get that invoice business straightened out with the greengrocer?" Charity asked.

"All taken care of. You got a couple of calls while you were out. And there's some papers you need to sign."

"I'll get to it." She checked her watch. "Now." She glanced over at Roman. "I'll be in the office off the lobby if there's anything you need to know."

"I'll be fine."

"Okay." She studied him for another moment. She couldn't quite figure out how he could be in a room with four other people and seem so alone. "See you later."

Roman took a long, casual tour of the inn before he began to haul tools into the west wing. He saw a young couple who had to be newlyweds locked in an embrace near the pond. A man and a young boy played one-on-one on a small concrete basketball court. The ladies, as he had come to think of them, had left their game to sit on the porch and discuss the garden. Looking exhausted, a family of four pulled up in a station wagon, then trooped toward the cabins. A man in a fielder's cap walked down the pier with a video camera on his shoulder.

There were birds trilling in the trees, and there was the distant sound of a motorboat. He heard a baby crying halfheartedly, and the strains of a Mozart piano sonata.

If he hadn't pored over the data himself he would have sworn he was in the wrong place.

He chose the family suite and went to work, wondering how long it would take him to get into Charity's rooms.

There was something soothing about working with his hands. Two hours passed, and he relaxed a little. A check of his watch had him deciding to take another, unnecessary trip to the shed. Charity had mentioned that wine was served in what she called the gathering room every evening at five. It wouldn't hurt for him to get another, closer look at the inn's guests.

He started out, then stopped by the doorway to his room. He'd heard something, a movement. Cautious, he eased inside the door and scanned the empty room.

Humming under her breath, Charity came out of the bath, where she'd just placed fresh towels. She unfolded linens and began to make the bed.

"What are you doing?"

Muffling a scream, she stumbled backward, then eased down on the bed to catch her breath. "My God, Roman, don't do that."

He stepped into the room, watching her with narrowed eyes. "I asked what you were doing."

"That should be obvious." She patted the pile of linens with her hand.

"You do the housekeeping, too?"

"From time to time." Recovered, she stood up and smoothed the bottom sheet on the bed. "There's soap and towels in the bath," she told him, then tilted her head. "Looks like you can use them." She unfolded the top sheet with an expert flick. "Been busy?"

"That was the deal."

With a murmur of agreement, she tucked up the corners at the foot of the bed the way he remembered his grandmother doing. "I put an extra pillow and blanket in the closet." She moved from one side of the bed to the other in a way that had him watching her with simple male appreciation. He couldn't remember the last time he'd seen anyone make a bed. It stirred thoughts in him that he couldn't afford. Thoughts of what it might be like to mess it up again—with her.

"Do you ever stop?"

"I've been known to." She spread a white wedding-ring quilt on the bed. "We're expecting a tour tomorrow, so everyone's a bit busy."

"Tomorrow?"

"Mmm. On the first ferry from Sidney." She fluffed his pillows, satisfied. "Did you—"

She broke off when she turned and all but fell against him. His hands went to her hips instinctively as hers braced against his shoulders. An embrace—unplanned, unwanted and shockingly intimate.

She was slender beneath the long, chunky sweater, he realized, even more slender than a man might expect. And her eyes were bluer than they had any right to be, bigger, softer. She smelled like the inn, smelled of that welcoming combination of lavender and woodsmoke. Drawn to it, he continued to hold her, though he knew he shouldn't.

"Did I what?" His fingers spread over her hips, drawing her just a fraction closer. He saw the dazed confusion in her eyes; her reaction tugged at him.

She'd forgotten everything. She could only stare, almost stupefied by the sensations that spiked through her. Involuntarily her fingers curled into his shirt. She got an impression of strength, a ruthless strength with the potential for violence. The fact that it excited her left her speechless.

"Do you want something?" he murmured.

"What?"

He thought about kissing her, about pressing his mouth hard on hers and plunging into her. He would enjoy the taste, the momentary passion. "I asked if you wanted something." Slowly he ran his hands up under her sweater to her waist.

The shock of heat, the press of fingers, brought her back. "No." She started to back away, found herself held still, and fought her rising panic. Before she could speak again, he had released her. Disappointment. That was an odd reaction, she thought, when you'd just missed getting burned.

"I was—" She took a deep breath and waited for her scattered nerves to settle. "I was going to ask if you'd found everything you needed."

His eyes never left hers. "It looks like it."

She pressed her lips together to moisten them. "Good. I've got a lot to do, so I'll let you get back."

He took her arm before she could step away. Maybe it wasn't smart, but he wanted to touch her again. "Thanks for the towels."

"Sure."

He watched her hurry out, knowing her nerves were as jangled as his own. Thoughtfully he pulled out a cigarette. He couldn't remember ever having been thrown off balance so easily. Certainly not by a woman who'd done nothing more than look at him. Still, he made a habit of landing on his feet.

It might be to his advantage to get close to her, to play on the response he'd felt from her. Ignoring a wave of self-disgust, he struck a match.

He had a job to do. He couldn't afford to think about
Charity Ford as anything more than a means to an end.
He drew smoke in, cursing the dull ache in his belly.

Chapter 2

It was barely dawn, and the sky to the east was fantastic. Roman stood near the edge of the narrow road, his hands tucked in his back pockets. Though he rarely had time for them, he enjoyed mornings such as this, when the air was cool and sparkling clear. A man could breathe here, and if he could afford the luxury he could empty his mind and simply experience.

He'd promised himself thirty minutes, thirty solitary, soothing minutes. The blooming sunlight pushed through the cloud formations, turning them into wild, vivid colors and shapes. Dream shapes. He considered lighting a cigarette, then rejected it. For the moment he wanted only the taste of morning air flavored by the sea.

There was a dog barking in the distance, a faint yap, yap, yap that only added to the ambience. Gulls, out for an early feeding, swooped low over the water, slicing the silence with their lonely cries. The fragrance of flowers, a celebration of spring, carried delicately on the quiet breeze.

He wondered why he'd been so certain he preferred the rush and noise of cities.

As he stood there he saw a deer come out of the trees and raise her head to scent the air. That was freedom, he thought abruptly. To know your place and to be content with it. The doe cleared the trees, picking her way delicately toward the high grass. Behind her came a gangly fawn. Staying upwind, Roman watched them graze.

He was restless. Even as he tried to absorb and accept the peace around him he felt the impatience struggling through. This wasn't his place. He had no place. That was one of the things that made him so perfect for his job. No roots, no family, no woman waiting for his return. That was the way he wanted it.

But he'd felt enormous satisfaction in doing the carpentry the day before, in leaving his mark on something that would last. All the better for his cover, he told himself. If he showed some skill and some care in the work he would be accepted more easily.

He was already accepted.

She trusted him. She'd given him a roof and a meal and a job, thinking he needed all three. She seemed to have no guile in her. Something had simmered between them the evening before, yet she had done nothing to provoke or prolong it. She hadn't—though he knew all females were capable of it from birth—issued a silent invitation that she might or might not have intended to keep.

She'd simply looked at him, and everything she felt had been almost ridiculously clear in her eyes.

He couldn't think of her as a woman. He couldn't think of her as ever being *his* woman.

He felt the urge for a cigarette again, and this time he deliberately suppressed it. If there was something you wanted that badly, it was best to pass it by. Once you gave in, you surrendered control.

He'd wanted Charity. For one brief, blinding instant the day before, he had craved her. A very serious error. He'd blocked the need, but it had continued to surface—when he'd heard her come into the wing for the night, when he'd listened to the sound of Chopin drifting softly down the stairway from her rooms. And again in the middle of the night, when he'd awakened to the deep country silence, thinking of her, imagining her.

He didn't have time for desires. In another place, at another time, they might have met and enjoyed each other for as long as enjoyments lasted. But now she was part of an assignment—nothing less, nothing more.

He heard the sound of running footsteps and tensed instinctively. The deer, as alert as he, lifted her head, then sprinted back into the trees with her young. His weapon was strapped just above his ankle, more out of habit than necessity, but he didn't reach for it. If he needed it it could be in his hand in under a second. Instead, he waited, braced, to see who was running down the deserted road at dawn.

Charity was breathing fast, more from the effort of keeping pace with her dog than from the three-mile run. Ludwig bounded ahead, tugged to the right, jerked to the left, tangled and untangled in the leash. It was a daily routine, one that both of them were accustomed to. She could have controlled the little golden cocker, but she didn't want to spoil his fun. Instead, she swerved with him, adjusting her pace from a flat-out run to an easy jog and back again.

She hesitated briefly when she saw Roman. Then, because Ludwig sprinted ahead, she tightened her grip on the leash and kept pace.

"Good morning," she called out, then skidded to a halt when Ludwig decided to jump on Roman's shins and bark at him. "He doesn't bite."

"That's what they all say." But he grinned and crouched down to scratch between the dog's ears. Ludwig immediately collapsed, rolled over and exposed his belly for rubbing. "Nice dog."

"A nice spoiled dog," Charity added. "I have to keep him fenced because of the guests, but he eats like a king. You're up early."

"So are you."

"I figure Ludwig deserves a good run every morning, since he's so understanding about being fenced."

To show his appreciation, Ludwig raced once around Roman, tangling his lead around his legs.

"Now if I could only get him to understand the concept of a leash." She stooped to untangle Roman and to control the now-prancing dog.

Her light jacket was unzipped, exposing a snug T-shirt darkened with sweat between her breasts. Her hair, pulled straight, almost severely, back from her face, accented her bone structure. Her skin seemed almost translucent as it glowed from her run. He had an urge to touch it, to see how it felt under his fingertips. And to see if that instant reaction would rush out again.

"Ludwig, be still a minute." She laughed and tugged at his collar.

In response, the dog jumped up and lapped at her face. "He listens well," Roman commented.

"You can see why I need the fence. He thinks he can

play with everyone." Her hand brushed Roman's leg as she struggled with the leash.

When he took her wrist, both of them froze.

He could feel her pulse skip, then sprint. It was a quick, vulnerable response that was unbearably arousing. Though it cost him, he kept his fingers loose. He had only meant to stop her before she inadvertently found his weapon. Now they crouched, knee to knee, in the center of the deserted road, with the dog trying to nuzzle between them.

"You're trembling." He said it warily, but he didn't release her. "Do you always react that way when a man touches you?"

"No." Because it baffled her, she kept still and waited to see what would happen next. "I'm pretty sure this is a first."

It pleased him to hear it, and it annoyed him, because he wanted to believe it. "Then we'll have to be careful, won't we?" He released her, then stood up.

More slowly, because she wasn't sure of her balance, she rose. He was angry. Though he was holding on to his temper, it was clear enough to see in his eyes. "I'm not very good at being careful."

His gaze whipped back to hers. There was a fire in it, a fire that raged and then was quickly and completely suppressed. "I am."

"Yes." The brief, heated glance had alarmed her, but Charity had always held her own. She tilted her head to study him. "I think you'd have to be, with that streak of violence you have to contend with. Who are you mad at, Roman?"

He didn't like to be read that easily. Watching her, he lowered a hand to pet Ludwig, who was resting his front paws on his knees. "Nobody at the moment," he told her, but it was a lie. He was furious—with himself.

She only shook her head. "You're entitled to your secrets, but I can't help wondering why you'd be angry with yourself for responding to me."

He took a lazy scan of the road, up, then down. They might have been alone on the island. "Would you like me to do something about it, here and now?"

He could, she realized. And he would. If he was pushed too far he would do exactly what he wanted, when he wanted. The frisson of excitement that passed through her annoyed her. Macho types were for other women, different women—not Charity Ford. Deliberately she looked at her watch.

"Thanks. I'm sure that's a delightful offer, but I have to get back and set up for breakfast." Struggling with the dog, she started off at what she hoped was a dignified walk. "I'll let you know if I can squeeze in, say, fifteen minutes later."

"Charity?"

She turned her head and aimed a cool look. "Yes?"

"Your shoe's untied."

She just lifted her chin and continued on.

Roman grinned at her back and tucked his thumbs in his pockets. Yes, indeed, the woman had one hell of a walk. It was too damn bad all around that he was beginning to like her.

He was interested in the tour group. It was a simple matter for Roman to loiter on the first floor, lingering over a second cup of coffee in the kitchen, passing idle conversation with the thick-armed Mae and the skinny Dolores. He hadn't expected to be put to work, but when he'd found himself with an armful of table linens he had made the best of it.

Charity, wearing a bright red sweatshirt with the inn's logo across the chest, meticulously arranged a folded napkin in a water glass. Roman waited a moment, watching her busy fingers smoothing and tapering the cloth.

"Where do you want these?"

She glanced over, wondering if she should still be annoyed with him, then decided against it. At the moment she needed every extra hand she could get. "On the tables would be a good start. White on the bottom, apricot on top, slanted. Okay?" She indicated a table that was already set.

"Sure." He began to spread the cloths. "How many are you expecting?"

"Fifteen on the tour." She held a glass up to the light and placed it on the table only after a critical inspection. "Their breakfast is included. Plus the guests already registered. We serve between seven-thirty and ten." She checked her watch, satisfied, then moved to another table. "We get some drop-ins, as well." After setting a chipped bread plate aside, she reached for another. "But it's lunch and dinner that really get hectic."

Dolores swooped in with a stack of china, then dashed out again when Mae squawked at her. Before the door had swung closed, the waitress they had passed on the road the day before rushed out with a tray of clanging silverware.

"Right," Roman murmured.

Charity rattled off instructions to the waitress, finished setting yet another table, then rushed over to a blackboard near the doorway and began to copy out the morning menu in a flowing, elegant hand.

Dolores, whose spiky red hair and pursed lips made Roman think of a scrawny chicken, shoved through the swinging door and set her fists on her skinny hips. "I don't have to take this, Charity."

Charity calmly continued to write. "Take what?"

"I'm doing the best that I can, and you know I told you I was feeling poorly."

Dolores was always feeling poorly, Charity thought as she added a ham-and-cheese omelet to the list. Especially when she didn't get her way. "Yes, Dolores."

"My chest's so tight that I can hardly take a breath."

"Um-hmm."

"Was up half the night, but I come in, just like always."

"And I appreciate it, Dolores. You know how much I depend on you."

"Well." Slightly mollified, Dolores tugged at her apron. "I guess I can be counted on to do my job, but you can just tell that woman in there—" She jerked a thumb toward the kitchen. "Just tell her to get off my back."

"I'll speak to her, Dolores. Just try to be patient. We're all a little frazzled this morning, with Mary Alice out sick again."

"Sick." Dolores sniffed. "Is that what they're calling it these days?"

Listening with only half an ear, Charity continued to write. "What do you mean?"

"Don't know why her car was in Bill Perkin's driveway all night again if she's sick. Now, with my condition—"

Charity stopped writing. Roman's brow lifted when he heard the sudden thread of steel in her voice. "We'll talk about this later, Dolores."

Deflated, Dolores poked out her lower lip and stalked back into the kitchen.

Storing her anger away, Charity turned to the waitress. "Lori?"

"Almost ready."

"Good. If you can handle the registered guests, I'll be back to give you a hand after I check the tour group in."

"No problem."

"I'll be at the front desk with Bob." Absently she pushed her braid behind her back. "If it gets too busy, send for me. Roman—"

"Want me to bus tables?"

She gave him a quick, grateful smile. "Do you know how?"

"I can figure it out."

"Thanks." She checked her watch, then rushed out.

He hadn't expected to enjoy himself, but it was hard not to, with Miss Millie flirting with him over her raspberry preserves. The scent of baking—something rich, with apples and cinnamon—the quiet strains of classical music and the murmur of conversation made it almost impossible not to relax. He carried trays to and from the kitchen. The muttered exchanges between Mae and Dolores were more amusing than annoying.

So he enjoyed himself. And took advantage of his position by doing his job.

As he cleared the tables by the windows, he watched a tour van pull up to the front entrance. He counted heads and studied the faces of the group. The guide was a big man in a white shirt that strained across his shoulders. He had a round, ruddy, cheerful face that smiled continually as he piloted his passengers inside. Roman moved across the room to watch them mill around in the lobby.

They were a mix of couples and families with small children. The guide—Roman already knew his name was Block—greeted Charity with a hearty smile and then handed her a list of names.

Did she know that Block had done a stretch in Leavenworth for fraud? he wondered. Was she aware that the man she was joking with had escaped a second term only because of some fancy legal footwork?

Roman's jaw tensed as Block reached over and flicked a finger at Charity's dangling gold earring.

As she assigned cabins and dealt out keys, two of the group approached the desk to exchange money. Fifty for one, sixty for the other, Roman noted as Canadian bills were passed to Charity's assistant and American currency passed back.

Within ten minutes the entire group was seated in the dining room, contemplating breakfast. Charity breezed in behind them, putting on an apron. She flipped open a pad and began to take orders.

She didn't look as if she were in a hurry, Roman noted. The way she chatted and smiled and answered questions, it was as though she had all the time in the world. But she moved like lightning. She carried three plates on her right arm, served coffee with her left hand and cooed over a baby, all at the same time.

Something was eating at her, Roman mused. It hardly showed…just a faint frown between her eyes. Had something gone wrong that morning that he'd missed? If there was a glitch in the system, it was up to him to find it and exploit it. That was the reason he was here on the inside.

Charity poured another round of coffee for a table of four, joked with a bald man wearing a paisley tie, then made her way over to Roman.

"I think the crisis has passed." She smiled at him, but again he caught something.... Anger? Disappointment?

"Is there anything you don't do around here?"

"I try to stay out of the kitchen. The restaurant has a three-star rating." She glanced longingly at the coffeepot. There would be time for that later. "I want to thank you for pitching in this morning."

"That's okay." He discovered he wanted to see her smile. Really smile. "The tips were good. Miss Millie slipped me a five."

She obliged him. Her lips curved quickly, and whatever had clouded her eyes cleared for a moment. "She likes the way you look in a tool belt. Why don't you take a break before you start on the west wing?"

"All right."

She grimaced at the sound of glass breaking. "I didn't think the Snyder kid wanted that orange juice." She hurried off to clean up the mess and listen to the parents' apologies.

The front desk was deserted. Roman decided that Charity's assistant was either shut up in the side office or out hauling luggage to the cabins. He considered slipping behind the desk and taking a quick look at the books but decided it could wait. Some work was better done in the dark.

An hour later Charity let herself into the west wing. She'd managed to hold on to her temper as she'd passed the guests on the first floor. She'd smiled and chatted with an elderly couple playing Parcheesi in the gathering room. But when the door closed behind her she let loose with a series of furious, pent-up oaths. She wanted to kick something.

Roman stepped into a doorway and watched her stride down the hall. Anger had made her eyes dark and brilliant.

"Problem?"

"Yes," she snapped. She stalked half a dozen steps past him, then whirled around. "I can take incompetence, and even some degree of stupidity. I can even tolerate an occasional bout of laziness. But I won't be lied to."

Roman waited a beat. Her anger was ripe and rich, but it wasn't directed at him. "All right," he said, and waited.

"She could have told me she wanted time off, or a different shift. I might have been able to work it out. Instead she lies, calling in sick at the last minute five days out of the last two weeks. I was worried about her." She turned again, then gave in and kicked a door. "I hate being made a fool of. And I *hate* being lied to."

It was a simple matter to put two and two together. "You're talking about the waitress… Mary Alice?"

"Of course." She spun around. "She came begging me for a job three months ago. That's our slowest time, but I felt sorry for her. Now she's sleeping with Bill Perkin—or I guess it's more accurate to say she's not getting any sleep, so she calls in sick. I had to fire her." She let out a breath with a sound like an engine letting off steam. "I get a headache whenever I have to fire anybody."

"Is that what was bothering you all morning?"

"As soon as Dolores mentioned Bill, I knew." Calmer now, she rubbed at the insistent ache between her eyes.

"Then I had to get through the check-in and the breakfast shift before I could call and deal with her. She cried." She gave Roman a long, miserable look. "I knew she was going to cry."

"Listen, baby, the best thing for you to do is take some aspirin and forget about it."

"I've already taken some."

"Give it a chance to kick in." Before he realized what he was doing, he lifted his hands and framed her face. Moving his thumbs in slow circles, he massaged her temples. "You've got too much going on in there."

"Where?"

"In your head."

She felt her eyes getting heavy and her blood growing warm. "Not at the moment." She tilted her head back and let her eyes close. Moving on instinct, she stepped forward. "Roman..." She sighed a little as the ache melted out of her head and stirred in the very center of her. "I like the way you look in a tool belt, too."

"Do you know what you're asking for?"

She studied his mouth. It was full and firm, and it would certainly be ruthless on a woman's. "Not exactly." Perhaps that was the appeal, she thought as she stared up at him. She didn't know. But she felt, and what she felt was new and thrilling. "Maybe it's better that way."

"No." Though he knew it was a mistake, he couldn't resist skimming his fingers down to trace her jaw, then her lips. "It's always better to know the consequences before you take the action."

"So we're being careful again."

He dropped his hands. "Yeah."

She should have been grateful. Instead of taking

advantage of her confused emotions he was backing off, giving her room. She wanted to be grateful, but she felt only the sting of rejection. He had started it, she thought. Again. And he had stopped it. Again. She was sick and tired of being jolted along according to his whims.

"You miss a lot that way, don't you, Roman? A lot of warmth, a lot of joy."

"A lot of disappointment."

"Maybe. I guess it's harder for some of us to live our lives aloof from others. But if that's your choice, fine." She drew in a deep breath. Her headache was coming back, doubled. "Don't touch me again. I make it a habit to finish whatever I start." She glanced into the room behind them. "You're doing a nice job here," she said briskly. "I'll let you get back to it."

He cursed her as he sanded the wood for the window trim. She had no right to make him feel guilty just because he wanted to keep his distance. Noninvolvement wasn't just a habit with him; it was a matter of survival. It was self-indulgent and dangerous to move forward every time you were attracted to a woman.

But it was more than attraction, and it was certainly different from anything he'd felt before. Whenever he was near her, his purpose became clouded with fantasies of what it would be like to be with her, to hold her, to make love with her.

And fantasies were all they were, he reminded himself. If things went well he would be gone in a matter of days. Before he was done he might very well destroy her life.

It was his job, he reminded himself.

He saw her, walking out to the van with those long,

purposeful strides of hers, the keys jingling in her hand. Behind her were the newlyweds, holding hands, even though each was carrying a suitcase.

She would be taking them to the ferry, he thought. That would give him an hour to search her rooms.

He knew how to go through every inch of a room without leaving a trace. He concentrated first on the obvious—the desk in the small parlor. It was common for people to be careless in the privacy of their own homes. A slip of paper, a scribbled note, a name in an address book, were often left behind for the trained eye to spot.

It was an old desk, solid mahogany with a few rings and scratches. Two of the brass pulls were loose. Like the rest of the room, it was neat and well organized. Her personal papers—insurance documents, bills, correspondence—were filed on the left. Inn business took up the three drawers on the right.

He could see from a quick scan that the inn made a reasonable profit, most of which she funneled directly back into it. New linens, bathroom fixtures, paint. The stove Mae was so territorial about had been purchased only six months earlier.

She took a salary for herself, a surprisingly modest one. He didn't find, even after a more critical study, any evidence of her using any of the inn's finances to ease her own way.

An honest woman, Roman mused. At least on the surface.

There was a bowl of potpourri on the desk, as there was in every room in the inn. Beside it was a framed picture of Charity standing in front of the mill wheel with a fragile-looking man with white hair.

The grandfather, Roman decided, but it was Char-

ity's image he studied. Her hair was pulled back in a ponytail, and her baggy overalls were stained at the knees.
From gardening, Roman guessed. She was holding an
armful of summer flowers. She looked as if she didn't
have a care in the world, but he noted that her free arm
was around the old man, supporting him.

He wondered what she had been thinking at that
moment, what she had done the moment after the picture had been snapped. He swore at himself and looked
away from the picture.

She left notes to herself: Return wallpaper samples.
New blocks for toy chest. Call piano tuner. Get flat re-
paired.

He found nothing that touched on his reason for
coming to the inn. Leaving the desk, he meticulously
searched the rest of the parlor.

Then he went into the adjoining bedroom. The bed,
a four-poster, was covered with a lacy white spread and
plumped with petit-point pillows. Beside it was a beautiful old rocker, its arms worn smooth as glass. In it sat
a big purple teddy bear wearing yellow suspenders.

The curtains were romantic priscillas. She'd left the
windows open, and the breeze came through billowing
them. A woman's room, Roman thought, unrelentingly
feminine with its lace and pillows, its fragile scents and
pale colors. Yet somehow it welcomed a man, made him
wish, made him want. It made him want one hour, one
night, in that softness, that comfort.

He crossed the faded handhooked rug and, burying
his self-disgust, went through her dresser.

He found a few pieces of jewelry he took to be heir-
looms. They belonged in a safe, he thought, annoyed
with her. There was a bottle of perfume. He knew ex-

actly how it would smell. It would smell the way her skin did. He nearly reached for it before he caught himself. Perfume wasn't of any interest to him. Evidence was.

A packet of letters caught his eye. From a lover? he wondered, dismissing the sudden pang of jealousy he felt as ridiculous.

The room was making him crazy, he thought as he carefully untied the slender satin ribbon. It was impossible not to imagine her there, curled on the bed, wearing something white and thin, her hair loose and the candles lit.

He shook himself as he unfolded the first letter. A room with a purple teddy bear wasn't seductive, he told himself.

The date showed him that they had been written when she had attended college in Seattle. From her grandfather, Roman realized as he scanned them. Every one. They were written with affection and humor, and they contained dozens of little stories about daily life at the inn. Roman put them back the way he'd found them.

Her clothes were casual, except for a few dresses hanging in the closet. There were sturdy boots, sneakers spotted with what looked like grass stains and two pairs of elegant heels on either side of fuzzy slippers in the shape of elephants. Like the rest of her rooms, they were meticulously arranged. Even in the closet he didn't find a trace of dust.

Besides an alarm clock and a pot of hand cream she had two books on her nightstand. One was a collection of poetry, the other a murder mystery with a gruesome cover. She had a cache of chocolate in the drawer and Chopin on her small portable stereo. There were candles, dozens of them, burned down to various heights. On one wall hung a seascape in deep, stormy blues and grays. On another was a collection of photos, most taken at the inn, many of her grandfather. Roman searched behind each one. He discovered that her paint was fading, nothing more.

Her rooms were clean. Roman stood in the center of the bedroom, taking in the scents of candle wax, potpourri and perfume. They couldn't have been cleaner if she'd known they were going to be searched. All he knew after an hour was that she was an organized woman who liked comfortable clothes and Chopin and had a weakness for chocolate and lurid paperback novels.

Why did that make her fascinating?

He scowled and shoved his hands in his pockets, struggling for objectivity as he had never had to struggle before. All the evidence pointed to her being involved in some very shady business. Everything he'd discovered in the last twenty-four hours indicated that she was an open, honest and hardworking woman.

Which did he believe?

He walked toward the door at the far end of the room. It opened onto a postage-stamp-size porch with a long set of stairs that led down to the pond. He wanted to open the door, to step out and breathe in the air, but he turned his back on it and went out the way he had come in.

The scent of her bedroom stayed with him for hours.

Chapter 3

"I told you that girl was no good."

"I know, Mae."

"I told you you were making a mistake taking her on like you did."

"Yes, Mae." Charity bit back a sigh. "You told me."

"You keep taking in strays, you're bound to get bit."

Charity resisted—just barely—the urge to scream. "So you've told me."

With a satisfied grunt, Mae finished wiping off her pride and joy, the eight-burner gas range. Charity might run the inn, but Mae had her own ideas about who was in charge. "You're too softhearted, Charity."

"I thought you said it was hardheaded."

"That too." Because she had a warm spot for her young employer, Mae poured a glass of milk and cut a generous slab from the remains of her double chocolate cake. Keeping her voice brisk, she set both on the table. "You eat this now. My baking always made you feel better as a girl."

Charity took a seat and poked a finger into the icing. "I would have given her some time off."

"I know." Mae rubbed her wide-palmed hand on Charity's shoulder. "That's the trouble with you. You take your name too seriously."

"I hate being made a fool of." Scowling, Charity took a huge bite of cake. Chocolate, she was sure, would be a better cure for her headache than an entire bottle of aspirin. Her guilt was a different matter. "Do you think she'll get another job? I know she's got rent to pay."

"Types like Mary Alice always land on their feet. Wouldn't surprise me if she moved in lock, stock and barrel with that Perkin boy, so don't you be worrying about the likes of her. Didn't I tell you she wouldn't last six months?"

Charity pushed more cake into her mouth. "You told me," she mumbled around it.

"Now then, what about this man you brought home?"

Charity took a gulp of her milk. "Roman DeWinter."

"Screwy name." Mae glanced around the kitchen, surprised and a little disappointed that there was nothing left to do. "What do you know about him?"

"He needed a job."

Mae wiped her reddened hands on the skirt of her apron. "I expect there's a whole slew of pickpockets, cat burglars and mass murderers who need jobs."

"He's not a mass murderer," Charity stated. She thought she had better reserve judgment on the other occupations.

"Maybe, maybe not."

"He's a drifter." She shrugged and took another bite

of the cake. "But I wouldn't say aimless. He knows where he's going. In any case, with George off doing the hula, I needed someone. He does good work, Mae."

Mae had determined that for herself with a quick trip into the west wing. But she had other things on her mind. "He looks at you."

Stalling, Charity ran a fingertip up and down the side of her glass. "Everyone looks at me. I'm always here."

"Don't play stupid with me, young lady. I powdered your bottom."

"Whatever that has to do with anything," Charity answered with a grin. "So he looks?" She moved her shoulders again. "I look back." When Mae arched her brows, Charity just smiled. "Aren't you always telling me I need a man in my life?"

"There's men and there's men," Mae said sagely. "This one's not bad on the eyes, and he ain't afraid of working. But he's got a hard streak in him. That one's been around, my girl, and no mistake."

"I guess you'd rather I spent time with Jimmy Loggerman."

"Spineless worm."

After a burst of laughter, Charity cupped her chin in her hands. "You were right, Mae. I do feel better."

Pleased, Mae untied the apron from around her ample girth. She didn't doubt that Charity was a sensible girl, but she intended to keep an eye on Roman herself. "Good. Don't cut any more of that cake or you'll be up all night with a bellyache."

"Yes'm."

"And don't leave a mess in my kitchen," she added as she tugged on a practical brown coat.

"No, ma'am. Good night, Mae."

Charity sighed as the door rattled shut. Mae's leaving usually signaled the end of the day. The guests would be tucked into their beds or finishing up a late card game. Barring an emergency, there was nothing left for Charity to do until sunrise.

Nothing to do but think.

Lately she'd been toying with the idea of putting in a whirlpool. That might lure a small percentage of the resortgoers. She'd priced a few solarium kits, and in her mind she could already see the sunroom on the inn's south side. In the winter guests could come back from hiking to a hot, bubbling tub and top off the day with rum punch by the fire.

She would enjoy it herself, especially on those rare winter days when the inn was empty and there was nothing for her to do but rattle around alone.

Then there was her long-range plan to add on a gift shop supplied by local artists and craftsmen. Nothing too elaborate, she thought. She wanted to keep things simple, in keeping with the spirit of the inn.

She wondered if Roman would stay around long enough to work on it.

It wasn't wise to think of him in connection with any of her plans. It probably wasn't wise to think of him at all. He was, as she had said herself, a drifter. Men like Roman didn't light in one spot for long.

She couldn't seem to stop thinking about him. Almost from the first moment she'd felt something. Attraction was one thing. He was, after all, an attractive man, in a tough, dangerous kind of way. But there was more. Something in his eyes? she wondered. In his voice? In the way he moved? She toyed with the rest of her cake, wishing she could pin it down. It might simply be that he was so different from herself. Taciturn, suspicious, solitary.

And yet…was it her imagination, or was part of him waiting, to reach out, to grab hold? He needed someone, she thought, though he was probably unaware of it.

Mae was right, she mused. She had always had a weakness for strays and a hard-luck story. But this was different. She closed her eyes for a moment, wishing she could explain, even to herself, why it was so very different.

She'd never experienced anything like the sensations that had rammed into her because of Roman. It was more than physical. She could admit that now. Still, it made no sense. Then again, Charity had always thought that feelings weren't required to make sense.

For a moment out on the deserted road this morning she'd felt emotions pour out of him. They had been almost frightening in their speed and power. Emotions like that could hurt…the one who felt them, the one who received them. They had left her dazed and aching—and wishing, she admitted.

She thought she knew what his mouth would taste like. Not soft, not sweet, but pungent and powerful. When he was ready, he wouldn't ask, he'd take. It worried her that she didn't resent that. She had grown up knowing her own mind, making her own choices. A man like Roman would have little respect for a woman's wishes.

It would be better, much better, for them to keep their relationship—their short-term relationship, she added—on a purely business level. Friendly but careful. She let her chin sink into her hands again. It was a pity she had such a difficult time combining the two.

He watched her toy with the crumbs on her plate. Her hair was loose now and tousled, as if she had pulled it out of the braid and ran impatient fingers through it. Her bare feet were crossed at the ankles, resting on the chair across from her.

Relaxed. Roman wasn't sure he'd ever seen anyone so fully relaxed except in sleep. It was a sharp contrast to the churning energy that drove her during the day.

He wished she were in her rooms, tucked into bed and sleeping deeply. He'd wanted to avoid coming across her at all. That was personal. He needed her out of his way so that he could go through the office off the lobby. That was business.

He knew he should step back and keep out of sight until she retired for the night.

What was it about this quiet scene that was so appealing, so irresistible? The kitchen was warm and the scents of cooking were lingering, pleasantly overlaying those of pine and lemon from Mae's cleaning. There was a hanging basket over the sink that was almost choked with some leafy green plant. Every surface was scrubbed, clean and shiny. The huge refrigerator hummed.

She looked so comfortable, as if she were waiting for him to come in and sit with her, to talk of small, inconsequential things.

That was crazy. He didn't want any woman waiting for him, and especially not her.

But he didn't step back into the shadows of the dining room, though he could easily have done so. He stepped toward her, into the light.

"I thought people kept early hours in the country."

She jumped but recovered quickly. She was almost

used to the silent way he moved. "Mostly. Mae was giving me chocolate and a pep talk. Want some cake?"

"No."

"Just as well. If you had I'd have taken another piece and made myself sick. No willpower. How about a beer?"

"Yeah. Thanks."

She got up lazily and moved to the refrigerator to rattle off a list of brands. He chose one and watched her pour it into a pilsner glass. She wasn't angry, he noted, though she had certainly been the last time they were together. So Charity didn't hold grudges. She wouldn't, Roman decided as he took the glass from her. She would forgive almost anything, would trust everyone and would give more than was asked.

"Why do you look at me that way?" she murmured.

He caught himself, then took a long, thirsty pull on the beer. "You have a beautiful face."

She lifted a brow when he sat down and pulled out a cigarette. After taking an ashtray from a drawer, she sat beside him. "I like to accept compliments whenever I get them, but I don't think that's the reason."

"It's reason enough for a man to look at a woman." He sipped his beer. "You had a busy night."

Let it go, Charity told herself. "Busy enough that I need to hire another waitress fast. I didn't get a chance to thank you for helping out with the dinner crowd."

"No problem. Lose the headache?"

She glanced up sharply. But, no, he wasn't making fun of her. It seemed, though she couldn't be sure why the impression was so strong, that his question was a kind of apology. She decided to accept it.

"Yes, thanks. Getting mad at you took my mind off

Mary Alice, and Mae's chocolate cake did the rest." She thought about brewing some tea, then decided she was too lazy to bother. "So, how was your day?"

She smiled at him in an easy offer of friendship that he found difficult to resist and impossible to accept. "Okay. Miss Millie said the door to her room was sticking, so I pretended to sand it."

"And made her day."

He couldn't prevent the smile. "I don't think I've ever been ogled quite so completely before."

"Oh, I imagine you have." She tilted her head to study him from a new angle. "But, with apologies to your ego, in Miss Millie's case it's more a matter of nearsightedness than lust. She's too vain to wear her glasses in front of any male over twenty."

"I'd rather go on thinking she's leering at me," he said. "She said she's been coming here twice a year since '52." He thought that over for a moment, amazed that anyone could return time after time to the same spot.

"She and Miss Lucy are fixtures here. When I was young I thought we were related."

"You been running this place long?"

"Off and on for all of my twenty-seven years." Smiling, she tipped back in her chair. She was a woman who relaxed easily and enjoyed seeing others relaxed. He seemed so now, she thought, with his legs stretched out under the table and a glass in his hand. "You don't really want to hear the story of my life, do you, Roman?"

He blew out a stream of smoke. "I've got nothing to do." And he wanted to hear her version of what he'd read in her file.

"Okay. I was born here. My mother had fallen in

love a bit later in life than most. She was nearly forty when she had me, and fragile. There were complications. After she died, my grandfather raised me, so I grew up here at the inn, except for the periods of time when he sent me away to school. I loved this place." She glanced around the kitchen. "In school I pined for it, and for Pop. Even in college I missed it so much I'd ferry home every weekend. But he wanted me to see something else before I settled down here. I was going to travel some, get new ideas for the inn. See New York, New Orleans, Venice. I don't know...." Her words trailed off wistfully.

"Why didn't you?"

"My grandfather was ill. I was in my last year of college when I found out *how* ill. I wanted to quit, come home, but the idea upset him so much I thought it was better to graduate. He hung on for another three years, but it was...difficult." She didn't want to talk about the tears and the terror, or about the exhaustion of running the inn while caring for a near-invalid. "He was the bravest, kindest man I've ever known. He was so much a part of this place that there are still times when I expect to walk into a room and see him checking for dust on the furniture."

He was silent for a moment, thinking as much about what she'd left out as about what she'd told him. He knew her father was listed as unknown—a difficult obstacle anywhere, but especially in a small town. In the last six months of her grandfather's life his medical expenses had nearly driven the inn under. But she didn't speak of those things; nor did he detect any sign of bitterness.

"Do you ever think about selling the place, moving on?"

"No. Oh, I still think about Venice occasionally. There are dozens of places I'd like to go, as long as I had the inn to come back to." She rose to get him another beer. "When you run a place like this, you get to meet people from all over. There's always a story about a new place."

"Vicarious traveling?"

It stung, perhaps because it was too close to her own thoughts. "Maybe." She set the bottle at his elbow, then took her dishes to the sink. Even knowing that she was overly sensitive on this point didn't stop her from bristling. "Some of us are meant to be boring."

"I didn't say you were boring."

"No? Well, I suppose I am to someone who picks up and goes whenever and wherever he chooses. Simple, settled and naive."

"You're putting words in my mouth, baby."

"It's easy to do, *baby,* since you rarely put any there yourself. Turn off the lights when you leave."

He took her arm as she started by in a reflexive movement that he regretted almost before it was done. But it was done, and the sulky, defiant look she sent him began a chain reaction that raced through his system. There were things he could do with her, things he burned to do, that neither of them would ever forget.

"Why are you angry?"

"I don't know. I can't seem to talk to you for more than ten minutes without getting edgy. Since I normally get along with everyone, I figure it's you."

"You're probably right."

She calmed a little. It was hardly his fault that she

had never been anywhere. "You've been around a little less than forty-eight hours and I've nearly fought with you three times. That's a record for me."

"I don't keep score."

"Oh, I think you do. I doubt you forget anything. Were you a cop?"

He had to make a deliberate effort to keep his face bland and fingers from tensing. "Why?"

"You said you weren't an artist. That was my first guess." She relaxed, though he hadn't removed his hand from her arm. Anger was something she enjoyed only in fast, brief spurts. "It's the way you look at people, as if you were filing away descriptions and any distinguishing marks. And sometimes when I'm with you I feel as though I should get ready for an interrogation. A writer, then? When you're in the hotel business you get pretty good at matching people with professions."

"You're off this time."

"Well, what are you, then?"

"Right now I'm a handyman."

She shrugged, making herself let it go. "Another trait of hotel people is respecting privacy, but if you turn out to be a mass murderer Mae's never going to let me hear the end of it."

"Generally I only kill one person at a time."

"That's good news." She ignored the suddenly very real anxiety that he was speaking the simple truth. "You're still holding my arm."

"I know."

So this was it, she thought, and struggled to keep her voice. "Should I ask you to let go?"

"I wouldn't bother."

She drew a deep, steadying breath. "All right. What do you want, Roman?"

"To get this out of the way, for both of us."

He rose. Her step backward was instinctive, and much more surprising to her than to him. "I don't think that's a good idea."

"Neither do I." With his free hand, he gathered up her hair. It was soft, as he'd known it would be. Thick and full and so soft that his fingers dived in and were lost. "But I'd rather regret something I did than something I didn't do."

"I'd rather not regret at all."

"Too late." He heard her suck in her breath as he yanked her against him. "One way or the other, we'll both have plenty to regret."

He was deliberately rough. He knew how to be gentle, though he rarely put the knowledge into practice. With her, he could have been. Perhaps because he knew that, he shoved aside any desire for tenderness. He wanted to frighten her, to make certain that when he let her go she would run, run away from him, because he wanted so badly for her to run to him.

Buried deep in his mind was the hope that he could make her afraid enough, repelled enough, to send him packing. If she did, she would be safe from him, and he from her. He thought he could accomplish it quickly. Then, suddenly, it was impossible to think at all.

She tasted like heaven. He'd never believed in heaven, but the flavor was on her lips, pure and sweet and promising. Her hand had gone to his chest in an automatic defensive movement. Yet she wasn't fighting him, as he'd been certain she would. She met his hard, almost brutal kiss with passion laced with trust.

His mind emptied. It was a terrifying experience for a man who kept his thoughts under such stringent control. Then it filled with her, her scent, her touch, her taste.

He broke away—for his sake now, not for hers. He was and had always been a survivor. His breath came fast and raw. One hand was still tangled in her hair, and his other was clamped tight on her arm. He couldn't let go. No matter how he chided himself to release her, to step back and walk away, he couldn't move. Staring at her, he saw his own reflection in her eyes.

He cursed her—it was a last quick denial—before he crushed his mouth to hers again. It wasn't heaven he was heading for, he told himself. It was hell.

She wanted to soothe him, but he never gave her the chance. As before, he sent her rushing into some hot, airless place where there was room only for sensation.

She'd been right. His mouth wasn't soft, it was hard and ruthless and irresistible. Without hesitation, without thought of self-preservation, she opened for him, greedily taking what was offered, selflessly giving what was demanded.

Her back was pressed against the smooth, cool surface of the refrigerator, trapped there by the firm, taut lines of his body. If it had been possible, she would have brought him closer.

His face was rough as it scraped against hers, and she trembled at the thrill of pleasure even that brought her. Desperate now, she nipped at his lower lip, and felt a new rush of excitement as he groaned and deepened an already bottomless kiss.

She wanted to be touched. She tried to murmur this new, compelling need against his mouth, but she managed only a moan. Her body ached. Just the anticipation of his hands running over her was making her shudder.

For a moment their hearts beat against each other in the same wild rhythm.

He tore away, aware that he had come perilously close to a line he didn't dare cross. He could hardly breathe, much less think. Until he was certain he could do both, he was silent.

"Go to bed, Charity."

She stayed where she was, certain that if she took a step her legs would give away. He was still close enough for her to feel the heat radiating from his body. But she looked into his eyes and knew he was already out of reach.

"Just like that?"

Hurt. He could hear it in her voice, and he wished he could make himself believe she had brought it on herself. He reached for his beer but changed his mind when he saw that his hand was unsteady. Only one thing was clear. He had to get rid of her, quickly, before he touched her again.

"You're not the type for quick sex on the kitchen floor."

The color that passion had brought to her cheeks faded. "No. At least I never have been." After taking a deep breath, she stepped forward. She believed in facing facts, even unpleasant ones. "Is that all this would have been, Roman?"

His hand curled into a fist. "Yes," he said. "What else?"

"I see." She kept her eyes on his, wishing she could hate him. "I'm sorry for you."

"Don't be."

"You're in charge of your feelings, Roman, not mine. And I am sorry for you. Some people lose a leg or a hand or an eye. They either deal with that loss or become bitter. I can't see what piece of you is missing, Roman, but it's just as tragic." He didn't answer; she hadn't expected him to. "Don't forget the lights."

He waited until she was gone before he fumbled for a match. He needed time to gain control of his head— and his hands—before he searched the office. What worried him was that it was going to take a great deal longer to gain control of his heart.

Nearly two hours later he hiked a mile and a half to use the pay phone at the nearest gas station. The road was quiet, the tiny village dark. The wind had come up, and it tasted of rain. Roman hoped dispassionately that it would hold off until he was back at the inn.

He placed the call, waited for the connection.

"Conby."

"DeWinter."

"You're late."

Roman didn't bother to check his watch. He knew it was just shy of 3:00 a.m. on the East Coast. "Get you up?"

"Am I to assume that you've established yourself?"

"Yeah, I'm in. Rigging the handyman's lottery ticket cleared the way. Arranging the flat gave me the opening. Miss Ford is…trusting."

"So we were led to believe. Trusting doesn't mean she's not ambitious. What have you got?"

A bad case of guilt, Roman thought as he lit a match. A very bad case. "Her rooms are clean." He paused and held the flame to the tip of his cigarette. "There's a tour group in now, mostly Canadians. A few exchanged money. Nothing over a hundred."

The pause was very brief. "That's hardly enough to make the business worthwhile."

"I got a list out of the office. The names and addresses of the registered guests."

There was another, longer pause, and a rustling sound that told Roman that his contact was searching for writing materials. "Let me have it."

He read them off from the copy he'd made. "Block's the tour guide. He's the regular, comes in once a week for a one-or two-night stay, depending on the package."

"Vision Tours."

"Right."

"We've got a man on that end. You concentrate on Ford and her staff." Roman heard the faint *tap-tap-tap* of Conby's pencil against his pad. "There's no way they can be pulling this off without someone on the inside. She's the obvious answer."

"It doesn't fit."

"I beg your pardon?"

Roman crushed the cigarette under his boot heel. "I said it doesn't fit. I've watched her. I've gone through her personal accounts, damn it. She's got under three thousand in fluid cash. Everything else goes into the place for new sheets and soap."

"I see." The pause again. It was maddening. "I suppose our Miss Ford hasn't heard of Swiss bank accounts."

"I said she's not the type, Conby. It's the wrong angle."

"I'll worry about the angles, DeWinter. You worry about doing your job. I shouldn't have to remind you that it's taken us nearly a year to come close to pinning this thing down. The Bureau wants this wrapped quickly, and that's what I expect from you. If you have a personal problem with this, you'd better let me know now."

"No." He knew personal problems weren't permitted. "You want to waste time, and the taxpayers' money, it's all the same to me. I'll get back to you."

"Do that."

Roman hung up. It made him feel a little better to scowl at the phone and imagine Conby losing a good night's sleep. Then again, his kind rarely did. He'd wake some hapless clerk up at six and have the list run through the computer. Conby would drink his coffee, watch the *Today* show and wait in his comfortable house in the D.C. suburbs for the results.

Grunt work and dirty work were left to others.

That was the way the game was played, Roman reminded himself as he started the long walk back to the inn. But lately, just lately, he was getting very tired of the rules.

Charity heard him come in. Curious, she glanced at the clock after she heard the door close below. It was after one, and the rain had started nearly thirty minutes before with a gentle hissing that promised to gain strength through the night.

She wondered where he had been.

His business, she reminded herself as she rolled over and tried to let the rain lull her to sleep. As long as he did his job, Roman DeWinter was free to come and go as he pleased. If he wanted to walk in the rain, that was fine by her.

How could he have kissed her like that and felt nothing?

Charity squeezed her eyes shut and swore at herself. It was her feelings she had to worry about, not Roman's. The trouble was, she always felt too much. This was one time she couldn't afford that luxury.

Something had happened to her when he'd kissed her. Something thrilling, something that had reached deep inside her and opened up endless possibilities. No, not possibilities, fantasies, she thought, shaking her head. If she were wise she would take that one moment of excitement and stop wanting more. Drifters made poor risks emotionally. She had the perfect example before her.

Her mother had turned to a drifter and had given him her heart, her trust, her body. She had ended up pregnant and alone. She had, Charity knew, pined for him for months. She'd died in the same hospital where her baby had been born, only days later. Betrayed, rejected and ashamed.

Charity had only discovered the extent of the shame after her grandfather's death. He'd kept the diary her mother had written. Charity had burned it, not out of shame but out of pity. She would always think of her mother as a tragic woman who had looked for love and had never found it.

But she wasn't her mother, Charity reminded herself as she lay awake listening to the rain. She was far, far less fragile. Love was what she had been named for, and she had felt its warmth all her life.

Now a drifter had come into her life.

He had spoken of regrets, she remembered. She was afraid that whatever happened—or didn't happen—between them, she would have them.

Chapter 4

The rain continued all morning, soft, slow, steady. It brought a chill, and a gloom that was no less appealing than the sunshine. Clouds hung over the water, turning everything to different shades of gray. Raindrops hissed on the roof and at the windows, making the inn seem all the more remote. Occasionally the wind gusted, rattling the panes.

At dawn Roman had watched Charity, bundled in a hooded windbreaker, take Ludwig out for his morning run. And he had watched her come back, dripping, forty minutes later. He'd heard the music begin to play in her room after she had come in the back entrance. She had chosen something quiet and floating with lots of violins this time. He'd been sorry when it had stopped and she had hurried down the hallway on her way to the dining room.

From his position on the second floor he couldn't

hear the bustle in the kitchen below, but he could imagine it. Mae and Dolores would be bickering as waffle or muffin batter was whipped up. Charity would have grabbed a quick cup of coffee before rushing out to help the waitress set up tables and write the morning's menu.

Her hair would be damp, her voice calm as she smoothed over Dolores's daily complaints. She'd smell of the rain. When the early risers wandered down she would smile, greet them by name and make them feel as though they were sharing a meal at an old friend's house.

That was her greatest skill, Roman mused. Making a stranger feel at home.

Could she be as uncomplicated as she seemed? A part of him wanted badly to believe that. Another part of him found it impossible. Everyone had an angle, from the mailroom clerk dreaming of a desk job to the CEO wheeling another deal. She couldn't be any different.

He wouldn't have called the kiss they'd shared uncomplicated. There had been layers to it he couldn't have begun to peel away. It seemed contradictory that such a calm-eyed, smooth-voiced woman could explode with such towering passion. Yet she had. Perhaps her passion was as much a part of the act as her serenity.

It annoyed him. Just remembering his helpless response to her infuriated him. So he made himself dissect it further. If he was attracted to what she seemed to be, that was reasonable enough. He'd lived a solitary and often turbulent life. Though he had chosen to live that way, and certainly preferred it, it wasn't unusual that at some point he would find himself pulled toward a woman who represented everything he had never had.

And had never wanted, Roman reminded himself as he tacked up a strip of molding.

He wasn't going to pretend he'd found any answers in Charity. The only answers he was looking for pertained to the job.

For now he would wait until the morning rush was over. When Charity was busy in her office, he would go down and charm some breakfast out of Mae. There was a woman who didn't trust him, Roman thought with a grin. There wasn't a naive bone in her sturdy body. And except for Charity there was no one, he was sure, who knew the workings of the inn better.

Yes, he'd put some effort into charming Mae. And he'd keep some distance between himself and Charity. For the time being.

"You're looking peaked this morning."

"Thank you very much." Charity swallowed a yawn as she poured her second cup of coffee. Peaked wasn't the word, she thought. She was exhausted right down to the bone. Her body wasn't used to functioning on three hours' sleep. She had Roman to thank for that, she thought, and shoved the just-filled cup aside.

"Sit." Mae pointed to the table. "I'll fix you some eggs."

"I haven't got time. I—"

"Sit," Mae repeated, waving a wooden spoon. "You need fuel."

"Mae's right," Dolores put in. "A body can't run on coffee. You need protein and carbohydrates." She set a blueberry muffin on the table. "Why, if I don't watch my protein intake I get weak as a lamb. 'Course, the doctor don't say, but I think I'm hydroglycemic."

"Hypoglycemic," Charity murmured.

"That's what I said." Dolores decided she liked the sound of it. At the moment, however, it was just as much fun to worry about Charity as it was to worry about herself. "She could use some nice crisp bacon with those eggs, Mae. That's what I think."

"I'm putting it on."

Outnumbered, Charity sat down. The two women could scrap for days, but when they had common cause they stuck together like glue.

"I'm not peaked," she said in her own defense. "I just didn't sleep well last night."

"A warm bath before bed," Mae told her as the bacon sizzled. "Not hot, mind you. Lukewarm."

"With bath salts. Not bubbles or oils," Dolores added as she plunked down a glass of juice. "Good old-fashioned bath salts. Ain't that right, Mae?"

"Couldn't hurt," Mae mumbled, too concerned about Charity to think of an argument. "You've been working too hard, girl."

"I agree," Charity said, because it was easiest that way. "The reason I don't have time for a long, leisurely breakfast is that I have to see about hiring a new waitress so I don't have to work so hard. I put an ad in this morning's paper, so the calls should be coming in."

"Told Bob to cancel the ad," Mae announced, cracking an egg into the pan.

"What? Why?" Charity started to rise. "Damn it, Mae, if you think I'm going to take Mary Alice back after she—"

"No such thing, and don't you swear at me, young lady."

"Testy." Dolores clucked her tongue. "Happens when you work too hard."

"I'm sorry," Charity mumbled, managing not to grind her teeth. "But, Mae, I was counting on setting up interviews over the next couple of days. I want someone in by the end of the week."

"My brother's girl left that worthless husband of hers in Toledo and came home." Keeping her back to Charity, Mae set the bacon to drain, then poked at the eggs. "She's a good girl, Bonnie is. Worked here a couple of summers while she was in school."

"Yes, I remember. She married a musician who was playing at one of the resorts in Eastsound."

Mae scowled and began to scoop up the eggs. "Saxophone player," she said, as if that explained it all. "She got tired of living out of a van and came home a couple weeks back. Been looking for work."

With a sigh, Charity pushed a hand through her bangs. "Why didn't you tell me before?"

"You didn't need anyone before." Mae set the eggs in front of her. "You need someone now."

Charity glanced over as Mae began wiping off the stove. The cook's heart was as big as the rest of her. "When can she start?"

Mae's lips curved, and she cleared her throat and wiped at a spill with more energy. "Told her to come in this afternoon so's you could have a look at her. Don't expect you to hire her unless she measures up."

"Well, then." Charity picked up her fork. Pleased at the thought of having one job settled, she stretched out her legs and rested her feet on an empty chair. "I guess I've got time for breakfast after all."

Roman pushed through the door and almost swore

out loud. The dining room was all but empty. He'd been certain Charity would be off doing one of the dozens of chores she took on. Instead, she was sitting in the warm, fragrant kitchen, much as she had been the night before. With one telling difference, Roman reflected. She wasn't relaxed now.

Her easy smile faded the moment he walked in. Slowly she slipped her feet off the chair and straightened her back. He could see her body tense, almost muscle by muscle. Her fork stopped halfway to her lips. Then she turned slightly away from him and continued to eat. It was, he supposed, as close to a slap in the face as she could manage.

He rearranged his idea about breakfast and gossip in the kitchen. For now he'd make do with coffee.

"Wondered where you'd got to," Mae said as she pulled bacon out of the refrigerator again.

"I didn't want to get in your way." He nodded toward the coffeepot. "I thought I'd take a cup up with me."

"You need fuel." Dolores busied herself arranging a place setting across from Charity. "Isn't that right, Mae? Man can't work unless he has a proper breakfast."

Mae poured a cup. "He looks like he could run on empty well enough."

It was quite true, Charity thought. She knew what time he'd come in the night before, and he'd been up and working when she'd left the wing to oversee the breakfast shift. He couldn't have gotten much more sleep than she had herself, but he didn't look any the worse for wear.

"Meals are part of your pay, Roman." Though her appetite had fled, Charity nipped off a bite of bacon. "I believe Mae has some pancake batter left over, if you'd prefer that to eggs."

It was a cool invitation, so cool that Dolores opened her mouth to comment. Mae gave her a quick poke and a scowl. He accepted the coffee Mae shoved at him and drank it black.

"Eggs are fine." But he didn't sit down. The welcoming feel that was usually so much a part of the kitchen was not evident. Roman leaned against the counter and sipped while Mae cooked beside him.

She wasn't going to feel guilty, Charity told herself, ignoring a chastising look from Dolores. After all, she was the boss, and her business with Roman was…well, just business. But she couldn't bear the long, strained silence.

"Mae, I'd like some petits fours and tea sandwiches this afternoon. The rain's supposed to last all day, so we'll have music and dancing in the gathering room." Because breakfast seemed less and less appealing, Charity pulled a notepad out of her shirt pocket. "Fifty sandwiches should do if we have a cheese tray. We'll set up an urn of tea, and one of hot chocolate."

"What time?"

"At three, I think. Then we can bring out the wine at five for anyone who wants to linger. You can have your niece help out."

She began making notes on the pad.

She looked tired, Roman thought. Pale and heavy-eyed and surprisingly fragile. She'd apparently pulled her hair back in a hasty ponytail when it had still been damp. Little tendrils had escaped as they'd dried. They seemed lighter than the rest, their color more delicate than rich. He wanted to brush them away from her temples and watch the color come back into her cheeks.

"Finish your eggs," Mae told her. Then she nodded at Roman. "Yours are ready."

"Thanks." He sat down, wishing no more fervently than Charity that he was ten miles away.

Dolores began to complain that the rain was making her sinuses swell.

"Pass the salt," Roman murmured.

Charity pushed it in his direction. Their fingers brushed briefly, and she snatched hers away.

"Thanks."

"You're welcome." Charity poked her fork into her eggs. She knew from experience that it would be difficult to escape from the kitchen without cleaning her plate, and she intended to do it quickly.

"Nice day," he said, because he wanted her to look at him again. She did, and pent-up anger was simmering in her eyes. He preferred it, he discovered, to the cool politeness that had been there.

"I like the rain."

"Like I said—" he broke open his muffin "—it's a nice day."

Dolores blew her nose heartily. Amusement curved the corners of Charity's mouth before she managed to suppress it. "You'll find the paint you need—wall, ceiling, trim—in the storage cellar. It's marked for the proper rooms."

"All right."

"The brushes and pans and rollers are down there, too. Everything's on the workbench on the right as you come down the stairs."

"I'll find them."

"Good. Cabin 4 has a dripping faucet."

"I'll look at it."

She didn't want him to be so damn agreeable, Charity thought. She wanted him to be as tense and out of sorts as she was. "The window sticks in unit 2 in the east wing."

He sent her an even look. "I'll unstick it."

"Fine." Suddenly she noticed that Dolores had stopped complaining and was gawking at her. Even Mae was frowning over her mixing bowl. The hell with it, Charity thought as she shoved her plate away. So she was issuing orders like Captain Bligh. She damn well felt like Captain Bligh.

She took a ring of keys out of her pocket. She'd just put them on that morning, having intended to see to the minor chores herself. "Make sure to bring these back to the office when you've finished. They're tagged for the proper doors."

"Yes, ma'am." Keeping his eyes on hers, he dropped the ring into his breast pocket. "Anything else?"

"I'll let you know." She rose, took her plate to the sink and stalked out.

"What got into her?" Dolores wanted to know. "She looked like she wanted to chew somebody's head off."

"She just didn't sleep well." More concerned than she wanted to let on, Mae set down the mixing bowl in which she'd been creaming butter and sugar. Because she felt like the mother of an ill-mannered child, she picked up the coffeepot and carried it over to Roman. "Charity's not feeling quite herself this morning," she told him as she poured him a second cup. "She's been overworked lately."

"I've got thick skin." But he'd felt the sting. "Maybe she should delegate more."

"Ha! That girl?" Pleased that he hadn't complained, she became more expansive. "It ain't in her. Feels responsible if a guest stubs his toe. Just like her grandpa." Mae added a stream of vanilla to the bowl and went back to her mixing. "Not a thing goes on around here she don't have a finger—more likely her whole hand—in. Except my cooking." Mae's wide face creased in a smile. "I shooed her out of here when she was a girl, and I can shoo her out of here today if need be."

"Girl can't boil water without scorching the pan," Dolores put in.

"She could if she wanted to," Mae said defensively, turning back to Roman with a sniff. "There's no need for her to cook when she's got me, and she's smart enough to know it. Everything else, though, from painting the porch to keeping the books, has to have her stamp on it. She's one who takes her responsibilities to heart."

Roman played out the lead she had offered him. "That's an admirable quality. You've worked for her a long time."

"Between Charity and her grandfather, I've worked at the inn for twenty-eight years come June." She jerked her head in Dolores's direction. "She's been here eight."

"Nine," Dolores said. "Nine years this month."

"It sounds like when people come to work here they stay."

"You got that right," Mae told him.

"It seems the inn has a loyal, hardworking staff."

"Charity makes it easy." Competently Mae measured out baking powder. "She was just feeling moody this morning."

"She did look a little tired," Roman said slowly, ignoring a pang of guilt. "Maybe she'll rest for a while today."

"Not likely."

"The housekeeping staff seems tight."

"She'll still find a bed to make."

"Bob handles the accounts."

"She'll poke her nose in the books and check every column." There was simple pride in her voice as she sifted flour into the bowl. "Not that she don't trust those who work for her," Mae added. "It would just make her heart stop dead to have a bill paid late or an order mixed up. Thing is, she'd rather blame herself than somebody else if a mistake's made."

"I guess nothing much gets by her."

"By Charity?" With a snicker, Mae plugged in her electric mixer. "She'd know if a napkin came back from the laundry with a stain on it. Watch where you sneeze," she added as Dolores covered her face with a tissue. "Drink some hot water with a squeeze of lemon."

"Hot tea with honey," Dolores said.

"Lemon. Honey'll clog your throat."

"My mother always gave me hot tea with honey," Dolores told her.

They were still arguing about it when Roman slipped out of the kitchen.

He spent most of his time closed off in the west wing. Working helped him think. Though he heard Charity pass in and out a few times, neither of them sought the other's company. He could be more objective, Roman realized, when he wasn't around her.

Mae's comments had cemented his observations and the information that had been made available to him.

Charity Ford ran the inn from top to bottom. Whatever went on in it or passed through it was directly under her eye. Logically that meant that she was fully involved with, perhaps in charge of, the operation he had come to destroy.

And yet…what he had said to Conby the night before still held true. It didn't fit.

The woman worked almost around the clock to make the inn a success. He'd seen her do everything from potting geraniums to hauling firewood. And, unless she was an astounding actress, she enjoyed it all.

She didn't seem the type who would want to make money the easy way. Nor did she seem the type who craved all the things easy money could buy. But that was instinct, not fact.

The problem was, Conby ran on facts. Roman had always relied heavily on instinct. His job was to prove her guilt, not her innocence. Yet, in less than two days, his priorities had changed.

It wasn't just a matter of finding her attractive. He had found other women attractive and had brought them down without a qualm. That was justice. One of the few things he believed in without reservation was justice.

With Charity he needed to be certain that his conclusions about her were based on more than the emotions she dragged out of him. Feelings and instincts were different. If a man in his position allowed himself to be swayed by feelings, he was useless.

Then what was it? No matter how long or how hard he thought it through, he couldn't pinpoint one specific reason why he was certain of her innocence. Because it was the whole of it, Roman realized. Her, the inn, the atmosphere that surrounded her. It made him want to believe that such people, such places, existed. And existed untainted.

He was getting soft. A pretty woman, big blue eyes, and he started to think in fairy tales. In disgust, he took the brushes and the paint pans to the sink to clean them. He was going to take a break, from work and from his own rambling thoughts.

In the gathering room, Charity was thinking just as reluctantly of him as she set a stack of records on the table between Miss Millie and Miss Lucy.

"What a lovely idea." Miss Lucy adjusted her glasses and peered at the labels. "A nice old-fashioned tea dance." From one of the units in the east wing came the unrelenting whine of a toddler. Miss Lucy sent a sympathetic glance in the direction of the noise. "I'm sure this will keep everyone entertained."

"It's hard for young people to know what to do with themselves on a rainy day. It makes them cross. Oh, look." Miss Millie held up a 45. "Rosemary Clooney. Isn't this delightful?"

"Pick out your favorites." Charity gave the room a distracted glance. How could she prepare for a party when all she could think of was the way Roman had looked at her across the breakfast table? "I'm depending on you."

The long buffet and a small server had been cleared off to hold the refreshments. If she could count on Mae—and she always had—they should be coming up from the kitchen shortly.

Would Roman come in? she wondered. Would he hear the music and slip silently into the room? Would he look at her until her heart started to hammer and she forgot there was anything or anyone but him?

She was going crazy, Charity decided. She glanced at her watch. It was a quarter to three. Word had been passed to all the guests, and with luck she would be ready for them when they began to arrive. The ladies were deep in a discussion of Perry Como. Leaving them to it, Charity began to tug on the sofa.

"What are you doing?"

A squeal escaped her, and she cursed Roman in the next breath. "If you keep sneaking around I'm going to take Mae's idea of you being a cat burglar more seriously."

"I wasn't sneaking around. You were so busy huffing and puffing you didn't hear me."

"I wasn't huffing or puffing." She tossed her hair over her shoulder and glared at him. "But I am busy, so if you'd get out of my way—"

She waved a hand at him, and he caught it and held it. "I asked what you were doing."

She tugged, then tugged harder, struggling to control her temper. If he wanted to fight, she thought, she'd be happy to oblige him. "I'm knitting an afghan," she snapped. "What does it look like I'm doing? I'm moving the sofa."

"No, you're not."

She could, when the occasion called for, succeed in being haughty. "I beg your pardon?"

"I said you're not moving the sofa. It's too heavy."

"Thank you for your opinion, but I've moved it before." She lowered her voice when she noticed the interested glances the ladies were giving her. "And if you'd get the hell out of my way I'd move it again."

He stood where he was, blocking her. "You really do have to do everything yourself, don't you?"

"Meaning?"

"Where's your assistant?"

"The computer sprang a leak. Since Bob's better equipped to deal with that, he's playing with components and I'm moving furniture. Now—"

"Where do you want it?"

"I didn't ask you to—" But he'd already moved to the other end of the sofa.

"I said, where do you want it?"

"Against the side wall." Charity hefted her end and tried not to be grateful.

"What else?"

She smoothed down the skirt of her dress. "I've already given you a list of chores."

He hooked a thumb in his pocket as they stood on either side of the sofa. He had an urge to put his hand over her angry face and give it a nice hard shove. "I've finished them."

"The faucet in cabin 4?"

"It needed a new washer."

"The window in unit 2?"

"A little sanding."

She was running out of steam. "The painting?"

"The first coat's drying." He angled his head. "Want to check it out?"

She blew out a breath. It was difficult to be annoyed when he'd done everything she'd asked. "Efficient, aren't you, DeWinter?"

"That's right. Got your second wind?"

"What do you mean?"

"You looked a little tired this morning." He skimmed a glance over her. The dark plum-colored dress swirled down her legs. Little silver buttons ranged down from the high neck to the hem, making him wonder how long it would take him to unfasten them. There was silver at her ears, as well, a fanciful trio of columns he remembered having seen in her drawer. "You don't now," he added, bringing his eyes back to hers.

She started to breathe again, suddenly aware that she'd been holding her breath since he'd started his survey. Charity reminded herself that she didn't have time to let him—or her feelings for him—distract her.

"I'm too busy to be tired." Relieved, she signaled to a waitress who was climbing the steps with a laden tray. "Just set it on the buffet, Lori."

"Second load's right behind me."

"Great. I just need to—" She broke off when the first damp guests came through the back door. Giving up, she turned to Roman. If he was going to be in the way anyway, he might as well make himself useful. "I'd appreciate it if you'd roll up the rug and store it in the west wing. Then you're welcome to stay and enjoy yourself."

"Thanks. Maybe I will."

Charity greeted the guests, hung up their jackets, offered them refreshments and switched on the music almost before Roman could store the rug out of sight. Within fifteen minutes she had the group mixing and mingling.

She was made for this, he thought as he watched her. She was made for being in the center of things, for making people feel good. His place had always been on the fringe.

"Oh, Mr. DeWinter." Smelling of lilacs, Miss Millie offered him a cup and saucer. "You must have some tea. Nothing like tea to chase the blues away on a rainy day."

He smiled into her blurred eyes. If even she could

see that he was brooding, he'd better watch his step. "Thanks."

"I love a party," she said wistfully as she watched a few couples dance to a bluesy Clooney ballad. "Why, when I was a girl, I hardly thought of anything else. I met my husband at a tea like this. That was almost fifty years ago. We danced for hours."

He would never have considered himself gallant, but she was hard to resist. "Would you like to dance now?"

The faintest of blushes tinted her cheeks. "I'd love to, Mr. DeWinter."

Charity watched Roman lead Miss Millie onto the floor. Her heart softened. She tried to harden it again but found it was a lost cause. It was a sweet thing to do, she thought, particularly since he was anything but a sweet man. She doubted that teas and dreamy little old ladies were Roman's style, but Miss Millie would remember this day for a long time.

What woman wouldn't? Charity mused. To dance with a strong, mysterious man on a rainy afternoon was a memory to be pressed in a book like a red rose. It was undoubtedly fortunate he hadn't asked her. She had already stored away too many memories of Roman. With a sigh, she herded a group of children into the television room and pushed a Disney movie into the VCR.

Roman saw her leave. And he saw her come back.

"That was lovely," Miss Millie told him when the music had stopped.

"What?" Quickly he brought himself back. "My pleasure." Then he made her pleasure complete by kissing her hand. By the time she had walked over to sigh with her sister he had forgotten her and was thinking of Charity.

She was laughing as an older man led her onto the floor. The music had changed. It was up-tempo now, something brisk and Latin. A mambo, he thought. Or a merengue. He wouldn't know the difference. Apparently Charity knew well enough. She moved through the complicated, flashy number as if she'd been dancing all her life.

Her skirt flared, wrapped around her legs, then flared again as she turned. She laughed, her face level and close to her partner's as they matched steps. The first prick of jealousy infuriated Roman and made him feel like a fool. The man Charity was matching steps with was easily old enough to be her father.

By the time the music ended he had managed to suppress the uncomfortable emotion but another had sprung up to take its place. Desire. He wanted her, wanted to take her by the hand and pull her out of that crowded room into someplace dim and quiet where all they would hear was the rain. He wanted to see her eyes go big and unfocused the way they had when he'd kissed her. He wanted to feel the incredible sensation of her mouth softening and heating under his.

"It's an education to watch her, isn't it?"

Roman jerked himself back as Bob eased over to pluck a sandwich from the tray. "What?"

"Charity. Watching her dance is an education." He popped the tiny sandwich into his mouth. "She tried to teach me once, hoping I'd be able to entertain some of the ladies on occasions like this. Trouble is, I not only have two left feet, I have two left legs." He gave a cheerful shrug and reached for another sandwich.

"Did you get the computer fixed?"

"Yeah. Just a couple of minor glitches." The little triangle of bread disappeared. Roman caught a hint of nerves in the way Bob's knuckle tapped against the server. "I can't teach Charity about circuit boards and software any more than she can teach me the samba. How's the work going?"

"Well enough." He watched as Bob poured a cup of tea and added three sugars to it. "I should be done in two or three weeks."

"She'll find something else for you to do." He glanced over to where Charity and a new partner were dancing a fox-trot. "She's always got a new idea for this place. Lately she's been making noises about adding on a sun-room and putting in one of those whirlpool tubs."

Roman lit a cigarette. He was watching the guests now, making mental notes to pass on to Conby. There were two men who seemed to be alone, though they were chatting with other members of the tour group. Block stood by the doors, holding a plateful of sand-wiches that he was dispatching with amazing ease and grinning at no one in particular.

"The inn must be doing well."

"Oh, it's stable." Bob turned his attention to the petits fours. "A couple of years ago things were a little rocky, but Charity would always find a way to keep the ship afloat. Nothing's more important to her."

Roman was silent for a moment. "I don't know much about the hotel business, but she seems to know what she's doing."

"Inside and out." Bob chose a cake with pink frost-ing. "Charity *is* the inn."

"Have you worked for her long?"

"About two and a half years. She couldn't really afford me, but she wanted to turn things around, modernize the bookkeeping. Pump new life into the place, was what she said." Someone put on a jitterbug, and he grinned. "She did just that."

"Apparently."

"So you're from back east." Bob paused for a moment, then continued when Roman made no comment. "How long are you planning to stay?"

"As long as it takes."

He took a long sip of tea. "As long as what takes?"

"The job." Roman glanced idly toward the west wing. "I like to finish what I start."

"Yeah. Well…" He arranged several petits fours on a plate. "I'm going to go offer these to the ladies and hope they let me eat them."

Roman watched him pass Block and exchange a quick word with him before he crossed the room. Wanting time to think, Roman slipped back into the west wing.

It was still raining when he came back hours later. Music was playing, some slow, melodic ballad from the fifties. The room was dimmer now, lit only by the fire and a glass-globed lamp. It was empty, too, except for Charity, who was busy tidying up, humming along with the music.

"Party over?"

She glanced around, then went hurriedly back to stacking cups and plates. "Yes. You didn't stay long."

"I had work to do."

Because she wanted to keep moving, she switched to emptying ashtrays. She'd held on to her guilt long enough. "I was tired this morning, but that's no excuse for being rude to you. I'm sorry if I gave you the impression that you couldn't enjoy yourself for a few hours."

He didn't want to accept an apology that he knew he didn't deserve. "I enjoy the work."

That only made her feel worse. "Be that as it may, I don't usually go around barking orders. I was angry with you."

"Was?"

She looked up, and her eyes were clear and direct. "Am. But that's my problem. If it helps, I'm every bit as angry with myself for acting like a child because you didn't let things get out of hand last night."

Uncomfortable, he picked up the wine decanter and poured a glass. "You didn't act like a child."

"A woman scorned, then, or something equally dramatic. Try not to contradict me when I'm apologizing."

Despite his best efforts, his lips curved against the rim of his glass. If he didn't watch himself he could find he was crazy about her. "All right. Is there more?"

"Just a little." She picked up one of the few petits fours that were left over, debated with herself, then popped it into her mouth. "I shouldn't let my personal feelings interfere with my running of the inn. The problem is, almost everything I think or feel connects with the inn."

"Neither of us were thinking of the inn last night. Maybe that's the problem."

"Maybe."

"Do you want the couch moved back?"

"Yes." Business as usual, Charity told herself as she walked over to lift her end. The moment it was in place she scooted around to plump the pillows. "I saw you dancing with Miss Millie. It thrilled her."

"I like her."

"I think you do," Charity said slowly, straightening and studying him. "You're not the kind of man who likes easily."

"No."

She wanted to go to him, to lift a hand to his cheek. That was ridiculous, she told herself. Apology notwithstanding, she was still angry with him for last night. "Has life been so hard?" she murmured.

"No."

With a little laugh, she shook her head. "Then again, you wouldn't tell me if it had been. I have to learn not to ask you questions. Why don't we call a truce, Roman? Life's too short for bad feelings."

"I don't have any bad feelings toward you, Charity."

She smiled a little. "It's tempting, but I'm not going to ask what kind of feelings you do have."

"I wouldn't be able to tell you, because I haven't figured it out." He was amazed that the words had come out. After draining the wine, he set the empty glass aside.

"Well." Nonplussed, she pushed her hair back with both hands. "That's the first thing you've told me I can really understand. Looks like we're in the same boat. Do I take it we have a truce?"

"Sure."

She glanced back as another record dropped onto the turntable. "This is one of my favorites. 'Smoke Gets in Your Eyes.'" She was smiling again when she looked back at him. "You never asked me to dance."

"No, I didn't."

"Miss Millie claims you're very smooth." She held out a hand in a gesture that was as much a peace offering as an invitation. Unable to resist, he took it in his. Their eyes stayed locked as he drew her slowly toward him.

Chapter 5

A fire simmered in the grate. Rain pattered against the windows. The record was old and scratchy, the tune hauntingly sad. Whether they wanted it or not, their bodies fitted. Her hand slid gently over his shoulder, his around her waist. With their faces close, they began to dance.

The added height from her heels brought her eyes level with his. He could smell the light fragrance that seemed so much a part of her. Seduced by it, he brought her closer, slowly. Their thighs brushed. Still closer. Her body melted against his.

It was so quiet. There was only the music, the rain, the hissing of the fire. Gloomy light swirled into the room. He could feel her heart beating against his, quick now, and not too steady.

His wasn't any too steady now, either.

Was that all it took? he wondered. Did he only have

to touch her to think that she was the beginning and the
end of everything? And to wish... His hand slid up her
back, fingers spreading until they tangled in her hair.
To wish she could belong to him.

He wasn't sure when that thought had sunk its roots
in him. Perhaps it had begun the first moment he had
seen her. She was—should have been—unattainable for
him. But when she was in his arms, warm, just border-
ing on pliant, dozens of possibilities flashed through
his head.

She wanted to smile, to make some light, easy comment. But she couldn't push the words out. Her throat
was locked. The way he was looking at her now, as
if she were the only woman he had ever seen or ever
wanted to see, made her forget that the dance was supposed to be a gesture of friendship.

She might never be his friend, she knew, no matter
how hard she tried. But with his eyes on hers she understood how easily she could be his lover.

Maybe it was wrong, but it didn't seem to matter as
they glided across the floor. The song spoke of love betrayed, but she heard only poetry. She felt her will ebb
away even as the music swelled inside her head. No,
it didn't seem to matter. Nothing seemed to matter as
long as she went on swaying in his arms.

She didn't even try to think, never attempted to reason. Following her heart, she pressed her lips to his.

Instant. Irresistible. Irrevocable. Emotions funneled
from one to the other, then merged in a torrent of need.
She didn't expect him to be gentle, though her kiss had
offered comfort, as well as passion. He dived into it,
into her, with a speed and force that left her reeling,
then fretting for more.

So this was what drove people to do mad, desperate acts, she thought as their tongues tangled. This wild, painful pleasure, once tasted, would never be forgotten, would always be craved. She wrapped her arms around his neck as she gave herself to it.

With quick, rough kisses he drove them both to the edge. It was more than desire, he knew. Desire had never hurt, not deeply. It was like a scratch, soon forgotten, easily healed. This was a raw, deep wound.

Lust had never erased every coherent thought from his mind. Still, he could only think of her. Those thoughts were jumbled, and all of them were forbidden. Desperate, he ran his lips over her face, while wild fantasies of touching, of tasting every inch of her whirled in his head. It wouldn't be enough. It would never be enough. No matter how much he took from her, she would draw him back. And she could make him beg. The certainty of it terrified him.

She was trembling again, even as she strained against him. Her soft gasps and sighs pushed him toward the brink of reason. He found her mouth again and feasted on it.

He hardly recognized the change, could find no reason for it. All at once she was like glass in his arms, something precious, something fragile, something he needed to protect and defend. He lifted his hands to her face, his fingers light and cautiously caressing. His mouth, ravenous only a moment before, gentled.

Stunned, she swayed. New, vibrant emotions poured into her. Weak from the onslaught, she let her head fall back. Her arms slipped, boneless, to her sides. There was beauty here, a soft, shimmering beauty she had never known existed. Tenderness did what passion had not yet accomplished. As freely as a bird taking wing, her heart flew out to him.

Love, first experienced, was devastating. She felt tears burn the back of her eyes, heard her own quiet moan of surrender. And she tasted the glory of it as his lips played gently with hers.

She would always remember that one instant when the world changed—the music, the rain, the scent of fresh flowers. Nothing would ever be quite the same again. Nor would she ever want it to be.

Shaken, she drew back to lift a hand to her spinning head. "Roman—"

"Come with me." Unwilling to think, he pulled her against him again. "I want to know what it's like to be with you, to undress you, to touch you."

With a moan, she surrendered to his mouth again.

"Charity, Mae wants to—" Lori stopped on a dime at the top of the stairs. After clearing her throat, she stared at the painting on the opposite wall as if it fascinated her. "Excuse me. I didn't mean to…"

Charity had jerked back like a spring and was searching for composure. "It's all right. What is it, Lori?"

"It's, well… Mae and Dolores… Maybe you could come down to the kitchen when you get a minute." She rushed down the stairs, grinning to herself.

"I should…" Charity paused to draw in a steadying breath but managed only a shaky one. "I should go down." She retreated a step. "Once they get started, they need—" She broke off when Roman took her arm. He waited until she lifted her head and looked at him again.

"Things have changed."

It sounded so simple when he said it. "Yes. Yes, they have."

"Right or wrong, Charity, we'll finish this."

"No." She was far from calm, but she was very determined. "If it's right, we'll finish it. I'm not going to pretend I don't want you, but you're right when you say things have changed, Roman. You see, I know what I'm feeling now, and I have to get used to it."

He tightened his grip when she turned to go. "What are you feeling?"

She couldn't have lied if she'd wanted to. Dishonesty was abhorrent to her. When it came to feelings, she had neither the ability nor the desire to suppress them. "I'm in love with you."

His fingers uncurled from her arm. Very slowly, very carefully, as if he were retreating from some dangerous beast, he released her.

She read the shock on his face. That was understandable. And she read the distrust. That was painful. She gave him a last unsmiling look before she turned away.

"Apparently we both have to get used to it."

She was lying. Roman told himself that over and over as he paced the floor in his room. If not to him, then certainly to herself. People seemed to find love easy to lie about.

He stopped by the window and stared out into the dark. The rain had stopped, and the moon was cruising in and out of the clouds. He jerked the window open and breathed in the damp, cool air. He needed something to clear his head.

She was working on him. Annoyed, he turned away from the view of trees and flowers and started pacing again. The easy smiles, the openhanded welcome, the casual friendliness...then the passion, the uninhibited

response, the seduction. He wanted to believe it was
a trap, even though his well-trained mind found the
idea absurd.

She had no reason to suspect him. His cover was solid.
Charity thought of him as a drifter, passing through long
enough to take in some sights and pick up a little loose
change. It was he who was setting the trap.

He dropped down on the bed and lit a cigarette, more
out of habit than because he wanted one. Lies were part
of his job, a part he was very good at. She hadn't lied to
him, he reflected as he inhaled. But she was mistaken.
He had made her want, and she had justified her desire
for a relative stranger by telling herself she was in love.

But if it was true...

He couldn't allow himself to think that way. Leaning back against the headboard, he stared at the blank
wall. He couldn't allow himself the luxury of wondering what it would be like to be loved, and especially not
what it would be like to be loved by a woman to whom
love would mean a lifetime. He couldn't afford any daydreams about belonging, about having someone belong
to him. Even if she hadn't been part of his assignment
he would have to sidestep Charity Ford.

She would think of love, then of white picket fences,
Sunday dinners and evenings by the fire. He was no
good for her. He would never be any good for her.
Roman DeWinter, he thought with a mirthless smile.
Always on the wrong side of the tracks. A questionable
past, an uncertain future. There was nothing he could
offer a woman like Charity.

But God, he wanted her. The need was eating away
at his insides. He knew she was upstairs now. He imagined her curled up in the big four-poster, under white

blankets, perhaps with a white candle burning low on the table.

He had only to climb the stairs and walk through the door. She wouldn't send him away. If she tried, it would take him only moments to break down her resistance. Believing herself in love, she would yield, then open her arms to him. He ached to be in them, to sink into that bed, into her, and let oblivion take them both.

But she had asked for time. He wasn't going to deny her what he needed himself. In the time he gave her he would use all his skill to do the one thing he knew how to do for her. He would prove her innocence.

Roman watched the tour group check out the following morning. Perched on a stepladder in the center of the lobby, he took his time changing bulbs in the ceiling fixture. The sun was out now, full and bright, bathing the lobby in light as a few members of the tour loitered after breakfast.

At the front desk, Charity was chatting with Block. He was wearing a fresh white shirt and his perpetual smile. Taking a calculator from his briefcase, he checked to see if Charity's tallies matched his own.

Bob poked his head out of the office and handed her a computer printout. Roman didn't miss the quick, uncertain look Bob sent in his direction before he shut himself away again.

Charity and Block compared lists. Still smiling, he took a stack of bills out of his briefcase. He paid in Canadian, cash. Having already adjusted the bill to take the exchange rate into account, Charity locked the cash away in a drawer, then handed Block his receipt.

"Always a pleasure, Roger."

"Your little party saved the day," he told her. "My people consider this the highlight of the tour."

Pleased, she smiled at him. "They haven't seen Mount Rainier yet."

"You're going to get some repeaters out of this." He patted her hand, then checked his watch. "Time to move them out. See you next week."

"Safe trip, Roger." She turned to make change for a departing guest, then sold a few postcards and a few souvenir key chains with miniature whales on them.

Roman replaced the globe on the ceiling fixture, taking his time until the lobby was clear again. "Isn't it strange for a company like that to pay cash?"

Distracted from her reservations list, Charity glanced up at him. "We never turn down cash." She smiled at him as she had promised herself she would. Her feelings, her problem, she reminded herself as he climbed down from the ladder. She only wished the hours she'd spent soul-searching the night before had resulted in a solution.

"It seems like they'd charge, or pay by check."

"It's their company policy. Believe me, with a small, independent hotel, a cash-paying customer like Vision can make all the difference."

"I'll bet. You've been dealing with them for a while?"

"A couple of years. Why?"

"Just curious. Block doesn't look much like a tour guide."

"Roger? No, I guess he looks more like a wrestler." She went back to her papers. It was difficult to make small talk when her feelings were so close to the surface. "He does a good job."

"Yeah. I'll be upstairs."

"Roman." There was so much she wanted to say, but she could feel, though they were standing only a few feet apart, that he had distanced himself from her. "We never discussed a day off," she began. "You're welcome to take Sunday, if you like."

"Maybe I will."

"And if you'd give Bob your hours at the end of the week, he generally takes care of payroll."

"All right. Thanks."

A young couple with a toddler walked out of the dining room. Roman left her to answer their questions on renting a boat.

It wasn't going to be easy to talk to him, Charity decided later. But she had to do it. She'd spent all morning on business, she'd double-checked the housekeeping in the cabins, she'd made every phone call on her list, and if Mae's comments were anything to go on she'd made a nuisance of herself in the kitchen.

She was stalling.

That wasn't like her. All her life she'd made a habit of facing her problems head-on and plowing through them. Not only with business, she thought now. Personal problems had always been given the same kind of direct approach. She had handled being parentless. Even as a child she had never evaded the sometimes painful questions about her background.

But then, she'd had her grandfather. He'd been so solid, so loving. He'd helped her understand that she was her own person. Just as he'd helped her through her first high-school crush, Charity remembered.

He wasn't here now, and she wasn't a fifteen-year-old mooning over the captain of the debating team. But if he had taught her anything, it was that honest feelings were nothing to be ashamed of.

Armed with a thermos full of coffee, she walked into the west wing. She wished it didn't feel so much like bearding the lion in his den.

He'd finished the parlor. The scent of fresh paint was strong, though he'd left a window open to air it out. The doors still had to be hung and the floors varnished, but she could already imagine the room with sheer, billowy curtains and the faded floral-print rug she'd stored in the attic.

From the bedroom beyond, she could hear the buzz of an electric saw. A good, constructive sound, she thought as she pushed the door open to peek inside.

His eyes were narrowed in concentration as he bent over the wood he had laid across a pair of sawhorses. Wood dust flew, dancing gold in the sunlight. His hands, and his arms where he'd rolled his sleeves up past the elbow, were covered with it. He'd used a bandanna to keep the hair out of his eyes. He didn't hum while he worked, as she did. Or talk to himself, she mused, as George had. But, watching him, she thought she detected a simple pleasure in doing a job and doing it well.

He could do things, she thought as she watched him measure the wood for the next cut. Good things, even important things. She was sure of it. Not just because she loved him, she realized. Because it was in him. When a woman spent all her life entertaining strangers in her home, she learned to judge, and to see.

She waited until he put the saw down before she pushed the door open. Before she could speak he whirled around. Her step backward was instinctive, defensive. It was ridiculous, she told herself, but she thought that if he'd had a weapon he'd have drawn it.

"I'm sorry." The nerves she had managed to get under control were shot to hell. "I should have realized I'd startle you."

"It's all right." He settled quickly, though it annoyed him to have been caught off guard. Perhaps if he hadn't been thinking of her he would have sensed her.

"I needed to do some things upstairs, so I thought I'd bring you some coffee on my way." She set the thermos on the stepladder, then wished she'd kept it, as her empty hands made her feel foolish. "And I wanted to check how things were going. The parlor looks great."

"It's coming along. Did you label the paint?"

"Yes. Why?"

"Because it was all done in this tidy printing on the lid of each can in the color of the paint. That seemed like something you'd do."

"Obsessively organized?" She made a face. "I can't seem to help it."

"I liked the way you had the paintbrushes arranged according to size."

She lifted a brow. "Are you making fun of me?"

"Yeah."

"Well, as long as I know." Her nerves were calmer now. "Want some of this coffee?"

"Yeah. I'll get it."

"You've got sawdust all over your hands." Waving him aside, she unscrewed the top. "I take it our truce is back on."

"I didn't realize it had been off."

She glanced back over her shoulder, then looked

around and poured the coffee into the plastic cup. "I made you uncomfortable yesterday. I'm sorry."

He accepted the cup and sat down on a sawhorse. "You're putting words in my mouth again, Charity."

"I don't have to this time. You looked as if I'd hit you with a brick." Restless, she moved her shoulders. "I suppose I might have reacted the same way if someone had said they loved me out of the blue like that. It must have been pretty startling, seeing as we haven't known each other for long."

Finding he had no taste for it, he set the coffee aside. "You were reacting to the moment."

"No." She turned back to him, knowing it was important to talk face-to-face. "I thought you might think that. In fact, I even considered playing it safe and letting you. I'm lousy at deception. It seemed more fair to tell you that I'm not in the habit of…what I mean is, I don't throw myself at men as a rule. The truth is, you're the first."

"Charity." He dragged a hand through his hair, pulling out the bandanna and sending more wood dust scattering. "I don't know what to say to you."

"You don't have to say anything. The fact is, I came in here with my little speech all worked out. It was a pretty good one, too…calm, understanding, a couple of dashes of humor to keep it light. I'm screwing it up."

She kicked a scrap of wood into the corner before she paced to the window. Columbine and bluebells grew just below in a bed where poppies were waiting to burst into color. On impulse, she pushed up the window to breathe in their faint, fragile scents.

"The point is," she began, hating herself for keeping her back to him, "we can't pretend I didn't say it. I can't pretend I don't feel it. That doesn't mean I expect you to feel the same way, because I don't."

"What do you expect?"

He was right behind her. She jumped when his hand gripped her shoulder. Gathering her courage, she turned around. "For you to be honest with me." She was speaking quickly now, and she didn't notice his slight, automatic retreat. "I appreciate the fact that you don't pretend to love me. I may be simple, Roman, but I'm not stupid. I know it might be easier to lie, to say what you think I want to hear."

"You're not simple," he murmured, lifting a hand and brushing it against her cheek. "I've never met a more confusing, complicated woman."

Shock came first, then pleasure. "That's the nicest thing you've ever said to me. No one's ever accused me of being complicated."

He'd meant to lower his hand, but she had already lifted hers and clasped it. "I didn't mean it as a compliment."

That made her grin. Relaxed again, she sat back on the windowsill. "Even better. I hope this means we're finished feeling awkward around each other."

"I don't know what I feel around you." He ran his hands up her arms to her shoulders, then down to the elbows again. "But awkward isn't the word for it."

Touched—much too deeply—she rose. "I have to go."

"Why?"

"Because it's the middle of the day, and if you kiss me I might forget that."

Already aroused, he eased her forward. "Always organized."

"Yes." She put a hand to his chest to keep some distance between them. "I have some invoices I have to go over upstairs." Holding her breath, she backed toward the door. "I do want you, Roman. I'm just not sure I can handle that part of it."

Neither was he, he thought after she shut the door. With another woman he would have been certain that physical release would end the tension. With Charity he knew that making love with her would only add another layer to the hold she had on him.

And she did have a hold on him. It was time to admit that, and to deal with it.

Perhaps he'd reacted so strongly to her declaration of love because he was afraid, as he'd never been afraid of anything in his life, that he was falling in love with her.

"Roman!" He heard the delight in Charity's voice when she called to him. He swung open the door and saw her standing on the landing at the top of the stairs. "Come up. Hurry. I want you to see them."

She disappeared, leaving him wishing she'd called him anyplace but that innocently seductive bedroom.

When he walked into her sitting room, she called again, impatience in her tone now. "Hurry. I don't know how long they'll stay."

She was sitting on the windowsill, her upper body out the opening, her long legs hooked just above the ankles. There was music playing, something vibrant, passionate. How was it he had never thought of classical music as passionate?

"Damn it, Roman, you're going to miss them. Don't just stand in the doorway. I didn't call you up to tie you to the bedposts."

Because he felt like a fool, he crossed to her. "There goes my night."

"Very funny. Look." She was holding a brass spy glass, and she pointed with it now, out to sea. "Orcas."

He leaned out the window and followed her guiding hand. He could see a pair of shapes in the distance, rippling the water as they swam. Fascinated, he took the spyglass from Charity's hand.

"There are three of them," he said. Delighted, he joined her on the windowsill. Their legs were aligned now, and he rested his hand absently on her knee. This time, instead of fire, there was simple warmth.

"Yes, there's a calf. I think it might be the same pod I spotted a few days ago." She closed a hand over his as they both stared out to sea. "Great, aren't they?"

"Yeah, they are." He focused on the calf, which was just visible between the two larger whales. "I never really expected to see any."

"Why? The island's named after them." She narrowed her eyes, trying to follow their path. She didn't have the heart to ask Roman for the glass. "My first clear memory of seeing one was when I was about four. Pop had me out on this little excuse for a fishing boat. One shot up out of the water no more than eight or ten yards away. I screamed my lungs out." Laughing, she leaned back against the window frame. "I thought it was going to swallow us whole, like Jonah or maybe Pinocchio."

Roman lowered the glass for a moment. "Pinocchio?"

"Yes, you know the puppet who wanted to be a real boy. Jiminy Cricket, the Blue Fairy. Anyway, Pop finally calmed me down. It followed us for ten or fifteen minutes. After that, I nagged him mercilessly to take me out again."

"Did he?"

"Every Monday afternoon that summer. We didn't always see something, but they were great days, the best days. I guess we were a pod, too, Pop and I." She turned her face into the breeze. "I was lucky to have him as long as I did, but there are times—like this— when I can't help wishing he were here."

"Like this?"

"He loved to watch them," she said quietly. "Even when he was ill, really ill, he would sit for hours at the window. One afternoon I found him sitting there with the spyglass on his lap. I thought he'd fallen asleep, but he was gone." There was a catch in her breath when she slowly let it out. "He would have wanted that, to just slip away while watching for his whales. I haven't been able to take the boat out since he died." She shook her head. "Stupid."

"No." He reached for her hand for the first time and linked his fingers with hers. "It's not."

She turned her face to his again. "You can be a nice man." The phone rang, and she groaned but slipped dutifully from the windowsill to answer it.

"Hello. Yes, Bob. What does he mean he won't deliver them? New management be damned, we've been dealing with that company for ten years. Yes, all right. I'll be right there. Oh, wait." She glanced up from the phone. "Roman, are they still there?"

"Yes. Heading south. I don't know if they're feeding or just taking an afternoon stroll."

She laughed and put the receiver at her ear again. "Bob— What? Yes, that was Roman." Her brow lifted.

"That's right. We're in my room. I called Roman up here because I spotted a pod out my bedroom window. You might want to tell any of the guests you see around. No, there's no reason for you to be concerned. Why should there be? I'll be right down."

She hung up, shaking her head. "It's like having a houseful of chaperons," she muttered.

"Problem?"

"No. Bob realized that you were in my bedroom— or rather that we were alone in my bedroom—and got very big-brotherly. Typical." She opened a drawer and pulled out a fabric-covered band. In a few quick movements she had her hair caught back from her face. "Last year Mae threatened to poison a guest who made a pass at me. You'd think I was fifteen."

He turned to study her. She was wearing jeans and a sweatshirt with a silk-screened map of the island. "Yes, you would."

"I don't take that as a compliment." But she didn't have time to argue. "I have to deal with a small crisis downstairs. You're welcome to stay and watch the whales." She started toward the door, but then she stopped. "Oh, I nearly forgot. Can you build shelves?"

"Probably."

"Great. I think the parlor in the family suite could use them. We'll talk about it."

He heard her jog down the stairs. Whatever crisis there might be at the other end of the inn, he was sure she would handle it. In the meantime, she had left him alone in her room. It would be a simple matter to go through her desk again, to see if she'd left anything that would help him move his investigation forward.

It should be simple, anyway. Roman looked out to

sea again. It should be something he could do without hesitation. But he couldn't. She trusted him. Sometime during the past twenty-four hours he reached the point where he couldn't violate that trust.

That made him useless. Swearing, Roman leaned back against the window frame. She had, without even being aware of it, totally undermined his ability to do his job. It would be best for him to call Conby and have himself taken off the case. It would simply be a matter of him turning in his resignation now, rather than at the end of the assignment. It was a question of duty.

He wasn't going to do that, either.

He needed to stay. It had nothing to do with being loved, with feeling at home. He needed to believe that. He also needed to finish his job and prove, beyond a shadow of a doubt, Charity's innocence. That was a question of loyalty.

Conby would have said that his loyalty belonged to the Bureau, not to a woman he had known for less than a week. And Conby would have been wrong, Roman thought as he set aside the spyglass. There were times, rare times, when you had a chance to do something good, something right. Something that proved you gave a damn. That had never mattered to him before, but it mattered now.

If the only thing he could give Charity was a clear name, he intended to give it to her. And then get out of her life.

Rising, he looked around the room. He wished he were nothing more than the out-of-work drifter Charity had taken into her home. If he were maybe he would have the right to love her. As it was, all he could do was save her.

Chapter 6

The weather was warming. Spring was busting loose, full of glory and color and scent. The island was a treasure trove of wildflowers, leafy trees and birdsong. At dawn, with thin fingers of fog over the water, it was a mystical, timeless place.

Roman stood at the side of the road and watched the sun come up as he had only days before. He didn't know the names of the flowers that grew in tangles on the roadside. He didn't know the song of a jay from that of a sparrow. But he knew Charity was out running with her dog and that she would pass the place he stood on her return.

He needed to see her, to talk to her, to be with her.

The night before, he had broken into her cash drawer and examined the bills she had neatly stacked and marked for today's deposit. There had been over two thousand dollars in counterfeit Canadian currency. His

first impulse had been to tell her, to lay everything he
knew and needed to know out in front of her. But he
had quashed that. Telling her wouldn't prove her innocence to men like Conby.

He had enough to get Block. And nearly enough, he
thought, to hang Bob along with him. But he couldn't
get them without casting shadows on Charity. By her
own admission, and according to the statements of her
loyal staff, a pin couldn't drop in the inn without her
knowing it.

If that was so, how could he prove that there had been
a counterfeiting and smuggling ring going on under her
nose for nearly two years?

He believed it, as firmly as he had ever believed anything. Conby and the others at the Bureau wanted facts.
Roman drew on his cigarette and watched the fog melt
away with the rising of the sun. He had to give them
facts. Until he could, he would give them nothing.

He could wait and make sure Conby dropped the ax
on Block on the guide's next trip to the inn. That would
give Roman time. Time enough, he promised himself,
to make certain Charity wasn't caught in the middle.
When it went down, she would be stunned and hurt.
She'd get over it. When it was over, and she knew his
part in it, she would hate him. He would get over that.
He would have to.

He heard a car and glanced over, then returned his
gaze to the water. He wondered if he could come back
someday and stand in this same spot and wait for Charity to run down the road toward him.

Fantasies, he told himself, pitching his half-finished
cigarette into the dirt. He was wasting too much time
on fantasies.

The car was coming fast, its engine protesting, its muffler rattling. He looked over again, annoyed at having his morning and his thoughts disturbed.

His annoyance saved his life.

It took him only an instant to realize what was happening, and a heartbeat more to evade it. As the car barreled toward him, he leaped aside, tucking and rolling into the brush. A wave of displaced air flattened the grass before the car's rear tires gripped the roadbed again. Roman's gun was in his hand even as he scrambled to his feet. He caught a glimpse of the car's rear end as it sped around a curve. There wasn't even time to swear before he heard Charity's scream.

He ran, unaware of the fire in his thigh where the car had grazed him and the blood on his arm where he had rolled into a rock. He had faced death. He had killed. But he had never understood terror until this moment, with her scream still echoing in his head. He hadn't understood agony until he'd seen Charity sprawled beside the road.

The dog was curled beside her, whimpering, nuzzling her face with her nose. He turned at Roman's approach and began to growl, then stood, barking.

"Charity." Roman crouched beside her, and felt for a pulse, his hand shaking. "Okay, baby. You're going to be okay," he murmured to her as he checked for broken bones.

Had she been hit? A sickening vision of her being tossed into the air as the car slammed into her pulsed through his head. Using every ounce of control he possessed, he blocked it out. She was breathing. He held on to that. The dog whined as he turned her head and examined the gash on her temple. It was the only spot of color on her face. He stanched the blood with his bandanna, cursing when he felt its warmth on his fingers.

Grimly he replaced his weapon, then lifted her into his arms. Her body seemed boneless. Roman tightened his grip, half afraid she might melt through his arms. He talked to her throughout the half mile walk back to the inn, though she remained pale and still.

Bob raced out the front door of the inn. "My God! What happened? What the hell did you do to her?"

Roman paused just long enough to aim a dark, furious look at him. "I think you know better. Get me the keys to the van. She needs a hospital."

"What's all this?" Mae came through the door, wiping her hands on her apron. "Lori said she saw—" She went pale, but then she began to move with surprising speed, elbowing Bob aside to reach Charity. "Get her upstairs."

"I'm taking her to the hospital."

"Upstairs," Mae repeated, moving back to open the door for him. "We'll call Dr. Mertens. It'll be faster. Come on, boy. Call the doctor, Bob. Tell him to hurry."

Roman passed through the door, the dog at his heels. "And call the police," he added. "Tell them they've got a hit-and-run."

Wasting no time on words, Mae led the way upstairs. She was puffing a bit by the time she reached the second floor, but she never slowed down. When they moved into Charity's room, her color had returned.

"Set her on the bed, and be careful about it." She yanked the lacy coverlet aside and then just as efficiently, brushed Roman aside. "There, little girl, you'll be just fine. Go in the bathroom," she told Roman. "Get me a fresh towel." Easing a hip onto the bed, she cupped Charity's face with a broad hand and examined her head wound. "Looks worse than it is." She let out a long breath. After taking the towel Roman offered, she pressed it against Charity's temple. "Head wounds bleed heavy, make a mess. But it's not too deep."

He only knew that her blood was still on his hands. "She should be coming around."

"Give her time. I want you to tell me what happened later, but I'm going to undress her now, see if she's hurt anywhere else. You go on and wait downstairs."

"I'm not leaving her."

Mae glanced up. Her lips were pursed, and lines of worry fanned out from her eyes. After a moment, she simply nodded. "All right, then, but you'll be of some use. Get me the scissors out of her desk. I want to cut this shirt off."

So that was the way of it, Mae mused as she untied Charity's shoes. She knew a man who was scared to death and fighting his heart when she saw one. Well, she'd just have to get her girl back on her feet. She didn't doubt for a moment that Charity could deal with the likes of Roman DeWinter.

"You can stay," she told him when he handed her the scissors. "But whatever's been going on between the two of you, you'll turn your back till I make her decent."

He balled his hands into impotent fists and shoved them into his pockets as he spun around. "I want to know where she's hurt."

"Just hold your horses." Mae peeled the shirt away and put her emotions on hold as she examined the scrapes and bruises. "Look in that top right-hand drawer and get me out a nightshirt. One with buttons. And keep your eyes to yourself," she added, "or I'll throw you out of here."

In answer, he tossed a thin white nightshirt onto the bed. "I don't care what she's wearing. I want to know how badly she's hurt."

"I know, boy." Mae's voice softened as she slipped Charity's limp arm into a sleeve. "She's got some bruises and scrapes, that's all. Nothing broken. The cut on her head's going to need some tending, but cuts heal. Why, she hurt herself worse when she fell out of a tree some time back. There's my girl. She's coming around."

He turned to look then, shirt or no shirt. But Mae had already done up the buttons. He controlled the urge to go to her—barely—and, keeping his distance, watched Charity's lashes flutter. The sinking in his stomach was pure relief. When she moaned, he wiped his clammy hands on his thighs.

"Mae?" As she struggled to focus her eyes, Charity reached out a hand. She could see the solid bulk of her cook, but little else. "What— Oh, God, my head."

"Thumping pretty good, is it?" Mae's voice was brisk, but she cradled Charity's hand in hers. She would have kissed it if she'd thought no one would notice. "The doc'll fix that up."

"Doctor?" Baffled, Charity tried to sit up, but the pain exploded in her head. "I don't want the doctor."

"Never did, but you're having him just the same."

"I'm not going to…" Arguing took too much effort. Instead, she closed her eyes and concentrated on clearing her mind. It was fairly obvious that she was in bed—but how the devil had she gotten there?

She'd been walking the dog, she remembered, and Ludwig had found a tree beside the road irresistible. Then…

"There was a car," she said, opening her eyes again.

"They must have been drunk or crazy. It seemed like they came right at me. If Ludwig hadn't already been pulling me off the road, I—" She wasn't quite ready to consider that. "I stumbled, I think. I don't know."

"It doesn't matter now," Mae assured her. "We'll figure it all out later."

After a brisk knock, the outside door opened. A short, spry little man with a shock of white hair hustled in. He carried a black bag and was wearing grubby overalls and muddy boots. Charity took one look, then closed her eyes again.

"Go away, Dr. Mertens. I'm not feeling well."

"She never changes." Mertens nodded to Roman, then walked over to examine his patient.

Roman slipped quietly out into the sitting room. He needed a moment to pull himself together, to quiet the rage that was building now that he knew she would be all right. He had lost his parents, he had buried his best friend, but he had never, never felt the kind of panic he had experienced when he had seen Charity bleeding and unconscious beside the road.

Taking out a cigarette, he went to the open window. He thought about the driver of the old, rusted Chevy that had run her down. Even as his rage cooled, Roman understood one thing with perfect clarity. It would be his pleasure to kill whoever had hurt her.

"Excuse me." Lori was standing in the hall doorway, wringing her hands. "The sheriff's here. He wants to talk to you, so I brought him up." She tugged at her apron and stared at the closed door on the other side of the room. "Charity?"

"The doctor's with her," Roman said. "She'll be fine."

Lori closed her eyes and took a deep breath. "I'll tell the others. Go on in, sheriff."

Roman studied the paunchy man, who had obviously been called out of bed. His shirttail was only partially tucked into his pants, and he was sipping a cup of coffee as he came into the room.

"You Roman DeWinter?"

"That's right."

"Sheriff Royce." He sat, with a sigh, on the arm of Charity's rose-colored Queen Anne chair. "What's this about a hit-and-run?"

"About twenty minutes ago somebody tried to run down Miss Ford."

Royce turned to stare at the closed door just the way Lori had done. "How is she?"

"Banged up. She's got a gash on her head and some bruises."

"Were you with her?" He pulled out a pad and a stubby pencil.

"No. I was about a quarter mile away. The car swerved at me, then kept going. I heard Charity scream. When I got to her, she was unconscious."

"Don't suppose you got a good look at the car?"

"Dark blue Chevy. Sedan, '67, '68. Muffler was bad. Right front fender was rusted through. Washington plates Alpha Foxtrot Juliet 847."

Royce lifted both brows as he took down the description. "You got a good eye."

"That's right."

"Good enough for you to guess if he ran you down on purpose?"

"I don't have to guess. He was aiming."

Without a flicker of an eye, Royce continued taking notes. He added a reminder to himself to do a routine check on Roman DeWinter. "He? Did you see the driver?"

"No," Roman said shortly. He was still cursing himself for that.

"How long have you been on the island, Mr. DeWinter?"

"Almost a week."

"A short time to make enemies."

"I don't have any—here—that I know of."

"That makes your theory pretty strange." Still scribbling, Royce glanced up. "There's nobody on the island who knows Charity and has a thing against her. If what you're saying's true, we'd be talking attempted murder."

Roman pitched his cigarette out the window. "That's just what we're talking about. I want to know who owns that car."

"I'll check it out."

"You already know."

Royce tapped his pad on his knee. "Yes, sir, you do have a good eye. I'll say this. Maybe I do know somebody who owns a car that fits your description. If I do, I know that that person wouldn't run over a rabbit on purpose, much less a woman. Then again, there's no saying you have to own a car to drive it."

Mae opened the connecting door, and he glanced up. "Well, now, Maeflower."

Mae's lips twitched slightly before she thinned them. "If you can't sit in a chair proper you can stand on your feet, Jack Royce."

Royce rose, grinning. "Mae and I went to school together," he explained. "She liked to bully me then, too.

I don't suppose you've got any waffles on the menu today, Maeflower."

"Maybe I do. You find out who hurt my girl and I'll see you get some."

"I'm working on it." His face sobered again as he nodded toward the door. "Is she up to talking to me?"

"Done nothing but talk since she came around." Mae blinked back a flood of relieved tears. "Go ahead in."

Royce turned to Roman. "I'll be in touch."

"Doc said she could have some tea and toast." Mae sniffled, then made a production out of blowing her nose. "Hay fever," she said roughly. "I'm grateful you were close by when she was hurt."

"If I'd been closer she wouldn't have been hurt."

"And if she hadn't been walking that dog she'd have been in bed." She paused and gave Roman a level look. "I guess we could shoot him."

She surprised a little laugh out of him. "Charity might object to that."

"She wouldn't care to know you're out here brooding, either. Your arm's bleeding, boy."

He looked down dispassionately at the torn, blood-stained sleeve of his shirt. "Some."

"Can't have you bleeding all over the floor." She walked to the door, waving a hand. "Well, come on down-stairs. I'll clean you up. Then you can bring the girl up some breakfast. I haven't got time to run up and down these steps all morning."

After the doctor had finished his poking and the sheriff had finished his questioning, Charity stared at the ceiling. She hurt everywhere there was to hurt. Her head especially, but the rest of her was throbbing right along in time.

The medication would take the edge off, but she wanted to keep her mind clear until she'd worked everything out. That was why she had tucked the pill Dr. Mertens had given her under her tongue until she'd been alone. As soon as she'd organized her thoughts she would swallow it and check into oblivion for a few hours.

She'd only caught a flash of the car, but it had seemed familiar. While she'd spoken with the sheriff she'd remembered. The car that had nearly run her over belonged to Mrs. Norton, a sweet, flighty lady who crocheted doilies and doll clothes for the local craft shops. Charity didn't think Mrs. Norton had ever driven over twenty-five miles an hour. That was a great deal less than the car had been doing when it had swerved at her that morning.

She hadn't seen the driver, not really, but she had the definite impression it had been a man. Mrs. Norton had been widowed for six years.

Then it was simple, Charity decided. Someone had gotten drunk, stolen Mrs. Norton's car, and taken it for a wild joyride around the island. They probably hadn't even seen her at the side of the road.

Satisfied, she eased herself up in the bed. The rest was for the sheriff to worry about. She had problems of her own.

The breakfast shift was probably in chaos. She thought she could rely on Lori to keep everyone calm. Then there was the butcher. She still had her list to complete for tomorrow's order. And she had yet to choose the photographs she wanted to use for the ad in the travel brochure. The deposit hadn't been paid, and the fireplace in cabin 3 was smoking.

What she needed was a pad, a pencil and a telephone. That was simple enough. She'd find all three at the desk in the sitting room. Carefully she eased her legs over the side of the bed. Not too bad, she decided, but she gave herself a moment to adjust before she tried to stand.

Annoyed with herself, she braced a hand on one of the bedposts. Her legs felt as though they were filled with Mae's whipped cream rather than muscle and bone.

"What the hell are you doing?"

She winced at the sound of Roman's voice, then gingerly turned her head toward the doorway. "Nothing," she said, and tried to smile.

"Get back in bed."

"I just have a few things to do."

She was swaying on her feet, as pale as the nightshirt that buttoned modestly high at the neck and skimmed seductively high on her thighs. Without a word, he set down the tray he was carrying, crossed to her and scooped her up in his arms.

"Roman, don't. I—"

"Shut up."

"I was going to lie back down in a minute," she began. "Right after—"

"Shut up," he repeated. He laid her on the bed, then gave up. Keeping his arms around her, he buried his face against her throat. "Oh, God, baby."

"It's all right." She stroked a hand through his hair. "Don't worry."

"I thought you were dead. When I found you I thought you were dead."

"Oh, I'm sorry." She rubbed at the tension at the back

of his neck, trying to imagine how he must have felt. "It must have been awful, Roman. But it's only some bumps and bruises. In a couple of days they'll be gone and we'll forget all about it."

"I won't forget." He pulled himself away from her. "Ever."

The violence she saw in his eyes had her heart fluttering. "Roman, it was an accident. Sheriff Royce will take care of it."

He bit back the words he wanted to say. It was best that she believe it had been an accident. For now. He got up to get her tray. "Mae said you could eat."

She thought of the lists she had to make and decided she had a better chance getting around him if she cooperated. "I'll try. How's Ludwig?"

"Okay. Mae put him out and gave him a ham bone."

"Ah, his favorite." She bit into the toast and pretended she had an appetite.

"How's your head?"

"Not too bad." It wasn't really a lie, she thought. She was sure a blow with a sledgehammer would have been worse. "No stitches." She pulled back her hair to show him a pair of butterfly bandages. A bruise was darkening around them. "You want to hold up some fingers and ask me how many I see?"

"No." He turned away, afraid he would explode. The last thing she needed was another outburst from him, he reminded himself. He wasn't the kind to fall apart—at least he hadn't been until he'd met her.

He began fiddling with bottles and bowls set around the room. She loved useless little things, he thought as he picked up a wand-shaped amethyst crystal. Feeling clumsy, he set it down again.

"The sheriff said the car swerved at you." She drank the soothing chamomile tea, feeling almost human again. "I'm glad you weren't hurt."

"Damn it, Charity." He whirled, then made an effort to get a handle on his temper. "No, I wasn't hurt." And he was going to see to it that *she* wasn't hurt again. "I'm sorry. This whole business has made me edgy."

"I know what you mean. Want some tea? Mae sent up two cups."

He glanced at the pretty flowered pot. "Not unless you've got some whiskey to go in it."

"Sorry, fresh out." Smiling again, she patted the bed. "Why don't you come sit down?"

"Because I'm trying to keep my hands off you."

"Oh." Her smile curved wider. It pleased her that she was resilient enough to feel a quick curl of desire. "I like your hands on me, Roman."

"Bad timing." Because he couldn't resist, he crossed to the bed to take her hand in his. "I care about you, Charity. I want you to believe that."

"I do."

"No." His fingers tightened insistently on hers. He knew he wasn't clever with words, but he needed her to understand. "It's different with you than it's ever been with anyone." Fighting a fresh wave of frustration, he relaxed his grip. "I can't give you anything else."

She felt her heart rise up in her throat. "If I had known I could get that much out of you I might have bashed my head on a rock before."

"You deserve more." He sat down and ran a gentle finger under the bruise on her temple.

"I agree." She brought his hand to her lips and watched his eyes darken. "I'm patient."

Something was moving inside him, and he was helpless to prevent it. "You don't know enough about me. You don't know anything about me."

"I know I love you. I figured you'd tell me the rest eventually."

"Don't trust me, Charity. Not so much."

There was trouble here. She wanted to smooth it from his face, but she didn't know how. "Have you done something so unforgivable, Roman?"

"I hope not. You should rest." Knowing he'd already said too much, he set her tray aside.

"I was going to, really. Right after I take care of a few things."

"The only thing you have to take care of today is yourself."

"That's very sweet of you, and as soon as I—"

"You're not getting out of bed for at least twenty-four hours."

"That's the most ridiculous thing I've ever heard. What possible difference does it make whether I'm lying down or sitting down?"

"According to the doctor, quite a bit." He picked up a tablet from the nightstand. "Is this the medication he gave you?"

"Yes."

"The same medication that you were supposed to take before he left?"

She struggled to keep from pouting. "I'm going to take it after I make a few phone calls."

"No phone calls today."

"Now listen, Roman, I appreciate your concern, but I don't take orders from you."

"I know. You give them to me."

Before she could respond, he lowered his lips to hers. Here was gentleness again, whisper-soft, achingly warm. With a little sound of pleasure, she sank into it.

He'd thought it would be easy to take one, only one, fleeting taste. But his hand curled into a fist as he fought the need to demand more. She was so fragile now. He wanted to soothe, not arouse...to comfort, not seduce. But in seconds he was both aroused and seduced.

When he started to pull back, she gave a murmur of protest and pressed him close again. She needed this sweetness from him, needed it more than any medication.

"Easy," he told her, clawing for his self-control. "I'm a little low on willpower, and you need rest."

"I'd rather have you."

She smiled at him, and his stomach twisted into knots. "Do you drive all men crazy?"

"I don't think so." Feeling on top of the world, she brushed his hair back from his brow. "Anyway, you're the first to ask."

"We'll talk about it later." Determined to do his best for her, he held out the pill. "Take this."

"Later."

"Uh-uh. Now."

With a sound of disgust, she popped the pill into her mouth, then picked up her cooling tea and sipped it. "There. Satisfied?"

He had to grin. "I've been a long way from satisfied since I first laid eyes on you, baby. Lift up your tongue."

"I beg your pardon?"

"You heard me. You're pretty good." He put a hand under her chin. "But I'm better. Let's have the pill."

She knew she was beaten. She took the pill out of her

mouth, then made a production out of swallowing it. She touched the tip of her tongue to her lips. "It might still be in there. Want to search me for it?"

"What I want—" he kissed her lightly "—is for you to stay in bed." He shifted his lips to her throat. "No calls, no paperwork, no sneaking downstairs." He caught her earlobe between his teeth and felt her shudder, and his own. "Promise."

"Yes." Her lips parted as his brushed over them. "I promise."

"Good." He sat back and picked up the tray. "I'll see you later."

"But—" She set her teeth as he walked to the door. "You play dirty, DeWinter."

"Yeah." He glanced back at her. "And to win."

He left her, knowing she would no more break her word than she would fly out of the window. He had business of his own to attend to.

Chapter 7

An important part of Roman's training had been learning how to pursue an assignment in a thorough and objective manner. He had always found it second nature to do both. Until now. Still, for very personal reasons, he fully intended to be thorough.

When he left Charity, Roman expected to find Bob in the office, and he hoped to find him alone. He wasn't disappointed. Bob had the phone receiver at his ear and the computer monitor blinking above his fingers. After waving a distracted hand in Roman's direction, he went on with his conversation.

"I'll be happy to set that up for you and your wife, Mr. Parkington. That's a double room for the nights of the fifteenth and sixteenth of July."

"Hang up," Roman told him. Bob merely held up a finger, signaling a short wait.

"Yes, that's available with a private bath and includes breakfast. We'd be happy to help you arrange the rentals of kayaks during your stay. Your confirmation number is—"

Roman slammed a hand down on the phone, breaking the connection.

"What the hell are you doing?"

"Wondering if I should bother to talk to you or just kill you."

Bob sprang out of his chair and managed to put the desk between him and Roman. "Look, I know you've had an upsetting morning—"

"Do you?" Roman didn't bother to try to outmaneuver. He simply stood where he was and watched Bob sweat. "Upsetting. That's a nice, polite word for it. But you're a nice, polite man, aren't you, Bob?"

Bob glanced at the door and wondered if he had a chance of getting that far. "We're all a bit edgy because of Charity's accident. You could probably use a drink."

Roman moved over to a stack of computer manuals and unearthed a small silver flask. "Yours?" he said. Bob stared at him. "I imagine you keep this in here for those long nights when you're working late—and alone. Wondering how I knew where to find it?" He set it aside. "I came across it when I broke in here a couple of nights ago and went through the books."

"You broke in?" Bob wiped the back of his hand over suddenly dry lips. "That's a hell of a way to pay Charity back for giving you a job."

"Yeah, you're right about that. Almost as bad as using her inn to pass counterfeit bills and slip undesirables in and out of the country."

"I don't know what you're talking about." Bob took

one cautious sideways step toward the door. "I want you out of here, DeWinter. When I tell Charity what you've done—"

"But you're not going to tell her. You're not going to tell her a damn thing—yet. But you're going to tell me." One look stopped Bob's careful movement cold. "Try for the door and I'll break your leg." Roman tapped a cigarette out of his pack. "Sit down."

"I don't have to take this." But he took a step back, away from the door, and away from Roman. "I'll call the police."

"Go ahead." Roman lit the cigarette and watched him through a veil of smoke. It was a pity Bob was so easily cowed. He'd have liked an excuse to damage him. "I was tempted to tell Royce everything I knew this morning. The problem with that was that it would have spoiled the satisfaction of dealing with you and the people you're with personally. But go ahead and call him." Roman shoved the phone across the desk in Bob's direction. "I can find a way of finishing my business with you once you're inside."

Bob didn't ask him to explain. He had heard the cell door slam the moment Roman had walked into the room. "Listen, I know you're upset...."

"Do I look upset?" Roman murmured.

No, Bob thought, his stomach clenching. He looked cold—cold enough to kill. Or worse. But there had to be a way out. There always was. "You said something about counterfeiting. Why don't you tell me what this is all about, and we'll try to settle this calm—" Before he got the last word out he was choking as Roman hauled him out of the chair by the collar.

"Do you want to die?"

"No." Bob's fingers slid helplessly off Roman's wrists.

"Then cut the crap." Disgusted, Roman tossed him back into the chair. "There are two things Charity doesn't do around here. Only two. She doesn't cook, and she doesn't work the computer. *Can't* would be a better word. She can't cook because Mae didn't teach her. Pretty easy to figure why. Mae wanted to rule in the kitchen, and Charity wanted to let her."

He moved to the window and casually lowered the shades so that the room was dim and private. "It's just as simple to figure why she can't work a basic office computer. You didn't teach her, or you made the lessons so complicated and contradictory she never caught on. You want me to tell you why you did that?"

"She was never really interested." Bob swallowed, his throat raw. "She can do the basics when she has to, but you know Charity—she's more interested in people than machines. I show her all the printouts."

"All? You and I know you haven't shown her all of them. Should I tell you what I think is on those disks you've got hidden in the file drawer?"

Bob pulled out a handkerchief with fumbling fingers and mopped at his brow. "I don't know what you're talking about."

"You keep the books for the inn, and for the little business you and your friends have on the side. I figure a man like you would keep backups, a little insurance in case the people you work for decided to cut you out." He opened a file drawer and dug out a disk. "We'll take a look at this later," he said, and tossed it onto the desk. "Two to three thousand a week washes through this place. Fifty-two weeks a year makes that a pretty good haul. Add that to the fee you charge to get someone back and forth across the border mixed with the tour group and you've got a nice, tidy sum."

"That's crazy." Barely breathing, Bob tugged at his collar. "You've got to know that's crazy."

"Did you know your references were still on file here?" Roman asked conversationally. "The problem is, they don't check out. You never worked for a hotel back in Ft. Worth, or in San Francisco."

"So I padded my chances a bit. That doesn't prove anything."

"I think we'll turn up something more interesting when we run your prints."

Bob stared down at the disk. Sometimes you could bluff, and sometimes you had to fold. "Can I have a drink?"

Roman picked up the flask, tossed it to him and waited while he twisted off the cap. "You made me for a cop, didn't you? Or you were worried enough to keep your ear to the ground. You heard me asking the wrong questions, were afraid I'd told Charity about the operation and passed it along to your friends."

"It didn't feel right." Bob wiped the vodka from his lips, then drank again. "I know a scam when I see one, and you made me nervous the minute I saw you."

"Why?"

"When you're in my business you get so you can spot cops. In the supermarket, on the street, buying underwear at a department store. It doesn't matter where, you get so you can make them."

Roman thought of himself and of the years he'd spent on the other side of the street. He'd made his share of cops, and he still could. "Okay. So what did you do?"

"I told Block I thought you were a plant, but he figured I was going loopy. I wanted to back off until you'd gone, but he wouldn't listen. Last night, when you went down for dinner, I looked through your room. I found a box of shells. No gun, just the shells. That meant you were wearing it. I called Block and told him I was sure you were a cop. You'd been spending a lot of time with Charity, so I figured she was working with you on it."

"So you tried to kill her."

"No, not me." Panicked, Bob pressed back in his chair. "I swear. I'm not a violent man, DeWinter. Hell, I like Charity. I wanted to pull out, take a breather. We'd already set up another place, in the Olympic Mountains. I figured we could take a few weeks, run legit, then move on it. Block just said he'd take care of it, and I thought he meant we'd handle next week's tour on the level. That would give me time to fix everything here and get out. If I'd known what he was planning..."

"What? Would you have warned her?"

"I don't know." Bob drained the flask, but the liquor did little to calm his nerves. "Look, I do scams, I do cons. I don't kill people."

"Who was driving the car?"

"I don't know. I swear it," he said. Roman took a step toward him, and he gripped the arms of his chair. "Listen, I got in touch with Block the minute this happened. He said he'd hired somebody. He couldn't have done it himself, because he was on the mainland. He said the guy wasn't trying to kill her. Block just wanted her out of the way for a few days. We've got a big shipment coming in and—" He broke off, knowing he was digging himself in deeper.

Roman merely nodded. "You're going to find out who was driving the car."

"Okay, sure." He made the promise without knowing if he could keep it. "I'll find out."

"You and I are going to work together for the next few days, Bob."

"But…aren't you going to call Royce?"

"Let me worry about Royce. You're going to go on doing what you do best. Lying. Only now you're going to lie to Block. You do exactly what you're told and you'll stay alive. If you do a good job I'll put in a word for you with my superior. Maybe you can make a deal, turn state's evidence."

After resting a hip on the desk, Roman leaned closer. "If you try to check out, I'll hunt you down. I'll find you wherever you hide, and when I'm finished you'll wish I'd killed you."

Bob looked into Roman's eyes. He believed him. "What do you want me to do?"

"Tell me about the next shipment."

Charity was sick of it. It was bad enough that she'd given her word to Roman and had to stay in bed all day. She couldn't even use the phone to call the office and see what was going on in the world.

She'd tried to be good-humored about it, poking through the books and magazines that Lori had brought up to her. She'd even admitted—to herself—that there had been times, when things had gotten crazy at the inn, that she'd imagined having the luxury of an idle day in bed.

Now she had it, and she hated it.

The pill Roman had insisted she swallow had made her groggy. She drifted off periodically, only to wake later, annoyed that she didn't have enough control to stay awake and be bored. Because reading made her headache worse, she tried to work up some interest in the small portable television perched on the shelf across the room.

When she'd found *The Maltese Falcon* flickering in black and white she'd felt both pleasure and relief. If she had to be trapped in bed, it might as well be with Bogart. Even as Sam Spade succumbed to the Fat Man's drug, Charity's own medication sent her under. She awoke in a very poor temper to a rerun of a sitcom.

He'd made her promise to stay in bed, she thought, jabbing an elbow at her pillow. And he didn't even have the decency to spend five minutes keeping her company. Apparently he was too busy to fit a sickroom call into his schedule. That was fine for him, she decided, running around doing something useful while she was moldering between the sheets. It wasn't in her nature to do nothing, and if she had to do it for five minutes longer she was going to scream.

Charity smiled a bit as she considered that. Just what would he do if she let out one long bloodcurdling scream? It might be interesting to find out. Certainly more interesting, she decided, than watching a blond airhead jiggle around a set to the beat of a laugh track. Nodding, she sucked in her breath.

"What are you doing?"

She let it out again in a long huff as Roman pushed open the door. Pleasure came first, but she quickly buried it in resentment. "You're always asking me that."

"Am I?" He was carrying another tray. Charity distinctly caught the scent of Mae's prize chicken soup and her biscuits. "Well, what were you doing?"

"Dying of boredom. I think I'd rather be shot." After

eyeing the tray, she decided to be marginally friendly. But not because she was glad to see him, she thought. It was dusk, and she hadn't eaten for hours. "Is that for me?"

"Possibly." He set the tray over her lap, then stayed close and took a long, hard look at her. There was no way for him to describe the fury he felt when he saw the bruises and the bandages. Just as there was no way for him to describe the sense of pleasure and relief he experienced when he saw the annoyance in her eyes and the color in her cheeks.

"I think you're wrong, Charity. You're going to live."

"No thanks to you." She dived into the soup. "First you trick a promise out of me, then you leave me to rot for the next twelve hours. You might have come up for a minute to see if I had lapsed into a coma."

He *had* come up, about the time Sam Spade had been unwrapping the mysterious bird, but she'd been sleeping. Nonetheless, he'd stayed for nearly half an hour, just watching her.

"I've been a little busy," he told her, and broke off half of her biscuit for himself.

"I'll bet." Feeling far from generous, she snatched it back. "Well, since you're here, you might tell me how things are going downstairs."

"They're under control," he murmured, thinking of Bob and the phone calls that had already been made.

"It's only Bonnie's second day. She hasn't—"

"She's doing fine," he said, interrupting her. "Mae's watching her like a hawk. Where'd all these come from?" He gestured toward half a dozen vases of fresh flowers.

"Oh, Lori brought up the daisies with the magazines.

Then the ladies came up. They really shouldn't have climbed all those stairs. They brought the wood violets." She rattled off more names of people who had brought or sent flowers.

He should have brought her some, Roman thought, rising and thrusting his hands into his pockets. It had never crossed his mind. Things like that didn't, he admitted. Not the small, romantic things a woman like Charity was entitled to.

"Roman?"

"What?"

"Did you come all the way up here to scowl at my peonies?"

"No." He hadn't even known the name for them. He turned away from the fat pink blossoms. "Do you want any more to eat?"

"No." She tapped the spoon against the side of her empty bowl. "I don't want any more to eat, I don't want any more magazines and I don't want anyone else to come in here, pat my hand and tell me to get plenty of rest. So if that's what you've got in mind you can leave."

"You're a charming patient, Charity." Checking his own temper, he removed the tray.

"No, I'm a miserable patient." Furiously, she tossed aside her self-control, and just as furiously tossed a paperback at his head. Fortunately for them both, her aim was off. "And I'm tired of being stuck in here as though I had some communicable disease. I have a bump on the head, damn it, not a brain tumor."

"I don't think a brain tumor's contagious."

"Don't be clever with me." Glaring at him, she folded her arms and dropped them over her chest. "I'm sick of being here, and sicker yet of being told what to do."

"You don't take that well, do you? No matter how good it is for you?"

When she was being unreasonable there was nothing she wanted to hear less than the truth. "I have an inn to run, and I can't do it from bed."

"Not tonight you don't."

"It's my inn, just like it's my body and my head." She tossed the covers aside. Even as she started to scramble out of bed her promise weighed on her like a chain. Swinging her legs up again, she fell back against the pillows.

Thumbs hooked in his pockets, he measured her. "Why don't you get up?"

"Because I promised. Now get out, damn it. Just get out and leave me alone."

"Fine. I'll tell Mae and the rest that you're feeling more like yourself. They've been worried about you."

She threw another book—harder—but had only the small satisfaction of hearing it slap against the closing door.

The hell with him, she thought as she dropped her chin on her knees. The hell with everything.

The hell with her. He hadn't gone up there to pick a fight, and he didn't have to tolerate a bad-tempered woman throwing things at him, especially when he couldn't throw them back. Roman got halfway down the stairs, turned around and stalked back up again.

Charity was moping when he pushed open the door. She knew it, she hated it, and she wished everyone would leave her in peace to get on with it.

"What now?"

"Get up."

Charity straightened her spine against the headboard. "Why?"

"Get up," Roman repeated. "Get dressed. There must be a floor to mop or a trash can to empty around here."

"I said I wouldn't get up—" she set her chin "—and I won't."

"You can get out of bed on your own, or I can drag you out."

Temper had her eyes darkening and her chin thrusting out even farther. "You wouldn't dare." She regretted the words even as she spoke them. She'd already decided he was a man who would dare anything.

She was right. Roman crossed to the bed and grabbed her arm. Charity gripped one of the posts. Despite her hold, he managed to pull her up on her knees before she dug in. Before the tug-of-war could get much further she began to giggle.

"This is stupid." She felt her grip slipping and hooked her arm around the bedpost. "Really stupid. Roman, stop. I'm going to end up falling on my face and putting another hole in my head."

"You wanted to get up. So get up."

"No, I wanted to feel sorry for myself. And I was doing a pretty good job of it, too. Roman, you're about to dislocate my shoulder."

"You're the most stubborn, hardheaded, unreasonable woman I've ever met," he said. But he released her.

"I have to go along with the first two, but I'm not usually unreasonable." Offering him a smile, she sat cross-legged. The storm was over. At least hers was, she thought. She recognized the anger that was still darkening his eyes. She let out a long sigh. "I guess you could

say I was having a really terrific pity party for myself
when you came in. I'm sorry I took it out on you."

"I don't need an apology."

"Yes, you do." She would have offered him a hand,
but he didn't look ready to sign any peace treaties. "I'm
not used to being cut off from what's going on. I'm
hardly ever sick, so I haven't had much practice in taking it like a good little soldier." She idly pleated the
sheet between her fingers as she slanted a look at him.
"I really am sorry, Roman. Are you going to stay mad
at me?"

"That might be the best solution." Anger had nothing to do with what he was feeling at the moment. She
looked so appealing with that half smile on her face,
her hair tousled, the nightshirt buttoned to her chin and
skimming her thighs.

"Want to slug me?"

"Maybe." It was hopeless. He smiled and sat down
beside her. He balled his hand into a fist and skimmed
it lightly over her chin. "When you're back on your feet
again I'll take another shot."

"It was nice of you to bring me dinner. I didn't even
thank you."

"No, you didn't."

She leaned forward to kiss his cheek. "Thanks."

"You're welcome."

After blowing the hair out of her eyes, she decided to
start over. "Did we have a good crowd tonight?"

"I bused thirty tables."

"I'm going to have to give you a raise. I guess Mae
made her chocolate mousse torte."

"Yeah." Roman found his lips twitching again.

"I don't suppose there was any left over."

"Not a crumb. It was great."

"You had some?"

"Meals are part of my pay."

Feeling deprived, Charity leaned back against the pillows. "Right."

"Are you going to sulk again?"

"Just for a minute. I wanted to ask you if the sheriff had any news about the car."

"Not much. He found it about ten miles from here, abandoned." He reached over to smooth away a line between her brows. "Don't worry about it."

"I'm not. Not really. I'm just glad the driver didn't hurt anyone else. Lori said you'd cut your arm."

"A little." Their hands were linked. He didn't know whether he had taken hers or she had taken his.

"Were you taking a walk?"

"I was waiting for you."

"Oh." She smiled again.

"You'd better get some rest." He was feeling awkward again, awkward and clumsy. No other woman had ever drawn either reaction from him.

Reluctantly she released his hand. "Are we friends again?"

"I guess you could say that. Good night, Charity."

"Good night."

He crossed to the door and opened it. But he couldn't step across the threshold. He stood there, struggling with himself. Though it was only a matter of seconds, it seemed like hours to both of them.

"I can't." He turned back, shutting the door quietly behind him.

"Can't what?"

"I can't leave."

Her smile bloomed, in her eyes, on her lips. She opened her arms to him, as he had known she would. Walking back to her was nearly as difficult as walking away. He took her hands and held them hard in his.

"I'm no good for you, Charity."

"I think you're very good for me." She brought their joined hands to her cheek. "That means one of us is wrong."

"If I could, I'd walk out the door and keep going."

She felt the sting and accepted it. She'd never expected loving Roman to be painless. "Why?"

"For reasons I can't begin to explain to you." He stared down at their linked hands. "But I can't walk away. Sooner or later you're going to wish I had."

"No." She drew him down onto the bed. "Whatever happens, I'll always be glad you stayed." This time she smoothed the lines from his brow. "I told you before that this wouldn't happen unless it was right. I meant that." Lifting her hands, she linked them behind his neck. "I love you, Roman. Tonight is something I want, something I've chosen."

Kissing her was like sinking into a dream. Soft, drugging and too impossibly beautiful to be real. He wanted to take care, such complete, such tender care, not to hurt her now, knowing that he would have no choice but to hurt her eventually.

But tonight, for a few precious hours, there would be no future. With her he could be what he had never tried to be before. Gentle, loving, kind. With her he could believe it was possible for love to be enough.

He loved her. Though he'd never known he was capable of that strong and fragile emotion, he felt it with her. It streamed through him, painless and sweet, healing wounds he'd forgotten he had, soothing aches he'd lived with forever. How could he have known when he'd walked into her life that she would be his salvation? In the short time he had left he would show her. And in showing her he would give himself something he had never expected to have.

He made her feel beautiful. And delicate, Charity thought as his mouth whispered over hers. It was as though he knew that this first time together was to be savored and remembered. She heard her own sigh, then his, as her hands slid up his back. Whatever she had wished they could have together was nothing compared to this.

He laid her back gently, barely touching her, as the kiss lengthened. Even loving him as she did, she hadn't known he'd possessed such tenderness. Nor could she know that he had just discovered it in himself.

The lamplight glowed amber. He hadn't thought to light the candles. But he could see her in the brilliance of it, her eyes dark and on his, her lips curved as he brought his to meet them. He hadn't thought to set the music. But her nightshirt whispered as she brought her arms around him. It was a sound he would remember always. Air drifted in through the open window, stirring the scent of the flowers others had brought to her. But it was the fragrance of her skin that filled his head. It was the taste of it that he yearned for.

Lightly, almost afraid he might bruise her with a touch, he cupped her breasts in his hands. Her breath caught, then released on a moan against the side of his neck. He knew that nothing had ever excited him more.

Then her hands were on his shirt, her fingers undoing his buttons as her eyes remained on his. They were as dark, as deep, as vibrant, as the water that surrounded her home. He could read everything she felt in them.

"I want to touch you," she said as she drew the shirt from his shoulders. Her heart began to sprint as she looked at him, the taut muscles, the taut skin.

There was a strength in him that excited, perhaps because she understood that he could be ruthless. There was a toughness to his body, a toughness that made her realize he was a man who had fought, a man who would fight. But his hands were gentle on her now, almost hesitant. Her excitement leaped higher, and there was no fear in it.

"It seems I've wanted to touch you like this all my life." She ran her fingertips lightly over the bandage on his arm. "Does it hurt?"

"No." Every muscle in his body tensed when she trailed her hands from his waist to his chest. It was impossible for him to understand how anyone could bring him peace and torment at the same time. "Charity..."

"Just kiss me again, Roman," she murmured.

He was helpless to refuse. He wondered what she would ask him for if she knew that he was powerless to deny her anything at this moment. Fighting back a flood of desperation, he kept his hands easy, sliding and stroking them over her until he felt the tremors begin.

He knew he could give her pleasure. The need to do so pulsed heavily inside him. He could ignite her passions. The drive to fan them roared through him like a brushfire. As he touched her he knew he could make her weak or strong, wild or limp. But it wasn't power that filled him at the knowledge. It was awe.

She would give him whatever he asked, without questions, without restrictions. This strong, beautiful, exciting woman was his. This wasn't a dream that would awaken him to frustration in the middle of the night. This wasn't a wish that he'd have to pretend he'd never made. It was real. She was real, and she was waiting for him.

He could have torn the nightshirt from her with one pull of his hand. Instead, he released button after tiny button, hearing her breath quicken, following the narrow path with soft, lingering kisses. Her fingers dug into his back, then went limp as her system churned. She could only groan as his tongue moistened her flesh, teasing and heating it. The night air whispered over her as he undressed her. Then he was lifting her, cradling her in his arms.

She was twined around him, her heart thudding frantically against his lips. He needed a moment to drag himself back, to find the control he wanted so that he could take her up, take her over. Murmuring to her, he used what skills he had to drive her past the edge of reason.

Her body was rigid against his. He watched her dazed eyes fly open. She gasped his name, and then he covered her mouth with his to capture her long, low moan as her body went limp.

She seemed to slide like water through his hands when he laid her down again. To his delight, her arousal burst free again at his lightest touch.

It was impossible. It was impossible to feel so much and still need more. Blindly she reached for him. Fresh pleasure poured into her until her arms felt too heavy to move. She was a prisoner, a gloriously willing prisoner, of the frantic sensations he sent tearing through her. She wanted to lock herself around him, to keep him there, always there. He was taking her on a long, slow journey to places she had never seen, places she never wanted to leave.

When he slid inside her she heard his low, breathless moan. So he was as much a captive as she.

With his face pressed against her neck, he fought the need to sprint toward release. He was trapped between heaven and hell, and he gloried in it. In her. In them. He heard her sob out his name, felt the strength pour into her. She was with him as no one had ever been.

Charity wrapped her arms around Roman to keep him from shifting away. "Don't move."

"I'm hurting you."

"No." She let out a long, long sigh. "No, you're not."

"I'm too heavy," he insisted, and compromised by gathering her close and rolling so that their positions were reversed.

"Okay." Satisfied, she rested her head on his shoulder. "You are," she said, "the most incredible lover."

He didn't even try to prevent the smile. "Thanks." He stroked a possessive hand down to her hip. "Have you had many?"

It was her turn to smile. The little trace of jealousy in his voice was a tremendous addition to an already-glorious night. "Define *many*."

Ignoring the quick tug of annoyance he felt, he played the game. "More than three. Three is a few. Anything more than three is many."

"Ah. Well, in that case." She almost wished she could lie and invent a horde. "I guess I've had less than a few. That doesn't mean I don't know an incredible one when I find him."

He lifted her head to stare at her. "I've done nothing in my life to deserve you."

"Don't be stupid." She inched up to kiss him briefly. "And don't change the subject."

"What subject?"

"You're clever, DeWinter, but not that clever." She lifted a brow and studied him in the lamplight. "It's my turn to ask you if you've had many lovers."

He didn't smile this time. "Too many. But only one who's meant anything."

The amusement faded from her eyes before she closed them. "You'll make me cry," she murmured, lowering her head to his chest again.

Not yet, he thought, stroking her hair. Soon enough, but not yet. "Why haven't you ever gotten married?" he wondered aloud. "Had babies?"

"What a strange question. I haven't loved anyone enough before." She winced at her own words, then made herself smile as she lifted her head. "That wasn't a hint."

But it was exactly what he'd wanted to hear. He knew he was crazy to let himself think that way, even for a few hours, but he wanted to imagine her loving him enough to forgive, to accept and to promise.

"How about the traveling you said you wanted to do? Shouldn't that come first?"

She shrugged and settled against him again. "Maybe I haven't traveled because I know deep down I'd hate to go all those places alone. What good is Venice if you don't have someone to ride in a gondola with? Or Paris if there's no one to hold hands with?"

"You could go with me."

Already half-asleep, she laughed. She imagined

Roman had little more than the price of a ferry ticket to his name. "Okay. Let me know when to pack."

"Would you?" He lifted her chin to look into her drowsy eyes.

"Of course." She kissed him, snuggled her head against his shoulder and went to sleep.

Roman switched off the lamp beside the bed. For a long time he held her and stared into the dark.

Chapter 8

Charity opened her eyes slowly, wondering why she couldn't move. Groggy, she stared into Roman's face. It was only inches from hers. He had pulled her close in his sleep, effectively pinning her arms and legs with his. Though his grip on her was somewhat guardlike, she found it unbearably sweet.

Ignoring the discomfort, she lay still and took advantage of the moment by looking her fill.

She'd always thought that people looked softer, more vulnerable, in sleep. Not Roman. He had the body of a fighter and the eyes of a man accustomed to facing trouble head-on. His eyes were closed now, and his body was relaxed. Almost.

Still, studying him, she decided that, asleep or awake, he looked tough as nails. Had he always been? she wondered. Had he had to be? It was true that smiling lent a certain charm to his face. It lightened the wariness in his eyes. In Charity's opinion, Roman smiled much too seldom.

She would fix that. Her own lips curved as she watched him. In time she would, gently, teach him to relax, to enjoy, to trust. She would make him happy. It wasn't possible to love as she had loved and not have it returned. And it wasn't possible to share what they had shared during the night without his heart being as lost as hers.

Sooner or later—sooner, if she had her way—he would come to accept how good they were together. And how much better they would become in all the years to follow. Then there would be time for promises and families and futures.

I'm not letting you go, she told him silently. *You don't realize it yet, but I've got a hold on you, and it's going to be mighty hard to break it.*

He had such a capacity for giving, she thought. Not just physically, though she wasn't ashamed to admit that his skill there had dazed and delighted her. He was a man full of emotions, too many of them strapped down. What had happened to him, she wondered, that had made him so wary of love, and so afraid to give it?

She loved him too much to demand an answer. It was a question he had to answer on his own…a question she knew he would answer as soon as he trusted her enough. When he did, all she had to do was show him that none of it mattered. All that counted, from this moment on, was what they felt for each other.

Inching over, she brushed a light kiss on his mouth. His eyes opened instantly. It took only a heartbeat longer for them to clear. Fascinated, Charity watched their expression change from one of suspicion to one of desire.

"You're a light sleeper," she began. "I just—"

Before she could complete the thought, his mouth, hungry and insistent, was on hers. She managed a quiet moan as she melted into his kiss.

It was the only way he knew to tell her what it meant to him to wake and find her close and warm and willing. Too many mornings he had woken alone in strange beds in empty rooms.

That was what he expected. For years he had deliberately separated himself from anyone who had tried to get close. The job. He'd told himself it was because of the job. But that was a lie, one of many. He'd chosen to remain alone because he hadn't wanted to risk losing again. Grieving again. Now, overnight, everything had changed.

He would remember it all, the pale fingers of light creeping into the room, the high echoing sound of the first birds calling to the rising sun, the scent of her skin as it heated against his. And her mouth…he would remember the taste of her mouth as it opened eagerly under his.

There were such deep, dark needs in him. She felt them, understood them, and met them unquestioningly. As dawn swept the night aside, he stirred her own until their needs mirrored each other's.

Slowly, easily, while his lips cruised over her face, he slipped inside her. With a sigh and a murmur, she welcomed him.

She felt as strong as an ox and as content as a cat with cream on its whiskers. With her eyes closed, Charity stretched her arms to the ceiling.

"And to think I used to consider jogging the best way

to start the day." Laughing, she curled over against him again. "I have to thank you for showing me how very wrong I was."

"My pleasure." He could still feel his own heart thudding like a jackhammer against his ribs. "Give me a minute and I'll show you the best reason for staying in bed in the morning."

Lord, it was tempting. Before her blood could begin to heat she shook her head. She took a quick nip at his chin before she sat up. "Maybe if you've got some time when I get back."

He took her wrist but kept his fingers light. "From where?"

"From taking Ludwig for his run."

"No."

The hand that had lifted to push back her hair paused. Deliberately she continued to lift it to finger-comb the hair away from her face. "No, what?"

He recognized that tone. She was the boss again, despite the fact that her face was still glowing from love-making and she was naked to where the sheets pooled at her waist. This was the woman who didn't take orders. Roman decided he would have to show her again that she was wrong.

"No, you're not taking the dog out for a run."

Because she wanted to be reasonable, she added a smile. "Of course I am. I kept my promise and stayed in bed all day yesterday. And all night, for that matter. Now I'm going to get back to work."

Around the inn, that was fine. In fact, the sooner everything got back to normal the better it would be. But there was no way he was having her walking down a deserted road by herself. "You're in no shape to go for a mile hike."

"Three miles, and yes, I am."

"Three?" Lifting a brow, he stroked a hand over her thigh. "No wonder you've got such great muscle tone."

"That's not the point." She shifted away before his touch could weaken her.

"You have the most incredible body."

She shoved at his seeking hands. "Roman... I do?"

His lips curved. This was the way she liked them best. "Absolutely. Let me show you."

"No, I..." She caught his hands as they stroked her thighs. "We'll probably kill each other if we try this again."

"I'll risk it."

"Roman, I mean it." Her head fell back and she gasped when he scraped his teeth over her skin. It was impossible, she thought, impossible, for this deep, dark craving to take over again. "Roman—"

"Fabulous legs," he murmured, skimming his tongue behind her knee. "I didn't pay nearly enough attention to them last night."

"Yes, you—" She braced a hand against the mattress as she swayed. "You're trying to distract me."

"Yeah."

"You can't." She closed her eyes. He could, and he was. "Ludwig needs the run," she managed. "He enjoys it."

"Fine." He sat up and circled her waist with his hands. "I'll take him."

"You?" Wanting to catch her breath, she turned her head to avoid his kiss, then shuddered as his lips trailed down her throat. "It's not necessary. I'm perfectly...

Roman." She said his name weakly as his thumbs circled her breasts.

"Yes, a truly incredible body," he murmured. "Long and lean and incredibly responsive. I can't seem to touch you and not want you."

She came up on her knees as he dragged another gasp out of her. "You're trying to seduce me."

"Nothing gets by you, does it?"

She was losing, weakening shamelessly. She knew it would infuriate her later, but for now all she could do was cling to him and let him have his way. "Is this your answer for everything?"

"No." He lifted her hips and brought her to him. "But it'll do."

Unable to resist, she wrapped her limbs around him and let passion take them both. When it was spent, she slid bonelessly down in the bed. She didn't argue when he drew the sheets over her shoulders.

"Stay here," he told her, kissing her hair. "I'll be back."

"His leash is on a hook under the steps," Charity murmured. "He gets two scoops of dog food when he gets back. And fresh water."

"I think I can handle a dog, Charity."

She yawned and tugged the blankets higher. "He likes to chase the Fitzsimmonses' cat. But don't worry, he can't catch her."

"That makes me breathe easier." He laced up his shoes. "Anything else I should know?"

"Mmm." She snuggled into the pillow. "I love you."

As always, it knocked him backward to hear her say it, to know she meant it. In silence, he stepped outside.

She wasn't tired, Charity thought as she stretched

under the sheets. But Roman was right. Sleep wasn't the best reason for staying in bed in the morning. Despite her bumps and bruises, she knew she'd never felt better in her life.

Still, she indulged herself, lingering in bed, half dreaming, until guilt finally prodded her out.

Moving automatically, she turned on the stereo, then tidied the bed. In the parlor she glanced over the notes she'd left for herself, made a few more. Then she headed for the shower. She was humming along to Tchaikovsky's violin concerto when the curtain swished open.

"Roman!" She pressed both hands to her heart and leaned back against the tile. "You might as well shoot me as scare me to death. Didn't you ever hear of the Bates Motel?"

"I left my butcher knife in my other pants." She had her hair piled on top of her head and a cake of some feminine scented soap in her hand. Her skin was gleaming wet and already soapy. He pulled off his shirt and tossed it aside. "Did you ever consider teaching that dog to heel?"

"No." She grinned as she watched Roman unfasten his jeans. "I guess you could use a shower." Saying nothing, he tossed his jeans on top of his shirt. Charity took a moment to make a long, thorough survey. "Well, apparently that run didn't...tire you out." She was laughing when he stepped in with her.

It was nearly an hour later when Charity made it down to the lobby. "I could eat one of everything." She pressed a hand to her stomach. "Good morning, Bob." She paused at the front desk to smile at him.

"Charity." Bob felt the sweat spring onto his palms

when he spotted Roman behind her. "How are you feeling? It's awfully soon for you to be up and around."

"I'm fine." Idly she glanced at the papers on the desk. "Sorry I left you in the lurch yesterday."

"Don't be silly." Fear ground in his stomach as he eyed the wound on her temple. "We were worried about you."

"I appreciate that, but there's no need to worry anymore." She slanted a smile at Roman. "I've never felt better in my life."

Bob caught the look, and his stomach sank. If the cop was in love with her, he thought, things were going to be even stickier. "Glad to hear it. But—"

She stopped his protest by raising a hand. "Is there anything urgent?"

"No." He glanced at Roman again. "No, nothing."

"Good." After setting the papers aside again, Charity studied his face. "What's wrong, Bob?"

"Nothing. What could be wrong?"

"You look a little pale. You're not coming down with anything, are you?"

"No, everything's fine. Just fine. We got some new reservations. July's almost booked solid."

"Great. I'll look things over after breakfast. Get yourself some coffee." She patted his hand and walked into the dining room.

Three tables were already occupied, the patrons enjoying Mae's coffee cake before their meal was served. Bonnie was busy taking orders. The breakfast menu was neatly listed on the board, and music was playing in the background, soft and soothing. The flowers were fresh, and the coffee was hot.

"Something wrong?" Roman asked her.

"No." Charity smoothed down the collar of her shirt. "What could be wrong? It looks like everything's just dandy." Feeling useless, she walked into the kitchen.

There was no bickering to referee. Mae and Dolores were working side by side, and Lori loaded up a tray with her first order.

"We need more butter for the French toast," Mae called out.

"Coming right up." Cheerful as a bird, Dolores began to scoop up neat balls of butter. As she offered the newly filled bowl to Lori, she spotted Charity standing inside the door. "Well, good morning." Her thin face creased with a smile. "Didn't expect to see you up."

"I'm fine."

"Sit down, girl." Hardly glancing around, Mae continued to sprinkle shredded cheese into an omelet. "Dolores will get you some tea."

Charity smiled with clenched teeth. "I don't want any tea."

"Want and need's two different things."

"Glad to see you're feeling better," Lori said as she rushed out with her tray.

Bonnie came in, pad in hand. "Oh, hi, Charity, we thought you'd rest another day. Feeling better?"

"I'm fine," Charity said tightly. "Just fine."

"Great. Two omelets with bacon, Mae. And an order of French toast with sausage. Two herb teas, an English muffin—crisp. And we're running low on coffee." After punching her order sheet on a hook by the stove, she took the fresh pot Dolores handed her and hurried out.

Charity walked over to get an apron, only to have Mae smack her hand away. "I told you to sit."

"And I told you I'm fine. That's *f-i-n-e*. I'm going to help take orders."

"The only orders you're taking today are from me. Now sit." She ran a hand up and down Charity's arm. Nobody recognized or knew how to deal with that stubborn look better than Mae. "Be a good girl, now. I won't worry so much if I know you've had a good breakfast. You don't want me to worry, do you?"

"No, of course not, but—"

"That's right. Now take a seat. I'll fix you some French toast. It's your favorite."

She sat down. Dolores set a cup of tea in front of her and patted her head. "You sure did give us all a fright yesterday. Have a seat, Roman. I'll get your coffee."

"Thanks. You're sulking," he murmured to Charity.

"I am not."

"Doc's coming by this morning to take another look at you."

"Oh, for heaven's sake, Mae—"

"You're not doing nothing till he gives the okay." With a nod, she began preparing Bonnie's order. "Fat lot of good you'll do if you're not a hundred percent. Things were hard enough yesterday."

Charity stopped staring into her tea and looked up. "Were they?"

"Everybody asking questions nobody had the answer to. Whole stacks of linens lost."

"Lost? But—"

"Found them." Mae made room at the stove for Dolores. "But it sure was confusing for a while. Then the dinner shift… Could have used an extra pair of hands for sure." Mae winked at Roman over Charity's head.

"We'll all be mighty glad when the doc gives you his okay. Let that bacon crisp, Dolores."

"It is crisp."

"Not enough."

"Want me to burn it?"

Charity smiled and sipped her tea. It was good to be back.

It was midafternoon before she saw Roman again. She had a pencil behind her ear, a pad in one pocket and a dust cloth in another, and she was dashing down the hallway toward her rooms.

"In a hurry?"

"Oh." She stopped long enough to smile at him. "Yes. I have some papers up in my room that should be in the office."

"What's this?" He tugged at the dust cloth.

"One of the housekeepers came down with a virus. I sent her home." She looked at her watch and frowned. She thought she could spare about two minutes for conversation. "I really hope that's not what's wrong with Bob."

"What's wrong with Bob?"

"I don't know. He just doesn't look well." She tossed her hair back, causing the slender gold spirals in her ears to dance. "Anyway, we're short a housekeeper, and we've got guests checking into units 3 and 5 today. The Garsons checked out of 5 this morning. They won't win any awards for neatness."

"The doctor said you were supposed to rest an hour this afternoon."

"Yes, but— How did you know?"

"I asked him." Roman pulled the dustcloth out of her pocket. "I'll clean 5."

"Don't be ridiculous. It's not your job."

"My job's to fix things. I'll fix 5." He took her chin in his hand before she could protest. "When I'm finished I'm going to go upstairs. If you aren't in bed I'm coming after you."

"Sounds like a threat."

He bent down and kissed her, hard. "It is."

"I'm terrified," she said, and dashed up the stairs.

It wasn't that she meant to ignore the doctor's orders. Not really. It was only that a nap came far down on her list of things to be done. Every phone call she made had to include a five-minute explanation of her injuries.

No, she was really quite well. Yes, it was terrible that someone had stolen poor Mrs. Norton's car and driven it so recklessly. Yes, she was sure the sheriff would get to the bottom of it. No, she had not broken her legs…her arm…her shoulder…. Yes, she intended to take good care of herself, thank you very much.

The goodwill and concern would have warmed her if she hadn't been so far behind in her work. To make it worse, Bob was distracted and disorganized. Worried that he was ill or dealing with a personal problem, Charity took on the brunt of his work.

Twice she'd fully intended to take a break and go up to her rooms, and twice she'd been delayed by guests checking in. Taking it on faith that Roman had spruced up unit 5, she showed a young pair of newlyweds inside.

"You have a lovely view of the garden from here," Charity said as a cover while she made sure there were fresh towels. Roman had hung them on the rack, exactly where they belonged. The bed, with its heart-shaped white wicker headboard, was made up with a military precision she couldn't have faulted. It cost her, but she resisted the temptation to turn up the coverlet and check sheets.

"We serve complimentary wine in the gathering room every evening at five. We recommend that you make a reservation for dinner if you plan to join us, particularly since it's Saturday night. Breakfast is served between seven-thirty and ten. If you'd like to—" She broke off when Roman stepped into the room. "I'll be with you in a minute," she told him, and started to turn back to the newlyweds.

"Excuse me." Roman gave them both a friendly nod before he scooped Charity up in his arms. "Miss Ford is needed elsewhere. Enjoy your stay."

As the first shock wore off she began to struggle. "Are you out of your mind? Put me down."

"I intend to—when I get you to bed."

"You can't just…" The words trailed off into a groan as he carried her through the gathering room.

Two men sitting on the sofa stopped telling fish stories. A family coming in from a hike gawked from the doorway. Miss Millie and Miss Lucy halted their daily game of Scrabble by the window.

"Isn't that the most romantic thing?" Miss Millie said when they disappeared into the west wing.

"You have totally embarrassed me."

Roman shifted her weight in his arms and carried her upstairs. "You're lucky that's all I did."

"You had no right interrupting me when I was welcoming guests. Then, to make matters worse, you decide to play Rhett Butler."

"As I recall, he had something entirely different in mind when he carried another stubborn woman up to bed." He dropped her, none too gently, on the mattress. "You're going to rest."

"I'm tempted to tell you to go to hell."

He leaned down to cage her head between his hands. "Be my guest."

She'd be damned if she'd smile. "My manners are too ingrained to permit it."

"Aren't I the lucky one?" He leaned a little closer. There was amusement in his eyes now, enough of it so she had to bite her lip to keep from laughing. "I don't want you to get out of this bed for sixty minutes."

"Or?"

"Or… I'll sic Mae on you."

"A low blow, DeWinter."

He brushed a kiss just below the fresh bandage on her temple. "Tune out for an hour, baby. It won't kill you."

She reached up to toy with the top button of his shirt. "I'd like it better if you got in with me."

"I said tuned out, not turned on." When the phone in the parlor rang, he held her down with one hand. "Not a chance. Stay here and I'll get it."

She rolled her eyes behind his back as he walked into the adjoining room.

"Yes? She's resting. Tell him she'll get back to him in an hour. Hold her calls until four. That's right." He glanced down idly at a catalog she'd left open on her desk. She had circled a carved gold bracelet with a square-cut purple stone. "You handle whatever needs to be handled for the next hour. That's right."

"What was it?" Charity called from the next room.

"I'll tell you in an hour."

"Damn it, Roman."

He stopped in the doorway. "You want the message, I'll give it to you in an hour."

"But if it's important—"

"It's not."

She sent him a smoldering look. "How do you know?"

"I know it's not more important than you. Nothing is." He closed the door on her astonished expression.

He needed to keep Bob on a tight leash, he thought as he headed downstairs. As long as he was more afraid of him than of Block, things would be fine. He only had to keep the pressure on for a few more days. Block and Vision Tours would be checking in on Tuesday. When they checked out on Thursday morning he would lock the cage.

Roman pushed open the door of the office to find Bob staring at the computer screen and gulping coffee. "For somebody who's made his living from scams you're a mess."

Bob gulped more coffee. "I never worked with a cop looking over my shoulder before."

"Just think of me as your new partner," Roman advised him. He took the mug out of his hand and sniffed at it. "And lay off the booze."

"Give me a break."

"I'm giving you more of one than you deserve. Charity's worried that you're coming down with something— something other than a stretch in federal prison. I don't want her worrying."

"Look, you want me to carry on like it's business as usual. I'm lying to Block, setting him up." His hand shook as he passed it over his hair. "You don't know what he's capable of. *I* don't know what he's capable of." He looked at the mug, which Roman had set out of reach. "I need a little something to help me through the next few days."

"Let this get you through." Roman calmly lit a cigarette. "You pull this off and I'll go to bat for you. Screw up and I'll see to it that you're in a cage for a long time. Now take a break."

"What?"

"I said, take a break, go for a walk, get some real coffee." Roman tapped the ash from his cigarette into a little mosaic bowl.

"Sure." As he rose, Bob rubbed his palms on his thighs. "Look, DeWinter, I'm playing it straight with you. When this goes down, I expect you to keep Block off me."

"I'll take care of Block." That was a promise he intended to keep. When the door closed behind Bob, he picked up the phone. "DeWinter," he said when the connection was made.

"Make it quick," Conby told him. "I'm entertaining friends."

"I'll try not to let your martini get warm. I want to know if you've located the driver."

"DeWinter, an underling is hardly important at this point."

"It's important to me. Have you found him?"

"A man answering the description your informant gave you was detained in Tacoma this morning. He's being held for questioning by the local police." Conby put his hand over the receiver. Roman heard him murmur something that was answered by light laughter.

"We're using our influence to lengthen the procedure," Conby continued. "I'll be flying out there on

Monday. By Tuesday afternoon I should be checked into the inn. I'm told I'll have a room overlooking a fish pond. It sounds very quaint."

"I want your word that Charity will be left out of this."

"As I explained before, if she's innocent she has nothing to worry about."

"It's not a matter of *if*." Struggling to hold his temper, Roman crushed out his cigarette. "She is innocent. We've got it on record."

"On the word of a whimpering little bookkeeper."

"She was damn near killed, and she doesn't even know why."

"Then keep a closer eye on her. We have no desire to see Miss Ford harmed, or to involve her any more deeply than necessary. There's a police officer out there who shares the same passionate opinion of Miss Ford as you do. Sheriff Royce managed to trace you to us."

"How?"

"He's a smart cop with connections. He has a cousin or brother-in-law or some such thing with the Bureau. He wasn't at all pleased at being left in the dark."

"I'll bet."

"I imagine he'll be paying you a visit before long. Handle him carefully, DeWinter, but handle him."

Just as Roman heard the phone click in his ear the office door opened. For once, Roman thought, Conby was right on target. He replaced the receiver before settling back in his chair.

"Sheriff."

"I want to know what the hell's going on around here, Agent DeWinter."

"Close the door." Roman pushed back in the chair and considered half a dozen different ways of handling

Royce. "I'd appreciate it if you'd drop the 'Agent' for now."

Royce just laid both palms on the surface of the desk. "I want to know what a federal agent is doing undercover in my territory."

"Following orders. Sit down?" He indicated a chair.

"I want to know what case you're working on."

"What did they tell you?"

Royce snorted disgustedly. "It got to the point where even my cousin started giving me the runaround, DeWinter, but I've got to figure that your being here had something to do with Charity being damn near run down yesterday."

"I'm here because I was assigned here." Roman waited a moment, sending Royce a long, direct look. "But my first priority is keeping Charity safe."

Royce hadn't been in law enforcement for nearly twenty years without being able to take the measure of a man. He took Roman's now, and was satisfied. "I got a load of bull from Washington about her being under investigation."

"She was. Now she's not. But she could be in trouble. Are you willing to help?"

"I've known that girl all her life." Royce took off his hat and ran his fingers through his hair. "Why don't you stop asking fool questions and tell me what's going on?"

Roman briefed him, pausing only once or twice to allow Royce to ask questions. "I don't have time to get into any more specifics. I want to know how many of your men you can spare Thursday morning."

"All of them," Royce said immediately.

"I only want your most experienced. I have information that Block will not only be bringing the counterfeit money, but also a man who'll register as Jack Marshall. His real name is Vincent Dupont. A week ago he robbed two banks in Ontario, killed a guard and wounded a civilian. Block will smuggle him out of Canada in the tour group, keep him here for a couple of days, then send him by short routes to South America. For his travel service to men like Dupont he takes a nice stiff fee. Both Dupont and Block are dangerous men. We'll have agents here at the inn, but we also have civilians. There's no way we can clear the place without tipping them off."

"It's a chancy game you're playing."

"I know." He thought of Charity dozing upstairs. "It's the only way I know how to play it."

Chapter 9

Charity drove back to the inn after dropping a trio of guests at the ferry. She was certain it was the most beautiful morning she'd ever seen. After the most wonderful night of her life, she thought. No, two of the most wonderful nights of her life.

Though she'd never considered herself terribly romantic, she'd always imagined what it would be like to really be in love. Her daydreams hadn't come close to what she was feeling now. This was solid and bewildering. It was simple and staggering. He filled her thoughts just as completely as he filled her heart. She couldn't wait to walk back into the inn, just knowing Roman would be there.

It seemed that every hour they spent together brought them closer. Gradually, step by step, she could feel the barriers he had placed around him lowering. She wanted to be there when they finally dropped completely.

He was in love with her. She was sure he was, whether he knew it or not. She could tell by the way he looked at her, by the way he touched her hair when he thought she was sleeping. By the way he held her so tightly all through the night, as if he were afraid she might somehow slip away from him. In time she would show him that she wasn't going anywhere—and that he wasn't going anywhere, either.

Something was troubling him. That was another thing she was sure of. Her eyes clouded as she drove along the water. There were times when she could feel the tension pulsing in him even when he was across the room. He seemed to be watching, waiting. But for what?

Since the accident he'd barely let her out of his sight. It was sweet, she mused. But it had to stop. She might love him, but she wouldn't be pampered. She was certain that if he had known she planned to drive to the ferry that morning he would have found a way to stop her.

She was right again. It had taken Roman some time to calm down after he had learned Charity wasn't in the office or the kitchen or anywhere else in the inn.

"She's driven up to drop some guests at the ferry," Mae told him, then watched in fascination as he let his temper loose.

"My, my," she said when the air was clear again. "You've got it bad, boy."

"Why did you let her go?"

"Let her go?" Mae let out a rich, appreciative laugh. "I haven't *let* that girl do anything since she could walk. She just does it." She stopped stirring custard to study him. "Any reason she shouldn't drive to the ferry?"

"No."

"All right, then. Just cool your britches. She'll be back in half an hour."

He sweated and paced, nearly the whole time she was away. Mae and Dolores exchanged glances across the room. There would be plenty of gossip to pass around once they had the kitchen to themselves.

Mae thought of the way Charity had been smiling that morning. Why, the girl had practically danced into the kitchen. She kept her eye on Roman as he brooded over a cup of coffee and watched the clock. Yes, indeed, she thought, the boy had it bad.

"You got today off, don't you?" Mae asked him.

"What?"

"It's Sunday," she said patiently. "You got the day off?"

"Yeah, I guess."

"Nice day, too. Good weather for a picnic." She began slicing roast beef for sandwiches. "Got any plans?"

"No."

"Charity loves picnics. Yes, sir, she's mighty partial to them. You know, I don't think that girl's had a day away from this place in better than a month."

"Got any dynamite?"

Dolores piped up. "What's that?"

"I figure it would take dynamite to blast Charity out of the inn for a day."

It took her a minute, but Dolores finally got the joke. She chuckled. "Hear that, Mae? He wants dynamite."

"Pair of fools," Mae muttered as she cut generous pieces of chocolate cheesecake. "You don't move that girl with dynamite or threats or orders. Might as well bash your head against a brick wall all day." She tried not to sound pleased about it, and failed. "You want her to do something, you make her think she's doing you a favor. Make her think it's important to you. Dolores, you go on in that back room and get me the big wicker hamper. Boy, if you keep walking back and forth you're going to wear out my floor."

"She should have been back by now."

"She'll be back when she's back. You know how to run a boat?"

"Yes, why?"

"Charity always loved to picnic on the water. She hasn't been out in a boat in a long time. Too long."

"I know. She told me."

Mae turned around. Her face was set. "Do you want to make my girl happy?"

He tried to shrug it off, but he couldn't. "Yes. Yes, I do."

"Then you take her out on the boat for the day. Don't let her say no."

"All right."

Satisfied, she turned around again. "Go down in the cellar and get a bottle of wine. French. She likes the French stuff."

"She's lucky to have you."

Her wide face colored a bit, but she kept her voice brisk. "Around here, we got each other. You're all right," she added. "I wasn't sure of it when you first came around, but you're all right."

He was ready for her when she came back. Even as she stepped out of the van he was walking across the gravel lot, the wicker hamper in his hand.

"Hi."

"Hi." She greeted him with a smile and a quick kiss.

Despite the two teenagers shooting hoops on the nearby court, Roman wrapped an arm around her and brought her hard against him for a longer, more satisfying embrace. "Well…" She had to take a deep breath and steady herself against the van. "Hello again." She noted then that he had pulled a loose black sweater over his jeans and was carrying a hamper. "What's this?"

"It's a basket," he told her. "Mae put a few things in it for me. It's my day off."

"Oh." She tossed her braid behind her back. "That's right. Where are you off to?"

"Out on the water, if I can use the boat."

"Sure." She glanced up at the sky, a bit wistfully. "It's a great day for it. Light wind, hardly a cloud."

"Then let's go."

"Let's?" He was already pulling her toward the pier. "Oh, Roman, I can't. I have dozens of things to do this afternoon. And I…" She didn't want to admit she wasn't ready to go out on the water again. "I can't."

"I'll have you back before the dinner shift." He laid a hand on her cheek. "I need you with me, Charity. I need to spend some time with you, alone."

"Maybe we could go for a drive. You haven't seen the mountains."

"Please." He set the hamper down to take both of her arms. "Do this for me."

Had he ever said "Please" before? she wondered. She didn't think so. With a sigh, she looked out at the boat rocking gently against the pier. "All right. Maybe for an hour. I'll go in and change."

The red sweater and jeans would keep her warm enough on the water, he decided. She would know that, too. She was stalling. "You look fine." He kept her hand in his as they walked down the pier. "This could use a little maintenance."

"I know. I keep meaning to." She waited until Roman stepped down into the boat. When he held up a hand, she hesitated, then forced herself to join him. "I have a key on my ring."

"Mae already gave me one."

"Oh." Charity sat down in the stern. "I see. A conspiracy."

It took him only two pulls to start the engine. Mae had told him Charity kept the boat for the staff to use. "From what you said to me the other day, I don't think he'd want you to grieve forever."

"No." As her eyes filled, she looked back toward the inn. "No, he wouldn't. But I loved him so much." She took a deep breath. "I'll cast off."

Before he sent the boat forward, Roman took her hand and drew her down beside him. After a moment she rested her head on his shoulder.

"Have you done much boating?"

"From time to time. When I was a kid we used to rent a boat a couple times each summer and take it on the river."

"Who's we?" She watched the shutters come down over his face. "What river?" she asked instead.

"The Mississippi." He smiled and slipped an arm over her shoulders. "I come from St. Louis, remember?"

"The Mississippi." Her mind was immediately filled with visions of steamboats and boys on wooden rafts. "I'd love to see it. You know what would be great? Taking a cruise all the way down, from St. Louis to New Orleans. I'll have to put that in my file."

"Your file?"

"The file I'm going to make on things I want to do."
With a laugh, she waved to a passing sailboat before
leaning over to kiss Roman's cheek. "Thanks."

"For what?"

"For talking me into this. I've always loved spending
an afternoon out here, watching the other boats, looking at the houses. I've missed it."

"Have you ever considered that you give too much
to the inn?"

"No. You can't give too much to something you
love." She turned. If she shielded her eyes with her hand
she could just see it in the distance. "If I didn't have
such strong feelings for it, I would have sold it, taken
a job in some modern hotel in Seattle or Miami or...or
anywhere. Eight hours a day, sick leave, two weeks paid
vacation." Just the idea made her laugh. "I'd wear a nice
neat business suit and sensible shoes, have my own office and quietly go out of my mind." She dug into her
bag for her sunglasses. "You should understand that.
You have good hands and a sharp mind. Why aren't
you head carpenter for some big construction firm?"

"Maybe when the time came I made the wrong
choices."

With her head tilted, she studied him, her eyes narrowed and thoughtful behind the tinted lenses. "No, I
don't think so. Not for you."

"You don't know enough about me, Charity."

"Of course I do. I've lived with you for a week. That
probably compares with knowing someone on a casual
basis for six months. I know you're very intense and
internal. You have a wicked temper that you seldom
lose. You're an excellent carpenter who likes to finish
the job he starts. You can be gallant with little old la-

dies." She laughed a little and turned her face into the wind. "You like your coffee black, you're not afraid of hard work…and you're a wonderful lover."

"And that's enough for you?"

She lifted her shoulders. "I don't imagine you know too much more about me. I'm starving," she said abruptly. "Do you want to eat?"

"Pick a spot."

"Head over that way," she told him. "See that little jut of land? We can anchor the boat there."

The land she'd indicated was hardly more than a jumble of big, smooth rocks that fell into the water. As they neared it he could see a narrow stretch of sand crowded by trees. Cutting back the engine, he maneuvered toward the beach, Charity guiding him in with hand signals. As the current lapped at the sides of the boat, she pulled off her shoes and began to roll up her jeans.

"You'll have to give me a hand." As she said it she plunged into the knee-high water. "God, it's cold!" Then she was laughing and securing the line. "Come on."

The water was icy on his bare calves. Together they pulled the boat up onto a narrow spit of sand.

"I don't suppose you brought a blanket."

He reached into the boat and took out the faded red blanket Mae had given him. "This do?"

"Great. Grab the basket." She splashed through the shallows and onto the shore. After spreading the blanket at the base of the sheltering rocks she rolled down the damp legs of her jeans. "Lori and I used to come here when we were kids. To eat peanut butter sandwiches and talk about boys." Kneeling on the blanket, she looked around.

There were pines at her back, deep and green and

thick all the way up the slope. A few feet away the water frothed at the rock, which had been worn smooth by wind and time. A single boat cruised in the distance, its sails full and white.

"It hasn't changed much." Smiling, she reached for the basket. "I guess the best things don't." She threw back the top and spotted a bottle of champagne. "Well." With a brow arched, she pulled it out. "Apparently we're going to have some picnic."

"Mae said you liked the French stuff."

"I do. I've never had champagne on a picnic."

"Then it's time you did." He took the bottle and walked back to dunk it in the water, screwing it down in the wet sand. "We'll let it chill a little more." He came back to her, taking her hand before she could explore deeper in the basket. He knelt. When they were thigh to thigh, he gathered her close and closed his mouth over hers.

Her quiet sound of pleasure came first, followed by a gasp as he took the kiss deeper. Her arms came around him, then slid up until her hands gripped his shoulders. Desire was like a flood, rising fast to drag her under.

He needed...needed to hold her close like this, to taste the heat of passion on his lips, to feel her heart thud against him. He dragged his hands through her hair, impatiently tugging it free of the braids. All the while his mouth ravaged hers, gentleness forgotten.

There was a restlessness in him, and an anger that she couldn't understand. Responding to both, she pressed against him, unhesitatingly offering whatever he needed. Perhaps it would be enough. Slowly his mouth gentled. Then he was only holding her.

"That's a very nice way to start a picnic," Charity managed when she found her voice again.

"I can't seem to get enough of you."

"That's okay. I don't mind."

He drew away to frame her face in his hands. The crystal drops at her ears swung and shot out light. But her eyes were calm and deep and full of understanding. It would be better, he thought, and certainly safer, if he simply let her pull out the sandwiches. They could talk about the weather, the water, the people at the inn. There was so much he couldn't tell her. But when he looked into her eyes he knew he had to tell her enough about Roman DeWinter that she would be able to make a choice.

"Sit down."

Something in his tone sent a frisson of alarm down her spine. He was going to tell her he was leaving, she thought. "All right." She clasped her hands together, promising herself she'd find a way to make him stay.

"I haven't been fair with you." He leaned back against a rock. "Fairness hasn't been one of my priorities. There are things about me you should know, that you should have known before things got this far."

"Roman—"

"It won't take long. I did come from St. Louis. I lived in a kind of neighborhood you wouldn't even understand. Drugs, whores, Saturday night specials." He looked out at the water. The spiffy little sailboat had caught the wind. "A long way from here, baby."

So the trust had come, she thought. She wouldn't let him regret it. "It doesn't matter where you came from, Roman. It's where you are now."

"That's not always true. Part of where you come from

stays with you." He closed a hand over hers briefly, then released it. It would be better, he thought, to break the contact now. "When he was sober enough, my father drove a cab. When he wasn't sober enough, he sat around the apartment with his head in his hands. One of my first memories is waking up at night hearing my mother screaming at him. Every couple of months she'd threaten to leave. Then he'd straighten up. We'd live in the eye of the hurricane until he'd stop off at the bar to have a drink. So she finally stopped threatening and did it."

"Where did you go?"

"I said she left."

"But...didn't she take you with her?"

"I guess she figured she was going to have it rough enough without dealing with a ten-year-old."

Charity shook her head and struggled with a deep, churning anger. It was hard for her to understand how a mother could desert her child. "She must have been very confused and frightened. Once she—"

"I never saw her again," Roman said. "You have to understand that not everyone loves unconditionally. Not everyone loves at all."

"Oh, Roman." She wanted to gather him close then, but he held her away from him.

"I stayed with my father another three years. One night he hit the gin before he got in the cab. He killed himself and his passenger."

"Oh, God." She reached for him, but he shook his head.

"That made me a ward of the court. I didn't much care for that, so I took off, hit the streets."

She was reeling from what he'd already told her, and she could barely take it all in. "At thirteen?"

"I'd been living there most of my life anyway."

"But how?"

He shook a cigarette out of his pack, lighting it and drawing deep before he spoke again. "I took odd jobs when I could find them. I stole when I couldn't. After a couple of years I got good enough at the stealing that I didn't bother much with straight jobs. I broke into houses, hot-wired cars, snatched purses. Do you understand what I'm telling you?"

"Yes. You were alone and desperate."

"I was a thief. Damn it, Charity, I wasn't some poor misguided youth. I stopped being a kid when I came home and found my father passed out and my mother gone. I knew what I was doing. I chose to do it."

She kept her eyes level with his, battling the need to take him in her arms. "If you expect me to condemn a child for finding a way to survive, I'll have to disappoint you."

She was romanticizing, he told himself, pitching his cigarette into the water.

"Do you still steal?"

"What if I told you I did?"

"I'd have to say you were stupid. You don't seem stupid to me, Roman."

He paused for a moment before he decided to tell her the rest. "I was in Chicago. I'd just turned sixteen. It was January, so cold your eyes couldn't water. I decided I needed to score enough to take a bus south. Thought I'd winter in Florida and fleece the rich tourists. That's when I met John Brody. I broke into his apartment and ended up with a .45 in my face. He was a cop." The memory of that moment still made him laugh. "I don't know who was more surprised. He gave me three choices. One, he could turn me over to Juvie. Two, he could beat the hell out of me. Three, he could give me something to eat."

"What did you do?"

"It's hard to play it tough when a two-hundred-pound man's pointing a .45 at your belt. I ate a can of soup. He let me sleep on the couch." Looking back, he could still see himself, skinny and full of bitterness, lying wakeful on the lumpy sofa.

"I kept telling myself I was going to rip off whatever I could and take off. But I never did. I used to tell myself he was a stupid bleeding heart, and that once it warmed up I'd split with whatever I could carry. The next thing I knew I was going to school." Roman paused a moment to look up at the sky. "He used to build things down in the basement of the building. He taught me how to use a hammer."

"He must have been quite a man."

"He was only twenty-five when I met him. He'd grown up on the South Side, running with the gangs. At some point he turned it around. Then he decided to turn me around. In some ways he did. When he got married a couple of years later he bought this old run-down house in the suburbs. We fixed it up room by room. He used to tell me there was nothing he liked better than living in a construction zone. We were adding on another room—it was going to be his workshop—when he was killed. Line of duty. He was thirty-two. He left a three-year-old son and a pregnant widow."

"Roman, I'm sorry." She moved to him and took his hands.

"It killed something in me, Charity. I've never been able to get it back."

"I understand." He started to pull away, but she held him fast. "I do. When you lose someone who was that much a part of your life, something's always going to be missing. I still think about Pop all the time. It still makes me sad. Sometimes it just makes me angry, because there was so much more I wanted to say to him."

"You're leaving out pieces. Look at what I was, where I came from. I was a thief."

"You were a child."

He took her shoulders and shook her. "My father was a drunk."

"I don't even know who my father was. Should I be ashamed of that?"

"It doesn't matter to you, does it? Where I've been, what I've done?"

"Not very much. I'm more interested in what you are now."

He couldn't tell her what he was. Not yet. For her own safety, he had to continue the deception for a few more days. But there was something he could tell her. Like the story he had just recounted, it was something he had never told anyone else.

"I love you."

Her hands went slack on his. Her eyes grew huge. "Would you—" She paused long enough to take a deep breath. "Would you say that again?"

"I love you."

With a muffled sob, she launched herself into his arms. She wasn't going to cry, she told herself, squeezing her eyes tight against the threatening tears. She wouldn't be red-eyed and weepy at this, the most beautiful and exciting moment of her life.

"Just hold me a moment, okay?" Overwhelmed, she pressed her face into his shoulder. "I can't believe this is happening."

"That makes two of us." But he was smiling. He could feel the stunned delight coil through him as he stroked her hair. It hadn't been so hard to say, he realized. In fact, he could easily get used to saying it several times a day.

"A week ago I didn't even know you." She tilted her head back until her lips met his. "Now I can't imagine my life without you."

"Don't. You might change your mind."

"Not a chance."

"Promise." Overwhelmed by a sudden sense of urgency, he gripped her hands. "I want you to make that a promise."

"All right. I promise. I won't change my mind about being in love with you."

"I'm holding you to that, Charity." He swooped her against him, then drained even happy thoughts from her mind. "Will you marry me?"

She jerked back, gaped, then sat down hard. "What? *What?*"

"I want you to marry me—now, today." It was crazy, and he knew it. It was wrong. Yet, as he pulled her up again, he knew he had to find a way to keep her. "You must know somebody, a minister, a justice of the peace, who could do it."

"Well, yes, but…" She held a hand to her spinning head. "There's paperwork, and licenses. God, I can't think."

"Don't think. Just say you will."

"Of course I will, but—"

"No buts." He crushed his mouth to hers. "I want you to belong to me. God, I need to belong to you. Do you believe that?"

"Yes." Breathless, she touched a hand to his cheek. "Roman, we're talking about marriage, a lifetime. I only intend to do this once." She dragged a hand through her hair and sat down again. "I guess everyone says that, but I need to believe it. It has to start off with more than a few words in front of an official. Wait, please," she said before he could speak again. "You've really thrown me off here, and I want to make you understand. I love you, and I can't think of anything I want more than to belong to you. When I marry you it has to be more than rushing to the J.P. and saying 'I do.' I don't have to have a big, splashy wedding, either. It's not a matter of long white trains and engraved invitations."

"Then what is it?"

"I want flowers and music, Roman. And friends." She took his face in her hands, willing him to understand. "I want to stand beside you knowing I look beautiful, so that everyone can see how proud I am to be your wife. If that sounds overly romantic, well, it should be."

"How long do you need?"

"Can I have two weeks?"

He was afraid to give her two days. But it was for the best, he told himself. He would never be able to hold her if there were still lies between them. "I'll give you two weeks, if you'll go away with me afterward."

"Where?"

"Leave it to me."

"I love surprises." Her lips curved against his. "And you…you're the biggest surprise so far."

"Two weeks." He took her hands firmly in his. "No matter what happens."

"You make it sound as though we might have to overcome a natural disaster in the meantime. I'm only going to take a few days to make it right." She brushed a kiss over his cheek and smiled again. "It will be right, Roman, for both of us. That's another promise. I'd like that champagne now."

She took out the glasses while he retrieved the bottle from the water. As they sat together on the blanket, he released the cork with a pop and a hiss.

"To new beginnings," she said, touching her glass to his.

He wanted to believe it could happen. "I'll make you happy, Charity."

"You already have." She shifted so that she was cuddled against him, her head on his shoulder. "This is the best picnic I've ever had."

He kissed the top of her head. "You haven't eaten anything yet."

"Who needs food?" With a sigh, she reached up. He linked his hand with hers, and they both looked out toward the horizon.

Chapter 10

Check-in on Tuesday was as chaotic as it came. Charity barreled her way through it, assigning rooms and cabins, answering questions, finding a spare cookie for a cranky toddler, and waited for the first rush to pass.

She was the first to admit that she usually thrived on the noise, the problems and the healthy press of people that proved the inn's success. At the moment, though, she would have liked nothing better than having everyone, and everything settled.

It was hard to keep her mind on the business at hand when her head was full of plans for her wedding.

Should she have Chopin or Beethoven? She'd barely begun her list of possible selections. Would the weather hold so that they could have the ceremony in the gardens, or would it be best to plan an intimate and cozy wedding in the gathering room?

"Yes, sir, I'll be glad to give you information on renting bikes." She snatched up a pamphlet.

When was she going to find an afternoon free so that she could choose the right dress? It *had* to be the right dress, the perfect dress. Something ankle-length, with some romantic touches of lace. There was a boutique in Eastsound that specialized in antique clothing. If she could just—

"Aren't you going to sign that?"

"Sorry, Roger." Charity pulled herself back and offered him an apologetic smile. "I don't seem to be all here this morning."

"No problem." He patted her hand as she signed his roster. "Spring fever?"

"You could call it that." She tossed back her hair, annoyed that she hadn't remembered to braid it that morning. As long as she was smelling orange blossoms she'd be lucky to remember her own name. "We're a little behind. The computer's acting up again. Poor Bob's been fighting with it since yesterday."

"Looks like you've been in a fight yourself."

She lifted a hand to the healing cut on her temple. "I had a little accident last week."

"Nothing serious?"

"No, just inconvenient, really. Some idiot joyriding nearly ran me down."

"That's terrible." Watching her carefully, he pulled his face into stern lines. "Were you badly hurt?"

"No, only a few stitches and a medley of bruises. Scared me more than anything."

"I can imagine. You don't expect something like that around here. I hope they caught him."

"No, not yet." Because she'd already put the incident

behind her, she gave a careless shrug. "To tell you the truth, I doubt they ever will. I imagine he got off the island as soon as he sobered up."

"Drunk drivers." Block made a sound of disgust. "Well, you've got a right to be distracted after something like that."

"Actually, I've got a much more pleasant reason. I'm getting married in a couple of weeks."

"You don't say!" His face split into a wide grin. "Who's the lucky man?"

"Roman DeWinter. I don't know if you met him. He's doing some remodeling upstairs."

"That's handy now, isn't it?" He continued to grin. The romance explained a lot. One look at Charity's face settled any lingering doubts. Block decided he'd have to have a nice long talk with Bob about jumping the gun. "Is he from around here?"

"No, he's from St. Louis, actually."

"Well, I hope he's not going to take you away from us."

"You know I'd never leave the inn, Roger." Her smile faded a bit. That was something she and Roman had never spoken of. "In any case, I promise to keep my mind on my work. You've got six people who want to rent boats." She took a quick look at her watch. "I can have them taken to the marina by noon."

"I'll round them up."

The door to the inn opened, and Charity glanced over. She saw a small, spare man with well-cut auburn hair, wearing a crisp sport shirt. He carried one small leather bag.

"Good morning."

"Good morning." He took a brief study of the lobby

as he crossed to the desk. "Conby, Richard Conby. I believe I have a reservation."

"Yes, Mr. Conby. We're expecting you." Charity shuffled through the papers on the desk and sent up a quick prayer that Bob would have the computer humming along by the end of the day. "How was your trip?"

"Uneventful." He signed the register, listing his address as Seattle. Charity found herself both amused and impressed by his careful manicure. "I was told your inn is quiet, restful. I'm looking forward to relaxing for a day or two."

"I'm sure you'll find the inn very relaxing." She opened a drawer to choose a key. "Either Roman or I will drive your group to the marina, Roger. Have them in the parking lot at noon."

"Will do." With a cheerful wave, he sauntered off.

"I'll be happy to show you to your room, Mr. Conby. If you have any questions about the inn, or the island, feel free to ask me or any of the staff." She came around the desk and led the way to the stairs.

"Oh, I will," Conby said, following her. "I certainly will."

At precisely 12:05, Conby heard a knock and opened his door. "Prompt as always, DeWinter." He scanned down to Roman's tool belt. "Keeping busy, I see."

"Dupont's in cabin 3."

Conby decided to drop the sarcasm. This was a big one, much too big for him to let his personal feelings interfere. "You made a positive ID?"

"I helped him carry his bags."

"Very good." Satisfied, Conby finished arranging his ebony-handled clothes brush and shoe horn on the oak dresser. "We'll move in as planned on Thursday morning and take him before we close in on Block."

"What about the driver of the car who tried to kill Charity?"

Always fastidious, Conby walked into the adjoining bath to wash his hands. "You're inordinately interested in a small-time hood."

"Did you get a confession?"

"Yes." Conby unfolded a white hand towel bordered with flowers. "He admitted to meeting with Block last week and taking five thousand to—to put Miss Ford out of the picture. A very minor sum for a hit." His hands dry, Conby tossed the towel over the lip of the sink before walking back into the bedroom. "If Block had been more discerning, he might have had more success."

Taking him by the collar, Roman lifted Conby to his toes. "Watch your step," he said softly.

"It's more to the point for me to tell you to watch yours." Conby pulled himself free and straightened his shirt. In the five years since he had taken over as Roman's superior he had found Roman's methods crude and his attitude arrogant. The pity was, his results were invariably excellent. "You're losing your focus on this one, Agent DeWinter."

"No. It's taken me a while—maybe too long—but I'm focused just fine. You've got enough on Block to pin him with conspiracy to murder. Dupont's practically tied up with a bow. Why wait?"

"I won't bother to remind you who's in charge of this case."

"We both know who's in charge, Conby, but there's a difference between sitting behind a desk and calling the shots in the field. If we take them now, quietly, there's less risk of endangering innocent people."

"I have no intention of endangering any of the guests. Or the staff," he added, thinking he knew where Roman's mind was centered. "I have my orders on this, just as you do." He took a fresh handkerchief out of his drawer. "Since it's apparently so important to you, I'll tell you that we want to nail Block when he passes the money. We're working with the Canadian authorities on this, and that's the way we'll proceed. As for the conspiracy charges, we have the word of a bargain-basement hit man. It may take a bit more to make it stick."

"You'll make it stick. How many have we got?"

"We have two agents checking in tomorrow, and two more as backup. We'll take Dupont in his cabin, and Block in the lobby. Moving on Dupont any earlier would undoubtedly tip off Block. Agreed?"

"Yes."

"Since you've filled me in on the checkout procedures, it should go very smoothly."

"It better. If anything happens to her—anything—I'm holding you responsible."

Charity dashed into the kitchen with a loaded tray. "I don't know how things can get out of hand so fast. When have you ever known us to have a full house on a Wednesday night?" she asked the room at large, whipping out her pad. "Two specials with wild rice, one with baked potato, hold the sour cream, and one child's portion of ribs with fries." She rushed over to get the drinks herself.

"Take it easy, girl," Mae advised her. "They ain't going anywhere till they eat."

"That's the problem." She loaded up the tray. "What a time for Lori to get sick. The way this virus is bouncing around, we're lucky to have a waitress still standing. Whoops!" She backed up to keep from running into Roman. "Sorry."

"Need a hand?"

"I need two." She smiled and took the time to lean over the tray and kiss him. "You seem to have them. Those salads Dolores is fixing go to table 5."

"Girl makes me tired just looking at her," Mae commented as she filleted a trout. She lifted her head just long enough for her eyes to meet Roman's. "Seems to me she rushes into everything."

"Four house salads." Dolores was humming the "Wedding March" as she passed him a tray. "Looks like you didn't need that dynamite after all." Cackling, she went back to fill the next order.

Five minutes later he passed Charity in the doorway again. "Strange bunch tonight," she murmured.

"How so?"

"There's a man at table 2. He's so jumpy you'd think he'd robbed a bank or something. Then there's a couple at table 8, supposed to be on a second honeymoon. They're spending more time looking at everyone else than each other."

Roman said nothing. She'd made both Dupont and two of Conby's agents in less than thirty minutes.

"And then there's this little man in a three-piece suit sitting at 4. Suit and tie," she added with a glance over her shoulder. "Came here to relax, he says. Who can relax in a three-piece suit?" Shifting, she balanced the tray on her hip. "Claims to be from Seattle and has an

Eastern accent that could cut Mae's apple pie. Looks like a weasel."

"You think so?" Roman allowed himself a small smile at her description of Conby.

"A very well-groomed weasel," she added. "Check it out for yourself." With a small shudder, she headed toward the dining room again. "Anyone that smooth gives me the creeps."

Duty was duty though, and the weasel was sitting at her station. "Are you ready to order?" she asked Conby with a bright smile.

He took a last sip of his vodka martini. It was passable, he supposed. "The menu claims the trout is fresh."

"Yes, sir." She was particularly proud of that. The stocked pond had been her idea. "It certainly is."

"Fresh when it was shipped in this morning, no doubt."

"No." Charity lowered her pad but kept her smile in place. "We stock our own right here at the inn."

Lifting a brow, he tapped a finger against his empty glass. "Your fish may be superior to your vodka, but I have my doubts as to whether it is indeed fresh. Nonetheless, it appears to be the most interesting item on your menu, so I shall have to make do."

"The fish," Charity repeated, with what she considered admirable calm, "is fresh."

"I'm sure you consider it so. However, your conception of fresh and mine may differ."

"Yes, sir." She shoved the pad into her pocket. "If you'll excuse me a moment."

She might be innocent, Conby thought, frowning at his empty glass, but she was hardly efficient.

"Where's the fire?" Mae wanted to know when Charity burst into the kitchen.

"In my brain." She stopped a moment, hands on hips. "That—that insulting pipsqueak out there tells me our vodka's below standard, our menu's dull and our fish isn't fresh."

"A dull menu." Mae bristled down to her crepe-soled shoes. "What did he eat?"

"He hasn't eaten anything yet. One drink and a couple of crackers with salmon dip and he's a restaurant critic."

Charity took a turn around the kitchen, struggling with her temper. No urban wonder was going to stroll into her inn and pick it apart. Her bar was as good as any on the island, her restaurant had a triple-A rating, and her fish—

"Guy at table 4 wants another vodka martini," Roman announced as he carried in a loaded tray.

"Does he?" Charity whirled around. "Does he really?"

He couldn't recall ever seeing quite that glint in her eye. "That's right," he said cautiously.

"Well, I have something else to get him first." So saying, she strode into the utility room and then out again.

"Uh-oh," Dolores mumbled.

"Did I miss something?" Roman asked.

"Man's got a nerve saying the food's dull before he's even had a taste of it." Scowling, Mae scooped a helping of wild asparagus onto a plate. "I've a mind to add some curry to his entrée. A nice fat handful of it. We'll see about dull."

They all turned around when Charity strolled back

in. She was still carrying the platter. On it flopped a very confused trout.

"My." Dolores covered her mouth with both hands, giggling. "Oh, my."

Grinning, Mae went back to her stove.

"Charity." Roman made a grab for her arm, but she evaded him and glided through the doorway. Shaking his head, he followed her.

A few of the diners looked up and stared as she carried the thrashing fish across the room. Weaving through the tables, she crossed to table 4 and held the tray under Conby's nose.

"Your trout, sir." She dropped the platter unceremoniously in front of him. "Fresh enough?" she asked with a small, polite smile.

In the archway Roman tucked his hands into his pockets and roared. He would have traded a year's salary for a photo of the expression on Conby's face as he and the fish gaped at each other.

When Charity glided back into the kitchen, she handed the tray and its passenger to Dolores. "You can put this back," she said. "Table 4 decided on the stuffed pork chops. I wish I had a pig handy." She let out a laughing squeal as Roman scooped her off the floor.

"You're the best." He pressed his lips to hers and held them there long after he'd set her down again. "The absolute best." He was still laughing as he gathered her close for a hug. "Isn't she, Mae?"

"She has her moments." She wasn't about to let them know how much good it did her to see them smiling at each other. "Now the two of you stop pawing each other in my kitchen and get back to work."

Charity lifted her face for one last kiss. "I guess I'd

better fix that martini now. He looked like he could use one."

Because she wasn't one to hold a grudge, Charity treated Conby to attentive and cheerful service throughout the meal. Noting that he hadn't unbent by dessert, she brought him a serving of Mae's Black Forest cake on the house.

"I hope you enjoyed your meal, Mr. Conby."

It was impossible for him to admit that he'd never had better, not even in Washington's toniest restaurants. "It was quite good, thank you."

She offered an easy smile as she poured his coffee. "Perhaps you'll come back another time and try the trout."

Even for Conby, her smile was hard to resist. "Perhaps. You run an interesting establishment, Miss Ford."

"We try. Have you lived in Seattle long, Mr. Conby?"

He continued to add cream to his coffee, but he was very much on guard. "Why do you ask?"

"Your accent. It's very Eastern."

Conby deliberated only seconds. He knew that Dupont had already left the dining room, but Block was at a nearby table, entertaining part of his tour group with what Conby considered rather boring stories. "You have a good ear. I was transferred to Seattle eighteen months ago. From Maryland. I'm in marketing."

"Maryland." Deciding to forgive and forget, she topped off his coffee. "You're supposed to have the best crabs in the country."

"I assure you, we do." The rich cake and the smooth coffee had mellowed him. He actually smiled at her. "It's a pity I didn't bring one along with me."

Laughing, Charity laid a friendly hand on his arm. "You're a good sport, Mr. Conby. Enjoy your evening."

Lips pursed, Conby watched her go. He couldn't recall anyone having accused him of being a good sport before. He rather liked it.

"We're down to three tables of diehards," Charity announced as she entered the kitchen again. "And I'm starving." She opened the refrigerator and rooted around for something to eat, but Mae snapped it closed again.

"You haven't got time."

"Haven't got time?" Charity pressed a hand to her stomach. "Mae, the way tonight went, I wasn't able to grab more than a stray French fry."

"I'll fix you a sandwich, but you had a call. Something about tomorrow's delivery."

"The salmon. Damn." She tilted her watch forward. "They're closed by now."

"Left an emergency number, I think. Message is upstairs."

"All right, all right. I'll be back in ten minutes." She cast a last longing glance at the refrigerator. "Make that two sandwiches."

To save time, she raced out through the utility room, rounded the side of the building and climbed the outside steps. When she opened the door, she could only stop and stare.

The music was pitched low. There was candlelight, and there were flowers and a white cloth on a table at the foot of the bed. It was set for two. As she watched, Roman took a bottle of wine from a glass bucket and drew the cork.

"I thought you'd never get here."

She leaned back on the closed door. "If I'd known this was waiting, I'd have been here a lot sooner."

"You said you liked surprises."

"Yes." There was both surprise and delight in her eyes as she brushed her tumbled hair back from her forehead. "I like them a lot." Untying her apron, she walked to the table while he poured the wine. It glinted warm and gold in the candlelight. "Thanks," she murmured when he offered her a glass.

"I wanted to give you something." He gripped her hand, holding tight and trying not to remember that this was their last night together before all the questions had to be answered. "I'm not very good with romantic gestures."

"Oh, no, you're very good at them. Champagne picnics, late-night suppers." She closed her eyes for a moment. "Mozart."

"Picked at random," he admitted, feeling foolishly nervous. "I have something for you."

She looked at the table. "Something else?"

"Yes." He reached down to the seat of his chair and picked up a square box. "It just came today." It was the best he could do. He pushed the box into her hand.

"A present?" She'd always liked the anticipation as much as the gift itself, so she took a moment to study and shake the box. But the moment the lid was off she snatched the bracelet out. "Oh, Roman, it's gorgeous." Thoroughly stunned, she turned the etched gold, watching the light glint off the metal and the square-cut amethyst. "It's absolutely gorgeous," she said again. "I'd swear I'd seen this before. Last week," she remembered. "In one of the magazines Lori brought me."

"You had it on your desk."

Overwhelmed, she nodded. "Yes, I'd circled this. I do that with beautiful things I know I'll never buy." She took a deep breath. "Roman, this is a wonderful, sweet and very romantic thing to do, but—"

"Then don't spoil it." He took the bracelet from the box and clasped it on her wrist. "I need the practice."

"No." She slipped her arms around him and rested her cheek against his shoulder. "I think you've got the hang of it."

He held her, letting the music, her scent, the moment, wash over him. Things could be different with her. He could be different with her.

"Do you know when I fell in love with you, Roman?"

"No." He kissed the top of her head. "I've thought more about why than when."

With a soft laugh, she snuggled against him. "I'd thought it was when you danced with me and you kissed me until every bone in my body turned to water."

"Like this?"

He turned his head, meeting her lips with his. Gently he set her on fire.

"Yes." She swayed against him, eyes closed. "Just like that. But that wasn't when. That was when I realized it, but it wasn't when I fell in love with you. Do you remember when you asked me about the spare?"

"The what?"

"The spare." Sighing, she tilted her head to give him easier access to her throat. "You wanted to know where the spare was so you could fix my flat." She leaned back to smile at his stunned expression. "I guess I can't call it love at first sight, since I'd already known you two or three minutes."

He ran his hands over her cheeks, through her hair, down her neck. "Just like that?"

"I'd never thought as much about falling in love and getting married as I suppose most people might. Because of Pop's being sick, and the inn. I always figured if it happened it would happen without me doing a lot of worrying or preparing. And I was right." She linked hands with him. "All I had to do was have a flat tire. The rest was easy."

A flat, Roman remembered, that had been deliberately arranged, just as her sudden need for a handyman had been arranged. As everything had been arranged, he thought, his grip tightening on her fingers. Everything except his falling in love with her.

"Charity..." He would have given anything to be able to tell her the truth, the whole truth. Anything but his knowledge that in ignorance there was safety. "I never meant for any of this to happen," he said carefully. "I never wanted to feel this way about anyone."

"Are you sorry?"

"About a lot of things, but not about being in love with you." He released her. "Your dinner's getting cold."

She tucked her tongue in her cheek. "If we found something else to do for an hour or so we could call it a midnight supper." She ran her hands up his chest to toy with the top button of his shirt. "Want to play Parcheesi?"

"No."

She flicked the button open and worked her way slowly, steadily down. "Scrabble?"

"Uh-uh."

"I know." She trailed a finger down the center of his

body to the snap of his jeans. "How about a rip-roaring game of canasta?"

"I don't know how to play."

Grinning, she tugged the snap open. "Oh, I have a feeling you'd catch on." Her laugh was muffled against his mouth.

Her heated thoughts of seducing him spun away as he dragged her head back and plundered her mouth. Her hands, so confident an instant before, faltered, then fisted hard at the back of his shirt. This wasn't the gentle, persuasive passion he had shown her since the night they had become lovers. This was a raw, desperate need, and it held a trace of fury, and a hint of despair. Whirling from the feel of it, she strained against him, letting herself go.

He'd needed her before. Roman had already come to understand that he had needed her long before he'd ever met her. But tonight was different. He'd set the stage carefully—the wine, the candles, the music—wanting to give her the romance she made him capable of. Then he'd felt her cool fingertips on his skin. He'd seen the promising flicker of desire in her eyes. There was only tonight. In a matter of hours she would know everything. No matter how often he told himself he would set things right, he was very much afraid she wouldn't forgive him.

He had tonight.

Breathless, she clung to him as they tumbled onto the bed. Here was the restless, ruthless lover she had known existed alongside the gentle, patient one. And he excited her every bit as much. As frantic as he, she pulled the loosened shirt from his shoulders and gloried in the feel of his flesh under her hands.

He was as taut as wire, as explosive as gunpowder. She felt his muscles tense and tighten as his mouth raced hungrily over her face. With a throaty laugh she tugged at his jeans while they rolled over the bed. If this was a game they were playing, she was determined they would both win.

A broken moan escaped him as her seeking hands drove him toward delirium. With an oath, he snagged her wrists, yanking them over her head. Breath heaving, he watched her face as he hooked a hand in the top of her shirt and ripped it down the center.

She had only time for a gasp before his hot, open mouth lowered to her skin to torment and tantalize. Powerless against the onslaught, she arched against him. When her hands were free, she only pressed him closer, crying out as he sucked greedily at her breast.

There were sensations here, wild and exquisite, that trembled on but never crossed the thin line that separated pleasure from pain. She felt herself dragged under, deep, still deeper, to windmill helplessly down some dark, endless tunnel toward unreasonable pleasures.

She couldn't know what she was doing to him. He was skilled enough to be certain that she was trapped by her own senses. Yet her body wrapped around his, her hands sought, her lips hungered.

In the flickering light her skin was like white satin. Under his hands it flowed like lava, hot and dangerous. Passion heated her light floral scent and turned it into something secret and forbidden.

Impatient, he yanked her slacks down her hips, frantically tasting each new inch of exposed flesh. This new intimacy had her sobbing out his name, shuddering as climax slammed impossibly into climax.

She held on to him, her nails digging in, her palms sliding damply over his slick skin. Her mind was empty, wiped clear of all but sensation. His name formed on her lips again and again. She thought he spoke to her, some mad, frenzied words that barely penetrated her clouded brain. Perhaps they were promises, pleas or prayers. She would have answered all of them if she could.

Then his mouth was on hers, swallowing her cry of release, smothering her groan of surrender, as he drove himself into her.

Fast, hot, reckless, they matched rhythms. Far beyond madness, they clung. Driven by love, locked in desire, they raced. Even when they tumbled back to earth, they held each other close.

Chapter 11

With her eyes half closed, her lips curved, she gave a long, lazy sigh. "That was wonderful."

Roman topped off the wine in Charity's glass. "Are you talking about the meal or the preliminaries?"

She smiled. "Both." Before he could set the bottle down, she touched his hand. It was just a skimming of her fingertip over his skin. His pulse doubled. "I think we should make midnight suppers a regular event."

It was long past midnight. Even cold fish was delicious with wine and love. He hoped that if he held on hard enough it could always be like this. "The first time you looked at me like that I almost swallowed my tongue."

She kept her eyes on his. Even in candlelight they were the color of morning. "Like what?"

"Like you knew exactly what I was thinking, and was trying not to think. Exactly what I wanted not to think. Exactly what I wanted, and was trying not to want. You scare the hell out of me."

Her lazy smile faltered. "I do?"

"You make too much difference. All the difference." He took both of her hands, wishing that just this once he had smooth words, a little poetry. "Every time you walk into a room..." But he didn't have smooth words, or poetry. "It makes a difference." He would have released her hands, but she turned them in his.

"I'm crazy about you. If I'd gone looking for someone to share my life, and my home, and my dreams, it would have been you."

She saw the shadow of concern in his eyes and willed it away. There was no room for worries in their lives tonight. With a quick, wicked smile, she nibbled on his fingers. "You know what I'd like?"

"More Black Forest cake."

"Besides that." Her eyes laughed at him over their joined hands. "I'd like to spend the night making love with you, talking with you, drinking wine and listening to music. I have a feeling I'd find it much more satisfying than the slumber parties I had as a girl."

She could, with a look and a smile, seduce him more utterly than any vision of black lace or white silk. "What would you like to do first?"

She had to laugh. It delighted her to see him so relaxed and happy. "Actually, there is something I want to talk with you about."

"I've already told you—I'll wear a suit, but no tuxedo."

"It's not about that." She smiled and traced a fingertip over the back of his hand. "Even though I know you'd look wonderful in a tux, I think a suit's more than adequate for an informal garden wedding. I'd like to talk to you about after the wedding."

"After-the-wedding plans aren't negotiable. I intend to make love with you for about twenty-four hours."

"Oh." As if she were thinking it through, she sipped her wine. "I guess I can go along with that. What I'd like to discuss is more long-range. It's something that Block said to me the other day."

"Block?" Alarm sprinted upward, then centered at the base of his neck.

"Just an offhand comment, but it made me think." She moved her shoulders in a quick, restless movement, then settled again. "I mentioned that we were getting married, and he said something about hoping you didn't take me away. It suddenly occurred to me that you might not want to spend your life here, on Orcas."

"That's it?" He felt the tension seep away.

"It's not such a little thing. I mean, I'm sure we can work it out, but you might not be crazy about the idea of living in a…well, a public kind of place, with people coming and going, and interruptions, and…" She let her words trail off, knowing she was rambling, as she did whenever she was nervous. "The point is, I need to know how you feel about staying on the island, living here, at the inn."

"How do you feel about it?"

"It isn't just a matter of what I feel any longer. It's what we feel."

It amazed him that she could so easily touch his heart. He supposed it always would. "It's been a long time since I've felt at home anywhere. I feel it here, with you."

She smiled and linked her fingers with his. "Are you tired?"

"No."

"Good." She rose and corked the wine. "Just let me get my keys."

"Keys to what?"

"The van," she told him as she walked into the next room.

"Are we going somewhere?"

"I know the best place on the island to watch the sun rise." She came back carrying a blanket and jiggling the keys. "Want to watch the sun come up with me, Roman?"

"You're only wearing a robe."

"Of course I am. It's nearly two in the morning. Don't forget the wine." With a laugh, she opened the door and crept down the steps. "Let's try not to wake anyone." She winced a little as she started across the gravel in her bare feet. With a muttered oath, Roman swung her up into his arms. "My hero," she murmured.

"Sure." He dumped her in the driver's seat of the van. "Where are we going, baby?"

"To the beach." She pushed her hair behind her shoulders as she started the van. Symphonic music blared from the radio before she twisted the knob. "I always play it too loud when I'm driving alone." She turned to look guiltily back at the inn. It remained dark and quiet. Slowly she drove out of the lot and onto the road. "It's a beautiful night."

"Morning."

"Whatever." She took a long, greedy gulp of air. "I haven't really had time for big adventures, so I have to take small ones whenever I get the chance."

"Is that what this is? An adventure?"

"Sure. We're going to drink the rest of the wine, make love under the stars and watch the sun come up over the water." She turned her head. "Is that all right with you?"

"I think I can live with it."

It was hours later when she curled up close to him. The bottle of wine was empty, and the stars were blinking out one by one.

"I'm going to be totally useless today." After a sleepy laugh, she nuzzled his neck. "And I don't even care."

He tugged the blanket over her. The mornings were still chilly. Though he hadn't planned it, the long night of loving had given him new hope. If he could convince her to sleep through the morning, he could complete his assignment, close the door on it and then explain everything. That would let him keep her out of harm's way and begin at the beginning.

"It's nearly dawn," she murmured.

They didn't speak as they watched day break. The sky paled. The night birds hushed. For an instant, time hung suspended. Then, slowly, regally, colors seeped into the horizon, bleeding up from the water, reflecting in it. Shadows faded, and the trees were tipped with gold. The first bird of the morning trumpeted the new day.

Roman gathered her to him to love her slowly under the lightening sky.

She dozed as he drove back to the inn. The sky was a pale, milky blue, but it was as quiet now as it had been when they'd left. When he lifted her out of the van, she sighed and nestled her head on his shoulder.

"I love you, Roman."

"I know." For the first time in his life he wanted to think about next week, next month, even next year—anything except the day ahead. He carried her up the stairs and into the inn. "I love you, Charity."

He had little trouble convincing her to snuggle between the sheets of the rumpled bed once he promised to take Ludwig for his habitual run.

Before he did, Roman went downstairs, strapped on his shoulder holster and shoved in his gun.

Taking Dupont was a study in well-oiled police work. By 7:45 his secluded cabin was surrounded by the best Sheriff Royce and the F.B.I. had to offer. Roman had ignored Conby's mutterings about bringing the locals into it and advised his superior to stay out of the way.

When the men were in position, Roman moved to the door himself, his gun in one hand, his shoulder snug against the frame. He rapped twice. When there was no response, he signaled for his men to draw their weapons and close in. Using the key he'd taken from Charity's ring, he unlocked the door.

Once inside, he scanned the room, legs spread, the gun held tight in both hands. The adrenaline was there, familiar, even welcome. With only a jerk of the head he signaled his backup. Guarding each other's flanks, they took a last circle.

Roman cautiously approached the bedroom. For the first time, a smile—a grim smile—moved across his face. Dupont was in the shower. And he was singing.

The singing ended abruptly when Roman yanked the curtain aside.

"Don't bother to put your hands up," Roman told him as he blinked water out of his eyes. Keeping the gun level, he tossed his first prize a towel. "You're busted, pal. Why don't you dry off and I'll read you your rights?"

"Well done," Conby commented when the prisoner was cuffed. "If you handle the rest of this as smoothly, I'll see that you get a commendation."

"Keep it." Roman holstered his weapon. There was only one more hurdle before he could finally separate past and future. "When this is done, I'm finished."

"You've been in law enforcement for over ten years, DeWinter. You won't walk away."

"Watch me." With that, he headed back to the inn to finish what he had started.

When Charity awoke, it was full morning and she was quite alone. She was grateful for that, because she couldn't stifle a moan. The moment she sat up, her head, unused to the generous doses of wine and stingy amounts of sleep, began to pound.

She had no one but herself to blame, she admitted as she crawled out of bed. Her feet tangled in what was left of the shirt she'd been wearing the night before.

It had been worth it, she thought, gathering up the torn cotton. Well worth it.

But, incredible night or not, it was morning and she had work to do. She downed some aspirin, allowed herself another groan, then dived into the shower.

Roman found Bob huddled in the office, anxiously gulping laced coffee. Without preamble, he yanked the mug away and emptied the contents into the trash can.

"I just needed a little something to get me through."

He'd had more than a little, Roman determined. His words were slurred, and his eyes were glazed. Even under the best of circumstances Roman found it difficult to drum up any sympathy for a drunk.

He dragged Bob out of his chair by the shirtfront. "You pull yourself together and do it fast. When Block comes in you're going to check him and his little group out. If you tip him off—if you so much as blink and tip him off—I'll hang you out to dry."

"Charity does the checkout," Bob managed through chattering teeth.

"Not today. You're going to go out to the desk and handle it. You're going to do a good job because you're going to know I'm in here and I'm watching you."

He stepped away from Bob just as the office door opened. "Sorry I'm late." Despite her heavy eyes, Charity beamed at Roman. "I overslept."

He felt his heart stop, then sink to his knees. "You didn't sleep enough."

"You're telling me." Her smile faded when she looked at Bob. "What's wrong?"

He grabbed at the thread of opportunity with both hands. "I was just telling Roman that I'm not feeling very well."

"You don't look well." Concerned, she walked over to feel his brow. It was clammy and deepened the worry in her eyes. "You're probably coming down with that virus."

"That's what I'm afraid of."

"You shouldn't have come in at all today. Maybe Roman should drive you home."

"No, I can manage." He walked on shaking legs to the door. "Sorry about this, Charity." He turned to give her a last look. "Really sorry."

"Don't be silly. Just take care of yourself."

"I'll give him a hand," Roman muttered, and followed him out. They walked out into the lobby at the same time Block strolled in.

"Good morning." His face creased with his habitual smile, but his eyes were wary. "Is there a problem?"

"Virus." Bob's face was already turning a sickly green. Fear made a convincing cover. "Hit me pretty hard this morning."

"I called Dr. Mertens," Charity announced as she came in to stand behind the desk. "You go straight home, Bob. He'll meet you there."

"Thanks." But one of Conby's agents followed him out, and he knew he wouldn't be going home for quite a while.

"This virus has been a plague around here." She offered Block an apologetic smile. "I'm short a housekeeper, a waitress and now Bob. I hope none of your group had any complaints about the service."

"Not a one." Relaxed again, Block set his briefcase on the desk. "It's always a pleasure doing business with you, Charity."

Roman watched helplessly as they chatted and went through the routine of checking lists and figures. She was supposed to be safe upstairs, sleeping deeply and dreaming of the night they'd spent together. Frustrated, he balled his hands at his side. Now, no matter what he did, she'd be in the middle.

He heard her laugh when Block mentioned the fish she'd carried into the dining room. And he imagined how her face would look when the agents moved in and arrested the man she thought of as a tour guide and a friend.

Charity read off a total. Roman steadied himself.

"We seem to be off by...22.50." Block began laboriously running the numbers through his calculator again. Brow furrowed, Charity went over her list, item by item.

"Good morning, dear."

"Hmm." Distracted, Charity glanced up. "Oh, good morning, Miss Millie."

"I'm just on my way up to pack. I wanted you to know what a delightful time we've had."

"We're always sorry to see you go. We were all pleased that you and Miss Lucy extended your stay for a few days."

Miss Millie fluttered her eyelashes myopically at Roman before making her way toward the stairs. At the top, he thought, there would now be an officer posted to see that she and the other guests were kept out of the way.

"I get the same total again, Roger." Puzzled, she tapped the end of her pencil on the list. "I wish I could say I'd run it through the computer, but..." She let her words trail off, ignoring her headache. "Ah, this might be it. Do you have the Wentworths in cabin 1 down for a bottle of wine? They charged it night before last."

"Wentworth, Wentworth..." With grating slowness, Block ran down his list. "No, nothing here."

"Let me find the tab." After opening a drawer, she flipped her way efficiently through the folders. Roman felt a bead of sweat slide slowly down his back. One of the agents strolled over to browse through some postcards.

"I've got both copies," she said with a shake of her head. "This virus is really hanging us up." She filed her copy of the receipt and handed Block his.

"No problem." Cheerful as ever, he noted the new

charge, then added up his figures again. "That seems to match."

With the ease of long habit, Charity calculated the amount in Canadian currency. "That's 2,330.00." She turned the receipt around for Block's approval.

He clicked open his briefcase. "As always, it's a pleasure." He counted out the money in twenties. The moment Charity marked the bill Paid, Roman moved in.

"Put your hands up. Slow." He pressed the barrel of his gun into the small of Block's back.

"Roman!" Charity gaped at him, the key to the cash drawer in her hand. "What on earth are you doing?"

"Go around the desk," he told her. "Way around, and walk outside."

"Are you crazy? Roman, for God's sake—"

"Do it!"

Block moistened his lips, keeping his hands carefully aloft. "Is this a robbery?"

"Haven't you figured it out by now?" With his free hand, Roman pulled out his ID. After tossing it on the desk, he reached for his cuffs. "You're under arrest."

"What's the charge?"

"Conspiracy to murder, counterfeiting, transporting known felons across international borders. That'll do for a start." He yanked one of Block's arms down and slipped the cuff over his wrist.

"How could you?" Charity's voice was a mere whisper. She held his badge in her hand.

He took his eyes off Block for only a second to look at her. One second changed everything.

"How silly of me," Miss Millie muttered as she waltzed back into the lobby. "I was nearly upstairs when I realized I'd left my—"

For a man of his bulk, Block moved quickly. He dragged Miss Millie against him and had a knife to her throat before anyone could react. The cuffs dangled from one wrist. "It'll only take a heartbeat," he said quietly, staring into Roman's eyes. The gun was trained in the center of Block's forehead, and Roman's finger was twitching on the trigger.

"Think about it." Block's gaze swept the lobby, where other guns had been drawn. "I'll slice this nice little lady's throat. Don't move," he said to Charity. Shifting slightly, he blocked her way.

Wide-eyed, Miss Millie could only cling to Block's arm and whimper.

"Don't hurt her." Charity stepped forward, but she stopped quickly when she saw Block's grip tighten. "Please, don't hurt her." It had to be a dream, she told herself. A nightmare. "Someone tell me what's happening here."

"The place is surrounded." Roman kept his eyes and his weapon on Block. He waited in vain for one of his men to move in from the rear. "Hurting her isn't going to do you any good."

"It isn't going to do you any good, either. Think about it. Want a dead grandmother on your hands?"

"You don't want to add murder to your list, Block," Roman said evenly. And Charity was much too close, he thought. Much too close.

"It makes no difference to me. Now take it outside. All of you!" His voice rose as he scanned the room. "Toss down the guns. Toss them down and get out before I start slicing into her. Do it." He nicked Miss Millie's fragile throat with the blade.

"Please!" Again Charity took a step forward. "Let her go. I'll stay with you."

"Damn it, Charity, get back."

She didn't spare Roman a glance. "Please, Roger," she said again, taking another careful step forward. "She's old and frail. She might get sick. Her heart." Desperate, she stepped between him and Roman's gun. "I won't give you any trouble."

The decision took Block only a moment. He grabbed Charity and dug the point of the blade into her throat. Miss Millie slid bonelessly to the floor.

"Drop the gun." He saw the fear in Roman's eyes and smiled. Apparently he'd made a much better bargain. "Two seconds and it's over. I don't have anything to lose."

Roman held his hands up, letting his weapon drop. "We'll talk."

"We'll talk when I'm ready." Block shifted the knife so that the length of the blade lay across Charity's neck. She shut her eyes and waited to die. "Get out, now. The first time somebody tries to get back in she dies."

"Out." Roman pointed to the door. "Keep them back, Conby. All of them. There's my weapon," he said to Block. "I'm clean." He lifted his jacket cautiously to show his empty holster. "Why don't I hang around in here? You can have two hostages for the price of one. A federal agent ought to give you some leverage."

"Just the woman. Take off, DeWinter, or I'll kill her before you can think how to get to me. Now."

"For God's sake, Roman. Get her out of here. She needs a doctor." Charity sucked in her breath when the point of the knife pierced her skin.

"Don't." Roman held up his hands again, palms out,

as he moved toward the crumpled form near the desk. Keeping his movements slow, he gathered the sobbing woman in his arms. "If you hurt her, you won't live long enough to regret it."

With that last frustrated threat he left Charity alone.

"Stay back." After bundling Miss Millie into waiting arms, he rushed off the porch, fighting to keep his mind clear. "Nobody goes near the doors or any of the windows. Get me a weapon." Before anyone could oblige him, he was yanking a gun away from one of Royce's deputies. With the smallest of gestures Royce signaled to his man to be silent.

"What do you want us to do?"

Roman merely stared down at the gun in his hand. It was loaded. He was trained. And he was helpless.

"DeWinter..." Conby began.

"Back off." When Conby started to speak again, Roman turned on him. "Back off."

He stared at the inn. He could hear Miss Millie crying softly as someone carried her to a car. The guests who had already been evacuated were being herded to safety. Roman imagined that Royce had arranged that. Charity would want to make sure they were well taken care of.

Charity.

Shoving the gun into his holster, he turned around. "Have the road blocked off a mile in each direction. Only official personnel in this area. We'll keep the inn surrounded from a distance of fifty feet. He'll be thinking again," Roman said slowly, "and when he starts thinking he's going to know he's blocked in."

He lifted both hands and rubbed them over his face. He'd been in hostage situations before. He was trained for them. With time and cool heads, the odds of getting a hostage out in a situation of this type were excellent. When the hostage was Charity, excellent wasn't nearly good enough.

"I want to talk to him."

"Agent DeWinter, under the circumstances I have serious reservations about you being in charge of this operation."

Roman rounded on him. "Get in my way, Conby, and I'll hang you up by your silk tie. Why the hell weren't there men positioned in the back, behind him?"

Because his palms were sweating, Conby's voice was only more frigid. "I thought it best to have them outside, prepared if he attempted to run."

Roman battled the red wave of fury that burst behind his eyes. "When I get her out," he said softly, "I'm going to deal with you, you bastard. I need communication," he said to Royce. "Can you handle it?"

"Give me twenty minutes."

With a nod, Roman turned back to study the inn. Systematically he considered and rejected points of entry.

Inside, Charity felt some measure of relief when the knife was removed from her throat. Somehow the gun Block was pointing at her now seemed less personal.

"Roger—"

"Shut up. Shut up and let me think." He swiped a beefy forearm over his brow to dry it. It had all happened so fast, too fast. Everything up to now he had done on instinct. As Roman had calculated, he was beginning to think.

"They've got me trapped in here. I should've used you to get to one of the cars, should've taken off." Then he laughed, looking wildly around the lobby. "We're on a damn island. Can't drive off an island."

"I think if we—"

"Shut up!" He shouted and had her holding her breath as he leveled the gun at her. "I'm the one who needs to think. Feds. That sniveling little wart was right all along," he muttered, thinking of Bob. "He made DeWinter days ago. Did you?" As he asked, he grabbed her by the hair and yanked her head back to hold the barrel against her throat.

"No. I didn't know. I didn't. I still don't understand." She could only give a muffled cry when he slammed her back against the wall. She'd never seen murder in a man's eyes before, but she recognized it. "Roger, think. If you kill me you won't have anything to bargain with." She tasted fear on her tongue as she forced the words out. "You need me."

"Yeah." He relaxed his grip. "You've been handy so far. You'll just have to go on being handy. How many ways in and out of this place?"

"I—I don't really know." She sucked in her breath when he gave her hair another cruel twist.

"You know how many two-by-fours are in this place."

"Five. There are five exits, not counting the windows. The lobby, the gathering room, the outside steps running to my quarters and a family suite in the east wing, and the back, through the utility room off the kitchen."

"That's good." Panting a bit, he considered the possibilities. "The kitchen. We'll take the kitchen. I'll have water and food there in case this takes a while. Come on." He kept a hand in her hair and the gun at the base of her neck.

* * *

His eyes on the inn, Roman paced back and forth behind the barricade of police cars. She was smart, he told himself. Charity was a smart, sensible woman. She wouldn't panic. She wouldn't do anything stupid.

Oh, God, she must be terrified. He lit a cigarette from the butt of another, but he didn't find himself soothed as the harsh smoke seared into him.

"Where's the goddamn phone?"

"Nearly ready." Royce pushed back his hat and straightened from where he'd been watching a lineman patch in a temporary line. "My nephew," he explained to Roman with a thin smile. "The boy knows his job."

"You got a lot of relatives."

"I'm lousy with them. Listen, I heard you and Charity were getting married. That part of the cover?"

"No." Roman thought of the picnic on the beach, that one clear moment in time. "No."

"In that case, I'm going to give you some advice. You're wrong," he said, before Roman could speak. "You do need it. You're going to have to get yourself calm, real calm, before you pick up that phone. A trapped animal reacts two ways. He either cowers back and gives up or he strikes out at anything in his way." Royce nodded toward the inn. "Block doesn't look like the type to give up easy, and Charity sure as hell's in his way. That line through yet, son?"

"Yes, sir." The young lineman's hands were sweaty with nerves and excitement. "You can dial right through." He passed the damp receiver to Roman.

"I don't know the number," Roman murmured. "I don't know the damn number."

"I know it."

Roman swung around to face Mae. In that one instant he saw everything he felt about himself mirrored in her eyes. There would be time for guilt later, he told himself. There would be a lifetime for it. "Royce, you were supposed to clear the area."

"Moving Maeflower's like moving a tank."

"I don't budge until I see Charity." Mae firmed her quivering lips. "She's going to need me when she comes out. Waste of time to argue," she added. "You want the number?"

"Yes."

She gave it to him. Tossing his cigarette aside, Roman dialed.

Charity jolted in the chair when the phone rang. Across the table, Block simply stared at it. He had had her pile everything she could drag or carry to block the two doors. Extra chairs, twenty-pound canisters of flour and sugar, the rolling butcher block, iron skillets, all sat in a jumble, braced against both entrances.

In the silent kitchen the phone sounded again and again, like a scream.

"Stay right where you are." Block moved across the room to answer it. "Yeah?"

"It's DeWinter. Thought you might be ready to talk about a deal."

"What kind of deal?"

"That's what we have to talk about. First I have to know you've still got Charity."

"Have you seen her come out?" Block spit into the phone. "You know damn well I've got her or you wouldn't be talking to me."

"I have to make sure she's still alive. Let me talk to her."

"You can go to hell."

Threats, abuse, curses, rose like bile in his throat. Still, when he spoke, his voice was dispassionate. "I verify that you still have a hostage, Block, or we don't deal."

"You want to talk to her?" Block gestured with the gun. "Over here," he ordered. "Make it fast. It's your boyfriend," he told Charity when she stood beside him. "He wants to know how you're doing. You tell him you're just fine." He brushed the gun up her cheek to rest it at her temple. "Understand?"

With a nod, she leaned into the phone. "Roman?"

"Charity." Too many emotions slammed into him for him to measure. He wanted to reassure her, to make promises, to beg her to be careful. But he knew he would have only seconds and that Block would be listening to every word spoken. "Has he hurt you?"

"No." She closed her eyes and fought back a sob. "No, I'm fine. He's going to let me fix some food."

"Hear that, DeWinter? She's fine." Deliberately Block dragged her arm behind her back until she cried out. "That can change anytime."

Roman gripped the phone helplessly as he listened to the sound of Charity's sobs. It took every ounce of control he had left to keep the terror out of his voice. "You don't have to hurt her. I said we'd talk about terms."

"We'll talk about terms, all right. My terms." He released Charity's arm and ignored her as she slid to the floor. "You get me a car. I want safe passage to the airport, DeWinter. Charity drives. I want a plane fueled up and waiting. She'll be getting on it with me, so any tricks and we're back to square one. When I get where I'm going, I turn her loose."

"How big a plane?"

"Don't try to stall me."

"Wait. I have to know. It's a small airport, Block. You know that. If you're going any distance—"

"Just get me a plane."

"Okay." Roman wiped the back of his hand over his mouth and forced his voice to level. He couldn't hear her any longer, and the silence was as anguishing as her sobbing. "I'm going to have to go through channels on this. That's how it works."

"The hell with your channels."

"Look, I don't have the authority to get you what you want. I need to get approval. Then I'll have to clear the airport, get a pilot. You'll have to give me some time."

"Don't yank my chain, DeWinter. You got an hour."

"I've got to get through to Washington. You know how bureaucrats are. It'll take me three, maybe four."

"The hell with that. You got two. After two I'm going to start sending her out in pieces."

Charity closed her eyes, lowered her head to her folded arms and wept out her terror.

Chapter 12

"We've got a couple of hours," Roman murmured, continuing to study the inn and the floor plan Royce had given him. "He's not as smart as I thought, or maybe he's too panicked to think it through."

"That could be to our advantage," Royce said when Roman shook his head at his offer of coffee. "Or it could work against us."

Two hours. Roman stared at the quiet clapboard building. He couldn't stand the idea of Charity being held at gunpoint for that long. "He wants a car, safe passage to the airport and a plane." He turned to Conby. "I want you to make sure he thinks he's going to get it."

"I'm aware of how to handle a hostage situation, DeWinter."

"Which one of your men is the best shot?" Roman asked Royce.

"I am." He kept his eyes steady on Roman's. "Where do you want me?"

"They're in the kitchen."

"He tell you that?"

"No, Charity. She told me he was going to let her fix some food. Since I doubt eating's on her mind, she was letting me know their position."

Royce glanced over to where Mae was pacing up and down the pier. "She's a tough girl. She's keeping her head."

"So far." But Roman remembered too well the sound of her muffled sobbing. "We need to shift two of the men around the back. I want them to keep their distance, stay out of sight. Let's see how close we can get." He turned to Conby again. "Give us five minutes, then call him again. Tell him who you are. You know how to make yourself sound important. Stall him, keep him on the phone as long as you can."

"You have two hours, DeWinter. We can call for a SWAT team from Seattle."

"We have two hours," Roman said grimly. "Charity may not."

"I can't take responsibility—"

Roman cut him off. "You'll damn well take it."

"Agent DeWinter, if this wasn't a crisis situation I would cite you for insubordination."

"Great. Just put it on my tab." He looked at the rifle Royce had picked up. It had a long-range telescopic sight. "Let's move."

She'd cried long enough, Charity decided, taking a long, deep breath. It wasn't doing her any good. Like her captor, she needed to think. Her world had whittled down to one room, with fear as her constant compan-

ion. This wouldn't do, she told herself, straightening
her spine. Her life was being threatened, and she wasn't
even sure why.

She rose from where she had been huddled on the
floor. Block was still sitting at the table, holding the gun
in one hand while the other tapped monotonously on
the scrubbed wood. The dangling cuffs jangled. He was
terrified, she realized. Perhaps every bit as much as she.
There must be some way to use that to her advantage.

"Roger…would you like some coffee?"

"Yeah. That's good, that's a good idea." He took a
firmer grip on the gun. "But don't get cute. I'm watching every move."

"Are they going to give you a plane?" She turned the
burner on low. The kitchen was full of weapons, she
thought. Knives, cleavers, mallets. Closing her eyes, she
wondered if she had the courage to use one.

"They're going to give me anything I want as long
as I have you."

"Why do they want you?" Stay calm, she told herself.
She wanted to stay calm and alert and alive. "I don't
understand." She poured the hot coffee into two cups.
She didn't think she could swallow, but she hoped that
sharing it would put him slightly more at ease. "They
said something about counterfeiting."

It didn't matter what she knew. In any case, he had
worked hard and was proud of it. "For over two years
now I've been running a nice little game back and forth
over the border. Twenties and tens in Canadian. I can
stamp them out like bottle caps. But I'm careful, you
know." He gulped at the coffee. "A couple thousand
here, couple thousand there, with Vision as the front.
We run a good tour, keep the clients happy."

"You've been paying me with counterfeit money?"

"You, and a couple other places. But you're the longest and most consistent." He smiled at her, as friendly as ever—if you didn't count the gun in his hand. "You have a special place here, Charity, quiet, remote, privately owned. You deal with a small local bank. It ran like a charm."

"Yes." She looked down at her cup, her stomach rolling. "I can see that." And Roman had come not to see the whales but to work on a case. That was all she had been to him.

"We were going to milk this route for a few more months," he continued. "Just lately Bob started getting antsy."

"Bob?" Her hand fisted on her lap. "Bob knew?"

"He was nothing but a nickel-and-dime con man before I took him on. Working scams and petty embezzlements. I set him up here and made him rich. Didn't do badly by you, either," he added with a grin. "You were on some shaky financial ground when I came along."

"All this time," she whispered.

"I'd decided to give it another six months, then move on, but Bob started getting real jumpy about your new handyman. The bastard set me up." He slammed the cup down. "Worked a deal with the feds. I should have caught it, the way he started falling apart after the hit-and-run."

"The accident—you tried to kill me."

"No." He patted her hand, and she cringed. "Truth is, I've always had a liking for you. But I wanted to get you out of the way for a while. Just testing the waters to see how DeWinter played it. He's good," Block mused.

"Real good. Had me convinced he was only interested in you. The romance was a good touch. Threw me off."

"Yes." Devastated, she stared at the grain in the wood of the tabletop. "That was clever."

"Sucked me in," Block muttered. "I knew you weren't stringing me along. You haven't got it in you. But DeWinter... They've probably already taken Dupont."

"Who?"

"We don't just run the money. There are people, people who need to leave the country quietly, who pay a lot for our services. Looks like I'm going to have to take myself on as a client." He laughed and drained his cup. "How about some food? One of the things I'll miss most about this place is the food."

She rose silently and went to the refrigerator. It had all been a lie, she thought. Everything Roman had said, everything he'd done...

The pain cut deep and had her fighting back another bout of weeping. He'd made a fool of her, as surely and as completely as Roger Block had. They had used her, both of them, used her and her inn. She would never forgive. She rubbed her hands over her eyes to clear them. And she would never forget.

"How about that lemon meringue pie?" Relaxed, pleased with his own cleverness, Roger tapped the barrel of the gun on the table. "Mae outdid herself on that pie last night."

"Yes." Slowly Charity pulled it out. "There's a little left."

Block had ripped the frilly tiebacks from the sunny yellow curtains, but there was a space two inches wide at the center. Silently Roman eased toward it. He could see Charity reach into a cupboard, take out a plate.

There were tears drying on her cheeks. It tore at him to see them. Her hands were steady. That was something, some small thing to hold on to. He couldn't see Block, though he shifted as much as he dared.

Then, suddenly, as if she had sensed him, their eyes met through the glass. She braced, and in that instant he saw a myriad of emotions run across her face. Then it was set again. She looked at him as she would have looked at a stranger and waited for instructions.

He held up a hand, palm out, doing his best to signal her to hold on, to keep calm. Then the phone rang and he watched her jolt.

"About time," Block said. He was almost swaggering as he walked to the phone. "Yeah? Who the hell's this?" After listening a moment, he gave a pleased laugh. "I like dealing with a title. Where's my plane, Inspector Conby?"

As quickly as she dared, Charity tugged the curtain open another inch.

"Over here," Block ordered.

She dropped her hand, and the plate rattled to the counter. "What?"

He gestured with the gun. "I said over here."

Roman swore as she moved between him and a clear shot.

"I want them to know I'm keeping up my end." Block took Charity by the arm, less roughly this time. "Tell the man I'm treating you fine."

"He hasn't hurt me," she said dully. She forced herself to keep her eyes away from the window. Roman was out there. He would do his best to get her out safely. That was his job.

"The plane'll be ready in an hour," Block told her after

he hung up. "Just enough time for that pie and another cup of coffee."

"All right." She crossed to the counter again. Panic sprinted through her when she looked out the window and saw no one. He'd left. Because her fingers were unsteady, she fumbled with the pie. "Roger, are you going to let me go?"

He hesitated only an instant, but that was enough to tell her that his words were just another lie. "Sure. As soon as I'm clear."

So it came down to that. Her heart, her inn and now her life. She set the pie in front of him and studied his face. He was pleased with himself, she thought, and she hated him for it. But he was still sweating.

"I'll get your coffee." She walked to the stove. One foot, then the other. There was a buzzing in her ears. It was more than fear now, she realized as she turned the burner up under the pot. It was rage and despair and a strong, irresistible need to survive. Mechanically she switched the stove off. Then, taking a cloth, she took the pot by the handle.

He was still holding the gun, and he was shoveling pie into his mouth with his left hand. He thought she was a fool, Charity mused. Someone who could be used and duped and manipulated. She took a deep breath.

"Roger?"

He glanced up. Charity looked directly into his eyes.

"You forgot your coffee," she said calmly, then tossed the steaming contents into his face.

He screamed. She didn't think she'd ever heard a man scream like that before. He was half out of his chair, groping blindly for the gun. It happened quickly. No matter how often she played back the scene in her mind, she would never be completely sure what happened first.

She grabbed for the gun herself. Block's flailing hand caught her across the cheekbone. Even as she staggered backward there was the sound of glass breaking.

Roman was through the window. Charity landed on the floor, stunned by the blow, as he burst through. There were men breaking through the barricaded doors and rushing into the room. Someone dragged her from the floor and pulled her out.

Roman held the gun to Block's temple. They were kneeling on the shattered glass—or rather Roman was kneeling and supporting the moaning Block. There were already welts rising up on his wide face. "Please," Roman murmured. "Give me a reason."

"Roman." Royce laid a hand on his shoulder. "It's over."

But the rage clogged his throat. It made his finger slippery on the trigger of the gun. He remembered the way Charity had looked at him when she had seen him outside the window. Slowly he drew back and holstered his gun.

"Yeah. It's over. Get him the hell out of here." He rose and went to find Charity.

He found her in the lobby, wrapped in Mae's arms.

"I'm all right," Charity murmured. "Really." When she saw Roman, her eyes frosted over. "Everything's going to be fine now. I need to speak with Roman for a minute."

"You say your piece." Mae kissed both of her cheeks. "Then you're going to get in a nice hot tub."

"Okay." She squeezed Mae's hand. Strange, but it felt more like a dream now, as if she were pushing her way through layers and layers of gauzy gray curtains. "I think we'll have more privacy upstairs," she said to Roman. Then she turned without looking at him and started up the stairs.

He wanted to hold her. His fingers curled tight into his palms. He needed to lift her against him, touch her hair, her skin, and convince himself that the nightmare was over.

Her knees were shaking. Reaction was struggling to set in, but she fought it off. When she was alone, Charity promised herself. When she was finally alone, she would let it all out.

In her sitting room she turned to face him. She would not, could not, speak to him in the intimacy of her bedroom. "I imagine you have reports to file," she began. Was that her voice? she wondered. It sounded so thin and cold, so foreign. Deliberately she cleared her throat. "I've been told I'll have to make a statement, but I thought we should get this out of the way first."

"Charity." He started toward her, only to be brought up short when her hands whipped out.

"Don't." Her eyes were as cold as her voice. It wasn't a dream, she told herself. It was as harsh and as brutal a reality as she had ever known. "Don't touch me. Not now, not ever again."

His hands fell uselessly to his sides. "I'm sorry."

"Why? You accomplished exactly what you came to do. From what I've been able to gather, Roger and Bob had quite a system going. I'm sure your superiors will be delighted with you."

"It doesn't matter."

She dug his badge out of her pocket, where she had shoved it. "Yes." She threw it at him. "Yes, it does."

Struggling for calm, he pushed it into his pocket. He noted dispassionately that his hands were bleeding. "I couldn't tell you."

"Didn't tell me."

There was a faint bruise on her cheekbone. For a moment all his guilt and impotent fury centered there. "He hit you."

She ran a fingertip lightly across the mark. "I don't break easily."

"I want to explain."

"Do you?" She turned away for a moment. She wanted to keep her anger cold. "I think I get the picture."

"Listen, baby—"

"No, *you* listen, baby." Her composure cracking, she whirled around again. "You lied to me, you used me from the first minute to the last. It was all one huge, incredible lie."

"Not all."

"No? Let's see, how can we separate one from the other? A convenient flat." She saw the anger in his eyes and shoved a chair out of her path. "And George, good old lucky George. I suppose it was worth a few thousand dollars to get him out of the way and leave you an opening. And Bob—you knew all about Bob, didn't you?"

"We couldn't be sure, not at first."

"Not at first," she repeated. As long as she kept her brain cold, she told herself, she could think. She could think and not feel. "I wonder, Roman, were you so sure of me? Or did you think I was part of it?" When he didn't answer, she spun around again. "You did. Oh, I see. I was under investigation all the time. And there you were, so conveniently on the scene. All you had to do was get close to me, and I made it so easy for you."

With a laugh, she pressed her hands to her face. "My God, I threw myself at you."

"I wasn't supposed to get involved with you." Fighting desperation, he paced his words carefully. "It just happened. I fell in love with you."

"Don't say that to me." She lowered her hands. Her face was pale and cool behind them. "You don't even know what it means."

"I didn't, until you."

"You can't have love without trust, Roman. I trusted you. I didn't just give you my body. I gave you everything."

"I told you everything I could," he shot back. "Damn it, I couldn't tell you the rest. The things I told you about myself, about the way I grew up, the way I felt, they were all true."

"Do I have your word on that? Agent DeWinter?"

With an oath, he strode across the room and grabbed her arms. "I didn't know you when I took the assignment. I was doing a job. When things changed, the most important part of that job became proving your innocence and keeping you safe."

"If you had told me I would have proven my own innocence." She jerked out of his hold. "This is my inn, and these are my people. The only family I have left. Do you think I would risk it all for money?"

"No. I knew that, I trusted that, after the first twenty-four hours. I had orders, Charity, and my own instincts. If I had told you who I was and what was going on, you would never have been able to keep up a front."

"So I'm that stupid?"

"No. That honest." Digging deep, he found his control again. "You've been through a lot. Let me take you to the hospital."

"I've been through a lot," she repeated, and nearly laughed. "Do you know how it feels to know that for two years, *two years*, people I thought I knew were using me? I always thought I was such a good judge of character." Now she did laugh. She walked to the window. "They made a fool out of me week after week. I'm not sure I'll ever get over it. But that's nothing." She turned, wrapping her fingers around the windowsill. "That's nothing compared to what I feel when I think of how I let myself believe you were in love with me."

"If it was a lie, why am I here now, telling you that I do?"

"I don't know." Suddenly weary, she dragged her hair away from her face. "And it doesn't seem to matter. I'm wrung dry, Roman. For a while today I was sure he was going to kill me."

"Oh, Charity." He gathered her close, and when she didn't resist he buried his face in her hair.

"I thought he would kill me," she repeated, her arms held rigidly at her sides. "And I didn't want to die. In fact, nothing was quite so important to me as staying alive. When my mother fell in love and that love was betrayed, she gave up. I've never been much like her." She stepped stiffly out of his hold. "Maybe I'm gullible, but I've never been weak. I intend to pick up where I left off, before all of this. I'm going to keep the inn running. No matter what it takes, I'm going to erase you and these last weeks from my life."

"No." Furious, he took her face in his hands. "You won't, because you know I love you. And you made me a promise, Charity. No matter what happened, you wouldn't stop loving me."

"I made that promise to a man who doesn't exist." It hurt. She could feel the pain rip through her from one end to the other. "And I don't love the man who does." She took a small but significant step backward. "Leave me alone."

When he didn't move, she walked into the bedroom and flipped the lock.

Mae was busily sweeping up glass in the kitchen. For the first time in over twenty years the inn was closed. She figured it would open again soon enough, but for now she was content that her girl was safe upstairs in bed and the coffee-guzzling police were on their way out.

When Roman came in, she rested her arms on her broom. Mae had rocked Charity for nearly an hour while she'd cried over him. She'd been prepared to be cold and dismissive. It only took one look to change her mind.

"You look worn out."

"I..." Feeling lost, he glanced around the room. "I wanted to ask how she was before I left."

"She's miserable." She nodded, content with the anguish she saw in his eyes. "And stubborn. You got a few cuts."

Automatically he lifted a hand to rub at the nick on his temple. "Will you give her this number?" He dropped a card on the table. "She can reach me there if— She can reach me there."

"Sit down. Let me clean you up."

"No, it's all right."

"I said sit down." She went to a cupboard for a bottle of antiseptic. "She's had a bad shock."

He had a sudden mental image of Block holding the knife to her throat. "I know."

"She bounces back pretty quick from most things. She loves you."

Roman winced a little as she dabbed on the antiseptic, but not from the sting. "Did."

"Does," Mae said flatly. "She just doesn't want to right now. You been an agent for long?"

"Too long."

"Are you going to make sure that slimy worm Roger Block's put away?"

Roman's hands curled into fists. "Yes."

"Are you in love with Charity?"

He relaxed his hands. "Yes."

"I believe you, so I'm going to give you some advice." Puffing a bit, she sat down next to him. "She's hurt, real bad. Charity's the kind who likes to fix things herself. Give her a little time." She picked up the card and slipped it into her apron pocket. "I'll just hold on to this for now."

She was feeling stronger. And not just physically, Charity decided as she jogged along behind Ludwig. In every way. The sweaty dreams that had woken her night after night were fading. It wasn't nearly as difficult to talk, or to smile, or to pretend that she was in control again. She had promised herself she would put her life back together, and she was doing it.

She rarely thought of Roman. On a sigh, she relented. She would never get strong again if she began to lie to herself.

She *always* thought of Roman. It was difficult not to, and it was especially difficult today.

They were to have been married today. Charity veered
into the grass as Ludwig explored. The ache came,
spread and was accepted. Just after noon, with the music
swelling and the sun streaming down on the garden, she
would have put her hand in his. And promised.

A fantasy, she told herself, and nudged her dog back
onto the shoulder of the road. It had been fantasy then,
and it was a fantasy now.

And yet... With every day that passed she remembered more clearly the times they had spent together.
His reluctance, and his anger. Then his tenderness and
concern. She glanced down to where the bracelet shim-
mered on her wrist.

She'd tried to put it back in the box, to push it into
some dark, rarely opened drawer. Every day she told
herself she would. Tomorrow. And every day she remembered how sweet, how awkward and how wonderful he'd been when he'd given it to her.

If it had only been a job, why had he given her so
much more than he had needed to? Not just the piece of
jewelry, but everything the circle of gold had symbol-
ized? He could have offered her friendship and respect,
as Bob had, and she would have trusted him as much.
He could have kept their relationship strictly physical.
Her feelings would have remained the same.

But he had said he loved her. And at the end he had
all but begged her to believe it.

She shook her head and increased her pace. She was
being weak and sentimental. It was just the day...the
beautiful spring morning that was to have been her
wedding day.

What she needed was to get back to the inn and keep
busy. This day would pass, like all the others.

At first she thought she was imagining it when she saw him standing beside the road, looking out at the sunrise over the water. Her feet faltered. Before she could think to prevent it, her knees weakened. Fighting her heart, she walked to him.

He'd heard her coming. As he'd stood in the growing light he'd remembered wondering if he came back, if he would stand just there and wait for Charity to run to him.

She wasn't running now. She was walking very slowly, despite the eager dog. Could she know, he wondered, that she held his life in her hands?

Nerves swarmed through her, making her fingers clench and unclench on the leash. She prayed as she stopped in front of him that her voice would be steadier.

"What do you want?"

He bent down to pat the squirming dog's head. "We'll get to that. How are you feeling?"

"I'm fine."

"You've been having nightmares." There were shadows under her eyes. He wouldn't make it easy on her by ignoring them.

She stiffened. "They're passing. Mae talks too much."

"At least she talks to me."

"We've already said all there is to say."

He closed a hand over her arm as she started by him. "Not this time. You had your say last time, and I had a lot of it coming. Now it's my turn." Reaching down, he unhooked the leash. Free, Ludwig bounded toward home. "Mae's waiting for him," Roman explained before Charity could call the dog back.

"I see." She wrapped the leash around her fisted hand. "You two work all this out?"

"She cares about you. So do I."

"I have things to do."

"Yeah. This is first." He pulled her close and, ignoring her struggling, crushed his mouth to hers. It was like a drink after days in the desert, like a fire after a dozen long cold nights. He plundered, greedy, as though it were the first time. Or the last.

She couldn't fight him, or herself. Almost sobbing, she clung to him, hungry and hurting. No matter how strong she tried to be, she would never be strong enough to stand against her own heart.

Aching, she started to draw back, but he tightened his hold. "Give me a minute," he murmured, pressing his lips to her hair. "Every night I wake up and see him holding a knife at your throat. And there's nothing I can do. I reach for you, and you're not there. For a minute, one horrible minute, I'm terrified. Then I remember that you're safe. You're not with me, but you're safe. It's almost enough."

"Roman." With a helpless sigh, she stroked soothing hands over his shoulders. "It doesn't do any good to think about it."

"Do you think I could forget?" He pulled back, keeping his hands firm on her arms. "For the rest of my life I'll remember every second of it. I was responsible for you."

"No." The anger came quickly enough to surprise both of them. She shoved at his chest. "*I'm* responsible for me. I was and I am and I always will be. And I took care of myself."

"Yeah." He ran his palm over her cheek. The bruise had faded, even if the memory hadn't. "It was a hell of a way to serve coffee."

"Let's forget it." She shrugged out of his grip and walked toward the water. "I'm not particularly proud of letting myself be duped, so I'd rather not dwell on it."

"They were pros, Charity. You're not the first person they've used."

She pressed her lips together. "And you?"

"When you're undercover you lie, and you use, and you take advantage of anything that's offered." Her eyes were closed when he turned her around to face him. "I came here to do a job. It had been a long time since I'd let myself think beyond anything but the next day. Look at me. Please."

Taking a steadying breath, she opened her eyes. "We've been through this already, Roman."

"No. I'd hurt you. I'd disappointed you. You weren't ready to listen." Gently he brushed a tear from her lashes. "I hope you are now, because I can't make it much longer without you."

"I was too hard on you before." It took almost everything she had, but she managed a smile. "I was hurt, and I was a lot shakier than I knew from being locked up with Roger. After I gave my statement, Inspector Conby explained everything to me, more clearly. About how the operation had been working, what my responsibilities were, what you had to do."

"What responsibilities?"

"About the money. It's put us in somewhat of a hole, but at least we only have to pay back a percentage."

"I see." Roman laughed and shook his head. "He always was a prince."

"The merchant's responsible for the loss." She tilted her head. "You didn't know about the arrangements I've made with him?"

"No."

"But you work for him."

"Not anymore. I turned in my resignation when I got back to D.C."

"Oh, Roman, that's ridiculous. It's like throwing out the baby with the bathwater."

He smiled appreciatively at her innate practicality. "I decided I like carpentry better. Got any openings?"

Running the leash through her hands, she looked over the water. "I haven't given much thought to remodeling lately."

"I work cheap." He tilted her face to his. "All you have to do is marry me."

"Don't."

"Charity." Calling on patience he hadn't been aware he possessed, he held her still. "One of the things I most admire about you is your mind. You're real sharp. Look at me, really look. I figure you've got to know that I'm not beating my head against this same wall for entertainment. I love you. You've got to believe that."

"I'm afraid to," she whispered.

He felt the first true spark of hope. "Believe this. You changed my life. Literally changed it. I can't go back to the way it was before. I can't go forward unless you're with me. How long do you want me to stand here, waiting to start living again?"

With her arms wrapped around her chest, she walked a short distance away. The high grass at the water's edge was still misted with dew. She could smell it, and the fragile fragrances of wildflowers. It occurred to her then that she had blocked such small things out of her life ever since she'd sent him away.

If it was honesty she was demanding from him, how could she give him anything less?

"I've missed you terribly." She shook her head quickly before he could touch her again. "I tried not to wonder if you'd come back. I told myself I didn't want you to. When I saw you standing in the road, all I wanted to do was run to you. No questions, no explanations. But it's not that simple."

"No."

"I do love you, Roman. I can't stop. I have tried," she said, looking back at him. "Not very hard, but I have tried. I think I knew under all the anger and the hurt that you weren't lying about loving me back. I haven't wanted to forgive you for lying about the rest, but— That's just pride, really." Perhaps it was simple after all, she thought. "If I have to make a choice, I'd rather choose love." She smiled and opened her arms to him. "I guess you're hired."

She laughed when he caught her up in his arms and swung her around. "We'll make it work," he promised her, raining kisses all over her face. "Starting today."

"We were going to be married today."

"Are going to be." He hooked his arm under her legs to carry her.

"But we—"

"I have a license." Closing his mouth over hers, he swung her around again.

"A marriage license?"

"It's in my pocket, with two tickets to Venice."

"To—" Her hand slid limply from his shoulder. "To *Venice*? But how—?"

"And Mae bought you a dress yesterday. She wouldn't let me see it."

"Well." The thrill was too overwhelming to allow her to pretend annoyance. "You were awfully sure of yourself."

"No." He kissed her again, felt the curve of her lips, and the welcoming. "I was sure of you."

* * * * *

WITHOUT A TRACE

To black sheep.

Prologue

"Pick up the beat on the intro, Tracey boy, you're dragging it."

Frank O'Hurley stood on his mark, stage right, and prepared to go through his opening routine again. The three-night run in Terre Haute might not be the highlight of his career, and it certainly wasn't the apex of his dreams, but he was going to give the audience their money's worth. Every two-bit gig was a dress rehearsal for the big break.

He counted off the beat, then swung into the routine with the enthusiasm of a man half his age. The calendar might put Frank's age at forty, but his feet would always be sixteen.

He'd written the little novelty number himself, with the wide-eyed hope that it would become the O'Hurley trademark. At the piano, his oldest child and only son tried to put some life into a melody he'd played too many times to count—and dreamed of other things and other places.

On cue, his mother spun onstage with his father. Even after endless routines, endless theaters, Trace still felt a tug of affection for them. Just as, after endless routines, endless theaters, he felt what had become a familiar tug of frustration.

Would he always be here, beating out a second-rate tune on a second-rate piano, trying to fill his father's big dreams that hadn't a hope in hell of coming true?

As she'd been doing most of her life, Molly matched her steps to Frank's. She could have done the number blindfold. As it was, while she dipped, spun and double-stepped, her mind was more on her son than her timing.

The boy wasn't happy, she thought. And he wasn't a child any longer. He was on the brink of manhood and straining to go his own way. It was that single fact, she knew, that terrified Frank to the point that he refused to acknowledge it.

The arguments had become more frequent, more heated. Soon, she thought, all too soon, something was going to explode, and she might not be able to pick up all the pieces.

Kick, ball change, dip, and her three daughters tapped onto the stage. With her heart close to Frank's, Molly could feel him swell with pride. She would hate for him to lose that pride or the hope that kept him the youthful dreamer she'd fallen in love with.

As Molly and Frank moved offstage, the routine eased smoothly into the opening song. The O'Hurley Triplets—Chantel, Abby and Maddy—launched into three-part harmony as if they'd been born singing.

They practically had, Molly thought. But, like Trace,

they weren't children any longer. Chantel was already using her wit and her wiles to fascinate the men in the audience. Abby, steady and quiet, was just marking time. And it wouldn't be long before they lost Maddy. As a mother, Molly felt both pride and regret at the thought that her youngest had too much talent to remain part of a roving troupe for long.

Yet it was Trace who concerned her now. He sat at the scarred piano in the dingy little club, his mind a thousand miles away. She'd seen the brochures he collected. Pictures and stories on places like Zanzibar, New Guinea, Mazatlán. Sometimes, on the long train or bus rides from city to city, Trace would talk of the mosques and caverns and mountains he wanted to see.

And Frank would brush those dreams off like dust, desperately clinging to his own—and to his son.

"Not bad, darlings." Frank bounced back to center stage to give each of his daughters a hug. "Trace, your mind's not on the music. You need to pump some life into it."

"There hasn't been any life in that number since Des Moines."

A few months before, Frank would have chuckled and rubbed a hand over his son's hair. But now he felt the sting of criticism, man to man. His chin came up to a stubborn point. "Nothing wrong with the song and never has been. It's your playing that's lacking. You lost tempo twice. I'm tired of you sulking over the keys."

Playing peacemaker, Abby stepped between her father and brother. The growing tension had been keeping the family on edge for weeks. "We're all a little tired, I think."

"I can speak for myself, Abby." Trace pushed away from the piano. "No one's sulking at the keys."

"Hah!" Frank brushed Molly's restraining hand away. Lord, the boy was tall, Frank thought. Tall and straight and almost a stranger. But Frank O'Hurley was still in charge, and it was time his son remembered it. "You've been in a black mood since I told you I wouldn't have a son of mine harking off to Hong Kong or God knows where like some Gypsy. Your place is here, with your family. Your responsibility is to the troupe."

"It's not my damn responsibility."

Frank's eyes narrowed. "Watch your tone, boy-o, you're not so big I can't take you down."

"It's time somebody took that tone with you," Trace went on, spewing out everything he'd held back for too long. "Year after year we play second-rate songs in second-rate clubs."

"Trace." Maddy said it quietly, adding a pleading look. "Don't."

"Don't what?" he demanded. "Don't tell him the truth? God knows he won't hear it anyway, but I'll have my say. The three of you and Ma have protected him from it long enough."

"Temper tantrums are so boring," Chantel said lazily, though her nerves were strung tight. "Why don't we all break to neutral corners?"

"No." Quivering with indignation, Frank stepped away from his daughters. "Go on, then, have your say."

"I'm tired of riding a bus to nowhere, of pretending the next stop's the brass ring. You drag us from town to town, year after year."

"Drag you?" Frank's face flushed with fury. "Is that what I'm doing?"

"No." Molly stepped forward, her eyes on her son. "No, it's not. We've all of us gone willingly, because it was what we wanted. If one of us doesn't want it, he has a right to say so, but not to be cruel."

"He doesn't listen!" Trace shouted. "He doesn't care what I want or don't want. I've told you. I've told you," he rounded on his father. "Every time I try to talk to you, all I get is how we have to keep the family together, how the big break is right around the corner, when there's nothing around the corner but another lousy one-night stand in another two-bit club."

It was too close to the truth, too close to what would make him feel like a failure when all he'd wanted was to give his family the best and the brightest. Temper was the only weapon Frank had, and he used it.

"You're ungrateful and selfish and stupid. All my life I've worked to pave the way for you. To open doors so you could step through. Now it's not good enough."

Trace felt tears of frustration burn his eyes, but didn't back down. "No, it's not good enough, because I don't want to walk through your doors. I want something else, I want something more, but you're so wrapped up in your own hopeless dream you can't see that I hate it. And that the more you push me to follow your dream instead of my own, the closer I come to hating you."

Trace hadn't meant to say that, and shocked himself speechless with his own bitter words. Before his stunned eyes, his father paled, aged and seemed to shrivel. If he could have taken the words back, he might have tried. But it was too late.

"Take your dream, then," Frank said in a voice rough with emotion. "Go where it takes you. But don't come back, Trace O'Hurley. Don't come back to me when it leaves you cold. There'll be no killing of the fatted calf for you."

He strode off, stage left.

"He didn't mean it," Abby said quickly, taking Trace's arm. "You know he didn't."

"Neither of them did." Her own eyes welling, Maddy looked helplessly at her mother.

"Everyone just needs to cool off." Even with her flair for the dramatic, Chantel was shaken. "Come on, Trace, we'll go for a walk."

"No." With a little sigh, Molly shook her head. "You girls go on now, let me talk to Trace." She waited until they were alone, then, feeling old and tired, sat on the piano bench. "I know you've been unhappy," she said quietly. "And that you've bottled things up. I should have done something about it."

"None of it's your fault."

"Mine as much as his, Trace. The things you said cut deep in him, and that won't heal for a while. I know some were said in temper, but others were true." She looked up, studying the face of her firstborn and only son. "I think it was true what you said about coming to hate him if he didn't let you go."

"Ma—"

"No. It was a hard thing to say, but harder if it came true. You want to go."

He opened his mouth, on the edge of caving in yet again. But the rage he had felt for his father was still too close, and it frightened him. "I have to go."

"Then do it." She stood again to put her hands on his shoulders. "And do it quick and clean, else he'll charm or shame you into staying and you'll never forgive him. Take your own road. We'll be here when you come back."

"I love you."

"I know. I want to keep it that way." She kissed him, then hurried away, knowing she had to hold off her own tears until she had comforted her husband.

That night, Trace packed his belongings—clothes, a harmonica, and dozens of brochures. He left a note that said simply, "I'll write." He had $327.00 in his pocket when he walked out of the motel and stuck out his thumb.

Chapter 1

The whiskey was cheap and had the bite of an angry woman. Trace sucked air through his teeth and waited to die. When he didn't, he poured a second shot from the bottle, tipped back in his chair and watched the open expanse of the Gulf of Mexico. Behind him, the little cantina was gearing up for the evening's business. Frijoles and enchiladas were frying in the kitchen. The smell of onions was coming on strong, competing with the odors of liquor and stale tobacco. The conversations were in rapid-fire Spanish that Trace understood and ignored.

He didn't want company. He wanted the whiskey and the water.

The sun was a red ball over the Gulf. There were low-lying clouds shimmering with pinks and golds. The fire of the whiskey was settling into a nice, comfortable heat in the pit of his stomach. Trace O'Hurley was on vacation, and by God he was going to enjoy it.

The States was only a short plane ride away. He'd stopped thinking of them as home years before—or at least he'd convinced himself he had. It had been twelve years since he'd sailed out of San Francisco, a young, idealistic man riddled with guilt, driven by dreams. He'd seen Hong Kong, and Singapore. For a year he'd traveled the Orient, living by his wits and the talent he'd inherited from his parents. He'd played in hotel lounges and strip joints at night and soaked up the foreign sights and smells by day.

Then there had been Tokyo. He'd played American music in a seedy little club with the idea of making his way across Asia.

It had simply been a matter of being in the right place at the right time. Or, as Trace thought when he was feeling churlish, the wrong place at the wrong time. A barroom brawl was a common enough occurrence. Frank O'Hurley had taught his son more than how to keep the beat. Trace knew when to swing and when to retreat.

He hadn't started out with the intention of saving Charlie Forrester's life. And he certainly hadn't known that Forrester was an American agent.

Fate, Trace thought now as he watched the red sun sinking closer to the horizon. It was fate that had caused him to deflect the knife meant for Charlie's heart. And it was fate and its wily ways that had embroiled him in the grim game of espionage. Trace had indeed made his way across Asia, and beyond. But he'd been bankrolled by the International Security System.

Now Charlie was dead. Trace poured himself another shot and drank a toast to his friend and mentor. It wasn't an assassin's bullet or a knife in a dark alley

Without a Trace

that had gotten him, but a stroke. Charlie's body had simply decided his time was up.

So Trace O'Hurley sat in a little dive on the Mexican coast and held his own wake.

The funeral was in fourteen hours in Chicago. Because he wasn't ready to cross the Rio Grande, Trace would stay in Mexico, drink to his old friend and contemplate life. Charlie would understand, Trace decided as he stretched out long legs clad in dingy khaki. Charlie had never been one for ceremony. Just do the job, have a drink and get on with the next one.

Trace pulled out a crushed pack of cigarettes and searched in the pocket of his dirt-streaked shirt for a match. His hands were long and wide palmed. At ten he'd dreamed of becoming a concert pianist. But he'd dreamed of becoming many things. A battered bush hat shadowed his face as he struck the match and touched it to the end of the cigarette.

He was very tanned, because his last job had kept him outdoors. His hair was thick and, because he hadn't bothered to have it trimmed, long enough to curl beyond the hat in dark blond disarray. His face was damp from the heat, and lean. There was a scar, small and white, along the left side of his jaw—an encounter with a broken bottle. His nose had been slightly out of alignment ever since he'd been sixteen. A fight over a girl's honor—or lack thereof.

His body was on the lanky side at the moment, due to a prolonged hospital stay. The last bullet he'd taken had nearly killed him. Even without the whiskey and the grief, he had a dangerous look. The bones were prominent, the eyes intense. Even now, when he was on his own time, they made occasional sweeps of the room.

He hadn't shaved in three days, and his beard was rough enough to give his mouth a surly look. The waiter was happy to leave him with his bottle and his solitude.

As dusk fell, the sky became quieter, and the cantina noisier. A radio played Mexican music interrupted by occasional bursts of static. Someone broke a glass. Two men started to argue about fishing, politics and women. Trace poured another shot.

He saw her the minute she walked in. Old habits had his eye on the door. Training had him taking in the details without seeming to look at all. A tourist who'd made a wrong turn, he thought as he took in the ivory skin dashed with freckles that went with her red hair. She'd burn to a crisp after an hour under the Yucatán sun. A pity, he thought mildly, and went back to his drink.

He'd expected her to back out the moment she realized the type of place she'd wandered into. Instead, she went up to the bar. Trace crossed his ankles and whiled away the time by studying her.

Her white slacks were spotless despite the dusty heat of the day. She wore them with a purple shirt that was loose enough to be cool. Even so, he noted that she was slender, with enough curve to give the baggy slacks some style. Her hair, almost the color of the setting sun, was caught back in a braid, but her face was turned away, so he could see only her profile. Classic, he decided without much interest. Cameo style. The champagne-and-caviar type.

He tossed back the rest of the drink and decided to get very drunk—for Charlie's sake.

He'd just lifted the bottle when the woman turned and looked directly at him. From the shadow of his hat,

Trace met the look. Tensed, he continued to pour as she crossed the room toward him.

"Mr. O'Hurley?"

His brow lifted only slightly at the accent. It had a trace of Ireland, the same trace his father's had taken on in anger or in joy. He sipped his whiskey and said nothing.

"You are Trace O'Hurley?"

There was a hint of nerves in the voice, as well, he noted. And, close up, he could see smudges of shadows under what were extraordinary green eyes. Her lips pressed together. Her fingers twisted on the handle of the canvas bag slung over her shoulder. Trace set the whiskey down and realized he was just a bit too drunk to be annoyed.

"Might be. Why?"

"I was told you'd be in Mérida. I've been looking for you for two days." And he was anything but what she'd expected. If she wasn't so desperate, she'd already have fled. His clothes were dirty, he smelled of whiskey, and he looked like a man who could peel the skin off you without drawing blood. She pulled in a deep breath and decided to take her chances. "May I sit down?"

With a shrug, Trace kicked a chair back from the table. An agent—from either side—would have approached him differently. "Suit yourself."

She wrapped her fingers around the back of the chair and wondered why her father believed this crude drunkard was the answer. But her legs weren't as steady as they might be, so she sat down. "It's very important that I speak with you. Privately."

Trace looked beyond her to the cantina. It was crowded now, and getting noisier by the minute. "This'll do. Now why don't you tell me who you are, how you knew I'd be in Mérida, and what the hell you want?"

She linked her fingers together because they were trembling. "I'm Dr. Fitzpatrick. Dr. Gillian Fitzpatrick. Charles Forrester told me where you were, and I want you to save my brother's life."

Trace kept his eyes on her as he lifted the bottle. His voice was quiet and flat. "Charlie's dead."

"I know." She thought she'd glimpsed something, some flash of humanity, in his eyes. It was gone now, but Gillian still responded to it. "I'm sorry. I understand you were close."

"I'd like to know how you understand anything or why you expect me to believe Charlie would have told you where to find me."

Gillian wiped a damp palm over the thigh of her slacks before reaching into her bag. In silence, she handed a sealed envelope to him.

Something told Trace he'd be better off not taking it. He should get up, walk out and lose himself in the warm Mexican night. It was only because she'd mentioned Charlie that he broke the seal and read the note inside.

Charlie had used the code they'd communicated with during their last assignment. As always, he'd kept the message brief: "Listen to the lady. No involvement with the organization at this time. Contact me."

Of course, there was no way to contact Charlie now, Trace thought as he folded the letter again. With the feeling that, even dead, Charlie was still guiding his moves, he looked at the woman again. "Explain."

"Mr. Forrester was a friend of my father's. I didn't know him well myself. I was away a lot. About fifteen years ago they worked together on a project known as Horizon."

Trace pushed the bottle aside. Vacation or not, he couldn't afford to dull his senses any further. "What's your father's name?"

"Sean. Dr. Sean Brady Fitzpatrick."

He knew the name. He knew the project. Fifteen years before, some of the top researchers and scientists in the world had been employed to develop a serum that would immunize man against the effects of ionizing radiation-injury—one of the nastier side effects of nuclear war. The ISS had been in charge of security and had monitored and maintained the project. It had cost hundreds of millions, and it had been a whopping failure.

"You'd have been a kid."

"I was twelve." She jolted and turned around nervously when something crashed in the kitchen. "Of course, I didn't know about the project then, but later…" The smell of onions and liquor was overpowering. She wanted to get up, wanted to walk along the beach, where the air would be warm and clear, but she forced herself to continue. "The project was dropped, but my father continued to work on it. He had other obligations, but whenever possible he resumed experimenting."

"Why? He wouldn't have been funded for it."

"My father believed in Horizon. The concept fascinated him, not as a defense, but as an answer to the insanity we're all aware exists. As to the money—well, my father has reached a point where he can afford to indulge his beliefs."

Not only a scientist, but a rich scientist, Trace thought as he watched her from under the brim of his hat. And this one looked as if she'd gone to a tidy convent school in Switzerland. It was the posture that usually gave it away. No one taught proper posture like a nun.

"Go on."

"In any case, my father turned all his notes and findings over to my brother five years ago, after he suffered his first heart attack. For the past few years, my father has been too ill to continue intense laboratory work. And now…"

For a moment, Gillian closed her eyes. The terror and the traveling were taking their toll. As a scientist, she knew she needed food and rest. As a daughter, a sister, she had to finish. "Mr. O'Hurley, might I have a drink?"

Trace shoved both bottle and glass across the table. He was nibbling, but he wasn't ready to bite yet. She interested him, certainly, but he'd learned long ago that you could be interested and uninvolved.

She'd have preferred coffee or at the most, a snifter of warm brandy. She started to refuse the whiskey, but then caught the look in Trace's eye. So he was testing her. She was used to being tested. Her chin came up automatically. Her shoulders straightened. Steady, she poured a double shot and downed it in one swallow.

She drew in breath through a throat that felt as if it had been blowtorched. Blinking the moisture from her eyes, she let it out again. "Thank you."

The light of humor flashed in his eyes for the first time. "Don't mention it."

Hot and bitter though it was, the whiskey helped. "My father is very ill, Mr. O'Hurley. Too ill to travel. He contacted Mr. Forrester but was unable to fly to Chicago himself. I went to Mr. Forrester in his place, and Mr. Forrester sent me to you. I was told that you're the best man for the job."

Trace lit another cigarette. He figured he hadn't been the best man for anything since he'd lain bleeding in the dirt, a bullet two inches from his heart. "Which is?"

"About a week ago, my brother was taken, kidnapped by an organization known as Hammer. You've heard of them?"

It was training that kept his face blank over a mix of fear and rage. His association with that particular organization had nearly killed him.

"I've heard of them."

"All we know is that they took my brother from his home in Ireland, where he had continued, and nearly completed, his work on the Horizon project. They intend to hold him until he has perfected the serum. You understand what the repercussions could be if a group like that possessed the formula?"

Trace tapped the ash of his cigarette onto the wooden floor. "I've been told I have a reasonably developed intelligence."

Driven, she grabbed his wrist. Because she was a woman in a man's field, physical contact was usually reserved for family and loved ones. Now she held on to Trace, and the only hope she had. "Mr. O'Hurley, we can't afford to joke about this."

"Careful how you use *we*." Trace waited until her fingers uncurled. "Let me ask you, Dr. Fitzpatrick, is your brother a smart man?"

"He's a genius."

"No, no, I mean does he have two grains of common sense to rub together?"

Her shoulders straightened again because she was all too ready to lay her head on the table and weep. "Flynn is a brilliant scientist, and a man who under normal circumstances can take care of himself quite nicely."

"Fine, because only a fool would believe that if he came up with the formula for Hammer, he'd stay alive. They like to call themselves terrorists, liberators, rebels. What they are is a bunch of disorganized fanatics, headed by a rich madman. They kill more people by mistake than they do on purpose." Frowning, he rubbed a hand over his chest. "They've got enough savvy to keep them going, and pots of money, but basically, they're idiots. And there's nothing more dangerous than a bunch of dedicated idiots. My advice to your brother would be to spit in their eye."

Her already pale skin was ghost white. "They have his child." Gillian placed a hand on the table for support as she rose. "They took his six-year-old daughter." With that, she fled the cantina.

Trace sat where he was. Not his business, he reminded himself as he reached for the bottle again. He was on vacation. He'd come back from the dead and intended to enjoy his life. Alone.

Swearing, he slammed the bottle down and went after her.

Her anger had her covering ground quickly. She heard him call her name but didn't stop. She'd been an idiot to believe that a man like him could help. She'd be better off attempting to negotiate with the terrorists. At least with them she wouldn't go in expecting any compassion.

When he grabbed her arm, she swung around. Temper gave her the energy that lack of sleep and food had depleted.

"I told you to wait a damn minute."

"You've already given me your considered opinion, Mr. O'Hurley. There doesn't seem to be any need for further discussion. I don't know what Mr. Forrester saw in you. I don't know why he sent me to look for a man who would rather sit in a seedy little dive swilling whiskey than help save lives. I came looking for a man of courage and compassion and found a tired, dirty drunk who cares about no one and nothing."

It stung, more than he'd expected. His fingers stayed firm on her arm as he waved away a small boy with a cardboard box filled with Chiclets. "Have you finished? You're making a scene."

"My brother and niece are being held by a group of terrorists. Do you think I care whether I embarrass you or not?"

"It takes more than an Irish redhead on a roll to embarrass me," he said easily. "But I have a policy against drawing attention to myself. Old habit. Let's take a walk."

She very nearly yanked her arm away. The part of her that was pride burned to do it. The part that was love triumphed, and she subsided. In silence she walked beside him, down the narrow planks that led to the water.

The sand was white here against a dark sea and a darker sky. A few boats were docked, waiting for tomorrow's fishing or tomorrow's tourists. The night was quiet enough that the music from the cantina carried to them. Trace noted that somebody was singing about love and a woman's infidelity. Somebody always was.

"Look, Dr. Fitzpatrick, you caught me at a bad time. I don't know why Charlie sent you to me."

"Neither do I."

He stopped long enough to cup his hands around a

match and a cigarette. "What I mean is, this situation should be handled by the ISS."

She was calm again. Gillian didn't mind losing her temper. It felt good. But she also knew that more was accomplished with control. "The ISS wants the formula as badly as Hammer. Why should I trust my brother's and my niece's lives to them?"

"Because they're the good guys."

Gillian turned toward the sea, and the wind hit her dead on. Though it helped clear her head, she didn't notice the first stars blinking to life. "They are an organization run by many men—some good, some bad, all ambitious, all with their own concept of what is necessary for peace and order. At the moment, my only concern is my family. Do you have family, Mr. O'Hurley?"

He drew hard on the cigarette. "Yeah." Over the border, he thought. He hadn't seen them in seven years, or was it eight? He'd lost track. But he knew Chantel was in L.A. filming a movie, Maddy was in New York starring in a new play. Abby was raising horses and kids in Virginia. His parents were finishing up a week's gig in Buffalo.

He might have lost track of the time, but not of his family.

"Would you trust the lives of any of the members of your family to an organization? One that, if they considered it necessary for the common good, might sacrifice them?" She closed her eyes. The wind felt like heaven, warm, salty and strong. "Mr. Forrester understood and agreed that what was needed to save my brother and his child was a man who would care more about them than the formula. He thought you were that man."

"He was off base." Trace pitched his cigarette into

the surf. "Charlie knew I was considering retiring. This was just his way of keeping me in the game."

"Are you as good as he told me?"

With a laugh. Trace rubbed a hand over his chin. "Probably better. Charlie was never much for back patting."

Gillian turned again, this time to face him. He didn't look like a hero to her, with the rough beard and the grimy clothes. But there had been strength in his hand when he'd taken her arm, and she'd sensed an undercurrent of violence. He'd be passionate when it was something he wanted, she thought, whether it was a goal, a dream or a woman. Under usual circumstances, she preferred men with cool, analytical minds, who attacked a problem with logic and patience. But it wasn't a scientist she needed now.

Trace dipped his hands into his pocket and fought the urge to squirm. She was looking at him as though he were a laboratory rat, and he didn't like it. Maybe it was the hint of Ireland in her voice or the shadows under her eyes, but he couldn't bring himself to walk away.

"Look, I'll contact the ISS. The closest field office is in San Diego. You can feed them whatever information you have. Inside of twenty-four hours, some of the best agents in the world will be looking for your brother."

"I can give you a hundred thousand dollars." Her mind was made up. She had discarded logic for instinct. Forrester had said this man could do it. Her father had agreed. Gillian was throwing her vote with theirs. "The price isn't negotiable, because it's all I have. Find my brother and my niece, and with a hundred thousand dollars you can retire in style."

He stared at her for a moment, and then, biting off an

oath, he walked toward the sea. The woman was crazy. He was offering her the skill of the best intelligence organization in the world, and she was tossing money in his face. A tidy sum.

Trace watched the sea roll up and recede. He'd never been able to hang on to more than a few thousand at a time. It just wasn't his nature. But a hundred thousand could mean the difference between retiring or just talking about retiring.

The spray flew over his face as he shook his head. He didn't want to get involved, not with her, not with her family, and not with some nebulous formula that might or might not save the world from the big blast.

What he wanted was to go back to his hotel, order up a five-star meal and go to bed on a full stomach. God, he wanted some peace. Time to figure out what to do with his life.

"If you're determined to have a freelancer, I can give you a couple of names."

"I don't want a couple of names. I want you."

Something about the way she said it made his stomach knot. The reaction made him all the more determined to get rid of her. "I just came off nine months of deep cover. I'm burned out, Doc. You need someone young, gung ho and greedy." For the second time he ran his hands over his face. "I'm tired."

"That's a cop-out," she said, and the sudden strength in her voice surprised him enough to have him turning around. She stood straight, loose tendrils of hair flying around her face, pale as marble in the light of the rising moon. It suddenly struck him that in fury and despair she was the most stunning woman he'd ever seen. Then he lost that thought as she advanced on him, her Irish leading the way.

"You don't want to get involved. You don't want to be responsible for the lives of an innocent man and a young child. You don't want to be touched by that. Mr. Forrester saw you as some kind of a knight, a man of principle and compassion, but he was wrong. You're a selfish shell of a man who couldn't have deserved a friend like him. He was a man who cared, who tried to help for nothing more than the asking, and who died because of his own standards."

Trace's head snapped up. "What the hell are you talking about?" His eyes caught the light and glittered dangerously. In one swift, silent move he had Gillian by both arms. "What the hell do you mean? Charlie had a stroke."

Her heart was beating hard in her throat. She'd never seen anyone look more capable of murder than Trace did at that moment. "He was trying to help. They'd followed me. Three men."

"What three men?"

"I don't know. Terrorists, agents, whatever you chose to call them. They broke into the house when I was with him." She tried to even her breathing by concentrating on the pain his fingers were inflicting on her arms. "Mr. Forrester pushed me through some kind of hidden panel in his library. I heard them on the other side. They were looking for me." She could remember even now how hot and airless it had been behind the panel. How dark. "He was putting them off, telling them I'd left. They threatened him, but he stuck by the story. It seemed that they believed him."

Her voice was shaking. Trace watched her dig her

teeth into her lower lip to steady herself. "It got very quiet. I was more frightened by the quiet and tried to get out to help him. I couldn't find the mechanism."

"Two inches down from the ceiling."

"Yes. It took me almost an hour before I found it." She didn't add that she'd fought hysteria the entire time, or that at one point she'd beaten against the panel and shouted, prepared to give herself up rather than stay in the suffocating dark. "When I got out, he was dead. If I'd been quicker, I might have been able to help him... I'll never be sure."

"The ISS said stroke."

"It was diagnosed as one. Such things can be brought on by a simple injection. In any case, they caused the stroke, and they caused it while looking for me. I have to live with that." Trace had dropped his grip, and she'd grabbed his shirtfront without realizing it, her fingers curled tight. "And so do you. If you won't help me for compassion or for money, maybe you'll do it for revenge."

He turned away from her again. He'd accepted Charlie's death once. A stroke, a little time bomb in the brain set to go off at a certain time. Fate had said: Charlie, you've got sixty-three years, five months, on earth. Make the best of it. That he'd accepted.

Now he was being told it wasn't fate, it was three men. Fate was something he was Irish enough to live with. But it was possible to hate men, to pay men back. It was something to think about. Trace decided to get a pot of black coffee and do just that.

"I'll take you back to your hotel."

"But—"

"We'll get some coffee and you can tell me everything Charlie said, everything you know. Then I'll tell you if I'll help you."

If it was all he'd give, she'd take it. "I checked into the same hotel as you. It seemed practical."

"Fine." Trace took her arm and began to walk with her. She wasn't steady, he noted. Whatever fire had pushed her this far was fading fast. She swayed once, and he tightened his grip. "When's the last time you ate?"

"Yesterday."

He gave a snort that might have been a laugh. "What kind of a doctor are you?"

"Physicist."

"Even a physicist should know something about nutrition. It goes like this. You eat, you stay alive. You don't eat, you fall down." He released her arm and slipped his around her waist. She would have protested if she'd had the energy.

"You smell like a horse."

"Thanks. I spent most of the day bumping around the jungle. Great entertainment. What part of Ireland?"

Fatigue was spreading from her legs to her brain. His arm felt so strong, so comforting. Without realizing it, she leaned against him. "What?"

"What part of Ireland are you from?"

"Cork."

"Small world." He steered her into the lobby. "So's my father. What room?"

"Two-twenty-one."

"Right next door to mine."

"I gave the desk clerk a thousand pesos."

Because the elevators were small and heated like ovens, he took the stairs. "You're an enterprising woman, Dr. Fitzpatrick."

"Most women are. It's still a man's world."

He had his doubts about that, but he didn't argue the point. "Key?"

She dug into her pocket, fighting off the weakness. She wouldn't faint. That she promised herself. Trace took the key from her palm and stuck it in the lock. When he opened the door, he shoved her against the wall in the hallway.

"What's wrong with you?" she asked. She swallowed the rest when she saw him draw a hunting knife out of his pocket.

It was all he had. He hadn't considered it necessary to strap on a gun while on vacation. His eyes were narrow as he stepped into the room and kicked aside some of the debris.

"Oh, God." Gillian braced herself in the doorway and looked. They'd done a thorough job. Even someone inexperienced in such matters could see that nothing had been overlooked.

Her suitcase had been cut apart, and the clothes she hadn't unpacked were strewn everywhere. The mattress and the cushions from the single chair had been slit, and hunks of white stuffing littered the floor. The drawers of the bureau had been pulled out and overturned.

Trace checked the bath and the access through the windows. They'd come in the front, he concluded, and a search of a room this size wouldn't have taken more than twenty minutes.

"You've still got your tail, Doc." He turned but didn't sheath the knife. "Pick up what you need. We'll talk next door."

She didn't want to touch the clothes, but she forced herself to be practical. She needed them, and it didn't matter that other hands had touched them. Moving quickly, she gathered up slacks and skirts and blouses. "I have cosmetics and toiletries in the bath."

"Not anymore you don't. They dumped the lot." Trace took her arm again. This time he checked the hall and moved quietly to the room next door. Again he braced Gillian against the wall and opened the door. His fingers relaxed on the handle of the knife, though only slightly. So they hadn't made him. That was good. He signaled to her to come in behind him, double-locked the door, then began a careful search.

It was an old habit to leave a few telltales, one he followed even off duty. The book on his nightstand was still a quarter inch over the edge. The single strand of hair he'd left on the bedspread hadn't been disturbed. He pulled the drapes, then sat on the bed and picked up the phone.

In perfect Spanish that had Gillian's brow lifting, he ordered dinner and two pots of coffee. "I got you a steak," he said when he hung up the phone. "But this is Mexico, so I wouldn't expect it for about an hour. Sit down."

With her clothes still rolled in her arms, she obeyed. Trace pushed himself back on the bed and crossed his legs.

"What are they after?"

"I beg your pardon?"

"They've got your brother. Why do they want you?"

"I occasionally work with Flynn. About six months ago I spent some time with him in Ireland on Horizon. We had a breakthrough." She let her head tilt back against the cushion. "We believed we'd found a way to immunize the individual cell. You see, in ionizing radiation injury the main structure affected is the single cell. Energy rays enter the tissue like bullets and cause localized injury in the cells. We were working on a formula that prevented molecular changes within the affected cells. In that way we could—"

"That's just fascinating, Doc. But what I want to know is why they're after you."

She realized she'd nearly been reciting the information in her sleep and tried to straighten in the chair. "I took the notes on this part of the project with me, back to the institute, to work on them more intensely. Without them it could take Flynn another year, maybe more, to reconstruct the experiment."

"So you're the missing piece of the puzzle, so to speak?"

"I have the information." The words began to slur as her eyes closed.

"You're telling me you carry that stuff with you?" God save him from amateurs. "Did they get it?"

"No, they didn't get it, and yes, I have it with me. Excuse me," she murmured, and went to sleep.

Trace sat where he was for a moment and studied her. Under other circumstances he would have been amused to have a woman he'd known for only a few hours fall asleep in the chair of his hotel room in the middle of a conversation. At the moment, his sense of humor wasn't what it might have been.

She was deathly pale from exhaustion. Her hair was a fiery halo that spoke of strength and passion. Clothes lay balled in her lap. Her bag was crushed between her hip and the side of the chair. Without hesitation, Trace got up and eased it out. Gillian didn't move a muscle as he dumped the contents on the bed.

He pushed aside a hairbrush and an antique hammered-silver compact. There was a small paperback phrase book—which told him she didn't speak the language—and the stub of a ticket for a flight from O'Hare. Her checkbook had been neatly balanced in a precise hand. Six hundred and twenty-eight dollars and eighty-three cents. Her passport picture was better than most, but it didn't capture the stubbornness he'd already been witness to. She'd worn her hair loose for it, he noted, frowning a bit at the thick riot of curls that fell beyond her shoulders.

He'd always had a weakness for long, luxuriant, feminine hair.

She'd been born in Cork twenty-seven years before, in May, and had kept her Irish citizenship, though her address was listed as New York.

Trace pushed the passport aside and reached for her wallet. She could use a new one, he decided as he opened it. The leather had been worn smooth at the creases. Her driver's license was nearly up for renewal, and the picture on it carried the same serious expression as the passport. She had three hundred and change in cash, and another two thousand in traveler's checks. He found a shopping list folded into the corner of the billfold along with a parking ticket. A long-overdue parking ticket.

A flip through the pictures she carried showed him a black-and-white snapshot of a man and a woman. From the clothes he judged that it had been taken in the late fifties. The woman's hair was as neat as the collar and cuffs on the blouse she wore, but she was smiling as though she meant it. The man, husky and full-faced, had his arm around the woman, but he looked a bit un-comfortable.

Trace flipped to the next and found a picture of Gil-lian in overalls and a T-shirt, her head thrown back, laughing, her arms around the same man. He was older by perhaps twenty years. She looked happy, delighted with herself, and nothing like a physicist. Trace flipped quickly to the next snapshot.

This was the brother. The resemblance to Gillian was stronger than with the people Trace assumed were her parents. His hair was a tamer red, almost a mahog-any, but he had the same wide-set green eyes and full mouth. In his arms he held a pixie of a girl. She would have been around three, he concluded, with that telltale mane of wildly curling red hair. Her face was round and pleased, showing a dimple near the corner of her mouth.

Before he realized it, Trace was grinning and holding the photo closer to the light. If a picture told a story, he'd bet his last nickel the kid was a handful. He had a weak-ness for cute kids who had the devil's gleam in their eyes. Swearing under his breath, he closed the billfold.

The contents of her bag might have told him a few things about her, but there hadn't been any notes. A few phone calls would fill in the blanks as far as Dr. Gil-lian Fitzpatrick was concerned. He glanced at her again as she sat sleeping, then, sighing, dumped everything back in her purse. He might have to wait until morning to get anything else out of her.

When the knock came at the door, she didn't budge. Trace let the room-service waiter set up the table. After giving Gillian three hefty shakes and getting no more than a murmur in response, he gave up. Muttering to himself, he slipped off her sandals, then gathered her up in his arms. She sighed, cuddled and caused him an uncomfortable pressure just under the ribs. She smelled like a meadow with the wildflowers just opening. By the time he'd gotten her into bed, he'd given up on the idea of sleeping himself.

Trace poured his first cup of coffee and settled down to eat his dinner—and hers.

Chapter 2

Gillian woke after a solid twelve hours of sleep. The room was dim, and she lay still, waiting for her mind to clear. Quickly, and in order, the events of the previous day came back to her. The bumpy, nerve-racking flight from Mexico City to Mérida. The fear and fatigue. The frustrating search from hotel to hotel. The dingy little cantina where she'd found the man she had to believe would save her brother and her young niece.

This was his room. This was his bed. Cautiously she turned her head—and let out a small groan. He was sleeping beside her, and in all probability he was as naked as the day he was born. The sheet slanted across his bare back, from below the shoulder blade to the waist. His face, a little less harsh, a little less forbidding, in sleep, was inches from hers. She felt then, as she had felt when she'd first seen him the evening before, that it was the face of a man a woman would never be safe with.

Yet she'd spent the night with him and had been safe—safe from him and from whatever forces were after her. More significantly, the moment she had stepped into the room and had finished unburdening herself, she had felt a wave of relief and confidence. He would help, reluctantly, resentfully, but he would help.

Sighing, she shifted in bed, preparing to get up. His hand shot out. His eyes opened. Gillian froze. Perhaps she wasn't as safe as she'd thought.

His eyes were clear and alert. His grip was firm, and just shy of being painful. Under his fingers, he felt her pulse speed up. Her hair was barely mussed, which told him that exhaustion had held her still through the night. The hours of sleep had faded the shadows under her eyes, eyes that watched him warily.

"You sleep like a rock," he said mildly, then released her and rolled over.

"The traveling caught up with me." Her heart was bumping as though she'd run up three flights of stairs. He was dangerous to look at, and too close. Perhaps it was the morning disorientation that caused her to feel that dull sexual pull.

Before she managed to resist it, her gaze had flicked down—the strong column of neck, the broad chest—and froze. A long red scar marred the tanned skin just right of his heart. It looked as though he'd been ripped open, then put back together. And recently.

"That looks...serious."

"It looks like a scar." His voice held no inflection at all as she continued to stare at the wound with horrified eyes. "You got a problem with scars, Doc?"

"No." She made herself look away, back at his face. It was as hard and blank as his voice. Not my business, she reminded herself. He was a violent man who lived by violent means. And that was exactly what she needed. She got out of bed to stand awkwardly, smoothing her clothes. "I appreciate you letting me sleep here. I'm sure we could have arranged for a cot."

"I've never had a problem sharing a bed." She was still pale. It gave her a delicate bone-china look that made him edgy. "Feel better?"

"Yes, I—" She reached a hand to her hair as she felt the first wave of embarrassment. "Thank you."

"Good, because we've got a lot of ground to cover today." He tossed the sheet aside and noted her instinctive flinch. His own discomfort turned to amusement. He wore flesh-colored briefs that left little room for modesty or imagination. Rising without any sign of self-consciousness, he gave her a slow, cocky grin. He liked the fact that she didn't avert her eyes. Whatever her thoughts, she stood where she was and watched him coolly.

Her throat had gone dry as dust, but she made a passable stab at casualness. "You could use a shower."

"Why don't you order up some breakfast while I do?" He turned toward the bath.

"Mr. O'Hurley…"

"Why don't you make it Trace, sweetheart?" He looked over his shoulder and grinned again. "After all, we just slept together."

The water was running in the shower before she managed to free the breath that was trapped in her lungs.

He'd done it on purpose, of course, she told herself as she sat on the edge of the bed. It was typical of the male of the species to flaunt himself. The peacock had his plumage, the lion his mane. Males were always strutting and preening so that the female would be impressed. But who would have guessed the man would be built like that?

With a shake of her head, Gillian lifted the phone. She didn't care how he was built as long as he helped her.

He'd have preferred it if she hadn't looked so frail and vulnerable. Trace kept the water cold to make up for three hours' sleep. His problem. Lathering his face, he began to shave in the shower by feel. He'd never been able to resist the damsel-in-distress routine. It had nearly gotten him killed in Santo Domingo. And nearly gotten him married in Stockholm. He wasn't sure which would have been worse.

It didn't help a hell of a lot that this one was beautiful. Beautiful women had an edge, no matter what modern-day philosophy said about intellect. He could admire a mind, but—call him weak—he preferred it packaged well.

By God, she was some package, and she'd dumped him into an international mess when all he wanted to do was wander around some ruins and go snorkeling.

Hammer. Why in the hell did it have to be Hammer? He'd thought he was done with the half-baked, destructive group of renegades. It had taken him more than six months to infiltrate the organization at one of the base levels. He'd been working his way up, nicely, keeping a low profile with a Slavic accent, his hair dyed black and a lot of facial hair to complete the disguise.

Ten miles out of Cairo, he'd made the mistake of discovering that the man he'd been working with on a small-arms deal had been making a few deals of his own on the side. Nothing to him, Trace thought now, bitterly. God knew he'd tried to tell the man he didn't give a damn about his private ventures. But in a panic, the terrified entrepreneur had blown a hole in Trace's chest and left him for dead rather than risk being reported.

It was well-known that the man who wielded the power and money at Hammer had little patience with private enterprise.

For nothing, Trace thought in disgust. The months of work, the careful planning, all for nothing because one half-crazed Egyptian had had a sweaty trigger finger.

As a result, he'd brushed close enough to death to want to spend some time appreciating life. Get drunk, hold a willing woman, lie on white sand and look at blue skies. He'd even started thinking about seeing his family.

Then she'd come along.

Scientists. He rubbed a hand over his chin and, finding it smooth enough, let the water beat over his head. Scientists had been screwing up the order of things since Dr. Frankenstein's day. Why couldn't they just work on a cure for the common cold and leave the destruction of the world to the military?

He turned off the taps, then reached for two undersized towels. Two phone calls the night before had given him enough information on Gillian Fitzpatrick to satisfy him. She was the genuine article, though he'd been wrong about the Swiss school. It was Irish nuns who'd taught her posture. She'd completed her education in Dublin, then gone on to work for her father until she'd accepted a position with the highly respected Random-Frye Institute in New York.

She was single, though there was a link between her and a Dr. Arthur Steward, head of research and development at Random-Frye. Three months ago she'd spent six weeks in Ireland, on her brother's farm.

A busman's holiday, Trace decided, if she had indeed worked on Horizon while she'd been there.

There was no reason to disbelieve her, no reason to refuse to do as she asked. He'd find Flynn Fitzpatrick and the angel-faced little girl. And while he was at it he'd find the men who'd killed Charlie. He'd get a hundred thousand for the first and a great deal of satisfaction for the second.

The towel covered him with the same nonchalance as the briefs. He walked back into the bedroom to find Gillian shaking out what was left of her clothes.

"Shower's yours, Jill."

"Gillian," she told him. Fifteen minutes alone had done a great deal to help her regain her composure. Since she was going to have to deal with Trace O'Hurley for some time, she'd decided to think of him as a tool rather than as a man.

"Suit yourself."

"I usually do. I don't have a toothbrush."

"Use mine." He pulled open a drawer of the bureau. He caught her look in the mirror and grinned. "Sorry, Doc. I don't have a spare. Take it or leave it."

"It's unhygienic."

"Yeah, but then, so's kissing if you do it right."

Gillian took her clothes and retreated to the bath without commenting.

She felt almost human when she came out again. Her hair was damp, her clothes were wrinkled, but the scent of food and coffee brought a very healthy pang to her stomach. He was already eating, poring over the newspaper as he did. When she moved to join him, he didn't bother to look up.

"I wasn't sure what you liked."

"This is fine," he told her over a mouthful of eggs.

"I'm so glad," she murmured, but the sarcasm bounced off him without making a dent. Because her hunger was urgent, she applied herself to her own plate and returned the compliment by ignoring him.

"They make it sound like it's only going to take a couple of nice chats to ratify the new SALT Treaty."

"Diplomacy is essential in any negotiation."

"Yeah, and—" He looked up. He knew exactly what it felt like to take a hard fist in the solar plexus. He knew how the body contracted, how the air vanished and the head spun. Until now he hadn't known he could experience the same sensation by looking at a woman.

Her hair curled damply past her shoulders, the color of a flame. Her skin was ivory, touched with a rose brought back by rest and food. Over the rim of her cup her eyes, as deep and rich a green as the hills of Ireland, looked into his questioningly.

He thought of mermaids. Of sirens. Of temptation.

"Is something wrong?" She was nearly tempted to reach out and take his pulse. The man looked as though he'd been struck on the back of the neck. "Trace, are you all right?"

"What?"

"Are you ill?" Now she did reach out, but he jerked back as if she'd stung him.

"No, I'm fine." No, he was an idiot, he told himself as he lifted his own coffee. She wasn't a woman, he reminded himself, she was his ticket to an early retirement and sweet revenge. "We need to clear up a few points. When did they snatch your brother?"

Relief came in a tidal wave. "You're going to help me."

He smeared more butter on a piece of toast. "You said a hundred thousand."

The gratitude in her eyes dulled. The warmth in her voice cooled. He preferred it that way. "That's right. The money is in a trust fund that came to me when I turned twenty-five. I haven't needed it. I can contact my lawyer and have it transferred to you."

"Fine. Now when did they take your brother?"

"Six days ago."

"How do you know who took him and why?"

It didn't matter that he was a mercenary, she told herself, only that he would save her family. "Flynn left a tape. He'd been recording some notes when they came for him. He left the tape on, and I suppose no one noticed during the struggle." She pressed a hand to her mouth for a moment. The sounds of the fight had come clearly over the tape, the crashing, the screams of her niece. "He didn't go easily. Then one of the men held a knife to Caitlin's throat. His daughter. I think it was a knife because Flynn said not to cut her. He said he'd go quietly if they didn't cut her."

She had to swallow again. The breakfast she'd eaten with such pleasure rolled toward her throat. "The man said he'd kill her unless Flynn cooperated. When Flynn asked what they wanted, he was told he was working for Hammer now. They instructed him to bring all his notes on the Horizon Project. Flynn said...he told them he'd go with them, he'd do whatever they wanted, but to let the child go. One of the men said they weren't inhuman, it would be too cruel to separate a child from her father. And he laughed."

Trace could see what this was doing to her. For both their sakes, he offered her no comfort. "Where's the tape?"

"Flynn's housekeeper had been at the market. She found the mess in the laboratory when she got back, and she phoned the police. They contacted me. Flynn's recorder had an automatic shutoff when he reached the end of the tape. The police hadn't bothered with it. I did." She linked her hands together as Trace lit a cigarette. "Ultimately I took the tape to Mr. Forrester. It was gone when I found him dead."

"How do you figure they know about you?"

"They would only have to have read Flynn's notes. It would have been recorded that I worked with him and took part of the project back with me."

"The men on the tape, they spoke English?"

"Yes, accented... Mediterranean, I think, except for the one who laughed. He sounded Slavic."

"Anyone use a name?"

"No." On a deep breath, she ran both hands through her hair. "I listened to the tape dozens of times, hoping I might catch something. They said nothing about where they were taking him, only why."

"Okay." Trace tipped back in his chair and blew smoke toward the ceiling. "I think we can get them out in the open."

"How?"

"They want you, don't they? Or the notes." He was silent for a moment as he watched that sink in. "You said you had them with you. I didn't find them in your bag."

The consideration in her eyes turned to indignation. "You looked through my belongings?"

"Just part of the service. Where are they?"

Gillian pushed away from the table to pace to the window. It seemed nothing was hers alone any longer. No part of her life could be private. "Mr. Forrester destroyed them."

"You told me you had them with you."

"I do." She turned back and placed a fingertip to her temple. "Right here. With a true photographic memory, one sees words. If and when it becomes necessary, I can duplicate the notes."

"Then that's what you're going to do, Doc, with a few alterations." He narrowed his eyes as he thought the plan through. It could work, but it all hinged on Gillian. "How are you fixed for guts?"

She moistened her lips. "It's not something I've had to test to any extent. But if you mean to use me as bait to find out where Flynn and Caitlin are being held, I'm willing."

"I don't want any grand sacrifices." He crushed out his cigarette before he rose and walked to her. "Do you trust me?"

She studied him in the hard, brilliant light of the Mexican sun. He was scrubbed and shaven and, she realized, no less dangerous than the man she'd met in the cantina. "I don't know."

"Then you'd better think it through, real careful." He cupped a hand under her chin. "Because if you want to stay alive, you're going to have to."

It was a long, mostly silent drive to Uxmal. Trace had made certain everyone in the hotel knew they were going. He'd asked for brochures, gotten directions in both English and Spanish, then gone to the gift shop to buy another guidebook and some film. He'd asked the clerk about mileage, restaurants along the way, and insect repellent. In general, he'd played the enthusiastic tourist and made a spectacle of himself.

Anyone looking for Gillian would know she could be found at the ruins of Uxmal.

The vegetation on either side of the road was thick and monotonous. The Jeep was canopied, but it didn't have air-conditioning. Gillian drank bottled lemonade and wondered if she'd be alive for the drive back.

"I don't suppose we could have found someplace closer."

"Uxmal's a natural tourist spot." The road was straight and narrow. Trace kept an eye on the rearview mirror. "We'll have some company, but not enough, I think, to put our friends off. Besides, one of the reasons I'm here is to check out the ruins." If they were being followed, the tail was first-class. Trace shifted in his seat and adjusted his dark glasses. "It's not as big or as popular as Chichén Itzá, but it's the most impressive site on the Puuc Route."

"I didn't think a man like you would be interested in ancient civilizations and pyramids."

"I have my moments." In truth, he'd always been fascinated by such things. He'd spent two months in Egypt and Israel using a cover as an anthropology major early in his career. It had given him a taste for both history and danger. "We should be able to pull this off, and soak up the atmosphere, as long as you follow orders."

"I agreed, didn't I?" Even with the thin buff-colored blouse and slacks she wore, the heat was irksome. Gil-

lian concentrated on it rather than the anxiety that was
gnawing at her gut. "What if they're armed?"

Trace took his eyes off the road long enough to shoot
her a grimly amused look. "Let me worry about that.
You're paying me to handle the details."

Gillian lapsed into silence again. She must be mad,
she thought, trusting her life and the lives of her family
to a man who was more interested in money than humanity. Taking another swig of warming lemonade, she
tried to comfort herself by remembering what Charles
Forrester had said of him.

"A bit of a renegade, and certainly not a man who
would be considered a good team player. If he was, he'd
be running the ISS by now. That's how good he is. If
you want a man who can find a needle in a haystack—
and you don't care if the hay gets a bit mangled in the
process—he's the one."

"This is my brother's life, Mr. Forrester. And the life
of a little girl, not to mention the possibility of nuclear
repercussions."

"If, out of all the agents I've worked with, I had to
pick one to trust my life to, it would be Trace O'Hurley."

Now she was trusting her life to him, a man she'd
known less than twenty-four hours. He was crude, and
more than a little rough around the edges. Since she'd
met him he hadn't offered one word of sympathy about
her family, and he hadn't expressed more than a passing interest in a formula that could change forever the
balance of power in the world.

And yet…there was the quietly supportive way he'd
slipped an arm around her waist when she'd been staggering with fatigue.

Who was he? A quick bubble of panic started in her

throat as the question finally broke through. Who was this man she was trusting everything to?

"How long have you been a spy?"

He looked at her again, then back at the road, before he burst out laughing. It was the first time she'd heard the sound from him. It was strong, careless, and more appealing than she'd counted on. "Honey, this ain't James Bond. I work in espionage—or, if you like a cleaner term, intelligence."

Unless she was mistaken, there was a trace of bitterness there. "You didn't answer my question."

"Ten years, more or less."

"Why?"

"Why what?"

"Why are you in this kind of work?"

Trace punched in the cigarette lighter and ignored the little voice in his head that reminded him he'd been smoking too much. "That's a question I've been asking myself lately. Why physics?"

She wasn't foolish enough to think he cared. It was simply a way to switch the conversation away from himself. "Family tradition, and I had a knack for it. I was all but born in a laboratory."

"You're not living in Ireland."

"No, I was offered a position at Random-Frye. It was an excellent opportunity." To finally slip out from under her father's shadow.

"Like the States?"

"Yes, very much. At first it seemed everything moved faster than it should, but you find yourself catching up. Where are you from?"

He pitched the cigarette out into the road. "Nowhere."

"Everyone's from somewhere."

His lips curved at some private joke. "No, they're not. We're nearly there. Want to go over anything?"

Gillian drew a long, steadying breath. The time for small talk was over. "No."

The parking lot was half full. When the winter season got under way, the ruins, less than a two-hour drive from Cancun, would do a brisk business. With his camera slung over his shoulder, Trace took Gillian's hand. Her initial resistance only caused him to tighten his grip.

"Try to look a little romantic. We're on a date."

"You'll understand if I find it a bit difficult to look starry-eyed."

"Shoot for interested." He pulled the guidebook out of his back pocket. "The place dates back to the sixth and seventh centuries. That's comforting."

"Comforting?"

"Over a thousand years and we haven't managed to destroy it. Up for a climb?"

She looked at him but couldn't see his eyes behind the dark lenses. "I suppose."

Hands linked, they started up the rough steps of the Pyramid of the Magician. She wasn't immune to the atmosphere. Even with sweat trickling down her back and her heart thudding with dull fear, she was moved by it. Ancient stones lifted by ancient hands to honor ancient gods. From the top she could look out over what had once been a community filled with people.

For a moment she indulged herself and held herself very still. The scientist in her would have cocked a brow, but her ancestors had believed in leprechauns. Life had been in this place. Spirits still were. With her eyes closed, Gillian felt the power of the atmosphere.

"Can you feel it?" she murmured.

It was captured memories, lingering passions, that drew him to places. The realist in him had never completely over-shadowed the dreamer. "Feel what?" he asked, though he knew.

"The age, the old, old souls. Life and death. Blood and tears."

"You surprise me."

She opened her eyes, greener now with the emotion that was in her. "Don't spoil it. Places like this never lose their power. You could raze the stone, put a high-rise on this spot, and it would still be holy."

"Is that your scientific opinion, Doctor?"

"You *are* going to spoil it."

He relented, though instinct told him they would both be better off it he kept the distance. "Have you ever been to Stonehenge?"

"Yes." She smiled, and her hand relaxed in his.

"If you close your eyes and stand in the shadow of a stone, you can hear the chanting." His fingers had linked with hers, intimately, though neither of them were aware of it. "In Egypt you can run your hand along the stone of a pyramid and all but smell the blood of slaves and the incense of kings. Off the coast of the Isle of Man there are mermaids with hair like yours."

He had a fistful of it, soft, silky. He imagined it heating his skin with the kind of fire magicians conjure without kindling or matches.

She could do nothing but stare at him. Though his eyes were still hidden, his voice had become soft and hypnotic. The hand on her hair seemed to touch every part of her, slowly, temptingly. The little twist of need she had felt that morning became an ache, that ache, a longing.

She leaned toward him. Their bodies brushed.

"The view better be worth it, Harry. I'm sweating like a pig."

Gillian jerked back as if she'd been caught with her hand in the till as a middle-aged couple dragged themselves up the last of the stairs.

"A pile of rocks," the woman said when she took off her straw hat to fan her flushed face. "God knows why we had to come all the way to Mexico to climb a pile of old rocks."

The magic of the place seemed to retreat. Gillian turned to look out over the ruins.

"Young man, would you mind taking a picture of my wife and me?"

Trace took the disc camera from the slightly overweight man, who had an Oklahoman accent. It was the least he could do after they'd prevented him from making a mistake. Letting his mind wander off the task at hand and into more personal matters wouldn't get him his revenge, and it wouldn't get Gillian her family.

"Little closer together," he instructed, then snapped the picture when the couple gave two wide, frozen grins.

"Kind of you." The man from Oklahoma took back his camera. "Want me to take one of you and the lady?"

"Why not?" It was a typical tourist device. After handing over his camera, he circled Gillian's waist. She went stiff as a board. "Smile, honey."

He wasn't sure, but he thought he heard her call him an unflattering name under her breath.

As they started back down, Trace maneuvered so that Gillian's bag was between them. Looking down from the pyramid, he'd seen three men come onto the site together, then separate.

"Stay close."

Gillian set her teeth and obeyed, though at the moment she would have liked nothing better than to put as much distance as possible between them. It must have been too much sun, she decided, that had made her go so soft and light-headed. It certainly hadn't had anything to do with genuine emotion. Sunstroke, she told herself. Add that to the fact that she had always been highly sensitive to atmosphere, and it made a plausible answer to why she had nearly kissed him, and wanted to kiss him, had felt as if she were meant to kiss him.

"This isn't the best time to be daydreaming." Swinging an arm around her shoulders, Trace drew her tight against his body and steered her under an arch into the Nun's Quadrangle.

The position pleased him. The grand plaza was flanked on all four sides by structures that were really a series of interior rooms and doors. It left them enough in the open, while providing cover if cover proved necessary. If he had a choice, he wanted to deal with their friends one at a time.

"You're supposed to be appreciating the detail work on the stones."

Gillian swallowed a little ball of fear. "The carved arches and facades are classic Mayan architecture. The Puuc construction is recognizable in the finely cut stone."

"Very good," Trace murmured. He saw one of the men slip into the quadrangle. Just one, he thought. So they had, as he'd hoped, spread out to find her. Turning, he pressed her against a column and ran his hands down her body.

"What are you—?"

"I'm making a lewd suggestion," he said softly as he leaned close to her ear. "Understand?"

"Yes." It was the signal for her to act, but she found herself frozen. His body was hard and hot and, for reasons she didn't want to dissect, made her feel safe.

"A very lewd suggestion, Gillian," Trace repeated. "It has something to do with you and me naked in a twenty-five-gallon tub of whipped cream."

"That's not lewd, that's pathetic." But she sucked in a deep breath. "You filthy-minded swine." Putting her heart into it, Gillian swung back and brought her palm hard—a bit harder than necessary—across his face. She shoved him away and made a production of smoothing her hair. "Just because I agreed to an afternoon's drive doesn't mean I intend to spend the night playing your revolting games."

Eyes narrowed, Trace ran a hand over his cheek. She packed a punch, but they'd discuss that later. "That's fine, sweetheart. Now why don't you find your own way back to Mérida? I've got better things to do than to waste my time on some skinny broad with no imagination." Swinging around, he left her alone. He passed the man who stood three yards away, ostensibly studying an arch.

Gillian had to bite her tongue to keep herself from calling Trace back. He'd asked her if she had guts, and now she was forced to admit she didn't have as many as she'd hoped. Her hands trembled as she cupped her elbows. It didn't take long.

"Are you all right, miss?"

This was it. She had no trouble recognizing the voice from her brother's tape. Gillian turned around, hoping her overbright eyes and unsteady voice would be taken as indignation. "Yes, thank you."

He was dark, and not much taller than herself, with olive skin and a surprisingly kind face. She forced herself to smile. "I'm afraid my companion wasn't as interested in Mayan architecture as he pretended."

"Perhaps I could offer you a ride back."

"No, that's kind of you, but—" She broke off when she felt the prick of a knife at her side, just above her waist.

"I believe it would be for the best, Dr. Fitzpatrick."

She didn't have to feign terror, but even as her mind threatened to freeze with it, Gillian remembered her instructions. Stall. Stall as long as possible so that Trace could even the odds.

"I don't understand."

"It will all be explained. Your brother sends his best."

"Flynn." Regardless of the knife, Gillian reached out and grabbed the man's shirt. "You have Flynn and Caitlin. Tell me if they're all right. Please."

"Your brother and niece are in good health and will remain so as long as we have cooperation." He put his left arm around her shoulders and began to walk.

"I'll give you whatever you want if you promise not to hurt them. I have some money. How much—?"

"We're not interested in money." The knife urged her forward. However kind his face had been, the hand on the knife was merciless. "There is a matter of the missing experiments and the notes."

"I'll give them to you. I have them right here." She

gripped the strap of her bag. "Please don't hurt me, or my family."

"It's to your advantage that you are more easily persuaded than your brother."

"Where is Flynn? Please, tell me where you're holding him."

"You'll be with him soon enough."

Trace found the second man behind the Governor's Palace. He strolled by, clicking his camera, then pressed the man's face into one of the twenty thousand intricately carved stones.

"Fascinating stuff, isn't it?" He had his hand around the man's neck in what would look like a brotherly embrace. They both knew it would take only a jerk to break bone. "If you want to keep the use of your right arm, don't look around. Let's make this quick while we've got some privacy. Where are you holding Flynn Fitzpatrick?"

"I don't know a Flynn Fitzpatrick."

Trace hitched the man's arm up another quarter inch. He could hear bone grinding against bone. "You're wasting my time." After a quick look around, Trace pulled out his hunting knife and placed the blade where ear met skull. "Ever heard of van Gogh? It only takes a few seconds to remove an ear. It won't kill you—unless you bleed to death. Now, once more—Flynn Fitzpatrick."

"We weren't told where he was taken." The blade nipped into flesh. "I swear it! Our instructions were to take him and the girl to the airport and turn them over. We were sent back for the woman, his sister."

"And your instructions for her?"

"A private plane at the airport in Cancun. We were not told of the final destination."

"Who killed Forrester?"

"Abdul."

Because time was pressing, Trace had to forgo the pleasure of making the man suffer. "Go to sleep," he said simply, and rammed his head into the stone.

Where was Trace? Gillian thought as she approached a small white compact. If he didn't come soon, she and the altered notes would be on their way to... She didn't even know where.

"Please, tell me where you're taking me." She stumbled, and the knife slashed through the cotton of her blouse to flesh. "I feel faint. I need a moment." When she leaned heavily against the hood of the car, the man relaxed enough to draw the knife away from her side.

"You can rest in the car."

"I'm going to be sick."

He made a sound of disgust and pulled her upright by the hair. Trace's fist sent him reeling back three feet. "She may be a bit of a bitch," he said mildly, "but I can't stand to see a woman manhandled. Look, honey, I just wanted to get you naked. No rough stuff."

Gillian let the bag slip out of her hands and fled.

"That's a woman for you. No appreciation." Trace shot the man, whose mouth was spurting blood, a grin. "Better luck next time."

The man swore. Trace knew enough Arabic to catch the drift. When a knife was drawn, he was ready. He wanted badly to pull out his own, to go head-to-head with this man he knew had killed his closest friend. But it wasn't the time, and it wasn't the place. He wanted not only the instrument, but also the man who'd given

the order. Keeping his gaze locked on the blade, Trace
lifted both hands and backed off.

"Listen, you want her that bad, she's all yours. One
woman's the same as another as far as I'm concerned."
When the man spit at his feet, Trace bent down as if to
wipe off his shoe. He came up with a nickel-plated .45
automatic. "Abdul, isn't it?" The half-amused light in
his eyes had become deadly. "I've already taken care
of your two friends. The only reason I'm not going to
put a hole in your head is that I want you to take a message to your boss. Tell him Il Gatto's going to pay him
a visit." Trace saw the quick widening of the dark eyes
and grinned. "You recognize the name. That's good.
Because I want you to know who kills you. Deliver the
message, Abdul, and put your affairs in order. You don't
have very long."

Abdul still had the knife in his hand, but he was
aware that a bullet was faster than a blade. He was also
aware that Il Gatto was quicker than most. "Il Gatto's
luck will run out, the same as his master's."

Trace leveled the gun to a point just under Abdul's
chin. "Yeah, but yours is ticking away right this minute. My finger's starting to sweat, Abdul. You'd better move."

He waited until the man had gotten behind the wheel
and driven off before he lowered the gun. It had been
close, Trace realized as he slipped the gun back into the
holster strapped to his calf. He'd nearly taken his revenge there and then. Trace straightened again. When
his blood was cool and his mind clear, revenge would
be that much sweeter.

He spun quickly when he heard footsteps behind.

Gillian had seen that look before—when she'd told

him that Forrester had been murdered. She thought she'd seen it again when her head had been jerked up by the hair. But even now, though she was seeing it for the third time, her skin prickled cold.

"I thought I told you to stay with a crowd."

"I saw," she began, then walked over to pick up her bag. It would sound foolish to say she'd stayed close in case he'd needed her help. "I didn't know you had a gun."

"You figure I was going to get your brother out with fast talk and a charming smile?"

"No." She couldn't meet his eyes now. She'd disliked but at least understood the world-weary, slightly grungy man she'd first met. She'd nearly liked and again had understood the cocky, smart-mouthed man she'd breakfasted with. But this one, this hard-eyed stranger who carried death within easy reach, she didn't understand at all. "Did you...the other two men, did you..."

"Kill them?" He said the word simply as he took her arm and led her back to the Jeep. He'd seen both fear and revulsion in her eyes. "No, sometimes it's better to leave people alive, especially when you know what's left of that life is going to be hell. I didn't get a lot out of either of them. They dropped your brother and the kid at the airport and were sent out for you. They didn't know where he was being held."

"How do you know they were telling you the truth?"

"Because these guys are the bottom of the food chain. They haven't got the brains to lie, especially when they know you'll slice off little pieces of their bodies."

The adrenaline washed out of her. "God, then how are we going to find him?"

"I've got some leads. And the word is *I*, not *we*. As soon as I find a safe house for you, you're going under."

"You're mistaken." She stopped in front of the Jeep. Her face was beaded with sweat but no longer pale.

"Sure, we'll discuss it later. Right now, I want a drink."

"And as long as you're working for me you'll drink in moderation."

He swore, but more good-naturedly than she'd expected. "Name ten Irishmen you know who drink in moderation."

"You, for one." She turned to walk around to her side of the Jeep when he swore again and grabbed her. She was about to snap at him when he pulled her shirt loose from the waistband of her slacks. "What the hell do you think you're doing?"

"You're bleeding." Before she could protest, he'd yanked her slacks down enough to expose her hipbone. The cut wasn't very deep, but it was rather long. Blood had seeped through to stain her shirt. For an instant— and an instant was often too long—the dull red haze of fury clouded his vision. "Why didn't you tell me he'd hurt you?"

"I didn't realize." She bent to examine the wound clinically. "I was trying to slow him down and stumbled. He gave me a jab, I guess for incentive. It isn't serious. Nearly stopped bleeding."

"Shut up." It didn't seem to matter at the moment that the cut was shallow. It was her skin, her blood. Trace half lifted her into the Jeep, then popped open the glove compartment. "Just be still," he ordered as he broke open a first-aid kit. "I told you not to take any chances, damn it."

"I only— For heaven's sake, that hurts worse than the cut. Will you stop fussing?"

"I'm cleaning it, damn it, and you're going to shut up." He worked quickly, and none too gently, until she was cleaned and bandaged.

"Congratulations, Doctor," she said dryly, and only smiled when he lifted angry eyes. "I never expected a man like you to get so flustered at the sight of a little blood. As a matter of fact, I would have taken bets that—"

She was cut off quickly and completely when his mouth covered hers. Stunned, she didn't move a muscle as his hands came to her throat and passed up into her hair. This was the promise, or the threat, she had glimpsed from the top of the pyramid.

His mouth, hard and hungry, didn't gently persuade, but firmly, unarguably possessed. The independence that was an innate part of her might have protested, but the need, the desire, the delight, overlapped and won.

He didn't know why in hell he'd started this. It seemed his mouth had been on hers before he'd even thought of it. It had just been. He'd been frightened when he'd seen her blood. And he wasn't used to being frightened—not for someone else. He'd wanted to stroke and soothe, and he'd fought that foolishness back with rough hands and orders.

But, damn it, why was he kissing her? Then her lips parted beneath his and he didn't ask any longer.

She tasted as she smelled, of meadows and wildflowers and early sunlight on cool morning dew. There was nothing exotic here, everything was soft and real. Home... Why was it she tasted of home and made him long for it as much as he did for her?

What he'd felt at the top of the pyramid came back a hundredfold. Fascination, sweetness, bewilderment.

He coated them all with a hard-edged passion he understood.

She didn't cringe from it. She lifted a hand to his face. The echo of her heartbeat was so loud in her head that she could hear nothing else. His kiss was so demanding, she could feel nothing else. When he drew away as abruptly as he had come to her, she blinked until her blurred vision cleared.

He was going to have to get rid of her, and fast, Trace thought as he stuck unsteady hands in his pockets. "I told you to shut up," he said briefly, and strode around the Jeep.

Gillian opened her mouth, then shut it again. Perhaps, until she could think clearly, she'd take his advice.

Chapter 3

Trace nursed a beer. He figured that if Abdul was smart the message would be delivered to the right people before nightfall. He intended to be out of Mexico in an hour. He gave a brief thought to warm Caribbean waters and lazy snorkeling, then picked up the phone.

"Make yourself useful and pack, will you, sweetheart?"

She turned from the window. "The name is Gillian."

"Yeah, well, toss the stuff in the suitcase. We're going to check out as soon as—Rory? Well, so how the devil are you? It's Colin."

Gillian's brows went up. In mid-sentence his voice had changed from a lazy American drawl to a musical Irish brogue. Colin, was it? she thought, folding her arms.

"Aye. No, I'm fit. Right as rain. How's Bridget? Not again. My God, Rory, do the two of you plan to populate Ireland by yourselves?" As he listened, Trace glanced up long enough to give her a mild look and gestured toward the bureau. With more noise than grace, Gillian began yanking out his clothes.

"I'm glad to hear it. No, I don't know when I might be back. No, no trouble, nothing to speak of, in any case, but I wondered if you'd do me a favor." He watched Gillian heap his clothes into the suitcase and took a pull on the beer. "I'm grateful. There was a plane, probably private, that left the airport in Cork ten days ago. I don't want you to ask who was on board or why. Understand? That's a lad. Just nose around and see if you can find out the destination. Lacking that, find out how many miles she was fueled for and where she might have put down to be refueled. I'll take it from there… Important enough," he went on after a pause, "but nothing you should take risks for… No." And this time he laughed. "Nothing to do with the IRA. It's more of a personal matter. No, I'm traveling. I'll get back to you. Kiss Bridget for me, but try to keep it at that. I don't want to be responsible for another baby."

He hung up and looked at the twisted, mangled clothes in his suitcase. "Nice job."

"And what was that all about… Colin?"

"That was about finding out where your brother is. You'd better toss whatever you want to keep in there, too. We'll deal with getting you another suitcase later." He was up and stuffing his snorkeling gear into a tote.

"Why the accent and the false name? It sounded to me as though that man was your friend."

"He is." Trace went to gather up the things in the bath.

"If he's your friend," Gillian insisted as she tailed behind him, "why doesn't he know who you are?"

Trace glanced up and caught his own reflection in the

mirror. His own face, his own eyes. Why was it that too often he didn't recognise himself? He dumped toothpaste and a bottle of aspirin into a travel kit. "I don't use my name when I'm working."

"You checked in as Trace O'Hurley."

"I'm on vacation."

"If he's your friend, why do you lie to him?"

He picked up his razor and examined the blade very carefully before he dropped it in the case. "He was a kid mixed up in a bad situation a few years ago. Gunrunning."

"That's what you meant by the IRA?"

"You know, Doc, you ask too many questions."

"I'm trusting the most precious things in my life to you. I'll ask questions."

He zipped the travel kit in one impatient movement. "I was on assignment when I ran into him, and I was using the name Colin Sweeney."

"He must be a very good friend to agree to do you this kind of a favor without any questions."

Trace had saved his life, but he didn't want to think about that. He'd saved lives, and he'd taken them. He didn't want to think about either at the moment. "That's right. Now can we finish packing and get out of here before someone pays us a visit?"

"I have another question."

He let out a little laugh. "Am I surprised?"

"What was the name you gave that man this afternoon?"

"Just a nickname I picked up a few years back in Italy." He stepped forward, but she didn't move away from the door.

"Why did you give it to him?"

"Because I wanted whoever gives the orders to know who was coming for him." Brushing past her, he dumped the rest of his things into the suitcase and snapped it shut. "Let's go."

"What does it mean?"

He walked to the door and opened it before turning back to her. There was a look in his eyes that both frightened and fascinated. "Cat. Just cat."

He'd known some day he would go back to the States. There had been times in a jungle, or a desert or a grimy hotel room in a town even God had forgotten when he'd imagined it: the prodigal son returns, brass band included. But that was the theatrical blood in him.

Other times he'd imagined slipping quietly into the country, the way he'd slipped out a million years before.

There were his sisters. At the oddest times he would think of them, want to be with them so badly he'd book a flight. Then he'd cancel it at the last minute. They were grown women now, with lives of their own, and yet he remembered them as they'd been the first time he'd seen them. Three scrawny infants, born in one surprising rush, nestled in incubators behind a glass nursery wall.

There had been a bond between them, as he supposed was natural between triplets, and yet he'd never felt excluded. They'd traveled together from the time they'd been born until he'd stuck out his thumb on a highway outside Terre Haute.

He'd seen them only once since then, but he'd kept track. Just as he'd kept track of his parents.

The O'Hurleys had never been the huge commercial success his father had dreamed of, but they'd gotten by. They were booked an average of thirty weeks of the year. Financially they were solvent. That was his mother's doing. She'd always had a knack for making five dollars stretch into ten.

It was Molly, he was certain, who had tucked a hundred dollars in fives and tens into the pocket of his suitcase a dozen years before. She'd known he was going. She hadn't wept or lectured or pleaded, but she had done what she could to make it easier for him. That was her way.

But Pop... Trace closed his eyes as the plane shuddered a bit with turbulence. Pop had never, would never, forgive him—not for leaving without a word, but for leaving.

He'd never understood Trace's need to find something of his own, to look for something other than the next audience, the next arrangement. Perhaps in truth he'd never been able to understand his son at all, or in understanding, hadn't been able to accept.

The only time Trace had gone back, hoping perhaps to mend a small portion of his fences, Frank had greeted him with tight-lipped disapproval.

"So you've come back." Frank had stood icily rigid in the tiny dressing room he'd shared with Molly. Trace hadn't known that his presence had made Frank see it for what it was. A dim little room in a second-rate club. "Three years since you walked out, and only a letter now and again. I told you when you left, there'd be no fatted calf for you."

"I didn't expect one." But he'd hoped for some understanding. Trace had worn a beard then, part of an affectation he'd grown for an assignment. The assignment had taken him to Paris, where he'd successfully broken up an international art fraud. "Since it was Mom's birthday, I thought... I wanted to see her." And you— but he couldn't say it.

"Then run off again so she can shed more tears?"

"She understood why I left," Trace had said carefully.

"You broke her heart." And mine. "You're not going to hurt her again. You're either a son to her, or you're not."

"Either the son you want me to be, or nothing," Trace had corrected, pacing the cramped little room. "It still doesn't matter to you what I need or feel, or what I am."

"You don't know what matters to me. I think you never did." Frank had to swallow the obstruction in his throat that was part bitterness and part shame. "The last time I saw you, you told me what I'd done for you hadn't been good enough. That what I could give you never would be. A man doesn't forget hearing that from his son."

He was twenty-three. He'd slept with a whore in Bangkok and gotten roaring drunk on ouzo in Athens, and he had eight stitches in his right shoulder from a knife wielded by a man he'd killed while serving his country. Yet at that moment he felt like a child being scolded without justice or cause.

"I guess that's the only thing I ever said to you that you really heard. Nothing's changed here. It never will."

"You've chosen your way, Trace." His son had no way of knowing that Frank wanted nothing more than to open his arms and take back what he'd thought he'd lost forever. And was afraid Trace would only turn away. "Now you'll have to make the best of it. At least have the decency to say goodbye to your mother and sisters this time."

It had been Frank, his eyes blurred with tears, who

had turned away. Trace had walked out of the dressing room and had never gone back.

He opened his eyes now to find Gillian watching him steadily. She looked different with the short, dark wig he'd made her wear. But she'd stopped complaining about it—and the horn-rimmed glasses and drab, dun-colored dress. It was padded to make her look frumpy, but he couldn't quite get his mind off what was hidden underneath. In any case, she'd blend into the scenery, which was just what he wanted.

No one would mistake the woman sitting beside him for the spectacular-looking Doctor Gillian Fitzpatrick.

He'd switched planes and airlines in San Diego, charging the tickets to a credit card under one of his cover names. After rerouting in Dallas, he'd picked up the fielder's cap and sideline jacket he was wearing. Now, as they headed into Chicago, they looked like a couple of dazed, weary tourists who wouldn't rate a second glance.

Except he could see her eyes, those deep, dark, intense green eyes through the clear lenses.

"Problem?" he asked.

"I was going to ask you the same thing. You know, you've been brooding ever since we boarded."

He pulled out a cigarette and played with it. "I don't know what you're talking about."

"I'm talking about the fact that you're ready to bite my head off if I so much as say pass the salt. I'm wearing this hideous wig, aren't I? And this very fashionable dress."

"Looks great."

"Then if you're not upset about my disguise, what is it?"

"Nothing's wrong with me," he said between his teeth. "Now back off."

Holding on to her temper, Gillian sipped the white wine she'd been served—with a pitying look from the flight attendant, she thought with some disgust. "There certainly is something wrong with you. I'm the one who should be having an anxiety attack, but I'm not, because we're actually doing something. But if there's a problem... I should be concerned about, I'd appreciate you telling me."

His finger tapped on the armrest between them. "Do you always nag?"

"When it's important. Lives are at stake, lives that mean the world to me. If you're worried about something, then I need to know."

"It's personal." Hoping to dismiss it, he pushed back his seat and closed his eyes.

"Nothing's personal now. How you feel will affect your performance."

He opened one eye. "You'd be the first woman to complain, sister."

She flushed, but didn't let up. "I consider myself your employer, and as such, I refuse to have you keep secrets from me."

He swore at her, quietly but with considerable imagination. "I haven't been back in a while. Even I have memories, and they're my business."

"I'm sorry." She took a deep breath. "I haven't been able to think about anything but Flynn and Caitlin. It never occurred to me that this might be difficult for you." He didn't seem like a man of deep feelings or genuine emotions. But she remembered the pain in his eyes when she'd spoken of Forrester. "Chicago…is it a special place for you?"

"Played Chicago when I was twelve, and again when I was sixteen."

"Played?"

"Nothing." He shook his head and tried to relax. "I spent a few days there with Charlie a few years back. Last thing I saw of the States was O'Hare Airport."

"Now it'll be the first thing you see again." She had a magazine in her lap, but instead of opening it she just ran a thumb along its edge. "I've never seen much of America except New York. I've always meant to. Flynn brought Caitlin to visit a couple of years ago, just after her mother died." She let out a long breath. "They were both like lost souls. We went up the Empire State Building and to Rockefeller Center and had tea at the Plaza. Flynn bought her a little windup dog from a street merchant. She slept with it every night." The emotion came so quickly, she could do nothing to block it. "Oh, God." She pressed both hands to her face. "Oh, God, she's only six."

There hadn't been a woman in his life to comfort in too many years to count, but he hadn't forgotten how. "Take it easy." His voice was soft as he put an arm around her. "They're not going to hurt her. They need your brother's cooperation too much to risk it."

"But what are they doing to her inside? She must be so frightened. The dark— She still can't sleep in the dark. Would they give her a light? Do you think they'd give her a light?"

"Sure they would." His hand stroked her hair just as his voice stroked her fears. "She's going to be fine, Gillian."

Tears ran down her cheeks even as she struggled to

calm herself. "I'm sorry. The last thing I want to do is make a fool of myself."

"Go ahead." His hand ran rhythmically over her shoulder. "I don't mind."

With a watery laugh, she fumbled for a tissue. "I try not to think of her too much. I try to concentrate on Flynn. He's very strong and capable."

"And he's with her. He's taking care of her."

"Aye, they're taking care of each other." God, she needed to believe that. She needed to believe that before long she'd see them, whole and healthy and safe. "We're going to get them out, aren't we?"

There were no promises in this kind of game. He knew that better than most. But she was looking at him now with brimming eyes and such desperate trust that he had no choice. "Sure we are. Didn't Charlie tell you I was the best?"

"He did." She let out a little breath. Control was back, but she didn't have as tight a grip on it as she would have liked. If she didn't think about something else, every minute that passed seemed like an hour. "Tell me about your family. Do you have brothers?"

"No." He drew his arm away, because it would have been entirely too easy to leave it around her. "Sisters."

"How many?"

"Three."

"That must have made life interesting."

"They were okay." His lips curved as he lit a cigarette. "Chantel was the brat."

"Every family has one," she began. Then it hit her, and she sat up straight. "Chantel O'Hurley? Chantel O'Hurley's your sister? I've seen her movies. She's wonderful."

The pride came, more intense than he'd expected. "She's okay. Always leaned toward the dramatic."

"She's the most beautiful woman I've ever seen."

"And knows it."

"Then Maddy O'Hurley's your sister, too." More than a little stunned, Gillian shook her head. "I saw her on Broadway a few months ago. She's very talented. The stage just lights up when she's on it."

It always did, Trace thought. "She's nominated for a Tony."

"She deserves it. Why, the audience nearly brought down the roof when she went into the number at the end of the first act. You should have seen…" Her words trailed off when she realized that he should indeed have seen, but, for reasons yet unknown to her, hadn't. "Your third sister?" she asked, wanting to give him both time and room.

"Abby raises horses in Virginia." He crushed out his cigarette and wondered how he'd ever gotten started on his family.

"Yes, I think I read something about her. She married Dylan Crosby, the writer, recently. There was a write-up in the *Times*. Oh, of course, triplets. Your sisters are triplets."

"I thought scientists would be too busy causing and solving the ills of the world to read gossip columns."

She lifted a brow and decided against taking offense. At least until she'd learned everything she wanted to know. "I don't keep my head buried in a test tube. The article mentioned that they grew up in show business, traveling around the country. Your parents still do. I don't remember reading anything about you."

"I've been gone a long time, remember?"

"But didn't you travel with them?" Intrigued by the idea, she smiled and shifted in her chair. "Did you sing and dance and live out of a trunk?"

"You know, for a doctor, you tend to glamorize the mundane." He felt the slight dip that meant they were starting their descent. "It's like going to the circus and seeing only the spangles and the red lights. Backstage there are elephant paddies up to your ankles."

"So you did travel with them." Gillian continued to smile. "Did you have a speciality?"

"God save me from plane rides with nosy women. I've been out of it for twelve years." He jerked his seat belt on. "I prefer thinking about today."

Gillian clicked her own belt into place. "I wanted to be a singer when I was a little girl. I always pictured myself in the spotlight." With a little sigh, she slipped the magazine back into the pocket of the seat. "Before I knew it, I was my father's lab assistant. Strange, isn't it, how our parents seem to map out our routes even before we're born?"

Charlie's house was behind a five-foot stone wall and was equipped with an elaborate security system. He left behind, as far as Trace knew, only an older sister who lived in Palm Beach and a nephew who ran a brokerage firm somewhere in the Midwest.

Gillian sat in the rented car while Trace pressed a series of buttons on the panel outside the gates. They opened soundlessly. He hadn't spoken since the airport, not once during all the cruising and backtracking, looking for signs of surveillance or a tail. She was holding back her questions now. It was grief that silenced him here, and she knew he'd have to deal with it in his own way.

The trees were fading as winter closed in, but they still held a stubborn touch of color. Wind tore at the leaves and moaned through the branches. The elms would shade the drive in the summer, she thought, giving the old brick house a stately, sturdy feel. It was something she'd barely noticed on her first trip here, and it was something that she tried to concentrate on now.

The house didn't look deserted, but as if it were simply waiting to be occupied again. She thought of the man who had listened to her, who had given her brandy and a sliver of hope.

"He was crazy about this place," Trace murmured. He shut off the engine but sat looking at the two stories of worn brick and white trim. "Whenever he was away, he'd always talk about coming back. I guess he'd have wanted to die here." He sat a moment longer, then pushed open his door. "Let's go."

He had keys. Charlie had given them to him once. "Use them sometime," he'd said. "Everybody has to have a home."

But he hadn't used them, not until now. The key slipped into the lock and turned with a quiet click.

The hallway was dim, but he didn't switch on the lights. He remembered the way well enough, and in truth he didn't yet have the heart to look at anything of Charlie's too closely.

He took her into a library that smelled of lemon and leather. The heat had been turned down because there was no one left to need the warmth. "You can wait here."

"Where are you going?"

"I told you I was coming here to find out where they

took your brother. I'm going to find out, and you're going to wait here."

"And I told you that I'm involved with anything that has to do with Flynn. Besides, I might be able to help."

"If I need a physicist, I'll let you know. Read a book."

"I'm not staying here."

She was two steps behind him when he reached the doorway. "Look, Doc, there's such a thing as national security. I'm already bending the rules because Charlie seemed to think it was worth it."

"Then bend them a little more." She took his arm. "I'm not interested in state secrets and international affairs. All I want is to know where my brother is. I've worked on sensitive projects, Trace. I have clearance."

"You keep interfering with me, it's going to take a lot longer."

"I don't think so."

"Have it your way. But keep your mouth shut for once." He went up the stairs, trying to convince himself he wasn't making a mistake.

The carpet was new since Trace had been there, but the wallpaper was the same. So was the room three doors from the top of the stairs that Charlie had used for an office. Without hesitating, Trace went to the desk and pushed a button under the second drawer. A four-foot span of paneling swung out.

"Another tunnel?" Gillian asked. Her courage was fading fast.

"Workroom," Trace said as he stepped through. He threw a switch and discovered that Charlie had updated his equipment.

Along the top of the far wall were clocks, still running, that gave the time in every zone around the globe.

The computer system spread beneath them, then continued in an L along the next wall. With the radio equipment opposite it, he could have contacted anyone from the local deejay to the Kremlin. "Pull up a stool, Doc. This could take a while."

Gillian jolted only a bit when the panel slid shut behind them. "What are you trying to do?"

"You want to bypass some paperwork, so I'm going to patch into the ISS computer."

"Do you think they know where Flynn was taken?"

"Maybe, maybe not." He switched on the terminal and sat. "But they should have a pretty good idea where Hammer's new headquarters are. Charlie had to go and get state-of-the-art on me." He punched a series of buttons. When the machine requested his code, he gave Charlie's. "Okay, that's a start. Let's see what this baby can do."

He worked in silence, but for the tapping of his fingers and the beeping of the machine, as Gillian looked on. He inched past one security block to ram into the next.

Patience, Gillian noted, more than a little surprised to find he had the quality, as he broke one code and slowly drew out more data. She began to find a rhythm to the numbers and symbols that appeared on the screen, then blinked out again, at Trace's command. As he worked, she began arranging and rearranging the system in her head.

"So damn close," Trace muttered as he tried another series. "The problem is there are enough variables to keep me at it for a week."

"Maybe if you—"

"I work alone."

"I was only going to say that—"

"Why don't you go down to the kitchen and dig up some coffee, sweetheart?"

Her eyes narrowed at the tone, and temper trembled on the tip of her tongue. "Fine." She whirled and faced the closed panel. "I don't know how to open the door."

"Button's on the left. Just put your finger on it and push."

Her mouth opened again, but, all too aware of what might come flying out, she pushed the button.

Typical hardheaded, egocentric male, Gillian decided as she marched down the stairs. Hadn't she lived with one, tried to please one, nearly all of her life? Why had fate decreed that in this, the most important thing she'd ever had to do, she'd be chained to another man who had no use for her opinion.

Make coffee, she thought as she found the kitchen. And if he called her sweetheart one more time, she'd give him what men like him deserved. The back of a woman's hand.

She started the coffee, too incensed to feel uncomfortable with rooting through a dead man's cupboards.

He'd had no business dismissing her. Just as he'd had no business kissing her the way he had. It had felt as if she were being devoured. And yet when it had finished she'd been whole. It had felt as if she'd been drugged. And yet her mind had been clear, her senses sharp.

However she'd felt, however it had finished, she would never be quite the same. She could admit that here, alone, to herself. She was too practical a woman for self-deception. Her feelings were perhaps more easily touched, perhaps more readily given, than she would have preferred, but they were her feelings, and she would never have denied them. She'd enjoyed the feel and taste of Trace's lips on hers. She would remember it for a long time. But she was also an expert on self-discipline. Enjoyable or not, she wouldn't allow it to happen again.

Trace was still working when she came back into the room. Without ceremony, she slammed the coffee cup down next to him. He acknowledged her with a grunt. Gillian took a turn around the room, told herself to keep her mouth shut, then jammed her hands into her pockets.

"Access, number 38537/BAKER. Tabulate access code five. Series ARSS28." Gillian blurted the series out almost like an obscenity. "And if you're not too pigheaded to try it, it may work. If not, switch the first number sequence with the second."

Trace lifted his coffee, pleased she'd left it black, surprised she'd made it well. "And what makes you think you can figure out the access code to one of the most sophisticated computer systems in the free world?"

"Because I've been watching you for the past hour and I do a little hacking as a hobby."

"A little hacking." He drank again. "Broken into any good Swiss bank accounts?"

She crossed the room slowly, almost, Trace thought not without admiration, the way a gunslinger might approach a showdown. "We're talking about my family, remember? Add to that the fact that I'm paying you, and the least you could do is try my suggestion."

"Fine." Willing to humor her to a point, Trace tapped out the sequence she'd recited.

ACCESS DENIED

With only a slight smirk, he gestured toward the screen.

"All right, then, transpose the numbers." Impatient,

she reached around him and began hitting the keys herself. The only thing Trace noticed for a moment was that his shampoo smelled entirely different on her.

REQUEST FILE

"There we are." Pleased with herself, Gillian leaned closer. "It's rather like working out a system for blackjack. A professor and I played around with that last semester."

"Remind me to take you with me the next time I go to Monte Carlo."

They were closer. One step closer. Smiling, she turned her face to his. "What now?"

There wasn't a hint of amber or gray in her eyes. They were pure green and brilliant now. Even as he watched them, they changed, filling with speculation, awareness, memory. "You talking about the computer?"

She needed to swallow badly. "Of course."

"Just checking." Trace turned away again. They both let out a quiet breath. He began typing, and within seconds data came up on the screen.

He moved from screen to screen. After all, he knew quite a bit about Hammer already. He'd been briefed intensely before he'd gone undercover, and had learned more during his stint as a low-level delivery boy. During his assignment, he'd managed to pass along names, places and dates to the ISS, and he'd been on the verge of being transferred to the newly implemented main base before he'd been shot.

Frowning at the screen, he rubbed a thumb over the scar.

But he'd been sedated for days, hanging between life and death. His recovery had taken two months of hospital care. He'd been debriefed, the assignment had been blown and he'd taken off for a long—supposedly peaceful—vacation.

Quite a bit could change in two or three months. Charlie, being Charlie, would have keyed into it.

He breezed by the basic data. Hammer had been founded in the Middle East in the early seventies. With a combination of luck and money, and a complete disregard for life, they had pulled off a number of bombings, taken hostages. The last hijacking the organization had attempted had ended with someone's itchy finger pushing a detonator and blowing eighty-five innocent people and six terrorists to oblivion.

That was their style, he thought. Win some, lose some.

"Husad," Gillian said, honing in on one name as Trace flipped screens. "Isn't he the leader?"

"He's the one with the bucks. Jamar Husad, political outcast, self-proclaimed general and complete lunatic. Come on, Charlie," he muttered at the machine. "Give me something."

"You're hardly looking," she began.

"I already know all this."

"How?"

"I worked for them for six months," he said half to himself.

"You *what*?" She took a step back.

Annoyance flickered in his eyes as he glanced up. "Relax, sweetheart, all for the good of the cause. I infiltrated."

"But if you were inside, then you should know where they would have taken Flynn and Caitlin. Why are we fooling with this computer when—"

"Because they moved. They were just getting set up in the new location when I got taken out."

"Taken out?" Puzzlement veered into horror. "You were shot?"

"Part of the job description."

"You were nearly killed—a scar like that..." She trailed off and laid a hand on his shoulder. "You were nearly killed by those people, but you're doing this."

He shook her hand away. He couldn't afford to let her feelings soften toward him. Then it would be too easy to let his soften toward her. "I got a personal investment here. There's a matter of a hundred thousand— my ticket to paradise."

She curled her fingers into her palm. "Do you expect me to believe you're only doing this for the money?"

"Believe what you like, but keep it to yourself. I've never known anybody who asks so many questions. I'm trying to concentrate. Yeah, yeah," he muttered. "I know they were in Cairo, that's old—

"All *right*. I knew I could count on Charlie." Trace leaned back. "New base of operations: Morocco."

"Morocco? Could they have taken Flynn and Caitlin all that way?"

"They'd want the best security for them. In Morocco, Hammer would have allies close." He continued to flip from screen to screen until he came to the end of the file. "Nothing on your brother here yet." He instructed the computer to print out the pages that interested him, then turned to Gillian. "It would only take a phone call to bring the ISS in on this. I want you to think about it."

She had thought about it, worried about it. "Why didn't Mr. Forrester do that?"

"I've got some ideas."

"But you're not going to tell me what they are."

"Not yet. Like you said, it's your family, you make the choice."

She moved away from him. It was more logical to call the ISS. They were an organization with sophisticated equipment, with manpower, with political clout. And yet... Every instinct told her to go with this one man, the man Charles Forrester had called a renegade. With her hands linked, Gillian turned to him. He still didn't look like a hero. And she was still going with her instincts.

"One hundred thousand, Mr. O'Hurley, and I go with you every step of the way."

"I told you I work alone."

"Perhaps you haven't seen me at my best, but I'm a very strong and capable woman. If I have to, I'll go to Morocco alone."

"You wouldn't last a day."

"Maybe not. Hammer's agents are looking for me. If they find me, they'll take me to my brother. At least that way I'd know he and my niece were all right. I'd rather do it another way."

He stood up to do some pacing himself. She'd slow him down, but not by much. And if she stayed with him, he'd be able to keep an eye on her. He couldn't deny she'd held up in Mexico. If he had to play that kind of game again, he could use her.

"We go together, it doesn't mean we're partners, it means you take orders."

Gillian inclined her head but didn't say anything.

"When the time comes for me to move, you stay out of the way. I won't be able to worry about you then."

"You won't have to worry about me." She took a deep breath. "What do we do now?"

"First I check with Rory." He moved to the phone. "But I have a feeling we're catching a plane."

Chapter 4

Casablanca. Bogart and Bergman. Pirates and intrigue. Foggy airports and sun-washed beaches. The name conjured up images of danger and romance. Gillian was determined to accept the first and avoid the second.

Trace had booked adjoining rooms in one of the more exclusive hotels near United Nations Square. Gillian remained silent while he spoke to the desk clerk in fluent French and was addressed as Monsieur Cabot.

André Cabot was the name on the passport he was using now. He wore a conservative three-piece suit and shoes that had a mirror gleam. His brown-rinsed hair was a bit mussed from the drive, but he'd shaved. He stood differently, too, she noted. Ramrod-straight, as though he'd come through some military academy. Even his personality had changed, she thought as she stood to the side and let him deal with the details of checking in. He'd slipped so effortlessly into the role of the brusque, slightly impatient French businessman, she could almost believe she'd lost Trace O'Hurley along the way and picked up someone else.

For the second time she felt as if she were putting her life into the hands of a stranger.

But the eyes were the same. A little shock passed through her when he turned and looked at her with the dark intensity she recognized but had yet to become accustomed to.

She remained silent as Trace took her arm and led her to a bank of elevators. Gillian still wore the wig, but the glasses were gone and the drab dress was replaced by an elegant silk outfit more suited to the image of Cabot's current mistress. Twenty stories later they were entering their suite and he hadn't said a word. Trace passed bills to the bell man in a slow, methodical fashion that indicated that he was a man who counted his francs.

She expected Cabot to disappear the moment the door was closed, but instead he spoke to her in lightly accented English. "For rooms of this price, the sheets should be threaded with gold."

"What—"

"See if the bar is stocked, *chérie*." He was moving around the room, checking lamps, lifting pictures from the wall. He turned to her only briefly, with a warning glance. "I would prefer a small glass of vermouth before I have the pleasure of undressing your lovely body." He picked up the phone, unscrewed the mouthpiece, and then, after a quick search, fastened it again.

"Would you?" She understood he was staying in character until he was certain there was no surveillance equipment in the rooms. Though it was unnerving, she accepted it. It was only the fact that he'd portrayed his character and hers as lovers that grated. Deciding two could play, she moved to a small wet bar and opened a cabinet door.

"I'm more than happy to fix you a drink, sweetheart." She saw his brow lift as he checked the headboard, then the mattress. "But, as to the rest, I'm a bit tired after the flight."

"Then we'll have to see what can be done to bring your energy back." Satisfied the first room was clean, Trace walked to her. There was a long moment of silence before he accepted the glass she'd poured. "Let's move into the next room," he murmured, then turned and left her to follow. "Perhaps you're not as tired as you think."

As he began the same procedure on the second room, Gillian sat on the bed. "It was a long flight."

"Then you should rest. Let me help you." He lifted a print of the Cathedral of the Sacré Coeur. His hands, long-fingered and sure, ran over the frame and the back. "You'll rest better unconfined."

Gillian slipped out of her shoes to massage her arches. "You seem to have only one thing on your mind."

"A man would be foolish to have more than one thing on his mind once alone with you."

Gillian considered a moment. Perhaps she could grow to like this André Cabot. "Really?" She lifted the glass he'd discarded and sipped from it. "Why?"

He'd come closer to check the headboard. Pausing a moment, he looked at her. There was a grin on her face that said, "I dare you." She should have known better. "Because you have skin like a white rose that grows only warmer and softer when I touch you." His hand brushed her thigh, making her jolt. Trace continued to

check the mattress, but his eyes stayed on hers. "Because your hair is fire and silk, and when I kiss you...
When I kiss you, *ma belle,* your lips are the same."

Her breath caught as he circled his hand around her neck. He leaned closer so that when it was released again it mingled with his. "Because when I touch you like this I can feel how much you want me. Because when I look at you I can see you're afraid."

She couldn't look away. She couldn't move away. "I'm not afraid of you." But she was fascinated. Whoever he was, he fascinated.

"No? You should be."

She didn't notice that his voice had changed, had become his own again, just before his mouth closed over hers. It was the same heat, the same strength, as before. Had it only been once before? she thought as her body went fluid, sliding beneath his onto the bed. Without a thought to reason, without a thought to consequences, she wrapped her arms around him.

Why did it seem so easy? His mouth was hard and hot, his hands were anything but gentle. And yet it seemed so easy to be with him now, so natural. So familiar. Surely his taste was a taste she'd woken to before. If she ran her hands over his back, she knew what muscles she would find. If she drew in a breath so that the scent of him filled her, it would be no surprise.

Perhaps she had known his face for only a matter of days. But there was something here that she had known all her life.

He must be going mad. It was as though she'd always been there for him. Would always be there. The feel of her body beneath his wasn't like that of any other woman. It was like that of the only woman. He knew, somehow, how her sigh would sound before he heard it, how her fingers would feel on his face before she lifted them to touch him.

He knew, he expected, yet it still stunned.

He could feel his pulse speed up until it beat in hundreds of points throughout his body. He could hear his own crazed murmuring of her name as he tore his mouth from hers to let it roam desperately over her face and throat. Then there was the need, growing to a rage inside him that was nothing like the desire he'd felt for other women.

He wanted all of her, mind, body, soul. He wanted her now. He wanted her for a lifetime.

It was that shocking thought that stopped him. There were no guaranteed lifetimes, especially not in the game he'd chosen to play. He'd learned to live for the moment. Tomorrow was up for grabs.

Whatever she was doing to him had to stop—if he wanted to live to collect his hundred thousand.

He ached. He could have hated her for that, but he rolled off her with a carelessness that left her still and speechless. "The room's clean." He picked up the glass to drain the last of the vermouth. And wished it was whiskey.

Her breathing was uneven, and her limbs were unsteady. There was nothing she could do about that, or about the unsated need crawling inside her. But she could hate him. With her whole heart and soul she could hate him.

"You bastard."

"You asked for it, sweetheart." He pulled out a cigarette and focused his mind on what lay ahead, instead of what had lain beneath him only moments before. "I've got some things to do. Why don't you take a nap?"

She came off the bed slowly, with the look in her eye that he'd noted before. It occurred to him that it was fortunate for both of them that his weapons were out of sight and reach.

She'd been humiliated before. She'd been rejected before. But she didn't intend to be either at his hands ever again. "Don't you ever touch me. I'll put up with your crude manners because I have no choice, but don't you ever put your hands on me again."

He wasn't sure why he did it. Anger had a way of urging a man to make a wrong and reckless move. He yanked her against him, even enjoying her fast and furious struggles as he clamped his mouth down on hers again. She was wildfire now, hot, volatile and dangerous. He had an image, steamy and strong, of pulling her to the bed and letting violence feed violence. Before he could top one mistake with another, he let her go.

"I don't take orders, Gillian. Remember that."

Her hands curled into fists. Only the knowledge that she'd lose kept her from landing a blow. "There'll come a time you'll pay for that."

"Probably. Right now, I'm going out. Stay inside."

When the door closed behind him, she had the small satisfaction of cursing him.

He was gone only an hour. Most of Casablanca was as he remembered it. The little shops along the Boulevard Hansali still catered to the tourist trade. The port was still busy with European ships. He had walked through the original Arab town, still surrounded by old rampart walls. But he hadn't gone sightseeing. His contact in the bidonville, the shantytown near the shopping district, had been pleased to see him again, and agreeable enough after an exchange of a few dirham to give birth to a certain rumor about a hijacked shipment of American arms.

Trace arrived back at the hotel, satisfied that the first step had been taken and ready to start the next. The rooms were empty. He didn't panic, not at first. His training was a natural extension of his mind, just as his arm was a natural extension of his body.

After unstrapping his revolver from his calf, he began to search both rooms and baths. The balcony doors were still locked from the inside, though the curtains had been drawn. She'd taken her things out of his suitcase. Trace found them neatly put away in closets and drawers. The cosmetics she'd bought to replace those she'd lost stood on the counter in the bath. There were bath salts the color of sea foam, and a short cotton robe shades darker hanging on the back of the door.

Her purse was gone, and so were the notes inside it. The drumming at the back of his neck, slow and steady, was growing louder.

There was no sign of a struggle. It was hard for him to believe that a woman like Gillian would have submitted to anyone without a fight. It was just as difficult for him to believe that anyone could have traced them so quickly.

So where the hell was she? Trace thought as he felt the first twinges of panic. He ran a hand through his hair and tried to think calmly. If they had her… If they had her, then he would…

He couldn't think calmly when he kept seeing how Abdul had dragged her up by the hair. He couldn't think calmly when he remembered how her blood had felt on his hands.

When he heard the key in the lock, he whirled. It took only an instant to pull back control. Before the knob turned, he was behind the door, gun pointed up, body tensed. As the door opened, he grabbed a wrist. And yanked Gillian inside. Both of them received a shock when he dragged her into his arms.

"Damn it, where were you? Are you all right?"

She'd drawn in her breath to scream. The collision with Trace had knocked the air out of her again. She managed to nod, and then, feeling the tension in his body, she soothed him automatically.

"I'm fine." She ran a hand over his back. "Did something happen? I was only gone a few minutes."

And in a few minutes his imagination had worked at top speed. Trace cursed himself, then her. "I told you to stay inside. What the hell's wrong with you?" Furious with himself, he shoved her away. "I don't have time to babysit, damn it. When I give an order, you're to follow it."

To think she'd felt a flow of concern, Gillian thought, berating herself. She'd even felt a warmth at what she'd thought was his concern for her. Both those emotions froze quickly enough. "I hired you to find my brother, not to spend every spare moment shouting at me."

"If you'd show some sense, I wouldn't have to shout at you. You've been cut once, sweetheart." He could only hope the memory of that would shake her as much as it did him. "Keep this up and I might not be around next time to make sure it's not any worse than that."

"You're not my bodyguard. In any case, you're the

one who went off without telling me where you were going or how long you'd be."

He didn't care to be reminded why he'd left so abruptly. "Listen, sister, the only reason you're here with me is because I might be able to use you to get your brother out. You won't be of much use if they've already got you."

"No one has me," she tossed back as she hurled her purse on the bed. "I'm here, aren't I?"

He hated to argue with logic. "I told you to stay inside. If you can't do what you're told, you're going to find yourself on the first plane back to New York."

"I go where I want, when I want." She planted her feet and almost hoped he'd try to put his hands on her again. "But, for your information, I did stay inside."

"That's strange. I could have sworn I pulled you into the room a few minutes ago."

"That you did, and nearly dislocated my shoulder in the process." She yanked a small bottle out of the bag she carried. "Aspirin, O'Hurley. There's a gift shop off the lobby downstairs, and I had a headache. Now, if you'll excuse me, I think I'm about ready to take the whole bottle." She stormed across the room. The bathroom door shut with a resounding slam.

Women, Trace thought as he strode into the adjoining room. He rarely thought they were more trouble than they were worth, but he was making an exception in Gillian's case.

After nearly a dozen years of fieldwork, he was still alive. And that was why he was considering retiring more and more seriously. The law of averages was against him. He was a man who believed in fate and believed in luck just as passionately. Sooner or later luck ran out. As it had for Charlie.

Lighting a cigarette, he stood at the window and looked out at Casablanca. The last time he'd been here it had had to do with smuggling. He'd nearly gotten his throat cut, but luck had still been with him. He'd been Cabot then, as well, the French businessman who didn't mind a shady—if profitable—deal.

His cover would hold. The ISS had invented it with the meticulousness they were best at. His nerve would hold, as long as he remembered that the woman in the next room was a means to an end and nothing more.

He heard the water running in Gillian's bath and checked his watch. He'd give her an hour to stew. Then they had business to attend to.

Gillian's temper wasn't the kind that flashed quickly and vanished. She knew how to hold it off, and how to nurse it along when it suited her. At the moment, she was reaping enormous satisfaction from keeping herself on the edge of fury. It gave her energy and blocked her fear.

She told herself she wasn't the least bit concerned about what was going on in the room next door as she changed into a simple blouse and skirt.

He probably intended to make her stay locked up in her room, eating a solitary dinner from room service. She attached a wide leather belt almost as if it were a holster. She'd be damned if she'd hole up here like a mouse. She might not be sure what she could do to help with Flynn's and Caitlin's release, but there had to be something. Trace O'Hurley was going to have to accept the fact that she was part of this thing. Starting now.

She moved to the door that joined the rooms and nearly ran into him.

"I was just coming in to see if you'd stopped sulking."

Her chin angled. "I never sulk."

"Sure you do, but since you've apparently finished we can go."

She opened her mouth, then shut it again. He'd said *we.* "Where?"

"To see a friend of mine." Eyes narrowed, he backed up to look at her. "Is that what you're wearing?"

Her automatic response was to look down at the wide circle skirt and blouse. "What's wrong with it?"

"Nothing, if you're going to tea at the rectory." While she sputtered and slapped at his hand, Trace unfastened two more buttons. He stood back, frowned, then nodded. "Helps a little."

"I've no desire to display myself for your benefit."

"Personally, I don't give a damn if you wear a cardboard box, but you've got a role to play. Don't you have any gaudy earrings?"

"No."

"Then we'll get some. And darker lipstick," he muttered before he stepped back. "Can you do anything with your eyes?"

"My eyes? What's wrong with my eyes?" Natural feminine vanity began to war with bafflement as Trace strode into her bath.

"Cabot's woman hasn't come straight out of a convent, know what I mean?" As he began to root through her cosmetics, she shoved him aside.

"No. Just what do you mean?"

"I mean you need a little more paint, a little more cleavage and a little less breeding." He picked up a smoky green eye shadow, examined it, then held it out. "Here, try for tart, will you?"

"Tart?" The word came out of her mouth with beautiful Irish indignation. "Tart, is it? Do you really believe I'd paint myself up so you can display me like a...like a..."

"Bimbo is what I had in mind. A nice-looking, empty-headed bimbo." He picked up her scent and gave the atomizer a squeeze. It smelled warmer on her skin, he thought, and he quickly pulled himself back. "This is drawing room stuff. Is this the only perfume you have?"

She unclenched her teeth only because it hurt to keep them clamped together. "It is."

"It'll have to do, then," he decided and sprayed it at her. "The hair, Doc."

She touched a hand to her wig almost protectively. "What's wrong with it?"

"Mess it up. The guy I'm going to see would expect me to travel with a pretty, empty-headed and very sexy woman. That's Cabot's style."

This time her eyes narrowed. "Oh, it is, is it?"

"Right. And you have to look the part. Don't you have anything slinky?"

"No, I don't have anything slinky." Her lower lip moved into a pout as she turned to look at herself in the mirror. "I wasn't coming on this trip to socialize."

"I've never known a woman not to have something slinky."

If looks really could have killed, he would have dropped like a stone. "You've never known this one."

Taking it in stride, Trace reached for her blouse again. "Well, maybe one more button."

"No." She pulled her blouse together. "I'm not parading around half dressed so you can keep up your image."

Teeth gritted, she snatched the eye shadow from him. "Go away. I don't want you hovering over me."

"Five minutes," he told her, and with his hands in his pockets he strolled out of the bath.

She took ten, but he decided not to quibble. Anger had brought on a flush that she'd added to with blusher. She'd used shadow and liner liberally so that her eyes were big as saucers and had that heavy bedroom look.

He'd wanted flamboyant, and she'd delivered. For the life of him, he couldn't figure out why it made him angry.

"Cheap enough for you, Monsieur Cabot?"

"It'll do," he said, already at the door. "Let's go."

She felt like a fool, and as far as she was concerned she looked the part. Still, she had to remind herself she wasn't being left behind to worry and fret while Trace went about the business of finding Flynn. Drawing a breath, Gillian told herself that if she was playing a part she should play it well.

As they stepped out of the hotel, Gillian tucked her arm through his and leaned against him. He gave her a quick, wary look that had her smiling. "Am I supposed to be crazy about you?"

"About my money, anyway."

"Oh, are you rich?"

"Loaded."

She looked over her shoulder as she stepped into a cab. "Then why don't I have any jewelry?"

A smart aleck, he thought, and wished he didn't like her better for it. He put his hand firmly on her bottom. "You haven't earned it yet, sweetheart."

The makeup couldn't disguise the fire and challenge that leaped into her eyes. Because he'd gotten the last word, he felt a great deal better as he settled into the cab beside her. He gave the driver an address, then turned to her. "Speak any French?"

"Only enough to know whether I'm ordering calf's brains or chicken in a restaurant."

"Just as well. Keep your mouth shut and let me do the talking. You're not supposed to be too bright, in any case."

He was telling her to keep her mouth shut too often for her taste. "I've already deduced that your taste in women runs to the type in men's magazines. Glossy and two-dimensional."

"As long as they don't talk back. If you have to say anything, ditch the Irish. You've lived in New York long enough to have picked up the tone."

They were driving out of the section of the city marked by hotels and large, modern shops. Inland from the port and harbor was the old medina, the original Arab town, enclosed by walls and mazed with narrow streets. At any other time, it would have fascinated her. She would have wanted to get out and look, smell, touch. Now it was only a place where a clue might be found.

Trace—or Cabot, as Gillian was training herself to think of him—paid off the cab. She stepped out to look at the hodgepodge of little shops and the mix of tourists they catered to.

The charm was there, the age, the Arab flavor. Exotic colors, open bazaars, men in robes. The avenue was shaded, the shop windows were crammed with souvenirs and silks and local crafts. The women she saw were for the most part European, unveiled and trousered. The wind was mild and carried the scents of the water, of spice, and of garbage left too long.

"It's so different." With her arm tucked through Trace's again, she began to walk. "You read about such places, but it's nothing like seeing them. It's so…exotic."

He thought of the bidonville he'd visited that afternoon, the squatters' shacks, the squalor hardly a stone's throw away from charming streets and neat shops. A slum was a slum, whatever the language or culture.

"We're going in here." Trace stopped in front of a jeweler's with gold and silver and brightly polished gems in the window. "Smile and look stupid."

Gillian lifted a brow. "I'm not sure I'm that talented, but I'll do my best."

The bells on the door of the shop jingled when it opened. Behind the counter was a man with a face like a burnt almond and hair growing white in patches. He glanced up, and recognition came quickly into his eyes before he went back to the customers bargaining over a bracelet. Trace simply linked his hands behind his back and studied the wares in a display case.

The shop was hardly more than ten feet by twelve, with a backroom closed off by a beaded curtain. There was music playing, something with pipes and flutes that made Gillian think of a tune shepherds might play to their flocks. The scent in here was all spice—cloves and ginger—and a paddle fan lazily twirled the air around and around.

The floor was wooden and scarred. Though the jewelry gleamed, most of the glass was dull and finger-marked. Remembering her role, Gillian toyed with necklaces of blue and red beads. She sighed, thinking how delighted little Caitlin would be with a few strands.

"Bon soir." His transaction completed, the shop-keeper cupped one hand in the other. "It's been a long time, old friend," he continued in French. "I did not expect to see you in my shop again."

"I could hardly come back to Casablanca without dropping in on an old and valued friend, al-Aziz."

The shopkeeper inclined his head, already wondering if a profit could be made. "You have come on business?"

"A little business…" Then he indicated Gillian by turning his palm upward. "A little pleasure."

"Your taste is excellent, as always."

"She's pretty," Trace said carelessly. "And not smart enough to ask too many questions."

"You would purchase her a bauble?"

"Perhaps. I also have a commodity to sell."

Annoyed with being shut out of the conversation, Gillian moved to Trace. She twined an arm around his neck, hoping the pose was sexy enough. She tried for the clipped New York accent of her assistant at the institute. "I might as well have stayed back at the hotel if you're going to speak in French all night."

"A thousand pardons, *mademoiselle*," al-Aziz said in precise English.

"No need to apologize," Trace told him after giving Gillian's cheek a light, intimate pat. The trace of Ireland was still there, but he doubted anyone who wasn't listening for it would have noticed. "There now, *chérie*, pick yourself out something pretty."

She wanted, quite badly, to spit in his eye, but she fluttered hers instead. "Oh, André, anything?"

"But of course, whatever you like."

She'd make it good, Gillian decided as she bent over

the display counter like a child in an ice cream parlor. Good and expensive.

"We can speak freely, *mon ami*," Trace went on. He too rested against the counter, but he moved his hands quickly, competently, then folded them together on the glass top. "My companion understands no French. I assume you're still...well connected."

"I am a fortunate man."

"You'll remember a few years ago we made a deal that was mutually profitable. I'm here to propose another."

"I am always happy to discuss business."

"I have a similar shipment. Something that was liberated from our capitalist friends. I find the shipment, shall we say, too volatile to store for any length of time. My sources indicate that a certain organization has relocated in Morocco. This organization might be interested in the supplies I can offer—at the going market rate, of course."

"Of course. You are aware that the organization you speak of is as volatile as the supplies you wish to sell?"

"It matters little to me, if the profit margin is agreeable. Are you interested in setting up the negotiations?"

"For the standard ten-percent commission?"

"Naturally."

"It's possible I can help you. Two days. Where can I reach you?"

"I'll reach you, al-Aziz." He smiled and ran a fingertip along the side of his jaw. It was a trait peculiar to Cabot. "There is a rumor I find interesting. A certain scientist is, let us say, employed, by this organization. If I had more information about him, the profit could very well increase, by perhaps twenty percent."

Al-Aziz's face was as bland as his voice. "Rumors are unreliable."

"But simple enough to substantiate." Trace drew out a money clip and extracted some bills. They disappeared like magic into the folds of al-Aziz's cloak.

"Such things are rarely impossible."

"Oh, darling, can I have these?" Gillian grabbed Trace's arm and drew him over to a pair of long gold earrings crusted with red stones. "Rubies," she said with a long, liquid sigh, knowing perfectly well they were colored glass. "Everyone at home will simply die of envy. Please, darling, can I have them?"

"Eighteen hundred dirham," the shopkeeper said with a complacent smile. "For you and the lady, sixteen hundred."

"Please, sweetheart. I just adore them."

Trapped in his own game, Trace nodded to al-Aziz. But he also managed to pinch Gillian hard as the shopkeeper drew the earrings out of their case.

"Oh, I'll wear them now." Gillian began to fasten them on as Trace took more bills from his clip.

"Two days," Trace added in French. "I'll be back."

"Bring your lady." The shopkeeper's face creased with a smile. "I can use the business."

Trace steered her out to the street. "You could have picked out some glass beads."

Gillian touched a fingertip to one earring and sent it spinning. "A woman like me would never be satisfied with glass beads, but would probably be foolish enough to believe paste was rubies. I wanted to do a good job."

"Yeah." The earrings glittered with a lot more style on her than they had in the case. "You did okay."

With a hand on his arm, Gillian pulled up short.

"Wait a minute. I'm nearly breathless after that compliment."

"Keep it up."

"There, that's better. Now are you going to tell me what that was all about?"

"Let's take a walk."

Chapter 5

At least she wasn't cooped up in a hotel room. Gillian tried to comfort herself with that as she sat in a noisy club that was fogged with smoke and vibrating with recorded music. Nursing a glass of wine, she sat observing the life around her. The clientele was young, and again mostly European. Though her traveling had been limited by her work, Gillian thought you could have found an almost identical place in London or Paris.

It occurred to her that she'd seen more of the world in the past two weeks than she had in all her life. Under other circumstances she might have enjoyed the noise and confusion, the edgy party atmosphere. Instead, she leaned closer to Trace.

"You have to tell me what was said, what's being done."

He'd chosen the club because it was loud and the clientele were self-absorbed. Whatever they said wouldn't carry beyond the table at which they sat. He'd chosen it for those reasons, and because he was postponing going back to the hotel, where he would be alone with her.

"Al-Aziz is a businessman. So is Cabot." Trace nibbled on a stale bread stick. "I made him a business proposition."

"What does that have to do with Flynn?"

"I get al-Aziz interested. With any luck he gets Hammer interested. We set up a meeting and I find out a hell of a lot more than we know now."

"You're going to meet with those people?" For some reason, her blood froze at the thought. For him, she realized. She was afraid for him. "But they know who you are."

Trace took a sip of his whiskey and wondered how long it would be before he was back in a country that served a proper drink. "Abdul knows who I am. Goons like him aren't generally in on arms transactions."

"Yes, but— Arms?" Her voice dropped to a passionate whisper. "You're going to sell them guns?"

"They damn well better think so."

"That's crazy. Setting up business transactions, pretending you'll be selling arms to terrorists. Certainly there has to be a better way."

"Sure. I could have walked into al-Aziz's and told him you were Dr. Gillian Fitzpatrick, whose brother had been kidnapped by Hammer. I could have appealed to his humanitarian instincts. Before the sun came up in the morning you'd be in the same position your brother's in now. And I'd be dead."

Gillian frowned into her wine. "It certainly seems a roundabout way of accomplishing something."

"You stick to your equations, Doc, I'll stick to mine.

In a few days I should be talking with the general himself. I have a feeling that wherever he is, your brother's close by."

"You really think Flynn's near here?" As she leaned closer, her fingers gripped his. "I wish I could be sure. I wish I could feel something."

"The computer said Morocco. Rory confirmed that the plane was logged for Casablanca. Wherever he is now, he was here. So we start here."

He seemed so confident, so sure of the plan of attack. There was nothing she wanted, needed, more than to believe in him. "You'd met al-Aziz before, hadn't you? He seemed to know you."

Trace felt an itch between his shoulder blades. He'd have preferred sitting with his back to the wall. "We've dealt before."

"You've used him to sell guns before."

"The ISS used him," Trace said. He broke another bread stick in half. "A few years back there were plans for a coup the ISS wanted to endorse. Anonymously. Cabot made a nice profit, al-Aziz made his commission, and democracy took a giant step forward."

She knew such things happened. She'd grown up in a country divided by war. She lived in a country whose faith had been strained by secret deals and political machinations. But that didn't make it right.

"It's wrong."

"This is the real world," he countered. "And most of it's wrong."

"Is that why you do it?" She'd drawn away from him, but she couldn't ignore the impulse to move closer. "To make things right?"

There'd been a time—it seemed a lifetime ago—

when he had been idealistic enough to believe that things could be made right. When he'd lost that, where he'd lost that, he couldn't have said. And he'd stopped looking.

"I just do my job, Gillian. Don't try to make a hero out of me."

"It didn't occur to me." She said it dryly enough to make his lips curve. "I just think it would make it easier if I understood you."

"Just understand that I'm going to get your brother and his kid out."

"And then?" She made a conscious effort to relax. There was nothing she could do now but wait. Wait, and try to probe beneath the surface of the man who held her life in his hands. "Will you retire?"

"That's the idea, sweetheart." The smoke around him was expensive—French, Turkish. The music was loud, the liquor just tolerable. He wondered when it had hit him that he'd spent too much time in places like this. He nearly laughed out loud. For all intents and purposes, he'd been born in a place like this. Sometime over the past year he'd realized he wanted out as badly as he'd wanted out a dozen years before. Only he was long past the point where he could just stick out his thumb.

"Trace?"

"What?"

She wasn't sure where he'd gone, but she knew it wasn't the time to ask. "What will you do…when you retire?"

"There's a place in the Canary Islands where a man can pick fruit right off the tree and sleep in a hammock with a warm woman. The water's clear as glass, and the fish jump right in your lap." He took another long sip. "A hundred thousand dollars in a place like that, I could be king."

"If you didn't die of boredom first."

"I've had enough excitement to last me the next thirty or forty years. Honey-skinned women and a salt-free diet." He clicked his glass against hers. "I'm going to enjoy myself."

"André!"

Trace twisted in his chair and found his mouth captured in a long, steamy kiss. About halfway through, recognition dawned. He could remember only one woman who smelled like a hothouse flower and kissed like a vampire.

"Désirée." Trace ran a hand down her bare arm as she snuggled into his lap. "Still in Casablanca."

"Of course." She gave a throaty laugh and tossed back a mane of spiky midnight hair. "I'm partners now in the club."

"Come up in the world."

"But yes." She had skin like a magnolia and a heart that pumped happily with poison. Despite it, Trace had maintained a distant affection for her. "I married Amir. He's in the back, or he'd slit your throat for putting your hands on me."

"Nothing's changed, I see."

"You haven't." Blithely ignoring Gillian, Désirée ran her fingertips over Trace's face. "Oh, André, I waited weeks for you to come back."

"Hours, anyway."

"Are you staying long?"

"Few days. I'm showing my friend the charms of North Africa."

Désirée glanced around, took a sweeping up-and-down look, then cast Gillian into oblivion. "There was a time when my charms were enough for you."

"Your charms were enough for any army." Trace lifted his drink and kept his eye on the door of the back room. He knew Désirée wasn't exaggerating about Amir. "I've got a little business, *ma belle*. Do you still listen well at keyholes?"

"For you—and a price."

"Flynn Fitzpatrick. Scientist. Irish, with a small daughter. How much will it cost me to find out if they're in Casablanca?"

"For such an old, dear friend…five thousand francs."

Trace shifted her off his lap before taking out his money clip. "Here's half now. As an incentive."

She bent down and slipped the money into her shoe. "It's always a pleasure to see you, André."

"And you, *chérie*." He rose and brushed his lips over her knuckles. "Don't give Amir my best."

With another laugh, Désirée weaved her way through the crowd.

"You have fascinating friends," Gillian commented.

"Yeah. I'm thinking of having a reunion. Let's go."

Gillian made her way out of the smoke and into the clear night. "What were you saying?"

"Just reminiscing about old times."

She lifted a brow. "I'm sure they were fascinating."

Despite himself, he had to smile. Désirée had a heart of coal, but what an imagination! "They had their moments."

She fell silent for a moment, struggling. At last she gave up. "That woman was your type? Slinky?"

Trace knew enough about women to know when

laughter was dangerous. He coughed instead. "Let's just say she's *a* type."

"I'm aware of that, and I doubt she's terribly attractive once you've scraped off the three layers of makeup."

"No need to be jealous, sweetheart. We're old news."

"Jealous?" She made the word sound like a joke and despised herself because it wasn't. "I would hardly be jealous of any woman you'd…you'd…"

"Come on, you can spit it out."

She shrugged off the arm he'd draped companionably around her shoulders. "Never mind. What did you pay her for?"

"To dig up some information."

"How would a woman like that be able to get any information?"

Trace looked down at her, saw that she was serious, and could only shake his head. "Diplomacy," he said.

She couldn't sleep. The energy that had been so sorely depleted only days before was back in full force. She was in Africa, a continent she had only read about in books. The Sahara was to the south. She was only steps away from the Atlantic, but from this side of the world it seemed a different ocean. Even the stars seemed different.

She didn't mind the strangeness. During her childhood she'd often dreamed of going to faraway places, but she'd contented herself with books. Her decision to emigrate to America had been the result of a craving to see something new, to be her own woman in a way she could never have been if she'd remained in Ireland with her father. So she'd gone to America to pursue her own goals, to live her own life. Now her father was ill and her brother was missing.

Gillian pulled on her robe, then threw open the terrace doors. How many times had she asked herself if things would somehow have been different if she'd stayed. It seemed foolish, even egotistical, to believe it. And yet the nagging doubt remained.

Now she was in Africa with a man who changed his identity in the blink of an eye. It would be through him and her own determination that things were put right again.

Put right. With a sigh, Gillian leaned on the railing and looked out at the lights and shadows of Casablanca. He said he didn't believe in putting things right, only in doing his job. Why didn't she believe that? It seemed to fit the style of the man. What it didn't fit were her feelings about him.

Almost from the first moment, she'd felt both drawn and repelled. There was something in his eyes, though only rarely, that told her he could be both kind and compassionate. There was the way he'd looked at her, looked to her, at the top of the Pyramid of the Magician. Part of him was a dreamer, part of him an icy realist. It seemed impossible to combine the two.

What he was, what he did, made her uneasy. All her life she'd believed in right and wrong, good and evil. Until she'd met him, she hadn't considered there could be so many shades in between. Nor had she realized until she'd met him that she could be attracted to a man who lived his life in those shades.

But it was a fact—not a theory, not a hypothesis, but a fact—that she was attracted, that she did trust, that she did believe. She couldn't take her emotions into a laboratory and dissect them, analyze them. For perhaps the first time in her life, she was stuck with a problem that no amount of logic or experimentation could solve. And the name of the problem was Trace O'Hurley.

She'd been jealous, quite fiercely jealous, when that woman had draped herself all over Trace in the club. When she'd murmured to him in intimate French and put her hands all over him, Gillian had wanted, badly, to grab her by the hair and yank out a few lacquered hunks. That simply wasn't in her nature. Or rather she'd never known it was.

She'd been jealous of Flynn from time to time, but only in the way a sister might be of a favored brother. And her love for him had always been much deeper than her envy. At university she'd had a few jealous pangs over girls with straight blond hair and blue eyes. But that had been very much a surface thing, without passion or depth.

The jealousy she'd felt tonight had been hot and violent and very difficult to control. It had also been unfamiliar. She hadn't been jealous of the woman's exotic looks or of her sinuous body, but of the fact that she'd twined that body around Trace's and kissed him as though she could have eaten him alive.

And he'd seemed to enjoy it.

Gillian crossed her arms over her chest and looked out at the smattering of lights that were still glowing in the city. She didn't care for jealousy any more than she cared for confusion. Trace O'Hurley apparently equaled both.

She jolted at a quick scraping sound, then whirled to see the flare of a match on the terrace beside hers.

He was in the shadows. They seemed to suit him

best. She wondered how long he'd been there, silently watching.

"I didn't know you were there." And she wouldn't have, she realized, unless he'd allowed her to. "I couldn't sleep." When he didn't respond, she fiddled with the tie of her robe and cleared her throat. "I thought you'd gone to bed."

"Time change throws your system off."

"Yes, I suppose that's it." She curled her fingers around the railing again, wishing it was that simple. "We've been in so many time zones in the past few days. I'd have thought you'd be used to it."

"I like the night." That was true enough, but he'd come onto the terrace because he'd been restless, and because he'd been thinking of her.

"Sometimes I'll go up on the roof of my building. It's the only way you can see the stars in New York." She looked up at them now. "Back in Ireland, all you had to do was walk outside." With a shake of her head, she looked out at the city again. "Do you ever miss it?"

"Miss what?"

"Your home."

He drew on the cigarette, and his face was washed in red light for an instant. "I told you, I don't have one."

She moved to the side of the terrace that ran along the side of his. "Just the Canary Islands? How long can a man live on fruit and fish?"

"Long enough."

Though the night had cooled, he wore only baggy drawstring pants. Gillian remembered, quite clearly, the wild thrill of being held against that body. And the confusing emptiness of being pushed away from it. No, emotions couldn't be analyzed, but she could try to analyze their source.

"I wonder what it is you're running from."

"Running to." Trace pitched his cigarette over the balcony and onto the street below. "A life of luxury, sweetheart. Coconut milk and half-naked women."

"I don't think you can do it. You've already given a chunk of your life to your country."

"That's right." Unconsciously he rubbed at the scar on his chest. "What's left is mine." Her scent was soft again. The breeze carried it from her skin to his.

"You know, one of the things Mr. Forrester told me about you was that if you played by the rules more regularly you'd be running the ISS."

"Charlie had delusions of grandeur."

"He was tremendously proud of you."

"He recruited me. He trained me." Trace moved restlessly to the railing. "He'd want to think he'd done a good job of it."

"I think it was more than that. Affection and pride don't always go together." She thought of her father. "You should have the satisfaction of knowing he liked who you were, as well as what he'd made you. I know you cared for him, and that you're doing this as much for him as for the money. The reasons shouldn't matter to me, but they do. Trace?"

He didn't want to look at her now, with the moonlight slanting down and her scent hanging in the air. He kept his eyes on the street below. "Yeah?"

"I know that Flynn and Caitlin will be all right. That they'll be safe soon because you're here." She wished he was close, that she could reach out and touch him. She was grateful he wasn't. "And when I have them back

I'll never be able to repay you. So I want you to know now that whatever happens in the meantime, whatever has to be done, I'm grateful."

"It's a job," he said, his teeth clenched, because the low, warm voice tended to make him forget that. "Don't make me out to be some knight on a white charger, Gillian."

"No, you're not that, but I think I'm beginning to understand what you are, Trace." She walked to the terrace doors. "Good night." Because she hadn't expected him to answer, she closed the door on his silence.

"But how can you expect me to browse through shops and snap pictures as if I were nothing more than a tourist?"

Trace steered Gillian toward another display window. "Because today you *are* nothing but a tourist. Show a little enthusiasm, will you?"

"My brother and my niece are prisoners. I'm afraid it's a little difficult for me to work up any enthusiasm over a bunch of crockery."

"Authentic North African Art," Trace said.

"We're wasting time poking around when we should be doing something."

"Any suggestions?" His voice was low as he continued to stroll, her arm caught firmly in his. Brightly striped awnings shaded the wares spread on outside tables. There was leather, and there was the flash of metal and the smell of horse. "You want me to break into where your brother's being held, guns blazing, maybe a knife between my teeth?"

He did a good job of making her feel like a fool. Gillian shrugged it off. "It makes better sense than buying trinkets and taking snapshots."

"In the first place I don't know where they're holding him. Hard to break into something until you've got the address. In the second place, if I tried that kind of TV tactics I'd be dead and your brother would be no better off. Let's sit." Satisfied with the position, he chose a shaded table on the terrace of a small café. "Why don't you tell me what's eating you?"

Gillian pushed her sunglasses more firmly on her nose. "Oh, I don't know. It might have something to do with the fact that Flynn and Caitlin have been kidnapped. Or perhaps I just got up on the wrong side of the bed."

"Sarcasm doesn't suit you." He ordered two coffees, then stretched out his legs. "You played the game well enough yesterday."

Gillian looked down at her hands. The sun glinted off the gold band of her watch. She studied the play of light until their coffee was served. "I couldn't sleep. Most of the night I just lay there waiting for morning. There was this feeling I couldn't shake. Something was wrong, dreadfully wrong, and I was going to be too late to put it right again." She looked up at him then, certain she would despise him if he laughed at her.

"You've been through a lot in the past few days." He said it easily, without the sympathy she would have bristled at or the edge she would have resented. "It wouldn't be normal for you to sleep like a baby."

"I suppose not, but if I just felt we were doing something…"

"We are." He put his hand on hers, then immediately drew it away again. "Drink your coffee."

The touch had been quick, and he was already resenting it. The fact that she thought she understood made her smile. "Being kind makes you uncomfortable."

"I'm not kind." He lit a cigarette, knowing he'd do better if he kept his hands occupied.

"Yes, you are." A little more relaxed, Gillian picked up her cup. "You'd prefer not to be, but it's difficult to change your nature. You can become other people." The coffee was hot and strong, and exactly what she'd needed. "But you can't change your nature. Whatever name you use, underneath it you're a kind man."

"You don't know me." He let smoke fill his lungs. "Or anything about me."

"As a scientist, I'm trained to observe, to analyze, categorize, hypothesize. Would you like to hear my hypothesis about you?"

"No."

The tension that had been locked in her muscles throughout the night eased. "You're a man who looked for adventure and excitement and undoubtedly found more than he'd bargained for. I'd say you believed in freedom and human rights strongly enough to spend a great deal of your life fighting for them. And you've been disillusioned and you nearly lost your life. I'm not certain which disturbs you more. I don't think you lied when you told me you were tired, Trace. But you lie every time you pretend not to care."

She was close, much too close, to the heart of things, much closer than anyone else had ever stepped. He'd found that life was more comfortable with distance. When he spoke, it was with the single goal of reestablishing it. "What I am is a trained liar, thief, cheat and killer. There's nothing pretty or glamorous or idealistic about what I do. I follow orders."

"I think the question isn't so much what you do as why you do it." For now, she stopped asking herself why it was so important for her to believe that, and just believed. "The whys became less clear, so you have a fantasy about retiring to some little island where you won't have to think about it."

Trace crushed out his cigarette. "You said physicist, not psychiatrist, right?"

"It's simply a matter of logic. I'm a very logical person." She set her cup back neatly in its saucer. "Then there's the matter of your behavior toward me. Apparently you're attracted."

"Is that so?"

She smiled then, always more secure when things were spelled out clearly. "I think it would be foolish to deny that a physical attraction exists. That can be listed as fact rather than theory. Yet, even on that basis, your behavior is contradictory. On each occasion when you've acted on that attraction, you've chosen to back off in favor of annoyance and frustration."

He didn't care to have his attractions, physical or otherwise, dissected like some embalmed frog. Trace waited until the waiter had freshened both cups before he leaned toward Gillian. "You can be grateful I backed off."

Their faces were very close over the little round table. Her heart began to drum, but she found the sensation more unique than unpleasant. "Because you're a dangerous man?"

"I'm the most dangerous man you'll ever meet."

She wasn't about to argue with that. "I explained to you before, I can take care of myself."

She reached for her coffee, and Trace closed his hand over her wrist. The grip was firm enough to make her eyes narrow. "You wouldn't know where to begin with me, Doc. And you sure as hell wouldn't know where to end. Count your blessings."

"My family's been kidnapped, I've seen a man die and had a knife to my back. There's little you could do to frighten me." She jerked her hand away and, with every outward appearance of calm, lifted her cup. Her heart beat fast and hard in her throat.

"You're wrong." This time he smiled. "If I decide to have you, you'll find out how wrong."

Her cup hit the saucer with a snap. "I'm ready to go."

"Sit." It was the sudden change in his voice that made her obey. "Drink your coffee," he said mildly as he picked up his camera.

"What is it?"

"Al-Aziz has a visitor." The camera was one of the few pieces of ISS equipment Trace was fond of. He pushed a button, and a man stepping out of a black car twenty yards away filled the viewfinder. He recognized the face from briefings, and he smiled again. Kendesa was the general's right hand, a man of taste and intelligence who just managed to balance the general's fanaticism.

"You know who it is?"

Trace took two shots out of habit. "Yeah." He lowered the camera.

"What does it mean?"

"It means they took the bait."

Gillian moistened her lips and struggled to stay calm. "What do we do now?"

Trace lit another cigarette. "We wait."

Al-Aziz's visitor stayed twenty minutes. When he came back out, Trace was up and moving. By the time Kendesa stepped into his car, Trace and Gillian were in a cab. "I want you to stay with that car," he told the driver, pulling out bills. "But keep a nice distance."

The driver pocketed the money before he started the engine. Gillian groped for Trace's hand and held on.

"He knows where Flynn is, doesn't he?"

"He knows."

She pressed her free hand to her lips as they drove. "What are you going to do?"

"Nothing."

"But if he—"

"Let's just see where he's going." Because her hand was icy, he kept it in his. The black car stopped at one of the more exclusive hotels in the business district. Trace waited until Kendesa was inside. "Stay here."

"But I want to—"

"Just stay here," he repeated, and then he was gone. As the minutes passed, fear became annoyance. Gillian slid to the door and had her fingers around the handle when Trace pulled it open.

"Going somewhere?" He let the door slam behind him. Settling back, he gave the driver the name of their hotel.

"Well?"

"He just checked in this morning. He hasn't given them a day of departure. I'd say that means he intends to stay until business is completed."

"Aren't you going to go in and make him tell you where Flynn is?"

Trace spared her a look. "Sure, I'll go on up to his room, rough him and his three guards up a bit and drag the truth out of them. Then I'll march up to wherever they're holding your brother and blast him out single-handed."

"Isn't that what I'm paying you for?"

"You're paying me to get him out—in one piece." As the cab pulled up at the curb, Trace handed the driver more bills. "Let's play this my way."

Knowing her temper couldn't be trusted, Gillian remained silent until they were in their rooms. "If you have a plan, I think it's time you filled me in."

Ignoring her, Trace walked over to the bed and began to fiddle with what Gillian had taken for a compact portable stereo.

"This is hardly the time to listen to music." When he continued to say nothing, she stormed over to him. "Trace, I want to know what you have in mind. I refuse to be kept in the dark while you sit here and listen to the radio. I want to know—"

"Shut up, will you?" When he played back the tape, the voices came out barely audible, and speaking Arabic. "Damn." He adjusted the volume and strained.

"What is that?"

"Our friends talking, almost out of reach of the bug I planted yesterday."

"You… I never saw you plant anything."

"That boosts my confidence." He rewound the tape to the beginning.

"I can't think of any place you could have hidden it."

"I left it out in plain view. People find things a lot

quicker if you hide them. Didn't you ever read Poe? Now be quiet."

The voices were barely distinguishable, but he recognized al-Aziz's. He could decipher the formal greetings, but from there on could translate only a few snatches. He heard Cabot's name, and some basic monetary negotiations.

"What does it say?" Gillian asked when he shut the tape off again.

"I don't know enough Arabic to make much sense of it."

"Oh." She tried to block off the disappointment. Running her hands over her face, she sat on the bed beside him. "I guess you'd hoped they speak in French or English."

"It would have been helpful." Trace removed the tape and slipped it into his pocket. "Now we need an interpreter."

Her hands dropped in her lap. "You know someone who'll help us?"

"Almost anyone's willing to help for a price." He checked his watch. "The club ought to be pretty quiet now. I think I'll go to see Désirée."

"I'm going with you."

He started to refuse, then thought better of it. "Just as well. I can use you as a cover in case Amir's around. With you hanging all over me, he won't think I'm trying to tickle his wife's fancy. Or anything else."

"I'm so glad I can be useful."

They found Désirée in the apartment above the club. Though it was nearly noon, she answered the door heavy-eyed and in a sexily rumpled robe that slipped provocatively off one shoulder. Her eyes brightened considerably at the sight of Trace.

"André. What a nice surprise." She spotted Gillian, pouted a moment, then stepped back to let them in. "You used to come visiting alone," she said in French.

"You used to be single." Trace glanced around the wide, dim room, with its fussy pillows and its china knicknacks. The room was crammed with furniture, and the furniture covered with things. Possessions had always been important to Désirée. Apparently she'd finally acquired them. "You've come up in the world, *chérie*."

"We make our own way in life." She walked to a table and chose a cigarette from a glass holder. "If you've come for your information, you haven't given me much time." She held the cigarette, waiting until Trace crossed the room to light it.

"Actually, I've come on other business." She smelled of perfume that clung from the night before, no longer strong, but still overpowering. "Is your husband in?"

Her brow lifted as she glanced in Gillian's direction. "You were never one for group games."

"No games at all." He took the cigarette from her and drew on it himself. "Amir. Is he here?"

"He had business. He's a busy man."

"Your Arabic was always excellent, Désirée." Trace drew the tape from his pocket. "Two thousand francs for a translation of this tape, and a memory lapse immediately afterward."

Désirée took the tape and turned it over in her palm. "Two thousand for the translation, and three more for the loss of memory." She smiled at him. "A woman must make a living where she can."

There had been a time when he would have enjoyed negotiating with her. He wondered why that time seemed to have passed. "Done."

"Cash, darling." She held out an empty hand. "Now."

When Trace handed her the money, she went over to a stereo. "Amir enjoys his toys," she said as she slipped the tape into the player. After switching it on, she adjusted the volume. Almost at once, her expression changed. With the touch of a finger, the player fell silent again. "Kendesa. You said nothing of Kendesa."

"You didn't ask." Trace sat and gestured for Gillian to join him. "The deal's struck, Désirée. Play it my way and your name will never be mentioned."

"You mix in very bad company, André. Very bad." But the money was still in her hand. After a moment's consideration, she slipped it into her pocket, then switched the machine back on. "Kendesa greets the swine al-Aziz. He asks if business is good." She listened for another moment, then turned the machine off again. "They speak of you, the Frenchman Cabot, who has an interesting business proposition for Kendesa's organization. Al-Aziz has humbly agreed to act as liaison."

She turned the machine on again, then repeated the process of listening before turning it off to translate. "Kendesa is very interested in your product. His sources have confirmed that you are in possession of a shipment of American arms intended for their Middle Eastern allies. A shipment of this size and—" she groped for the word a moment "—quality is of interest to Kendesa's superior. And so are you."

She switched the tape on again and lit a cigarette as the two voices murmured through the speakers. "Your reputation is satisfactory, but Kendesa is cautious. His organization is most concerned with another project at this time, and yet your product is tempting. Kendesa has agreed to have al-Aziz arrange a meeting. They discuss commission. Then it becomes interesting. Al-Aziz asks of this Fitzpatrick. He tells Kendesa he has heard rumors. Kendesa tells him to mind his shop and his tongue."

Désirée turned the tape off. It ejected smoothly. "Tell me, André, are you interested in guns or in this Irishman?"

"I'm interested in the largest profit." He rose to take the tape from her. "And your memory, Désirée?"

She fondled the bills in her pocket. "Quite blank." She smiled, then ran a hand up his chest. "Come back for a drink tonight. Alone."

Trace cupped her chin in his hand and kissed her. "Amir is a large, jealous man who has a talent with knives. Let's just treasure the past."

"It was an interesting one." She sighed and watched him walk to the door. "André, the Irishman was in Casablanca."

He stopped, clamping his hand around Gillian's arm before she could speak. "And now?"

"He was taken east, into the mountains. That's all I know."

"There was a child."

"A girl. She's with him. It would have to be a great deal more profitable to ask questions now that I know who is involved."

"You've asked enough." He drew out bills and set them on the table by the door. "Forget this, too, Désirée, and enjoy your large husband."

When he closed the door, Désirée considered for a long moment, then walked to the phone.

"He was here," Gillian said, torn between relief and fresh terror. "They were both here. There has to be a way of finding out where they were taken. Oh, God, they were so close."

"Don't get ahead of yourself. The mountains to the east isn't a street address."

"But it's another step. What do we do now?"

"We get some lunch. And we wait for Kendesa to move."

Chapter 6

"I want to go with you."

Trace straightened the knot of the hated tie. "It's out of the question."

"You haven't given me a reason." Gillian stood planted behind him, scowling at his reflection. He looked so smooth, she thought, a world away from the man she'd found in the cantina. She wondered what dramatic turn her life had taken to make her prefer the rough, unshaven and slightly dirty man she'd first met to the urbane and cologned one who stood in front of her.

"I don't have to give you reasons, just results."

At least that much hadn't changed, she thought wryly, standing her ground. "I explained to you right from the beginning that I'd be going through this step-by-step with you."

"You're going to miss this step, sweetheart." Trace checked the plain brushed-gold links at his cuffs. "You

just stay here and keep a light burning in the window."
Turning, he gave her a friendly pat on the cheek.

"You look like a stockbroker," she muttered.

"No need for insults." Trace picked up a briefcase
filled with papers and inventories he'd spent the better
part of the night putting together.

"You're meeting with Kendesa, and I think I should
be there."

"It's a business meeting—bad business. I take a
woman along to a meeting where I'm talking about
dealing arms to terrorists, Kendesa's going to wonder
why. He wonders hard enough and he could check you
out. He checks deep enough, he could find out that my
woman is the sister of Hammer's most prized possession." He stopped long enough to wipe away a smudge
on his shoe. "It's not a good bet."

It was because it was too logical to argue with that
Gillian was angry. "I'm not your woman."

"They better think you are."

"I'd rather be buried up to my neck in hot sand."

He glanced at her. She stood by the window, spitting
mad and stunning. "I'll keep that in mind. Why don't
you spend a couple hours making up a list of alterna-
tives? It might put you in a better mood."

When he opened the door, she prepared to hurl abuse.
"Be careful," she said instead, hating herself for it.

He paused again. "Concern. I'm touched."

"It's nothing personal." But her palms were sweaty
at the idea of him going alone. "If anything happened
to you I'd have to start from scratch."

With a little laugh, he stepped into the hall. "Stay
inside, Doc."

The moment the door closed at his back, he left Trace

O'Hurley behind. He had a certain affection for each of his covers. Without that, it would have been difficult for him to play any of them convincingly for what were often long stretches of time. André Cabot was fussy, and often pompous, but he had excellent taste and extraordinary luck with women. Trace felt that redeemed him.

Still, Cabot's charm hadn't made a dent in Gillian's defenses. So she doesn't like Frenchmen, Trace decided as he settled into a cab. Apparently she preferred stodgy American scientists like that Arthur Steward she spent so much time with in New York. The man was fifteen years older than she, and more interested in white mice than romance. Trace had told himself it was simply standard procedure to check him out. Nothing personal.

Trace shifted his briefcase and reminded himself that Cabot was concerned only with making a profit. He wouldn't have given a woman like Gillian a second thought once she was out of sight. The trouble was, Trace O'Hurley was thinking about her entirely too much.

She was still a puzzle to him, and he was used to figuring any angle, any woman. They shared the same set of rooms, yet she gave the arrangement a sense of innocence and propriety. She was vulnerable and passionate, frightened and determined. She was logical, yet enough of a dreamer to feel the power of a Mayan ruin. She spoke easily, even clinically, of his attraction to her. But there had been a fire, hot and vital, when he'd kissed her.

She was right about one thing—he wanted her, and bad. What she didn't know, what he couldn't explain even to himself, was that he was terrified of what might happen if he acted on that need.

When the cab drew up to the curb, Trace pulled himself back. He was right about something, too. He was thinking about her too much.

He counted out bills as Cabot would, carefully. With obvious reluctance, he added the minimum tip. After straightening the line of his jacket, he walked into the lobby of Kendesa's hotel.

He spotted one of the bodyguards but walked to the bank of elevators without pausing. He was on time to the minute. That was another of Cabot's traits. The elevator took him to the top floor, to the executive suite, often reserved for dignitaries and visiting heads of state.

The door was opened at the first knock by a burly guard who looked uncomfortable in his dark Western suit. "Your weapon, monsieur," he said in stilted French.

Trace reached inside his jacket and removed a .25 automatic. Cabot carried a small pistol rather than chance ruining the line of his jacket.

The guard pocketed it before gesturing him into the parlor of the suite. A bottle of wine was open on the table. Fresh roses stood in a vase beside it. The room was cushioned from the noise and heat of the day. Noting that the terrace doors were not only shut but locked, Trace took his seat. Kendesa didn't keep him waiting.

He wasn't an imposing man. Whatever passions stirred him were kept firmly strapped down and controlled. He was small in stature and impeccably and conservatively dressed. Unlike the man he represented, he wore no ostentatious jewelry, no vivid colors. He was dark and blandly handsome, rather like a news anchorman, and moved with the steady grace of a career soldier.

He was a man who exuded trust and moderation,

and in the past eighteen months he had been responsible for the execution of three political hostages. He was holding the wildly fanatical Hammer together by the skin of his teeth.

"Monsieur Cabot." Kendesa offered his hand. "It's a pleasure to meet you."

"*Monsieur.* Business is always my pleasure."

With a politely interested smile, Kendesa took his seat. "Our mutual friend indicated you have some supplies that may be of interest to me. Some wine? I think you'll find it agreeable." Kendesa poured two glasses. Trace let him drink first.

"I've recently acquired certain military supplies that I believe your organization would find useful." Trace sipped and found the wine dry and light. Cabot's preference. He smiled. Kendesa had done his homework.

"My sources tell me that these supplies were intended for the Zionists."

Trace lifted a shoulder, pleased that the money he'd spent in the bidonville had been invested wisely. "I'm a businessman, *monsieur.* I have no politics, only a profit margin. The supplies could still be shipped where the Americans originally intended, if the price was right."

"You're frank." Kendesa tapped a finger on the side of his glass. "The United States had not admitted openly that these supplies were…confiscated. In fact, it's difficult to prove that they ever existed."

"Such things are embarrassing. For myself, I prefer that the entire business be kept quiet until the final transactions are complete." Setting his wine aside, Trace lifted his suitcase. "This is a list of the arms my associates are holding. I can assure you they are top-quality. I've checked samples myself."

Kendesa took the papers but continued to watch Trace. "Your reputation in such matters is unimpeachable."

"Merci."

Kendesa's brows lifted slightly as he scanned the list. Trace had made it irresistible. "This particular weapon, the TS-35. My sources tell me it was not to be completed for several months."

"It was completed and tested five weeks ago," Trace told him, knowing the news would be out in a matter of weeks in any case. "It is a beautiful piece of work. Very lightweight, and compact. The Americans are very clever in some areas." He drew out another sheet of paper. "My associates and I have settled on a price. Shipping can, of course, be arranged."

"The total seems high."

"Overhead. Inflation." He spread his hands in a purely Gallic gesture. "You understand."

"And I am a cautious man, you understand. Before negotiations can be initiated, it would be necessary to inspect a portion of your product."

"Naturally, I can deal with that myself, if you like." He moved his fingertip over his jawline consideringly. "It will take me a few days to make the arrangements. I prefer to do so in a place you have secured. In today's atmosphere, transactions of this nature have become only more delicate."

"The general is residing in the east. Such a transaction cannot be completed without his approval."

"Understood. Though I'm aware much of the buying and selling are your province, I would prefer discussing the matter with the general."

"You will bring your samples to us, in one week." In

a week he would have a complete report on Cabot and the enterprise. "The general has established his head-quarters in an area east of Sefrou that he has christened el Hasad. It will be arranged for you to be met in Se-frou. From there, your transportation will be seen to."

"I will contact my associates, but I see no problem with those arrangements. One week, then." Trace rose.

Kendesa rose, as well. "A question on another mat-ter, *monsieur*. You inquired about a scientist who has recently joined our organization. I would ask what your interest is."

"Profit. There are several parties interested in Dr. Fitzpatrick and his particular skills. The Horizon proj-ect, once completed, could generate an incredible amount of income."

"We are not only interested in money."

"I am," Trace said with a cool smile. "You might think of what the scientist is worth, if you can persuade him to complete the project. The arms we are currently negotiating over would be little more than toys." He folded his hands, and the gold at his wrists winked dully. "If your organization finds the proper partner, you could not only be rich, but as powerful politically as any developed country."

It was something he had considered already, though he would have preferred making the first move. "Your outlook is intriguing."

"Only speculation, *monsieur*, unless you can indeed convince the man to produce for you."

Kendesa brushed that aside easily. He was a man who was accustomed to cooperation—or submission. "That is only a matter of time. I will speak with the general on this, as well. Perhaps it can be discussed."

Kendesa led him to the door. "I would tell you, Monsieur Cabot, that you might be more cautious in choosing your associates."

"I beg your pardon?"

"I speak of the French woman, Désirée. She thought a greater profit could be made through blackmail. She was mistaken."

Trace merely lifted a brow, but he felt a cold gnawing at his stomach. "She is as greedy as she is beautiful."

"And now she is dead. Good afternoon, *monsieur*."

Trace gave a slight bow. He held on to Cabot until he was back in his room. There he gave way to fury by slamming a fist into the wall.

"Damn the woman!" Couldn't she have been satisfied with the easy money he'd passed her? She'd killed herself. He could tell himself she'd killed herself, and yet he felt the weight of another life on his hands.

For a moment he closed his eyes and forced the image of his island into his mind. Soft breezes, warm fruit, warmer women. The minute he had the cash in his hand he was getting out.

Trace went to the bottle of whiskey on his dresser, poured a double and washed the taste of Kendesa's wine from his mouth. It didn't help. Slamming the glass down again, he went into the next room to tell Gillian they were a step closer.

She was sitting on the bed, her back very straight, her hands folded in her lap. She didn't glance over as he came in, but continued to stare out the window at a slice of sky.

"Still sulking?" The whiskey hadn't helped, but maybe dumping a little excess temper on her would. "I don't know which is more tiresome, listening to you bitch or putting up with your moods." Yanking off his tie, he tossed it in the general direction of a chair. "Snap out of it, Doc, unless you don't want to hear what I found out about your brother."

She looked at him then, but he didn't see recrimination or temper in her eyes. There wasn't the anticipation he'd expected, but grief, raw and dry-eyed. He'd started to peel out of his jacket, and now he drew it off slowly.

"What is it?"

"I called my father." Her voice was quiet, hardly more than a whisper, but steady. It was the tone that stopped him from nagging at her for using an unsecured line. "I thought he should know we were close to finding Flynn. I wanted to give him some hope, some comfort. I know he felt helpless having to send me instead of doing it himself." She closed her eyes and waited for her strength to rebuild. "I got his nurse. She's staying at the house, looking after it. He died three days ago." She unlinked her fingers, then curled them together again. "Three days. I didn't know. I wasn't there. They buried him this morning."

He came to her in silence to sit beside her, to slip an arm around her. She resisted only a moment, then allowed herself to lean against him. The tears didn't come. She wondered why she felt so cold and numb, when hot, raging grief would have been a relief.

"He was all alone when he died. No one should die alone, Trace."

"You said he'd been ill."

"He was dying. He knew it, and he really didn't want to live the way he'd become. Weak and feeble. All his research, all his brilliance, couldn't help him. He only wanted one thing—for me to bring Flynn home before he died. Now it's too late."

"You're still going to bring Flynn home."

"He loved Flynn so. I was a disappointment to him, but Flynn was everything he wanted. The worry of the past days only made him worse. I wanted him to die easy, Trace. Even after everything, I wanted him to die easy."

"You did everything you could. You're doing what he wanted."

"I never did what he wanted." Her cheeks were hot and wet now, but she didn't notice. "He never forgave me for going to America, for leaving him. He never understood that I needed to breathe, needed to look for my own life. He only understood that I was going away, rejecting him and his plans for me. I loved him." Her voice caught on the first sob. "But I could never explain myself to him. And I never will. Oh, God, I didn't get to say goodbye. Not even that."

She didn't object when he drew her closer, to rock, to stroke, to soothe. He didn't speak, only held, as the tears came, fast and violent. He understood grief, the fury and the ache of it, and knew it wasn't words that dulled both, it was time. Gathering her close, he lay down with her while she wept out the first pains.

He understood the guilt. He and Gillian were as different as black and white, but he, too, had had a father who had made plans, who hadn't understood and hadn't forgiven. And he knew that guilt made grief more painful even than love.

He brushed his lips across her temple and held on.

When she was quiet, he continued to stroke her hair. The light was still strong through the windows. Wanting to draw the curtains closed, he started to rise. Gillian tightened her hold.

"Don't go," she murmured. "I don't want to be alone."

"I'll close the drapes. Maybe you can sleep."

"Just stay with me a little while longer." She brushed a hand over her face to wipe away the tears. Emotional outbursts were something she'd always been prone to, and one more thing her father hadn't understood. "He was a hard man, my father, especially after my mother died. She knew how to reach him. I'll always regret that I couldn't." Taking a long breath, she shut her eyes again. "Flynn and Caitlin are the only family I have left. I have to find them, Trace. I have to see that they're safe."

"I have a pretty good idea where they are."

She nodded. All her faith, all her hopes, were tied up in him now. "Tell me."

He gave her a brief sketch of his meeting with Kendesa, but stopped short of mentioning Désirée. That was still on his conscience. She listened but didn't move away. Her head stayed on his shoulder, her hand on his chest. As he spoke, something he'd closed off long before began to crack open. He couldn't explain why he felt stronger because his arms were around her. He couldn't explain why, even knowing what had to be done in the next few days, he felt almost at peace lying in the bright room with her hair against his cheek.

"You think Flynn and Caitlin are with this General Husad?"

"I'd give odds on it."

"And in a week you'll meet with him."

"That's the plan."

"But he'll expect you to have some of these guns. What will happen when you don't?"

"Who says I won't?"

She did move then, slowly drawing her head back so that she could see his face. His eyes were half closed, but the grimness around his mouth hadn't faded. "Trace, I don't understand. You told them you had a shipment of American arms. You don't. How can you take them samples of what you don't have?"

"I have to go shopping for a few M-16s, 40-millimeter grenade launchers and odds and ends."

"I don't think the local department stores carry them."

"The black market does, and I've got connections." He let the silence hang for a moment. "Gillian, it's time to let the ISS in on this."

"Why? Why now?"

"Because I've established cover, I've made contact. They'll be annoyed, but they aren't stupid enough to blow the operation at this stage. If something goes wrong, they'll need to have the information so they can move on it."

She was silent for a long time. "You mean if you're killed."

"If I'm taken out, a lot of time will be wasted in getting to your brother. With ISS backing from this point, we cover more bases."

"Why should they hurt you? You're selling them the guns they want."

He thought of Désirée. "The guns are one thing, Horizon is another. These people aren't businessmen, and they don't have the honor of a Manhattan street gang. If they think I know too much, or might infringe on their territory, eliminating me would be the best way of protecting their interest. It's a toss of the dice which way they'll play it. You don't want to risk your brother's life on a toss of the dice."

Nor did she want to risk his. It came to her now as they lay close, without passion, without anger, that she'd become as concerned for him as for her family. He wasn't simply an instrument to free Flynn and Caitlin with any longer, but he was a man who drew her, infuriated her, aroused her.

She looked down and saw that her hand had curled against his chest. Holding on, she thought, to something that wasn't hers. "Maybe we should let the ISS take over from here."

"Let's not go overboard."

"No, I mean it." She shifted away and sat up. She wanted more now. She wanted him to hold her, not in comfort, not in reassurance, but in desire. "The more I think about it, the crazier it seems for you to go in alone. Anything could happen to Flynn and Caitlin...to you."

"I've worked alone and come out in one piece before."

"And the last time you worked against them you nearly died."

Because this sudden attack of nerves intrigued him, Trace sat up and took her by the shoulders. "Don't you believe in destiny, Gillian? We do things to move it along, to protect ourselves from it, but in the end, what's meant is meant."

"You were just talking about luck."

"Yeah, I don't figure there's a contradiction there. If my luck's in, and I'm meant to come out, I will."

"You're not a fatalist."

"Depends on the mood. But I'm always a realist. This job is mine, for a lot of reasons." And she wasn't the least of them. "But I'm practical enough to know when it's time for backup."

"I don't want anything to happen to you." She said it quickly, knowing it was as foolish as it was useless.

His look sharpened. Before she could turn away, he cupped her chin in his hand. "Why?"

"Because... I'd feel responsible."

It wasn't wise to push, but he wasn't always wise. "Why else?"

"Because I'd be alone, and I've nearly gotten used to you, and..." Her voice trailed off as she lifted a hand to his cheek. "And there's this," she murmured, bringing her lips to his.

The light was still bright, but it seemed to her that the room went dim, the colors softened and the world tipped out of focus. The emotional roller coaster she'd already experienced went speeding around an unexpected curve, leaving her giddy and exhilarated. She pressed against him, already anticipating the next plunge.

She was as warm and sweet as any fantasy. She was real and vital. More than he'd ever wanted freedom or wealth or peace of mind, he wanted her. He felt reason slipping against the pull of need, and he held himself back. To need anything too much was to risk losing.

But her hands were so soft, so soothing. His own were in her hair, dragging her closer, even as he told himself it was wrong for both of them. Her scent was like a quiet promise, lulling him into believing he could have and keep. He ached from needing to touch her, to feel how her body might move against his hands.

He had to remind himself that there was no promise, neither from her nor to her. There couldn't be.

When he drew her away, she reached out again. Trace tightened his grip and held her back. "You listen to me. This is all wrong. You know it and I know it."

"No, I don't."

"Then you're an idiot."

She knew how to handle rejection. She braced herself for it. "You don't want me?"

He swore, once, then twice. "Of course I want you. Why shouldn't I? You're beautiful. You've got brains and guts. You're everything I've ever wanted."

"Then why—?"

He dragged her out of the bed. Before she could draw in the breath to protest, he was holding her in front of the mirror. "Look at yourself, you're a nice, well-bred woman. A physicist, for God's sake. You came from a nice upper-class family, went to good schools and did what you were told." When temper had her pulling away, he yanked her back again. "Look at me, Gillian." He gave her one hard shake until her head snapped up and her eyes met his in the mirror. "I spent most of my life dancing from second-rate club to second-rate club. I never spent more than a handful of days a year in a real school. I never learned to play by the rules. I've never owned a car or a piece of property, and I've never stayed with a woman for long. Do you want to know how many people I've killed in twelve years? Do you want to know how many ways there are to do it?"

"Stop it." She pulled away from him, only to whirl back. "You're trying to scare me, and it won't work."

"Then you *are* an idiot."

"Maybe I am, but at least I'm an honest one. Why

don't you just admit that you don't want to be involved? You don't want to feel anything for me."

He drew out a cigarette. "That's right."

"But you do." She tossed her head back, daring him to deny it. "You do feel, and you're the one who's scared."

Her point, he thought as he blew out smoke. But he'd be damned if he'd let her know it. "Let's get something straight, sweetheart. I don't have time to give you the hearts and flowers you'd like. We've got a priority, and it's in the mountains east of here. Let's concentrate on that."

"You can't run forever."

"When I stop, you'll wish to God I'd kept going. I've got some things to do." He walked out.

Gillian did something she hadn't done in years. She picked up the nearest breakable and heaved it at the door.

Chapter 7

"After the number of years you've had in service, Agent O'Hurley, I'm sure you're aware that there's such a thing as procedure."

Captain Addison—British, balding and straight-line ISS—sat in Trace's room, drinking coffee and looking annoyed. It was his job to oversee and coordinate operations in this part of the world. After nearly fifteen years of field duty, he was quite content to do so from behind a desk. Under these particular circumstances, he'd been ordered to handle the business face-to-face. The break in routine did nothing to please him.

He'd been set to go back to London on holiday when the call had reached him at his Madrid base. Now he was in godforsaken Morocco, in the middle of an incident that would very likely keep him from his steak-and-kidney pie for some time to come.

"You have, I presume, some sort of valid explanation?"

"I was on vacation, Captain." Trace drew easily on his cigarette. Types like Addison amused him more than they annoyed him. It was the possibility that he could become similarly straitlaced that had kept him away from desks and paperwork. "My own time. I thought the ISS might be interested in what I stumbled into."

"Stumbled into," Addison repeated. He pushed his rimless glasses up on his nose and gave Trace a very cool and very clear stare. "We both know you didn't stumble into anything, Agent O'Hurley. You acted on your own, without ISS sanction."

"The woman came to me." Trace didn't bother to put any emphasis into the explanation. He knew very well that men of Addison's type preferred agents to sweat. "I followed up an interesting story and came by some even more interesting information. If you don't want what I've got, it doesn't matter to me. I've still got a week before I punch in."

"The correct procedure would have been to inform the ISS the moment Dr. Fitzpatrick contacted you."

"I consider that a judgment call, Captain. My judgment."

Addison folded his hands. Though he'd been divorced for five years, he still wore a gold wedding band. He'd gotten used to the weight on his finger. "Your record shows a high percentage of infractions."

"Am I fired?"

A creature of habit and order, Addison bristled at Trace's careless arrogance. But he, too, had his orders. "Fortunately—or unfortunately, depending on one's viewpoint—your record also shows a high percentage of successful assignments. To be frank, O'Hurley, I don't care for showboating of this kind, but the Horizon project and Dr. Fitzpatrick and his daughter take precedence over personal feelings."

Trace hadn't missed the order of importance. Nor had he expected anything else. "Then I take it I'm not fired."

"You will maintain your cover as André Cabot, but from this point on we go by the book. You will keep in constant contact with the ISS base in Madrid on your progress. You will report directly to me." This, too, gave him no pleasure. One didn't easily keep a rogue agent under one's thumb. "We have arranged for one crate of American-made weapons to be delivered to you in Sefrou in four days. Your contact there will be Agent Breintz. Once you have confirmed Dr. Fitzpatrick's location and assessed the situation, you'll be given further orders. Headquarters feels you should keep the arms negotiations straightforward. If you do find yourself in Husad's lair, it's code blue."

Again, it was nothing he hadn't expected. Code blue meant simply that if his cover didn't hold the ISS would destroy his files, his identity. It would be as if Trace O'Hurley had never existed.

"I need a TS-35 in the crate."

"A—" Addison laid his hands carefully on the arms of his chair. "You told them about the TS-35?"

"The Soviets will know about it in a week—if they don't already. Everyone else will know before the month is out. If I dangle one in front of their noses, Husad might decide I'm a useful ally. He might loosen up enough about Fitzpatrick to let me have a tour, especially if I tell him that my associates are willing to help finance Horizon."

"They may be maniacs, but they're not fools. If they had a prototype, it wouldn't take them long to duplicate the weapon."

"If we don't get Fitzpatrick out and secure the Horizon project, the TS-35 isn't much more than a peashooter."

Addison rose and paced to the window. He didn't like it. He didn't like O'Hurley. He didn't like having his plans interfered with. But he hadn't reached his position by not knowing when and how to play his cards. "I'll arrange it. But the weapon is to be brought back out or destroyed."

"Understood."

With a nod, Addison turned back. "Now, about the woman." He glanced toward the door that led to Gillian's room. "Since Agent Forrester saw fit to tell her about you and she's now aware of the operation, she'll have to be debriefed."

Trace lifted the pot of coffee and poured himself a cup. "Good luck."

"Your humor eludes me, O'Hurley. I'd like to speak with her now."

With a shrug, Trace rose to walk to the door. He pushed it open and stuck his head inside. Gillian stopped pacing and looked at him. "Your turn."

Gillian swallowed, wiped her hands on her slacks, then walked through the doorway.

"Dr. Fitzpatrick." With the first congenial smile Trace had ever seen on his face, Addison crossed to offer her his hand. "I'm Captain Addison."

"How do you do?"

"Please, sit down. Can I offer you a cup of coffee?"

"Yes, thank you." Gillian sat, back straight, chin up, while Trace lounged in the chair beside her.

"Cream, Doctor?"

"No, black, please."

Addison handed her a cup, then sat down cozily with his own. Gillian was almost afraid he was going to talk about the weather. "Dr. Fitzpatrick, I must tell you how concerned the ISS is about your family's welfare. Our organization is dedicated to ensuring the freedom and basic human rights of people everywhere. A man like your brother is of great importance to us."

"My brother is of even greater importance to me."

"To be sure." He smiled again, almost avuncularly. "Though we believe you and Agent O'Hurley acted impulsively, we think we can turn these impulses to our advantage."

Gillian looked at Trace, saw by the lazy way he moved his shoulders that he would be no help and looked back at Addison. "I acted in what I believed, and still believe, is my brother's best interests, Captain. He and Caitlin are my only concern."

"Of course, of course. I can assure you that even now the ISS is putting all its skill and experience into freeing your brother. We hope that will be accomplished quickly. In the meantime, I'd like you to come back to Madrid with me and remain under ISS protection."

"No."

"I beg your pardon?"

"I appreciate the offer, Captain, but I'm staying with Agent O'Hurley."

Addison put his arms on either side of his cup and linked his hands. "Dr. Fitzpatrick, for your own safety, and for the security of this operation, I must insist you come under ISS protection."

"My brother and my niece are in the mountains east

of here. I won't sit in Madrid and wait. I'm quite confident that Agent O'Hurley can protect me, if you feel
protection is warranted. As to the operation's security,
I was involved long before you or the ISS, Captain. I'm
sure my clearance can be upgraded if necessary."

"My orders are to take you to Madrid."

"Your orders are of no concern to me, Captain." It
was that tone of voice, used rarely but effectively, that
had helped secure her a top position at the institute.
"I have no ties to the ISS, or to anyone but my family.
General Husad wants me, as well. As long as there's a
chance that that can be used to get Flynn out, I'm willing to take the risk."

"Dr. Fitzpatrick, I understand and appreciate your
emotional involvement, but it's simply not possible—"

"It is possible, unless the ISS also indulges in kidnapping private citizens."

Addison sat back to collect his thoughts, then tried
another tactic. "Agent O'Hurley is highly trained, certainly one of our best." Trace merely lifted a brow,
knowing that had stuck in Addison's throat. "However,
his energies will be centered on the operation."

"And so will mine, as long as I can be useful."

"Agent O'Hurley will tell you himself that it's against
policy to use a civilian."

"Go to Madrid, Gillian." Trace said it quietly, and
broke a promise to himself by putting a hand over hers.
It wasn't a matter of policy. He'd already said to hell
with policy. But it was a matter of what would be best,
and safest, for her.

"I'm going with you." She turned her hand over so
that their palms met. "That was the deal."

"Don't be stupid. It could get ugly from here."

"That doesn't matter."

Because he thought he understood, he drew his hand away again. Rising, he walked to the window and lit a cigarette. What the hell had he done to earn that kind of trust? He didn't know the answer to that any more than he knew how to make her see reason. "I told you before, I don't have time to babysit."

"And I told you, I can take care of myself." She put the hand, still warm from his, in her lap as she turned back to Addison. "I've established myself as Cabot's woman. There wouldn't be any reason to question my traveling with him as far as Sefrou. If I have to wait there, I'll wait. Unless you intend to forcibly detain me, which I assure you would cause some nasty publicity, I'm going."

Addison hadn't expected resistance. His files on Gillian had indicated that she was a dedicated scientist, a woman who lived quietly and followed the rules. "I have no intention of forcibly detaining you, Dr. Fitzpatrick, but let me ask you this—what would happen if you were discovered and taken to Husad?"

"Then I'd try to find a way to kill him." She said it passionlessly. It was a decision she'd come to at dawn, after spending the night searching her soul. And it was because of the lack of passion, because of the simplicity, that Trace turned from the window to stare at her. "I would never allow him to use my knowledge or the skill I've worked all my life to attain against me. The Horizon project was never intended for a man like him. One of us would die before he got it."

Addison pulled off his glasses and began polishing them with a white handkerchief. "I admire your dedication, Doctor, and I appreciate your feelings. However, Agent O'Hurley will have his hands full over the next few days."

"She holds her own," Trace said from the window.

Addison pushed his glasses back on. "She's a civilian, and a target."

"She holds her own," Trace repeated as he and Gillian looked at each other. "I can use her. Cabot's been traveling with a woman. He always does."

"Then we'll assign another agent."

"Gillian's already established. She'll go with or without ISS sanction, so we might as well make the best of it."

It wasn't the fact that he was outnumbered. Addison had been outnumbered before. There was, however, the fact that any change of routine at this point could endanger the operation. Gillian Fitzpatrick wasn't one of his people, but if she insisted on risking her life, the ISS would use her.

"Very well. I can't stop you, but I can't approve. I hope you won't live to regret this decision, Doctor."

"I won't regret it."

"The notes. Since you refuse to come to Madrid with me, I must insist you give me your notes on Horizon so that I can secure them."

"Of course. I wrote them—"

"She wrote them in technical terms," Trace said, interrupting her. He aimed a long, cool glance at her that had her subsiding. "You probably won't be able to make much out of them."

"I'm sure our scientists will be able to interpret them. If you'll get them for me?"

"Of course."

"She's your responsibility," Addison said in an undertone when Gillian left the room. "I don't want any civilian casualties."

"I'll take care of her."

"See that you do." Addison rose and brushed back what was left of his hair. "At least without the notes she won't be able to make things worse than they are."

Gillian came back with her neatly folded papers. "This is all I have on the area I worked on."

"Thank you." Addison took them and slipped them into his briefcase. He turned the combination lock before straightening again. "If you change your mind, you have only to ask O'Hurley to contact us."

"I won't change my mind."

"Then goodbye, Doctor." He shook his head. "I hope that when this is over you and your brother can work on Horizon in peace." He gave a brief nod to Trace. "Report at six-hour intervals."

Gillian waited until the door had closed before she sat on the edge of the bed. "What an unfortunate man to work for. Do you deal with him often?"

"No, thank God." He went back to the coffee, but it was only lukewarm. "Not all ISS brass are like him."

"That's good news for the free world." She waited until he'd paced the room twice before speaking again. "I have some questions."

"Am I supposed to be surprised?"

"Could you sit?" In a gesture that might have been of annoyance or amusement, she waved toward a chair. "Over there. There's no danger of you touching me accidentally from that distance."

He paused long enough to give her a level look. "I don't touch accidentally."

"Well, that clears that up." She waited. Restless and

edgy, he took the chair. "Why did you change your mind?"

"About what?"

"About taking me with you."

"Agreeing with Addison went against the grain."

Gillian folded her hand and spoke with the patience of a Sunday-school teacher. "I think I'm entitled to a genuine answer."

"That's genuine enough." He lit a cigarette. "And I meant what I said. I think you'll do okay."

"Your flattery leaves me speechless."

"Look, I figure you've got the biggest stake in this. Maybe you've got a right to stick around." He watched her through a haze of smoke. "That's all there is."

Or all she'd get, Gillian thought. She opted to accept it. For now. "All right. Now tell me why you didn't want me to tell Addison the notes had been doctored."

"Because the real ones are in your head. I figure that's where they belong."

"He's your superior. Don't you have an obligation to be straight with him?"

"First I go with the gut, then I go with regulations."

Gillian said nothing for a moment. She respected what he'd said, admired him because she knew he meant it. Hadn't that been the reason she'd chosen to trust him? "Once before you told me you thought you understood why Mr. Forrester didn't go directly to the ISS. I think it's time you tell me."

Trace tapped the ashes of his cigarette. The sun was dropping lower in the sky. Twilight was nearly on them. He remembered he'd been watching another sunset just before he'd seen her the first time. Perhaps he was doomed to think of her whenever night approached.

"Why don't you want Hammer to have the formula?"

"That's a ridiculous question. They're a group of terrorists headed by a madman. If they had the serum, nuclear war would be almost inevitable." She fell silent as he simply sat and looked at her. "Surely you're not comparing the ISS with one of the most radical organizations on the globe? The ISS is dedicated to ensuring international law and order, to saving lives, to protecting democracy." This time it was she who rose to pace. "I don't have to tell you what they represent. You're one of them."

"Yeah, I'm one of them. Weren't you the one who said it was an organization run by men, some good, some bad?"

"Yes." She couldn't have said why her nerves were beginning to fray. The room was dimmer, the light soft and pleasant. "And I still believe that if I had gone to them in the beginning, the project would have come first, my brother and my niece second. Meeting Captain Addison did nothing to change my mind. Still, the project was done under their auspices, and it was always intended to be handed over when completed. My father believed in the system."

Trace took one last long drag. "And you?"

"My family comes first. When they're safe, we'll go from there."

"Complete the project and hand it over to the ISS?"

"Yes, of course." A little paler, she turned back to him. "That was what my father was working toward. What are you saying, Trace?"

"Just that I figure the intent of the ISS is one thing and possible results another. Think about it, Gillian, a serum that protects you from the effects of nuclear fallout. A miracle, a shield, a scientific breakthrough, whatever you want to call it. Once it's proven, how much easier is it going to be for someone to decide to push the button?"

"No." She hugged her chest and turned away again. "Horizon is a defense, only a defense, one that could save millions of lives. My father— None of us who have worked on it ever intended for it to be used destructively."

"Do you figure the scientists involved in the Manhattan Project ever expected Hiroshima? Or maybe they did. They had to know they were busy creating a bomb in the name of a scientific breakthrough."

"We're creating a defense, not a weapon."

"Yeah, a defense. And some German physicists were just fooling around with experiments fifty years ago. I wonder if they'd have gone on with it if they'd known they were forming the basis of a weapon that has the power to wipe life off the planet."

"But the weapon's there, Trace. We can't go back and prevent its creation." She'd turned back to him now. The light coming through the window behind her had gone a pure rose. "Horizon's meant to balance that, to ensure that life will go on if that final button is pushed. Horizon is a promise of life, not a threat."

"Who decides who gets the serum, Gillian?"

She moistened dry lips. "I don't know what you mean."

"Do you plan to inoculate everyone? That's not practical, probably not even feasible. Maybe we should only shoot for the countries in the United Nations. Better yet, just the countries whose political beliefs mesh with ours. Do we use it on the very old or the terminally ill?

It's bound to be expensive. Who pays for it, anyway? The taxpayers? Well, do the taxpayers want to foot the bill for the inoculation of criminals? Do we go in and give the mass murderers a shot in the arm, or do we get selective?"

"It doesn't have to be that way."

"Doesn't have to, but it usually is, isn't it? The world's not perfect, Doc. It ain't ever going to be."

She wanted to believe it could be, but she'd been fighting off those very same questions and doubts for a long time. "My father devoted most of his life to Horizon. My brother might lose his because of it. What is it you're asking me to do?"

"I'm not asking you to do anything—I'm just theorizing."

She came to him then, knowing he would distance himself, however hard she struggled to close the gap. "What disillusioned you, Trace? What made you stop believing that what you do can make a difference?"

"Because it doesn't. Oh, maybe for a while, maybe here and there, but in the long view, none of it really means a damn." He started to reach for another cigarette but pushed the pack aside instead. "I'm not ashamed of anything I've done, but that doesn't mean I'm proud, either. I'm just tired of it."

She sat across from him, no longer sure of her own thoughts, her own goals. "I'm a scientist, Trace, not a politician. As far as Horizon goes, my input has been minimal. My father didn't share a great many of his hopes with me. I do know that it was his belief, his dream, that his work would bring some lasting good. Perhaps the kind of peace we all claim to want but do so little to secure."

"You don't get peace from a serum, Doc."

"No, perhaps not. Some of the questions you've asked I've asked myself, but I haven't gone very far with them. Maybe I haven't done enough with my life to be disillusioned." She closed her eyes a moment, because nothing seemed clear, and especially not her life. "I don't know enough of what you do—or have done— to understand. I have to take it on faith. I believe, in the long view, you have made a difference. If you're tired, if you're dissatisfied, it may be because you're more of a dreamer than you'll admit. You can't change the world—none of us can—only little pieces of it."

She wanted to offer him a hand, but she held back, knowing that rejection now would prevent her from finishing. "These last few days with you have made a difference with me."

He wanted to believe. And wanting, he discovered, could hurt. "You're romanticizing again, Doc."

"No, I'm being as honest as I know how. As logical as the situation permits. You've made a difference in the way I think, the way I feel, the way I act." She pressed her lips together. Did he have any idea how difficult it was for her to strip herself bare this way? She cleared her throat, telling herself it didn't matter. She was going for broke. "I've never thrown myself at a man before."

"Is that what you're doing?" He picked up a cigarette but only ran it through his fingers. He wanted to be casual, even amused, but the ache was spreading.

"It would be obvious to anyone but you." She had to get up, to move. Why did it always seem she had to beg and bargain for affection? "I haven't asked you for a commitment." Though she wanted one. "I haven't asked for a pledge of love or fidelity." But she would give one to him if he asked. "I've only asked you to be honest enough to...to..."

"Sleep with you?" When the cigarette snapped in his fingers, Trace dropped the pieces in the ashtray. "I've already given you the reasons why that's not in the cards."

"You gave me a bunch of foolishness about our differences. I don't want you to be my twin." She had to take a quick, steadying breath. "I want you to be my lover."

Need and longing twined so tightly inside him that he had to make a conscious effort to stand and walk toward her. He would make it quick, he promised himself, he would make it cruel and save both of them. "A fast tussle in the sheets, no strings attached? Some nice uncomplicated sex without the pretty words?"

Color flooded her face, but she kept her eyes steady. "I expect no pretty words from you."

"That's good, because I don't have any." He curled his fingers into the V of her blouse and dragged her closer. She was trembling. Good. Her fear would make it that much easier. "You're out of your league, Doc. A one-night stroll through paradise isn't your style."

She started to back away but made herself stand firm. "What difference does it make? You said you wanted me."

"Sure, and maybe I'd get a kick out of showing you what life's all about. But you're the permanent kind, sweetheart. If I ever start thinking about a house in a nice neighborhood, I'll give you a call. Meanwhile, you're just not my type."

It was, as he'd intended, a solid slap in the face. She backed away, turned and started toward her room. She heard the sound of liquid hitting glass as she grasped the doorknob.

All her life, Gillian thought on a sudden wave of fury. All her life she'd taken that kind of casual criticism without a murmur. She'd grown up with it, come to expect it. But she was a grown woman. Her shoulders straightened. Her own woman, she added with a touch of malice as she turned back. It was time to stop freezing up or walking away and take the next risk.

Trace sipped warm whiskey and braced himself for what he thought would be a rousing argument. He'd have preferred it if she'd just gone into her room and slammed the door, but she was entitled to take a few shots. If she needed to, he'd let her aim and fire. He lifted the whiskey a second time. And choked on it.

"What the hell are you doing?"

Gillian calmly finished unbuttoning her blouse. "Proving you're wrong."

"Stop it." She let the blouse slide to the floor, then reached for the hook of her slacks. "Damn it, Gillian. Put your shirt on and get out of here."

She stepped out of her slacks. "Nervous?"

The teddy was virgin white, without lace, without frills. Her legs were creamier, with long thighs. Despite the whiskey, his mouth went dry as dust. "I'm not in the mood for one of your experiments." With damp hands he fumbled for a cigarette.

"Nervous, definitely." She tossed her hair back. One strap fell down her shoulder as she started toward him.

"You're making a mistake."

"That's more than a possibility." She stood in front of him so that the last light of day streamed over her hair and face. "But it'll be mine, won't it?"

If he'd ever seen anything more beautiful, he couldn't remember it. If he'd ever wanted anything more intensely, he'd long since forgotten it. But he was sure he'd never feared anything more than this small, lovely, half-naked woman with eyes like jade and hair like fire.

"I'm not going to touch you." He lifted his glass and drained the last drop. His hand trembled. It was all she needed to complete her confidence.

"All right. I'll touch you."

She had no guide to work with, no standard formula she had tested. Her experience with men wasn't non-existent, but it had been limited by a strict upbringing and a demanding career. Somehow she understood that even if she'd known hundreds of men this time would have been different. Relying on instinct and need, she stepped closer.

Her hands were steadier than his as she ran them up over his chest. With her eyes on his, she enjoyed the firm, hard feel of muscle as she moved them over his shoulders. She had to rise on her toes to reach his mouth. Then her lips were soft and coaxing as they played across his. With her body pressed against his, she felt his heart thudding.

He held his body tense, as if he were expecting a blow. Once he caught himself reaching for her, but he dropped his hands again and curled them against the dresser at his back. He thought he knew her well enough to be sure a lack of response would humiliate her to the point where she would leave. To keep her safe from him. What he hadn't counted on was that she'd come to understand him, as well.

While her lips toyed with his, she unbuttoned his shirt so that her hands could move freely over the flesh beneath. Her own heart was drumming, her vision clouding, as she murmured her approval. If she had been an accomplished seductress, she could have done no better.

"I want you, Trace." Her lips trailed over his jaw to his throat. "I have since the beginning. I tried not to." On a shuddering breath, she wrapped her arms around his waist, then ran them up his back. "Make love with me."

He put his hands to her shoulders before she could kiss him again. He knew that if his mouth was on hers a second time there would be no reason, no chance. "This isn't a game you can win." His voice had thickened. The words seemed to burn his throat. "Back off, Gillian, before it's too late."

The room was dark. The moon had yet to rise. He could see only the glimmer of her eyes as she looked at him. "You said you believe in destiny. Don't you recognize me, Trace? I'm yours."

Perhaps it was that and that alone he feared most. She was as inescapable as fate, as elusive as dreams. And now, just now, she was wrapped around him like a promise.

"Then I'm yours. God help you."

He lowered his mouth to hers with all the fire, all the force, all the fury, that he'd held back. He'd wanted to save her, and himself. Now it was up to fate, and luck. Whatever promises he'd made he'd break. He would touch her, would have his fill of her. The night would take care of itself.

He let his hands roam over her. The thin material slid under his palms. More enticement. It rose high on the thigh, so he could move from texture to texture, arousing them both. Her skin was like cream, cool, white, rich. Fascinated, he slipped his fingers under the material and found the heat. At once she dug her fingers into his back. Bracing her against him, he drove her up until her knees buckled. When she was limp, he swept her into his arms.

"This is just the beginning," he told her as he laid her on the bed. "Tonight I'm going to do all the things to you I imagined the first time I saw you." Her hair spread out like a fan of flame on the plain white cover. The first sprinkling of moonlight filtered in, along with a breeze that smelled faintly of the sea. "I can take you places you've never been. Places you may wish tomorrow you hadn't gone."

She believed him. Excited, afraid, she reached up to him. "Show me."

She hadn't known anyone could kiss that way. Before he'd shown her passion, temper, restraint. Now the restraint had been lifted, to be replaced by a devastating skill. His tongue teased and tormented, his teeth aroused and provoked. She found herself responding with a totality she'd never experienced. Already more involved than she'd ever been before, she dragged him back again and again.

Then he began to touch.

He had the hands of a musician, and he knew how to play a woman. Fingertips stroked, pressed, lingered, until she was breathless beneath him. Her murmurs were soft, then urgent, then delirious. She reached for him, held him, demanded with a strength that seemed to have been born of the moment. She fumbled for the snap of his pants, ready to take him to her, ready to give back this pleasure that she thought could reach no higher. Then his fingers found a new secret. Her body tensed, shuddered, then went lax.

No, she'd never been to this place before. It was dark,

and the air was thick and sweet. Her arms felt so heavy, her head so light. She felt the trace of his lips down her throat to where the material lay on her breast. He dipped his tongue beneath to run over the peak. She could only moan.

He caught the strap in his teeth and lowered it slowly while his hands continued to work their magic. This was how he'd wanted her, weak from pleasure, drugged with desire. He could taste where he chose. Such sweetness. Even as her skin grew hot and damp, there was such sweetness. He could have fed on it for days.

The moonlight grew brighter, the passion darker.

He drew the material down and down, following the path with his mouth. He could make her shudder. And did. He could make her moan. And did. He let her sigh with quiet delight, murmur with easy pleasure, then shot her back to desperation.

Catapulted up, Gillian reached for him. They rolled together, caught in a need that was so close to being fulfilled. Again she struggled to undress him, and this time he made no protest. She moved quickly. When they were naked, he moved more quickly.

When he plunged into her, she let out a strangled cry. Half mad, she grabbed his hair and dragged his mouth to hers. He took her hard and fast, but she found herself more than able to match her rhythm to his. More than that, it seemed to her that their hearts beat in the same rhythm. She felt him form her name against her mouth, heard the sudden shudder of his breath as emotion merged with passion. She saw as her eyes fluttered open the dark intensity of his.

Then he buried his face in her hair and they took each other.

Chapter 8

It had been a mistake to stay with her. To sleep with her through the night. To wake beside her in the morning. Trace had known when they'd wrapped themselves around each other in the night that he'd pay. A man always paid for his mistakes.

The problem was, it felt so damn good.

In sleep she was as warm, as soft, as pliable, as she had been in passion. Her head was nestled on his shoulder as if it belonged there. Her hand, curled loosely in a fist, lay over his heart as if a claim had been staked. He wished, in those early morning moments, that such things were true. Knowing better wasn't easy, it just was.

The odd and uneasy thing was that the desire hadn't dissipated. He still needed, still craved, just as sharply as he had the night before, when she'd put her hands on him for the first time.

He wanted to gather her close, to wake her slowly,

erotically, and send them both spinning back to where they'd gone before sleep had claimed them. He wanted, somehow more intensely, to gather her close, to stroke her hair and absorb the quiet excitement of dozing with her through the morning.

He couldn't do either. Though Trace would never have considered himself noble, he was thinking of her. He was a man who did his job and did as he chose. He lived as hard as he worked and had no ties to anyone. In Gillian he recognized a woman to whom home and hearth and family came first. He had no doubt she was good at what she did, that she was devoted to her work, but there were white picket fences and flower gardens buried inside her. A man who'd never had a home, who'd chosen never to have one, could only complicate the life of a woman who made one wherever she went.

But she felt so good curled around him.

He drew away more abruptly than he'd intended. When she stirred and murmured something, he rose to pull on his loose drawstring pants. He didn't have to turn around to know she was awake and watching him.

"You can sleep a while longer," he told her. "I've got some things to do."

Gillian drew the sheet with her as she sat up. She'd been half awake, or thought she had been. Perhaps she'd dreamed that he'd been stroking her hair. "I'll go with you."

"Well-bred ladies don't belong where I'm going."

Strange how quickly a chill could come. She'd lain half dreaming, warm and secure. Now she was cold and alone again. Her fingers tensed on the sheet, but her voice came out calmly. "I thought we were going to work together."

"When it suits, sweetheart."

Her fingers began to work on the sheet. "When it suits whom?"

"Me." He reached for a cigarette before he turned back to her. It was just as he'd thought. She looked more beautiful now than she had any right to, with her skin pale, her hair vivid, her eyes dark and heavy. "You'd get in the way."

"Apparently I already am." She fought back humiliation as she tossed the sheets aside to gather up what she could find of her clothes. Holding them in front of her, she paused long enough to look at him. She would say what she had to say, she told herself. Too often in the past she'd taken an emotional slap with a bowed head. No more.

"I don't know what you're afraid of, O'Hurley, except yourself and your own feelings, but there's no need to behave this way."

"I'm just doing what comes naturally." He drew on the cigarette. It tasted as bitter as his thoughts. "Look, if you're going to order breakfast, get me some coffee. I'm going to take a shower before I go out."

"It's fine to regret what happened. That's your privilege." She wouldn't cry. That she promised herself. "But it isn't fine to be cruel about it. Were you thinking I'd expect a pledge of undying love? Did you have it in your mind that I'd be waiting for you to fall on your knees and tell me I'd changed your life? I'm not the fool you think I am."

"I've never thought you were a fool."

"That's good, because I'm not." It was satisfying, she'd discovered, very satisfying, to bite back. "I didn't expect those things from you. But I didn't expect that you'd treat me as if I were something you'd bought and paid for and had the right to discard in the morning. I didn't expect that, either, Trace. Maybe I should have."

She walked quickly into her room and, tossing the crumpled clothes aside, headed straight for her shower. She wouldn't weep for him. No, by the saints, there wouldn't be one tear wasted on him. Turning the spray up to near scalding, she stepped into the shower. All she needed was to be warm again, to wash the scent of him from her skin, to rinse the taste of him from her mouth. Then she would be fine again.

She wasn't a fool, she told herself. She was simply a woman who'd made an error in judgment and now had to deal with it. She was an adult, one who made her own decisions and accepted fully and freely the consequences of her own actions.

But she was a fool. As big and as stupid as they came. Gillian pressed the heels of her hands against her eyes as the water streamed over her. Damn him, and her. Who else but a fool fell in love with a man who would never give anything back?

When the curtain whipped back, her head snapped up. She turned and gave Trace a cool, disinterested stare. The hurt wasn't his problem, she told herself. And she'd see him in hell before she'd let it show. "I'm busy at the moment."

"Let's get something straight. Just because I didn't babble over you like an idiot this morning doesn't mean I think of you as someone I could have picked up off the street."

Gillian picked up the soap to rub it in slow circles over her shoulder. So he was angry. It was there, darkening his eyes and his voice. That, too, was satisfying.

"It occurs to me that I'm better off not giving a damn what you think. Your pitiful excuses don't interest me, O'Hurley, and you're getting water all over the floor." She snatched the curtain back into place. It didn't even have time to settle before he tore it open again.

His eyes were furious, and his voice entirely too soft and steady. "Don't ever close a door in my face."

She wondered why she should feel like laughing at this point in her life. "It's not a door I'm closing, it's a curtain. A door would be more effective, but this will have to do." She pulled it closed again. Trace ripped it from the rod in one angry tug. As the little metal hooks jingled against the rod, Gillian tossed wet hair out of her eyes. "Well, now, that was a brilliant move. If you've finished taking out your foulness on an inanimate object, you can go."

He kicked the torn curtain aside. "What the hell do you want?"

"At the moment, to wash my hair in peace." Deliberately she stuck her head under the spray. Despite her determination, she let out a quick yelp when she was dragged back. He stood in the tub with her now, his cotton pants plastered to his legs. Water bounced off them both and onto the tile.

"I don't have time for this guilt trip. I've got a job to do, and we're going to clear the air so I can concentrate on doing it."

"Fine. The air's clear." She smacked the soap back in its holder. "You want absolution? You've got it."

"I've got nothing to feel guilty about." He stepped closer, and the spray hit his chest. "You threw yourself at me."

With one hand, Gillian dragged her hair back from

her face. The steam rose, clouding the room. "Aye, that I did. You fought like a tiger, but I overpowered you." She shoved a hand into his chest. "Better clear out, O'Hurley, before I force myself on you again."

"You smart-mouthed little—" He'd started forward, then had the breath knocked out of him as her fist connected with his stomach. As the water beat down on both of them, they stared at each other in equal surprise. All at once Gillian let out a gurgle of laughter and covered her mouth with her hand.

"What the hell's so funny?"

"Nothing." She choked back another laugh. "Nothing at all, except you look like a bloody fool, and I feel like one." Still laughing, she turned her face into the spray. "Be on your way, O'Hurley, before I really get tough."

He touched a hand to his stomach for a moment, amazed that she'd gotten one in under his guard. He was slipping. Then, because the anger had disappeared, he laid a hand on her shoulder to turn her around again. "You pack a hell of a punch, Doc."

It might have been her imagination, or wishful thinking, but she thought he was speaking of more than her fist. "Thank you."

"You know you run the water too hot."

"I was in the mood for hot."

"Uh-huh." He touched her cheek, running his thumb over the light sprinkling of freckles. She wondered if he knew he was apologizing. "Why don't I wash your back?"

"No."

He slipped his arms around her. "Then you can wash mine."

"Trace." She brought her hands up in a small defensive gesture. "This isn't the answer."

"It's the only one I've got." He lowered his head to rub his lips over hers. "I want you. Isn't that what you wanted to hear?"

If only it were so simple. If only she cared less. She let the sigh come as she pressed her cheek to his. "Last night was special. I can accept that it didn't mean anything to you, but I can't afford to get in any deeper, because it did mean something to me."

He was silent for a moment, knowing they would both be better off without the words even as he understood that they had to be said. "It meant something to me, Gillian." He framed her face in his hands so that he could look at her as he took the risk. "It meant too damn much."

Her heart broke a little. "And that makes things hard for you."

"Hard for me, maybe impossible for you." He would have let his hands drop, but she caught them in hers. "I'm no good for you."

"No, you're not." She smiled as she pulled his arms around her. "Neither's chocolate cake, but I can never resist that, either."

He wasn't sure it was wise to take Gillian to the bidonville, but he'd nearly convinced himself it was necessary. She might be better off seeing how low he had to sink in his job, and what kind of people he often did business with. What had happened between them that morning hadn't changed his mind about the senselessness of their relationship, but it had made him realize that a bond had formed, like it or not. It was up to him to be certain she had a clear-eyed view of what she was getting into.

So he took her on a roundabout route until he'd lost both Kendesa's tail and the shadow Addison had assigned to him. The first he not only expected but accepted as part of the game. The second proved to him that the ISS, or perhaps Addison alone, had decided against giving him a free hand. That only meant he had to take it.

Once he was certain he'd ditched both teams, Trace took one last circle before heading toward the shacks and squalor of the bidonville.

Because he wanted to go on foot, he carried a pistol under his jacket, another strapped to his calf, and a silent and very effective switchblade. Though his visit this trip had been brief, he knew his way here, just as he knew his way through so many other slums and ghettos.

There were plenty of unemployed men loitering in the narrow streets and cramped alleyways. But the two of them were never approached. Trace didn't walk like a tourist who'd lost his way or a curiosity seeker who'd come to take snapshots of the other side of Casablanca.

It stank. Gillian said nothing as she walked beside Trace. She wondered if he sensed it as she did. The smell was more than sweat, animal and rot. Over that there was the scent of anger and hatred. She'd seen poverty in Ireland, she'd witnessed the homeless and destitute in New York, but she'd never seen such misery and squalor as this.

There was blood here, newly spilled. There was disease waiting patiently to take hold. And there was death, more easily understood than life. She saw men watching her with hard black eyes. Veiled women never lifted theirs.

Trace approached a shack. It couldn't be called anything else, though it had glass in the windows and an excuse for a yard. A scrawny dog bared its teeth but backed away when Trace continued forward. There was a vegetable garden scratched into the ground. Someone had weeded it, and the rows were straight.

Trace knocked on the door of the shack before taking a long, sweeping view of the street. They were still watched, that was expected, but what went on in the bidonville stayed in the bidonville. Kendesa wouldn't find out about his visit unless Trace arranged it himself.

The door was opened by a small woman in a dark dress and veil. Her eyes showed the quick light of fear as she looked at Trace.

"Good morning. I've come to speak to your husband." His Arabic was rusty but competent enough. Gillian watched the woman's eyes dart here and there before she bowed the door the rest of the way open.

"If you would be pleased to sit."

Whatever filth and dirt were outside, the inside of the shack was neat as a pin. The floors and walls were scrubbed and still smelled lightly of the harsh soap used. The furniture was sparse, but without a speck of dust. In the center of the room sat a small boy in a cloth diaper. He grinned up at Trace and Gillian and pounded on the floor with a wooden spoon.

"I will bring my husband." The woman scooped up the child and disappeared through the back door.

Gillian bent to pick up the wooden spoon. "Why is she afraid of you?"

"Because she's smarter than you are. Sit down, Doc, and look a little bored. This shouldn't take too long."

With the spoon still in her hand, Gillian sat on a spindly chair. "Why are we here? Why did we come to this place?"

"Because Bakir has something for me. I've come to collect it." Trace slipped a hand inside his jacket as the door opened. He let it relax again when he saw that the man was alone.

Bakir was a little weasel of a man with a thin build and a narrow face. His eyes were small and dark. When he smiled, his teeth gleamed white and sharp. He was dressed in a gray robe that might have started off as spotless as the room. Now it was grimy at the hem. Two fresh grease stains spoiled the sleeve. Gillian felt an instant and uncontrollable revulsion.

"Ah, old friend. You were not expected until tomorrow."

"Sometimes the unexpected is preferable."

Though they spoke in English—Trace wasn't feigning an accent—Gillian said nothing. She wished quite fiercely that she had remained behind. The shack didn't seem clean and harmless now that Bakir had come inside.

"You are in a hurry to complete our business?"

"Do you have the merchandise, Bakir? I have other matters to attend to today."

"Of course, of course, you're a busy man." He glanced at Gillian and, with a grin, said something in Arabic. Trace's eyes went hard as stone. His reply was only a murmur, but whatever he said was enough to make Bakir blanch and bow. Pushing a table aside, he lifted a portion of the floor to reveal a wide trench beneath.

"Your assistance, please."

Trace bent to the task. Between the two of them, they hauled up a long wooden crate. Moving in silence now, Bakir pulled a crowbar from the trench and pried off the lid. Gillian's fingers tensed when Trace pulled out the first rifle.

It was black and oiled. She knew by the ease with which he lifted and sighted that he'd used one before. He broke it open and, in the practical manner of a man who understood guns, examined it.

"Almost like new," Bakir offered.

Instead of acknowledging him, Trace put the rifle back and drew out another. He performed the same careful examination on it, then on the next and the next, as he pulled them out of the crate. Each time he lifted a new one, Gillian's heart jolted.

He looked so natural with a gun in his hands. The same hands that had held and stroked and aroused her only a short time before. He was the same man. And yet as she looked at him now she wondered how he could seem so different in this place, with a crate of weapons at his feet and one in his hand.

Satisfied that the guns and ammunition were in order, Trace nodded. "You'll have the merchandise shipped to Sefrou. This address." He passed Bakir a sheet of paper. "Shipment tomorrow."

He reached into his jacket for an envelope fat with ISS money. He wondered what Addison's reaction would be when he learned Trace had requisitioned it.

The envelope disappeared into the folds of Bakir's cloak, but his hand remained on it. "As you wish. It may interest you that certain powers have offered great rewards for information on Il Gatto."

"Make the shipment, Bakir, and remember what would be done to anyone found to have done business with Il Gatto."

Bakir only grinned. "My memory is excellent."

"I don't understand." Gillian stayed close to Trace's side as they started down the narrow street. "Where did you get that money?"

"From taxpayers." As he walked he let his gaze swing right and left. "This is an ISS-backed operation now."

"But you gave him money for those guns. I thought Captain Addison was arranging for the weapons."

"He is." He took her arm to steer her around a corner.

"Well, if Addison's arranging for the weapons you're to show Husad, why did you pay that man for more?"

"Backup. If things don't go Addison's way, I don't figure on trying to get your brother out with a pistol and a charming smile."

Gillian felt the knot of tension in her stomach tighten. "I see. Then they're for you."

"That's right, sweetheart. Keep walking," he said when she hesitated. "This isn't the neighborhood for window-shopping."

"Trace, what good are those weapons going to do you, one man, alone?"

"Isn't that what you hired me for?"

"Yes." She pressed her lips together as she kept pace with him. "Yes, but—"

"Having second thoughts?"

She was having more than second thoughts. But how could she explain to him that the past few days had changed everything? How could she tell him that he was now every bit as important to her as the man and the child she wanted so desperately to see safe? He would laugh at her concern—or, worse, be annoyed by it.

"I don't know what I think anymore," she murmured. "The longer this goes on, the less real it seems. When it first started, I thought I knew exactly what had to be done. Now I'm not sure of anything."

"Just let me do the thinking."

A man in a grimy white robe stumbled in front of them. He only had time to gesture toward Gillian and mutter something in a drunken slur before Trace had the switchblade out. Gillian saw the sun glint off steel as Trace issued a quiet warning. Still grinning, the man lifted both hands palms up and teetered out of the way again.

"Don't look back," Trace ordered as he pulled Gillian along with him.

"Did he want money?"

He'd stopped believing anyone could be that naive. She was good for him, he thought. Too damn good. "For starters," he said simply.

"This is an awful place."

"There are worse."

She looked at him then as the beat of her heart began to calm again. "You know how to walk here, how to talk here, but that doesn't make you like that man back in that shack."

"We both make a living."

They skirted around the walls and went into the shopping district. "You know, I think you'd like me to believe you were like him. That would be more comfortable for you."

"Maybe. We'll get some coffee, hang around here long enough for the tails to pick us up again."

"Trace." Though it shamed her, she felt safe again away from the sights and smells of the slums. "Is it just me, or do you fight off anyone who gets too close?"

He didn't know how to answer her. Worse, he wasn't sure he could afford to dig too deeply for the real answer. "Seems to me we were pretty close last night."

She met his look levelly, her eyes clear and serene. "Yes, we were, and you still haven't dealt with it."

"I've got a lot on my mind, Doc." He pulled out a chair at a small café and sat down. After a moment's hesitation, Gillian joined him.

"So have I. More than I bargained for." She let him order coffee and hoped that before long she would be back in her room, where she could pull down the shades, close her eyes and block out the morning, if only for a little while. "I have another question."

"Sweetheart, I've never known you not to."

She put a hand on his before he could light a cigarette. "That man, Bakir, he didn't know you as Cabot."

"No, I used him in an operation a few years back."

"He's an agent?"

Trace laughed but waited until their coffee was served before speaking again. "No, Doc, he's a snake. But reptiles have their uses."

"He knows who you are. Why would he deliver the shipment instead of simply keeping the money you've given him and telling Husad who and where you are?"

"Because he knows that if Husad didn't manage to kill me I'd come back and slit his throat." Trace lifted his coffee. Out of the corner of his eye he noted that the first tail had picked them up again. "Bad business risk."

Gillian stared at her coffee. It was black and thick. She knew that if she drank it it would take the chill from her skin, but she didn't pick up the cup. "I was raised to respect life," she said quietly. "All life. So much of the work I've done has been to try to make life better, easier. I can't deny that science has had too much to do with destruction, but the goal has always been to preserve and advance. I've never in my life hurt anyone intentionally. It's not that I'm such a saint, but more, I think, that I've never had to make that choice."

She wrapped both hands around her cup but still didn't pick it up as she lifted her gaze to Trace's. "When Captain Addison asked me what I would do if Husad took me, I was telling the truth. I know in my heart that I could take a life. And it frightens me."

"You're not going to find yourself in the position where you have to put that to the test." He put a hand over hers briefly, because no matter how hard he tried he couldn't keep himself from offering comfort.

"I hope not, because I know not only what I would do, but that I could live with it afterward. I suppose what I'm trying to say is that we're not so different, you and I."

He looked away from her, because the need to believe she was right was too sharp. "Don't bet on it."

"I already have," she murmured, and drank her coffee.

Chapter 9

Gillian told herself that the move to Sefrou was bringing her another step closer to Flynn. He was close now. She could look out at the unfamiliar streets and mountains and almost feel how close.

It was a rare thing now for her to allow herself more than a few moments alone. Alone she would think too clearly of what had happened, what could be happening, to her brother and niece. The fear that she was too late, or would ultimately be too late, was a dark secret she kept buried inside her heart.

She didn't spend her nights weeping. The emotional release of tears wouldn't help Flynn. There were the nightmares, the sometimes hideous, often violent dreams she pulled herself out of on almost a nightly basis. Thus far she had been able to bring herself out of the nightmares without causing a disturbance that woke Trace. At least she could be grateful for that. She didn't want him to know she was weak enough to be frightened into cold chills by dreams. He had to think of her as strong and capable. Otherwise he might change his mind about letting her play any part in freeing Flynn.

Strange how well she had come to know him. Gillian watched a small compact car wind through the streets below while the silence of her hotel room hung around her. It was at times like this, when she was alone, that she worked hardest to concentrate on the practical aspects of Flynn's release. When that didn't work, she concentrated instead on Trace. Who he was, what made him tick, what secrets he kept locked in his heart.

She had come to understand him, though he told her little with words. More than once she had imagined them meeting socially in New York, under normal, even pedestrian, circumstances. A dinner date, a show, a cocktail party. She knew they would have become lovers wherever they'd met, but she also knew that under other circumstances it would have happened slowly and with more caution.

Destiny. She had never really thought about her own before Trace. Now she believed, as he did, that some things were meant. *They* were meant. She wondered how long he would continue to fight his feelings, the feelings she sensed in him whenever he held her. Words of affection wouldn't come easily from a man who'd deliberately shut those doors in his life. She was certain the reason for that had to do with his family.

If there was one thing Gillian was accustomed to, it was reticent males. She could be patient until he opened up to her. And she was optimistic enough not to doubt that he would.

She was so in love. She leaned on the windowsill

with a sigh. All her life she'd waited for this feeling, the one that made the heart pound and the brain giddy, the one that made everything seem more vivid. True, she'd never expected to experience love for the first time in the midst of the biggest crisis of her life. But, crisis or not, the feeling was there, big and bold and beautiful.

Gillian knew she would have to wait to share it. There'd come a time when she could speak of it freely, laugh and steep herself in the feelings between them. She hadn't waited all her life to fall in love only to be denied the pleasure of expressing it. But she could wait.

One day, when Flynn and Caitlin were safe, when the violence, the fear, the intrigue, were nothing more than a vague memory, she would have her time with Trace. A lifetime. She couldn't afford to doubt that. What had happened in the past few weeks had taught her that happiness had to be grabbed with both hands and treasured with a full heart.

Yes, she would bide her time, and accept her destiny.

But how she wished he'd come back. How she hated being left alone.

Gillian understood he had a role to play and a job to do. Neither Cabot's mistress nor Dr. Gillian Fitzpatrick had a place in the morning meeting between Flynn and his ISS contact in eastern Morocco. The ISS agent would see that André Cabot received his supply of arms, just as Bakir would see that Il Gatto received his.

She could only wait while the man she loved armed himself and stepped into the hornet's nest.

Because her nerves were building quickly, Gillian searched for something to do. She had already unpacked and rearranged her belongings three times. Trace's case was open, but his clothes were jumbled inside. He'd taken out only what he needed that morning. For lack of something better to do, Gillian began to shake out, refold and put away his clothes.

She found she could enjoy the small task, smoothing out a shirt, wondering where he'd bought it, how he looked wearing it. She could draw in his scent from his rumpled garments. His taste in clothes was certainly eclectic. There was everything from denim to silk, from bargain basement to Saville Row.

How many men did he carry around in this case? she wondered as she folded a T-shirt that was thin to the point of transparency at the shoulders. She wondered if he ever had to stop and think, to bring back to the front of his mind who he really was.

Then she found the flute, wrapped carefully in felt beneath a tailored shirt of satin piqué. It was polished but had the look of something old and well used. Experimentally Gillian lifted it to her lips and blew. The note came clear and sweet and had her smiling.

He came from a family that made its living making music. He hadn't left that behind, not completely, no matter how hard he pretended he had. She imagined he played when he was alone and lonely in some foreign place. Perhaps it reminded him of the home he claimed not to have, of the family he'd chosen not to see for years.

She placed her fingers over the holes, then lifted two at random, enjoying the sound that came when she blew into the mouthpiece. She'd always had an affection for music, though her father had considered the study of chemicals more important than the piano lessons she'd once hoped for. She wondered if someday Trace would teach her to play a real melody, something sentimental, from the country she'd left behind.

She set the flute on the bed, but didn't rewrap it. There were books in the case, as well, Yeats and Shaw and Wilde. Gillian picked one and leafed through familiar passages. A man who described himself in such harsh terms carried Yeats along with a weapon. She'd sensed that contradictory combination long before she'd seen evidence it existed; indeed, she'd fallen in love with the many sides of the enigma that was Trace O'Hurley.

Nerves forgotten, fears banked, she set the books on the table beside the bed. She was humming to herself as she put the last of the shirts away. When she started to close the case, she noticed a notebook tucked in one of the side pockets. Without thinking, she drew it out and set it on the edge of the dresser. She put the case in the closet beside hers, fussed to be sure the trousers were hung by the crease, then wandered back toward the window. As she passed the dresser, she knocked the notebook to the floor. The words and musical notes caught her eye as she bent to pick it up.

The sun rises, the sun sets, but I wait for the dream.
The nights are too long to be alone.
Days pass without sweetness in sunlight that streams.
The nights are too dark to be far from home.

Enchanted, she sat on the bed to read. Her hand went to the flute and rested there.

It had been a few years since Trace had worked with Breintz. They'd put together a tidy little job in Sri Lanka five or six years before, and then, in the way of people in their business, they'd lost touch. Outwardly Breintz had changed. His hair had thinned, his face had widened. There were folds of wrinkles under his eyes that gave him a lazy basset-hound look. He sported a sapphire stud in his ear and wore the robe of the desert people.

After an hour's discussion, Trace was reassured. However much Breintz's appearance had changed, inside he was still the same sharp-witted agent he'd worked with in the past.

"It was decided against using the usual routes for the shipment." Breintz's clipped English had a controlled musicality Trace had always found agreeable. "It would be too possible for another terrorist group to trace it, or even for an overenthusiastic customs official to cause problems. In this I have used my contacts. The shipment comes by private plane to an airstrip a few miles east of here. Those who need to be paid off have been."

Trace nodded. In the dim rear booth of the nearly empty restaurant he indulged in one of Breintz's Turkish cigarettes. Over the scent of rich smoke he could smell meat—some sort of sausage—grilling. "And once the shipment arrives, I move accordingly. The whole thing should be over in a week."

"If the gods permit."

"Still superstitious?"

Breintz's lips curved, more in patience than in humor. "We all hold on to what works." Breintz let out smoke in three puffs, watching the rings form and vanish. "I don't believe in advice, but in information. Understand?"

"Yes."

"Then I will pass on this information, though you are likely aware already. I am in my fourth year of association with terrorists in this small, beleaguered part of the world. Some are fanatically religious, some politically ambitious, some simply blinded by anger. Such things, when accompanied by a disregard for human life, are dangerous, and, as we have too often found, not easily controllable. There is a reason, old friend, why none of the more established revolutionary organizations recognize Hammer. Religion, politics and anger become unpalatable even to the radical when they are driven by madness. Husad is a madman—a clever and magnetic one, but a madman. If he discovers your deception, he will kill you in any of several unpleasant ways. If he does not discover your deception, he will still kill you."

Trace drew again on the Turkish cigarette. "You're right, I'm already aware. I'm going to get the scientist and the kid out. Then I'm going to kill Husad."

"Assassination attempts have failed before, to the disappointment of many."

"This one won't."

Breintz spread his hands. "I am at your service."

With a last nod, Trace rose. "I'll be in touch."

Trace knew he would be moving toward a conclusion in a matter of days. He was grateful for it. Since his first assignment with the ISS, he'd accepted the fact that any job he agreed to take could kill him. It hadn't been a matter of his not caring whether he lived or died. Trace had always had a definite preference for living. It had simply been a matter of his acknowledging the risks and making damn sure he was around to collect his pay. Over the past few days, staying alive had become even more important.

He hadn't changed his mind concerning himself and Gillian, but he'd had to accept the fact that he wanted more time with her. He wanted time to hear her laugh, as she'd done so rarely since they'd met. He wanted time to watch her relax, as she did only when she'd convinced herself she could let go for short snatches of time. He wanted, more than he cared to admit, to have her care for him with the same depth and devotion that she cared for her family.

It was stupid. It was certainly wrong for her. But that was what he wanted.

He would give her back her brother, and the child she sometimes murmured for in her sleep. He would do what he had come to Morocco to do, and then he would have one clear night with her. One night, all night, without the tensions, the fears, the doubts, that hovered around her now. She thought he didn't sense them, but he did. He wanted to give her peace.

She hadn't wanted his sympathy, so he didn't offer it. The passion he did give should have been easy, yet it was tinted with the sweetest, sharpest ache he'd ever known. The ache was longing, a longing to give more than was asked, to take more than was given. To make promises, and to accept them.

He couldn't do that, but he could have that one night with her when her family was safe and the threat was past. Then he could give her the gift of backing out of her life.

To have that one night, to walk away with more than he'd ever had before, all he had to do was stay alive.

Kendesa's tail dropped him in the lobby. Trace felt secure knowing Kendesa was taking precautions. He felt even better knowing that his meeting with Breintz would be reported. The other agent's cover was as tight as they came. Trace strolled down the corridor to his room, thinking how glad he would be to get out of the suffocating suit and tie.

When he opened the door he was stunned, then furious.

Gillian looked up at him, her eyes damp and her smile brilliant. "Trace, I'm so glad you're back. These songs are so lovely. I've read them all twice and still haven't decided if I have a favorite. You have to play them for me so I can—"

"What the hell are you doing digging around in my things?"

The tone caught her so off guard that she simply stared at him, the notebook open in her lap. When he crossed to her to snatch the notebook, she felt the full brunt of his fury. She didn't cringe away. She just sat very still.

"I don't suppose it occurred to you that even though I'm working for you, even though I'm sleeping with you, I'm still entitled to my privacy."

She went very pale, as she did whenever stress took over. "I'm sorry," she managed in a very careful voice. "You were gone so long, and I needed something to do, so I thought I'd put your things away for you. I came across the flute and the notebook as I was finishing up."

"And didn't stop to think that what was written in the notebook might be private?" He stood, holding the book in his hand, as thoroughly embarrassed as he'd ever been in his life. What he'd written had come straight from the heart and was nothing he'd ever intended to share with anyone.

"I beg your pardon." Her voice was stiff with formality now. She didn't bother to tell him how the notebook had fallen open, since he was so obviously interested only in the end result. "You're right, of course. I had no business messing about with your things."

He'd hoped for an argument. A good shouting match would have helped him turn the embarrassment into something more easily dealt with. Instead, her quiet apology only made him feel more embarrassed and a great deal like a moron. Opening a drawer, he tossed the book in, then slammed it shut again.

"Next time you're bored, read a book."

She rose as her own temper bristled. She'd gotten such pleasure, such innocent pleasure, out of the words the man was capable of writing. Now she was being punished for discovering this secret part of him. But it was his secret, she reminded herself before she could open her mouth in anger. It was his, and she'd intruded on it.

"I can only repeat that I'm sorry, I was completely in the wrong, and you have my word that the mistake won't be repeated."

No, she wasn't going to argue with him, Trace realized as he walked over to wrap the flute in felt. There was too much hurt in her eyes, hurt he'd put there by being so unreasonably hard about an innocent act. "Forget it." He set the flute in the drawer beside the book and shut them both away. "The meeting with Breintz went according to plan. The guns are here. I figure Kendesa will make contact tomorrow, the next day at the latest."

"I see." She looked around for something to do, something to occupy her hands. She settled on clasping them together. "Then it should all be over soon."

"Soon enough." For reasons that escaped him, he wanted to apologize, to hold her and tell her he was sorry for being an idiotic ass. He stuck his hands in his pockets. "We can go down for lunch. There's not much to see in this place, but you could get out of the room awhile."

"Actually, I thought I'd lie down, now that you're back and I know everything's all right. I've really been more wound up than hungry." And though she'd thought never to feel that way again, she wanted desperately to be alone.

"All right. I'll bring you something back."

"Some fruit, maybe." They kept their distance, because neither had the nerve to take the first step. "I never seem to have much of an appetite when I'm traveling."

He remembered the first night, when she'd fallen asleep without dinner, how pale and drained she'd been when he'd carried her to bed. She was pale now, too. He wanted, very badly, to stroke the color back into her cheeks. "I won't be long."

"Take your time."

She waited until he was gone before she lay down on the bed. Curling into a ball always seemed to help somehow. It concentrated the hurt into one tight place where it was more easily dealt with. She wouldn't weep. She let her eyes close and tried hard to concentrate on nothing. She wouldn't let her emotions swing wild, the way they had when she'd been young and had thought to surprise her father.

She'd tidied up his office, polishing wood and shining glass. He'd been furious, too. She sighed and struggled to clear the memory from her mind. Furious that she'd infringed on his private space, touched his personal things. She might have broken something, misplaced something. It hadn't mattered that she'd done neither.

Sean Brady Fitzpatrick had been a hard man, and loving him had been one long exercise in frustration. Gillian sighed again. Apparently she was a very slow learner.

He hadn't eaten anything. Nor had he finished the whiskey he'd ordered. Trace had never known a woman who could make a man feel more of a fool when she was clearly in the wrong. Those songs had never been intended for anyone but himself. He wasn't ashamed of them, it was just that he'd indulged himself, or parts of himself, in the writing of them. They were his innermost thoughts, innermost feelings, dreams he admitted to having only on the rarest of occasions. He wasn't sure he could handle her knowing what was inside him, what he sometimes longed for on the longest of lonely nights. The songs could erase the differences and the distance between them, whether he wanted them to or not.

He shouldn't have hurt her. Only the stupid or the heartless hurt the defenseless. Discovering he could be both left an unpleasant taste in his mouth. He'd have liked to blame that on her, too, but he thought too clearly once anger had passed.

He laid the rose on the little basket of fruit and opened the door.

She was sleeping. He'd hoped she would be awake so that he could make his gesture of apology quick and painless. Growing up with women had taught him that they forgave easily, often smugly, as though men's cloddish behavior was to be expected. It wasn't a sweet pill to swallow, but at least it was a small one.

Trace set the basket on the dresser before moving toward her. She was curled up tight, as if to ward off another blow. That was one more brick on his back. Muttering a curse, he pulled the spread up over her. She'd left the shade up. He walked over to draw it down and dim the room. It made a quiet sound that had her stirring in sleep.

"Caitlin."

Though the little girl's name came in a murmur, Trace heard the fear in it. Not sure what to do, he sat on the edge of the bed and began to stroke her hair. "She'll be all right, Gillian. Just a few more days."

But his touch and his reassurance seemed to set off a new reaction. He felt her begin to tremble. Even as he stroked the hair from her temple, sweat pearled cold on her skin. Though he let no more than a second pass, he could see she was fighting to pull herself out of the dream. Her face went a deathly white as he took her by the shoulders and drew her up.

"Gillian, wake up." He gave her a squeeze that had her muffling a scream. "Come on, Doc, knock it off." Her eyes were wide and terrified when they flew open. Trace kept his grip firm until he saw comprehension come into them. "You okay?"

"Yes, yes, I'm fine." But she couldn't stop shaking. All the other times she'd been able to control the shaking. "I'm sorry."

"You don't have to apologize for having a nightmare."

"For making a fool out of myself, then." She drew away, just a little, but enough to make him realize what a twist rejection gave the heart.

"Want some water?"

"Yes. I'll get it."

"Sit down, damn it. I'll get it." He felt like a ham-handed jerk. Giving the tap a violent twist, he filled a glass to the rim with tepid water. Gillian sat on the bed, fighting back tears she was certain would put a cap on her humiliation and struggling to ignore a roiling stomach that came from holding back too long. "Take a couple of sips and relax."

But her hands were shaking, and she only managed to spill water on both of them. "I'm—"

"If you apologize again, I swear I'll belt you." He took the glass and set it aside and then, feeling an awkwardness he'd never experienced with women, slipped an arm around her. "Just relax. Why don't you tell me about it? It usually helps."

She wanted to lean her head against his shoulder. She wanted him to hold her, really hold her, murmuring something sweet and foolish, until the terror passed. She wanted a miracle, she told herself. As a scientist, she knew that the world was fresh out.

"It was just a dream, unpleasant, that's all. Like the rest of them."

"What rest of them?" He cupped her face in his hand so that he could turn it up to his. "Have you been having nightmares all along?"

"It's not surprising. The unconscious mind—"

He swore and tightened his grip. He remembered how she had trembled, how the sweat had beaded cold and clammy on her skin, how glazed with fear her eyes had been. "Why didn't you tell me?"

"I didn't see the point."

He let her go then, slowly, and rose to his feet. If she had aimed a blow directly at his solar plexus, she wouldn't have been any more accurate. He gave a brief, humorless laugh. "Well, I guess I had that one coming, didn't I?"

A new fear was growing, one that warned her that she might be suddenly, violently, physically sick. She was too afraid to try to stand, too restless to stay where she was. "You'd just have been annoyed, as you are now. And I'd just have been embarrassed, as I am now." She shifted so that she could press a hand against the churning of her stomach.

"Seems you've got me pegged," he murmured. He opened his mouth to say more but was surprised to see that she'd gone even paler. Moving instinctively, he turned her toward the edge of the bed and pushed her head between her knees. "Just breathe deep. It'll pass in a minute. Come on, love, nice deep breaths."

Even as the faintness faded, the tears burned in her eyes. "Just leave me alone, will you? Just go away and leave me alone."

There'd been a time, not so long before, when he would've been only too happy to oblige her. Now he simply ran a hand up and down her spine, murmuring to her, until he felt her breathing even out. "I think we've both taken the easy way for too long." Gathering her up, he lay down beside her and held her close. He recognized more surprise than resistance and decided he deserved that, as well. "I think you should know I don't expect Superwoman. I know what you're going through, and I know that even someone as strong as you needs an outlet. Let me help."

She tightened her arms around him. Though the tears fell quietly, the release was complete. "I need you." Her body absorbed the warmth of his as tension fled. "I've tried so hard not to be afraid, and to believe everything really is going to be all right. Then the dreams... They kill all of you. And I can't stop them."

"The next time you have a dream, remember, I'm right here. I'm not going to let it happen."

She could almost believe in miracles when he moved his fingers gently through her hair, his lips gentle at her temple. "I don't want to lose you, either." She tilted her face up to his, hoping she would at least see acceptance.

"I've come through tighter spots than this." He touched his mouth to her forehead, realizing how comforting it could be to give comfort. "Besides, my retirement fund's riding on this one."

Her lips curved a little. "The Canary Islands."

"Yeah." Oddly, he couldn't picture the palm trees and calm waters. "I'm not going to let you down, Gillian."

She touched a hand to his face. "When this is over, I wonder if it would be an intrusion if I visited you there for a few days."

"I might be up to some company. The right company." He nestled her head in the curve of his shoulder again. The glass on the table beside them vibrated against the wood. Water sloshed over the edge again. Beneath them, the bed shook.

"What—"

"Earth tremor." He tightened his grip. "Just a little one. Morocco's prone to earthquakes."

"Is that all?" When the vibration ceased, Gillian let out the breath she'd been holding. "I could give you some scientific data on earthquakes, crustal plates, faults." She let out a calmer breath when the world stayed steady. "But I can't say I've ever experienced one firsthand."

"It's quite a show."

"One I wouldn't mind missing."

"Gillian..."

"Yes?"

"I'm...ah... About before... I guess I didn't have to come down so hard on you."

"I didn't think before I acted. That's always a mistake."

"Not always. Anyway, I overreacted about something that wasn't that big a deal."

"Your songs are a very big deal." She liked the way he brushed his hand under her hair to her neck. He'd held her so close when the earth had shaken. There was a need in him to protect. She wondered how long it would take before he recognized it. "I know you didn't like me looking at them, but I can't be sorry I did. They were so beautiful."

"They're only... Really?"

Because the question touched her, she shifted again so that she could look down at him. How nice it was, how sweet, to discover that he, too, knew self-doubt and the need for reassurance. "Now and again, and very briefly, I've seen true sensitivity in you. A real gift for seeing things, feeling things. I like that man very much. After reading those songs, I felt closer to him."

He moved his shoulders uncomfortably. "You're making me into something I'm not again."

"No. I'm just accepting that there's more than one side of you." She kissed him softly, reaching out as much to the man he was as to the man he'd had to be.

She moved him too much, too deeply. Trace drew her away again, though he knew they'd passed the last border. "I'm going to disappoint you."

"How, when I'm willing to take you as you are?"

"I guess there's no use reminding you you're making a mistake?"

"None," she answered, just as her lips met his.

He'd never kissed her like this, softly, quietly, as if he had a lifetime to indulge himself. The passion and skill that always excited and overwhelmed her was banked. Instead, he gave her the affection she'd always fantasized about but had never expected to receive. She wondered if he realized how beautiful that gift was or how desperately she needed it now. Her sigh, as much from gratitude as pleasure, stole into the room.

He undressed her slowly, experimenting with the feelings that he'd finally let have their freedom. Strong, solid, inescapable feelings that filled him with power and serenity.

He could love and be loved, he could give and receive love, taste it, savor it, hoard it. For one day he could believe that a woman like her was meant for him, to keep, to cherish, to last.

By necessity the future had always been kept very close to the present. He could never allow himself to think in months, much less years. So even now, with her warm and willing in his arms, he refused to acknowledge the tomorrows. Today was timeless and theirs, and he would remember it.

His hands were the hands of an artist now. Skillful, yes, but sensitive. She hadn't known a man could love a woman with such restraint and still stir unbearably. His body was familiar now, so that when she undressed him she knew how to touch, where to stroke, when to linger. It was an adventure in itself to discover she could arouse him, make his body tense, his muscles bunch. It was thrilling to learn that even when aroused he could take care.

He held her differently, and though the difference was subtle, she reveled in it. Desire took on such fascinating, such miraculous angles when touched with emotion. Her name came almost musically through his lips as they glided over her. His murmurs were like quiet promises as she caressed.

He loved her. She wanted to laugh and shout it out with triumph, but she knew the words had to come from him, in his time, in his way.

Such patience. She hadn't known he had such patience in him for a woman. For her. Given it, she felt herself blossom in his hands. All that she had, all that she felt, all that she'd hoped to feel, was his for the asking.

Such generosity. He hadn't known anyone could possess such a bounty of it. He hadn't expected anyone to offer it to him with such freedom. Whatever he could give, whatever was coming to life inside him, was for her. And only her.

When they offered, and accepted, they both understood that some miracles were possible.

The light crept around the edges of the shades but did little to chase away the shadows in the room. He'd never felt so at ease with anyone. They'd slept awhile—only minutes, really—but he'd found himself refreshed and renewed. Trace rolled over on his stomach, one arm wrapped around her, and thought that the best thing to do with his energy was to make love with her again.

"Remember that shower we took the other day, when you were in a snit?"

Lazily she shifted so that she lay half over him, her

cheek on his back. "I don't recall being in a snit. I do remember being justifiably annoyed."

"Whatever, the result was the same." He closed his eyes on a sigh as she began to knead the muscles at the base of his neck. "I was just thinking how nice you felt, all hot and wet, particularly when you were mad enough to spit in my eye."

"Oh? Do you have plans to make me mad again?"

"Whatever it takes. A little lower, Doc. Yeah." He sighed as her fingers moved down his spine. "That's the spot."

"I could be persuaded to take a shower." She pressed her lips to his shoulder blade, then moved them down to follow the path of her hands.

"I don't think it would take much persuasion."

"Really." She looked up at the back of his head. "Are you saying I'm easy, O'Hurley?"

"No." He grinned to himself. "I'm saying I'm good." He winced only a little when she pinched him.

"Such arrogance usually precedes a fall. Perhaps I should—" She broke off when she made a new discovery. "Trace, why do you have a beetle tattooed on your bottom?"

He opened one eye. "A scorpion."

"I beg your pardon?"

"It's a scorpion."

Willing to give him the benefit of the doubt, Gillian leaned closer. "I realize the light's a bit dim, but... No, this is definitely a beetle. A squashed beetle, at that." She gave it a quick, friendly kiss. "Trust me, I'm a scientist."

"It's a scorpion. Symbolic of a quick sting."

She pressed a hand to her mouth to muffle a chuckle. "I see. How appropriate. However, since my view is undoubtedly better than yours could be, let me assure you that your very attractive posterior is adorned with a squashed beetle."

"It's just a little out of focus," he told her, refusing to take offense, because her hands felt so good. "The tattoo artist was drunk."

Gillian sat up, resting one hand on his hip. "Are you saying you were mad enough to trust this very sensitive area of your body to a drunk tattoo artist?"

Trace rolled over. In a move that reminded her how quick he could be, he had her beneath him. "I was drunk, too. Do you think I'd let anyone come near me with a needle if I was sober?"

"You're mad."

"Yeah. And I was twenty-two." He began to indulge in the taste of her skin. "Nursing a broken heart and a dislocated shoulder."

"Did you have your heart broken, then?" Curious, she lifted his face to hers. "Was she pretty?"

"Gorgeous," he said instantly, though he couldn't really remember. "With a body that was almost as good as her imagination." He kept his face bland as her eyes narrowed.

"Is that the truth?"

"If it's not, it should be. Anyway, I did have a dislocated shoulder."

"Aw." Gillian ran her hand up to it. "Would you like another?"

"Threats?" Delighted, Trace grinned down at her. "You know, Doc, you sound suspiciously like a jealous woman."

Now the heat came into her eyes. "I don't know what

you're talking about. I'd hardly waste any healthy jealousy I might have on the likes of you."

"Are you getting justifiably annoyed?"

"And why shouldn't I, when I'm lying naked in bed with a man who's cloddish enough to tell me about another woman?"

"Good." Trace rolled off the bed. Then, ignoring her struggles, he tossed Gillian over his shoulder.

"Just what do you think you're doing?"

"Now that I've got you in a snit, I thought we'd take that shower."

Gillian caught the beetle between her thumb and forefinger and twisted hard. "Bastard."

"I love it when you talk dirty."

He carried her laughing into the bath.

Chapter 10

When the arrangements had been made for Trace to meet Husad's men and be driven into the mountains, Gillian was torn in two directions. She wanted Trace to get to Flynn, to see him, to come back and tell her that her brother and her little niece were well and that he'd found a safe and simple way to free them.

It was because she knew there was no safe and simple way that she wanted to tell him not to go, not to risk being killed or captured. She was well aware that if she hadn't interfered in his life Trace would have spent these past weeks basking in the Mexican sun. Whatever happened to him now was her responsibility. When she'd tried to explain her feelings to him, he'd brushed her off.

"No one's ever been responsible for me, sweetheart. It would be stupid for you to start now."

So she kept silent about her fears, knowing they were of little use to her, and of no use whatever to Trace.

When they made love, it was with a quiet madness, a restrained desperation that spoke of what neither of them had said aloud. This might be the last time. She wanted to beg him for promises, but she settled for moonlight and rough caresses. He wanted to make her a pledge, but he settled for her warmth and generosity. She could have no idea what risks were involved when he walked into the lion's den armed only with a lie. Though he knew a lie could be as lethal a weapon as any, he would have preferred the cold company of his .45.

As Cabot, he would get nowhere near Husad with a gun or a blade. As Il Gatto... But Il Gatto would have to wait. He would go to Husad's mountain headquarters, and he would come back with Flynn and Caitlin Fitzpatrick. Or he would not come back.

Shifting, he listened to Gillian's quiet breathing beside him. No nightmares, he thought, grateful. In a day, perhaps two, it would be done. Then she could go back to her life in New York, her institute, her experiments. There would be no need for nightmares once her world had been put in order again.

He stroked her hair, but lightly, wanting to touch but not to awaken. He'd never asked her about her work. To ask would have brought himself another step closer. But he tried to imagine her now, laboring over some impossibly complicated calculations, a white coat covering some neat business suit, her hair tied back or pinned up, her eyes intense with concentration.

She really believed she could change the world with knowledge and logic and science. He let the tangled silk of her hair drift between his fingers. Maybe it was good that she did, that she refused to face the hard reality that nothing ever really changed. The grimness of that fact would steal something from her, as it had from him. He wanted to remember her as she was—strong, naive, full of hope.

He didn't know how to tell her what she'd meant to him, what, if he'd been different, they might have meant to each other. So he drew his hand away and left her sleeping.

But she was awake. She'd known he was restless and lost in his own thoughts, so she'd lain quietly. There was something so tender and sweet about the way he touched her when he thought she was unaware. That was something she could hold on to the next day, when he walked out the door.

If he couldn't sleep, she thought, perhaps if she reached out and offered to hold him he would rest. But when she heard him pick up the phone, she kept her silence.

He spoke in French, which left her in the dark, then lapsed into silence. She heard him strike a match as he waited.

"This is O'Hurley, number 8372B. Patch this call through Paris to New York, code three, phase twelve."

He needed to make the call, though he knew it was against regulations when he was on assignment. Going through the Paris operation would secure it. He knew the phone wasn't bugged or tapped, and if Kendesa was tracing his calls he would know only that Cabot had called Paris. From there, the call would be scrambled.

Now he could only hope she was home.

"Hello."

"Maddy." The sound of her voice had him smiling into the shadows. "No show tonight?"

"Trace? Trace!" Her quick, infectious laugh bubbled over oceans and miles. "How are you? Where are you? I was wondering if I'd get my semiannual call. I'm so glad I did. There's so much to tell you. Are you in New York?"

"No, I'm not in the States. I'm fine. How's the toast of Broadway?"

"Terrific. I don't know what the Great White Way is going to do without me when I take a year off."

"A year? You and Valentine going traveling?"

"No… I don't know, maybe. Trace, I'm going to have a baby." Her excitement was all but sizzling the wires. "In six and a half months. In fact, they're going to be doing some tests, because it looks like I'm having more than one."

A baby. He thought of the skinny, long-legged redhead, who had always seemed to have more energy than any one person was entitled to. She'd still been a teenager when he'd seen her last. And now…a baby. He thought of Abby and her sons, the nephews he'd never seen.

"You okay?" And he wished, more intensely than he'd wished before, that he could link hands with her and see for himself.

"Never better. Oh, Trace, I wish you could make it home, even for a little while, and meet Reed. He's so terrific, so upstanding and stable. I don't know how he tolerates me. And Abby, she's going to have the baby in just a few months. You should see her. I can't believe how beautiful, how content she is, since she married Dylan. The boys are growing like weeds. Did you get the pictures she sent you?"

"Yeah." He'd gotten them, pored over the faces of his

sister's sons, then destroyed them. If something happened to him, he couldn't leave behind anything that could be traced to his family. "Nice-looking boys. The little one looks like a heartbreaker."

"That's because he looks like you."

She couldn't know how the statement shook him. Trace closed his eyes a moment and brought the face in the photo back into his mind. Maddy was right, of course. Family ties might be thin, almost invisible, but they were strong.

"You hear from Chantel?"

"That's the big news." Maddy paused automatically for dramatic impact. "Big sister's getting married."

"What?" He wasn't often thrown completely off balance, but Trace nearly choked on the smoke he'd dragged into his lungs. There had been rumors, of course. There were always rumors. But he hadn't believed them. "You want to say that again?"

"I said Chantel, femme fatale, star of stage and screen, has met her match. She's getting married in just a couple of weeks. We wanted to let you know, but we didn't know how to get in touch."

"Yeah. I've been—" he glanced over to where Gillian lay quiet in the bed "—tied up."

"In any case, she's really taking the plunge. It should be the glitziest wedding this side of the Windsors."

"So Chantel's getting married. I'd like to meet the guy," he said, half under his breath.

"He's perfect for her. Rough and tough and just cynical enough to keep Chantel on her toes. Trace, she's absolutely crazy about him. Seems there was a writer who'd developed an obsession about her, a dangerous one. Anyway, to keep the story short, she'd hired Quinn as a sort of bodyguard, and when the air cleared, she was making wedding plans."

"Is she all right?"

"She's fine, better than fine."

He wanted to dig deeper. He could use his contacts and sources to learn the details Maddy was leaving out. It would have to wait until he came out of the mountains—if he came out of the mountains.

"Trace, you know how much it would mean if you could come back for the wedding. It's been a long time."

"I know. You know I'd like to see you again, kid, all of you, but I'm just not suited to playing prodigal son."

"It doesn't have to be like that." She knew better than to press, but something told her she might not get another chance. "Things have changed. We've all changed. Mom misses you. She still has that little music box you sent her from Austria, and Pop…" Here she hesitated, because the ground was shakier. "Pop would give anything to see you again. He won't admit it—you know he can't—but I can see it every time your name's mentioned. Trace, every time we manage to get together, there's this hole. You could fill it."

"Mom and Pop still touring?" he asked, already knowing the answer, only to redirect the conversation.

"Yes." Maddy bit off a sigh. The son was as stubborn as the father. "They've got a gig coming up on public television. Folk dancing, traditional music. Pop's in heaven."

"I bet. Is he…is he okay?"

"I swear, he gets younger every year. If I had to make a bet I'd say music is the fountain of youth. He can still dance a teenager into the ground. Come see for yourself."

"We'll see how things go. Listen, tell Chantel and Abby I called. And Mom."

"I will." Maddy tightened her grip on the phone, knowing she was losing him. "Can you tell me where you'll be?"

"I'll let you know."

"Trace, I love you. We all love you."

"I know." He wanted to say more, but he knew there was nothing left. "Maddy?"

"Yes?"

"Break a leg."

He hung up the phone but didn't go back to bed for a very long time.

In the morning, Gillian watched Trace dress in Cabot's conservative European suit. She waited, nerves stretching, in silence while he deliberated over the proper tie.

What difference does it make? She wanted to shout it at him, rage it at him, while she tossed the hated, well-laundered clothes around the room. She watched him slip Cabot's little derringer into his pocket. It wouldn't do any good, she thought. He took it only because Cabot would take it. The pistol might as well have been filled with water for all the protection it would afford him.

He turned, and the man who had loved her so fiercely the night before had become André Cabot. He was sleek, well groomed and cold-eyed. She'd wanted to put off this moment, to push it back until it couldn't be pushed any longer. Now it was here, and she had to face it.

"If there is another way…" she began.

"There isn't." He answered with the same finality

she'd heard when he'd spoken to his sister the night before. But then Gillian had been sure she'd heard a trace
of regret. Perhaps he'd been too tired to stamp it out.
But this morning he was in complete control.

"I have to ask. Is there some way you can take me
with you?"

"You know there isn't."

She pressed her lips together, hating being helpless
on the ground while everyone she loved walked a tight-
rope. "Is there some way I can contact this other agent,
if things…if there's anything he should know?"

"You won't have to contact him."

She'd known that, too, and that she was dragging
something out that should be done quickly. "So all I
can do is wait."

"That's right." He hesitated a moment. "Gillian, I
know that waiting is the hardest part."

"At least I'm allowed to pray, as well."

"It wouldn't hurt." He wished he didn't need to, but
he reached out to take both of her hands. Things had
changed, he realized, too much and too fast. For the
first time in a dozen years, leaving was painful. "I'm
going to get them out."

"And yourself." Her fingers tightened on his. "Will
you promise me that, too?"

"Sure." He knew that often lies were needed. "Tell
you what, once this is over, we'll take a little vacation.
A couple of weeks, a month, pick the spot."

"Anywhere?"

"Sure." He bent to kiss her but only brushed his lips
over her forehead. He was afraid that if he held her, if
he really kissed her, he wouldn't be able to turn away.
But he did give himself a moment, one long moment, to

memorize her face—the milky skin dashed with freck-les, the dark green eyes, the mouth that could be so sweet, so passionate. "Give it some thought while I'm gone." He let her go then and picked up his briefcase. "You've got two ISS guards, Doc, but don't do any sightseeing. I shouldn't be gone more than a day or two."

"I'll be waiting."

As he walked toward the door, she struggled to keep a promise to herself. She'd sworn she wouldn't say it. But he was leaving. In a moment he'd be gone and—

"Trace."

He stopped, impatience just beginning to show as he turned.

"I love you."

She saw his expression change, his eyes darken, deepen. It seemed, for a heartbeat it seemed, that he would come to her. Then his face went carefully blank. He opened the door, and left without another word.

She could have thrown herself on the bed and wept. She could have thrown all the breakables in the room and raged. It was a huge temptation to do both. Instead, Gillian stood where she was and waited for calm.

The fact that he hadn't answered her was no more than she had expected. But he was gone now, and the wheels that had been put into motion couldn't be stopped. She could pray, and would, but for now there was something else she could do. Whenever it seemed there would be no tomorrow, it was best to make plans for the next day.

She went to the phone and asked for the number Trace had called the night before. Gillian dialed it and, calling on her photographic memory, gave the person who answered the same sequence Trace had recited.

Her heart beating a bit unsteadily, she waited for someone to pick up. She winced when a sleepy and irritated masculine voice did.

"Hello, I'd like to speak with Madeline O'Hurley."

There was an oath, and a feminine murmur in the distance. "Do you know what time it is?"

"No." Gillian rolled her eyes and nearly laughed. Trace was on his way to Husad, and she didn't have the least idea what time it was in New York. "I'm sorry, I'm out of the country."

"It's 4:15 a.m.," Reed said helpfully. "And my wife is trying to sleep. So am I."

"I'm really terribly sorry. I'm a friend of her brother's. I don't know if I can make the call again." And Trace would surely murder her if he found out she'd made it at all. "If I could just speak with her for a moment."

There was static, and more muttering. Then the connection became so clear that Gillian could hear the bedsprings squeak. "Hello? Is Trace all right? Has something happened?"

"No." Gillian cursed herself for not waiting. "No, Trace is fine." She hoped. "I'm Gillian Fitzpatrick. A friend."

"Is Trace in Ireland?"

"No." She nearly smiled. "Ms. O'Hurley, well, I suppose it's best to be frank. I'm in love with your brother, and I think it would do him a lot of good to come home. I thought you might help me arrange it."

Maddy gave a shout of laughter, threw one arm around her very cranky husband and decided Gillian Fitzpatrick had been sent from heaven. "Tell me what I can do."

* * *

Trace sat silently in the car as it traveled east. He had directed the driver to the warehouse where Breintz had arranged for the ISS weapons to be stored. Retrieving them had been as simple as signing a form and passing a few bills. Now they were deep in the mountains. The ride was far from smooth. In the way that Cabot had, he muttered a few complaints but exchanged no conversation. There were no questions asked, no answers given. Trace sat back and, behind tinted glasses, marked the route as carefully as if he'd drawn a map.

He'd be back.

He knew the villagers in the scattered settlements they passed would keep to themselves. They had their own way of life, and their own way of dealing with what came. A man like him, passing through their land, was only so much wind. To be noticed, tolerated, then forgotten.

Trace glanced at his watch with a slight sniff of impatience. The homing device inside it would be transmitting his location to Breintz. If his luck—and ISS technology—held, Husad's security wouldn't detect it. If they did…he'd take that as it came.

There were times when it didn't pay to think too far ahead. It clouded the present, and it was always the instant that had to be coped with. That was why he tried not to think of Gillian, how she'd looked, what she'd said. If she meant it.

She loved him. Trace felt the emotion move through him, warm and strong and not a little frightening. She'd meant it. He'd seen it in her eyes then, and before, though he'd tried to tell himself that it was the intensity of the moment that had made her feel it, had made him want it.

When she'd said it he'd wanted to go to her, to hold her hard and tight and endlessly. He'd wanted to make promises he couldn't be sure he could keep. And, though he wasn't sure she would understand, it was because he loved her that he hadn't.

He'd never loved a woman before, so he hadn't known what a tug-of-war it could be between the selfish and the unselfish. Part of him wanted to take what she so recklessly offered. Another part of him felt it would be wrong, even sinful, for a man like him to take such pure emotion from her when he'd long since forgotten how to give it back.

Because he knew no other way at the moment, Trace decided to treat it as an assignment. He would give her what she had come to him for. Once she had her family back, he would…he would play it as it came.

Trace got his first sight of Husad's headquarters as the car drove over a rise. It was large, even larger than he'd expected, and built into the side of a cliff with rock carved from the mountains. Another ten miles in any direction and it would have been easily detected by air or land surveillance. But here it was isolated, almost merging into the wild desolation of the countryside. There was no land fit to farm here, no river to settle beside, no town to spread out from.

This was country for outlaws and renegades—and the hopeless.

Security seemed light, but Trace's eyes were sharp enough to spot the armed men stationed on the ridges. It was windowless and unfenced. Wise, because the reflection of glass or high-voltage wire could have been spotted from miles away. The driver signaled by punching out a code on a small box fixed to the dash. After a few seconds' delay, a wide door opened into the rock. The car drove into the mountain.

He was inside. Trace adjusted his cuff. His finger slid over and pressed on the stem of his watch to turn off the homing device. Either Breintz had his location now or he was on his own.

As he stepped out of the car, Trace took a long look around. The floor and the walls were rock. The tunnel seemed to go on endlessly and was dimly lit and cool. The door behind them had already closed, shutting out the sun and the heat. From somewhere came a low mechanical whine, telling him the air was circulated and processed. He heard, too, the sound of a door and footsteps. It was Kendesa who came to greet him.

"Again you are prompt. I trust your journey was not too unpleasant."

Trace inclined his head. "Business often causes some physical discomfort. The roads in your country are not yet as civilized as those in Europe."

"My pardon. Perhaps you would join me for a drink. I have an excellent chardonnay that should ease the memory of the journey."

"My samples?"

"Of course." Kendesa signaled. Two men seemed to come straight out of the rock wall. "They will be taken directly to the general, if you have no objection." His brow lifted at Trace's hesitation. "Surely you would not demand a receipt. We have no need to steal trifles from guests."

They both knew that the "trifles" included a TS-35. Still, his orders were to proceed with straightforward negotiations. "I would enjoy the chardonnay before meeting with the general."

"Excellent." Kendesa gave another signal, and the crate in the car's trunk was off-loaded. He gestured Trace forward. "I'm afraid a man of your taste will find our establishment crude. You will understand, of course, that we are a military operation and look not for comfort but revolution."

"I understand, though for myself I prefer comfort."

He led Trace into a small room whose walls had been paneled in light wood. The floor was carpeted, and, although the furniture was sparse, what was there was tasteful.

"We entertain rarely." Kendesa smiled as he drew the cork from the bottle. "When the general becomes more widely accepted, this will change." He poured wine into two Waterford glasses. "I confess that I have an affection for beautiful things, and the comfort and pleasure they bring."

"To profit, then," Trace said as he lifted his glass. "Because money gives the most comfort."

"I find you an interesting man, Cabot." Kendesa sipped his wine. Over the past few days he had employed the best equipment at his disposal in his search through Cabot's background. What he had found had pleased him a great deal. Such a man, and his connections, would be very useful during a period of transition.

"You've reached a level in power and wealth most men only wish for, yet you crave still more."

"I shall have still more," Trace countered.

"I believe so. You will understand that before doing business I used my resources to look into your current situation, as well as your background."

Trace merely sipped again. "Standard procedure."

"Indeed. What fascinates me, Cabot, is that you've reached this level of power while remaining almost unknown."

"I prefer subtlety to celebrity."

"Wise. There are some, even in our own organization, who criticize the general for maintaining such a high profile. Power amassed quietly is something more useful."

"The general is political. I am not." Trace continued to drink, wondering what Kendesa was fishing for.

"All of us are political, even if the politics is money. You expressed interest in Horizon."

"I did. And do."

"I have considered discussing this further with you. You are interested in the profit from Horizon. I am interested in the power."

"And the general?"

Kendesa lifted his glass again. He was nearly ready to play his cards. "Is interested in the revolution."

Unless Kendesa was playing a part, Trace sensed a slight disenchantment, and more than a little ambition. "Perhaps, with a kind of partnership, we could gain all three."

Kendesa studied Trace for a long, silent moment. "Perhaps."

The knock on the door echoed dully. "Come."

"The general is ready."

With a nod, Kendesa set down his glass. "I will take you to him myself. The general speaks no French, I'm afraid, but is quite proud of his adeptness with English. You will oblige him?"

"Certainly." Trace set his glass beside Kendesa's and prepared for the next step.

* * *

Gillian felt she'd waited for days, though it was only a matter of hours. She tried, unsuccessfully, to pass the time with Trace's books. Every time she started to read, she thought of him, and worried.

So she paced. And when she tired of that she sat and reminded herself of her conversation with Maddy. She would take Trace back to the States. In doing so, she would be able to give him what he'd promised her only a short time ago—a family.

For as long as she was able to hold off worry, Gillian concentrated on that. In a few days, a week at most, both she and Trace would have their families back.

And where would they go from there?

The Canary Islands? she thought, and nearly laughed out loud. She wondered what Trace would say when she told him that if he insisted on hiding from the world for the next fifty years or so she would be hiding right alongside him.

She wasn't going to lose him now, not to Husad, not to the ISS or his own stubbornness. If he wanted life in a hammock, it would be a hammock for two.

Gillian had learned a lot about herself in the past few weeks. She could do what needed to be done. She could face what needed to be faced. More, she could change what needed to be changed to find the happiness that had always remained just out of her reach.

When the fear began to edge back, she wondered what she would do if Trace didn't walk through the door again. Her life wouldn't be over. She knew you could lose what you loved and go on, but you could never go on in quite the same way. She knew there was no way to prepare herself for losing Trace. He'd opened doors in her, he'd caused the blossoming of love in her that had pushed her to open doors in him. She wouldn't lose him. Gillian promised herself that.

And went back to watching the clock.

She ordered room service only because she wanted something to do. Then she asked herself how in the world she could eat anything. She'd nearly decided to cancel the order when the knock came.

Experience had taught her caution. Even knowing she was guarded, Gillian checked the peephole for the uniformed waiter. Satisfied, she opened the door and looked disinterestedly at the tray.

"Just set it over there," she told him, gesturing because she wasn't certain he spoke English. Still, a check was a check in any language. Gillian leaned over to sign it.

She felt the prick in her arm and jerked back. The drug worked quickly, and she was staggering even as she grabbed for the table knife. The world went gray and dissolved to black before she could even think Trace's name.

Chapter 11

General Husad liked beautiful things, too. He liked to look at them, touch them, wear them. Still, the austerity of his headquarters pleased him. A military establishment required a certain ambience. A soldier's life could never be a soft one, or discipline was lost. He believed that, even when he dressed in silks and admired his wife's emeralds.

He was a small, spare man in his prime, with a mesmerizing voice and a glint in his eyes some took for genius and others took for madness. The title of general was self-bestowed, and, though he had indeed fought in wars, most of the medals he had pinned on his chest were self-awarded. By turns he treated his men like an indulgent father and a heartless dictator. They didn't love him, but they feared him enough to follow his orders without question.

He was dressed in a gold cloak for his meeting with

Cabot. It was tied at the neck to reveal the medal-be-decked uniform beneath and the twin handguns at his hips. He had a striking face, hawkish, with silvered hair combed straight back. He photographed very well and spoke like an evangelist. His mind was slipping into a dark, violent area that even his medication no longer controlled completely.

His office wasn't sparsely furnished, as Kendesa's had been. The desk was huge, of polished oak, and dominated the room from its center. Sofas and chairs plump with pillows formed a circle around it. There were bookshelves and display cabinets. Trace studied them with what appeared to be a detached interest.

No windows, he thought, and only one door. Not likely.

There were a pair of épées crossed on the wall over an enormous aquarium in which colorful tropical fish glided in clear blue water.

"Monsieur Cabot." Husad held out a hand with the warmth and sincerity of a car salesman one sale away from his monthly quota. "Welcome."

"General." Trace accepted the hand and looked into the face of the man he'd sworn to kill. The eyes were black and full of odd lights. Madness. Could anyone stand this close to it and not smell it?

"I hope you didn't find the journey too inconvenient."

"Not at all."

"If you would be pleased to sit."

Trace took a chair and waited while the general stood with his hands folded behind his back. Kendesa stood silently at the door. For some moments, Husad paced, the sound of his highly polished boots absorbed by the carpet.

"The revolution needs both allies and arms," he began. "We wage a holy battle for the people, a battle that requires us to destroy the unworthy and the unbeliever. In Europe and the Middle East we have often been successful in bringing destruction to those who oppose us." He turned to Trace, head high, eyes blazing. "It is not enough. We have our duty, a sacred duty, to overthrow the oppressive governments of the world. Many will die in righteousness and sacrifice before we succeed. And we will succeed."

Trace sat calmly, noting that, as reported, Husad had a stirring voice, a strong presence. But even though he went on in the same vein for ten minutes, he basically said nothing. Trace noted, as well, that once the speech was over he glanced toward Kendesa. For approval? he wondered. For guidance?

"Your mission, General, if you will pardon me, interests me only as it concerns my associates and myself. I am not a patriot or a soldier, but a man of business." Trace folded his hands and continued. "You require arms, and I can supply them, for a price."

"Your price is high," the general said as he walked to his desk.

"My price includes the risk factor for securing, storing and delivering the merchandise. This same price can be quoted to others."

Husad reached down and came up with the TS-35. Even as Trace tensed, he heard Kendesa make a quick, surprised movement behind him.

"I find this weapon of particular interest."

The TS-35 was slim and amazingly lightweight. Even on a forced march, a soldier could carry it as easily as his food rations. The clips were slimmer than the average pack of cigarettes. Husad balanced its spearlike shape in his hands, then brought it up to sight it. In the middle of Trace's forehead.

If it was loaded, and Trace was certain that it was, the projectile would obliterate him where he sat, then go on to kill Kendesa and anyone unlucky enough to be standing in its path for the next fifty yards.

"The Americans talk and talk of peace while they make such brilliant weapons." Husad was speaking almost dreamily now. "We are considered madmen because we talk of war. Such a weapon was made for a man of war. And the war is holy, the war is righteous, the war is food and drink."

Trace felt the sweat roll cold down his back. To die here, now, would be foolish, pitiful. "With all respect, General Husad, the weapon isn't yours until it's paid for."

The finger hovered on the trigger a moment, flexed, then retreated. With a charming smile, Husad lowered the gun. "Of course. We are warriors, but we are honest. We will take your shipment, Monsieur Cabot, and we ask, in the name of friendship, that you lower your price by half a million francs."

Trace's hands were damp as he reached for a cigarette. For survival's sake he wanted to agree and be done with it and get on with what he had come to do. But the man Cabot would never have agreed so easily. Nor would Husad, or Kendesa, expect it.

"In the name of expediency, General, we will lower the price by a quarter of a million, payment on delivery."

The weapon lay on Husad's desk now, and he stroked it as he might have a small child, or a pet. Again Trace saw his gaze shift briefly to Kendesa. "The papers will be drawn up. You will be driven back to Sefrou. In three days you will make the delivery, personally."

"It will be my pleasure." Trace rose.

"I am told you have an interest in our guest." Husad smiled. His teeth shone, and his eyes. "Personal interest?"

"Business is always personal to me, General."

"Perhaps you would be interested in observing the doctor. Kendesa will arrange it."

"Of course, General." Kendesa opened the door. Trace saw him give both Husad and the weapon an uneasy look before they walked back into the corridor.

"The general amuses himself in odd ways," Trace commented as they walked.

"Were you afraid, Monsieur Cabot?"

"I have, as you have not, observed the power of that weapon. You may choose to die for your cause, Kendesa. I do not. My associates might find it unpalatable to continue to do business with one so unstable."

"The general is under some stress."

Trace crushed out his cigarette on the stone floor and decided to take the risk. "I am said to be observant. Who is it that wields the hammer, Kendesa? Who is it that I am actually doing business with?"

Kendesa paused. As was his habit, he wore a Western suit, without frills or jewelry. The decision came easily, because he had considered it for some time. If Cabot didn't continue to satisfy him, it would be a simple matter to arrange his disposal. "As is often the case, the one with the title is but a figurehead. The general's mental condition has become frail over the past year. It has become my duty to assume more responsibility."

He waited to be certain Trace understood. "Does this change your position?"

Not the general, Trace thought, but Kendesa. Kendesa had ordered Charlie's death, Fitzpatrick's kidnapping. So he would deal with Kendesa rather than a half-mad puppet. "It satisfies me," Trace replied.

"Excellent." For the general's usefulness was almost at an end. Once Fitzpatrick had completed his task, Kendesa would take full power. And how much sweeter it would be with the backing of Cabot's organization, and the wealth that went with it.

Kendesa waved aside two armed guards. Taking a key from his pocket, he unlocked a door.

No research-and-development lab could have been better equipped. The lighting was brilliant, every surface was spotless. Trace spotted two surveillance cameras before he turned his attention to Gillian's brother.

It was the man from the snapshot, but he'd grown thinner, older. Strain had dug lines in his face and bruised the skin around his eyes. He was clean-shaven, but his hair, darker and deeper than Gillian's, was unkempt. His white lab coat hung loosely over jeans and a plain blue shirt.

Flynn pushed away from the microscope and stood. The hatred in his eyes brought Trace a wave of relief. He hadn't given up or given in. He was hanging on, and not by a thread, but by his teeth. If the man had enough strength to hate, he had enough strength to escape.

"Dr. Fitzpatrick, your work goes well today?"

"I haven't seen my daughter in two days."

"We discussed incentive, Doctor."

Flynn's hand closed into a fist. He had withstood their torture. He was all but certain Kendesa had known he would withstand it. It was only the threat that they would take his Caitlin into that dark little room that kept him in the lab.

"I'm here." His Irish brogue had barbs in it. "I'm working. I was promised that she wouldn't be harmed and that I would see her daily if I cooperated."

"I'm afraid the general feels you work too slowly. When there is progress, we will bring your daughter to you. In the meantime, I will introduce you to Monsieur Cabot. He is interested in your work."

Flynn turned dark, hate-filled eyes on Trace. "Go to hell."

Trace wanted to congratulate him, but he only nodded stiffly. "Your work here will put your name in the history books, Dr. Fitzpatrick." Trace looked around, osstensibly interested in the lab, while he searched for another exit. "Fascinating. My organization feels the profit from your serum will be enormous."

"Your money will do you little good once a madman has destroyed the world."

Trace smiled. So he understood. He kept his voice mild. "Your serum will ensure power and profit for those clever enough to earn it. There is progress?" he asked Kendesa.

"It is slow." This time Kendesa smiled and watched Trace carefully. "The missing link is Fitzpatrick's sister. She has in her possession certain notes, certain knowledge that will expedite the completion of this work. She'll be joining you, Doctor."

Trace felt the air stop pumping into his lungs. Before he could speak, Flynn was rushing forward.

"Gillian? What have you done with her?"

Kendesa had his gun out quickly. "Calm yourself,

Doctor. She is unharmed." He turned a curious smile on Trace. "Were you aware, *monsieur*, that you traveled with the good doctor's sister?"

"I?" He could play it two ways. But if he went with instinct and attacked, Flynn Fitzpatrick would be dead. "I'm afraid you're mistaken."

"The woman you brought to Casablanca was Dr. Gillian Fitzpatrick."

"The woman I brought to Casablanca was a little American tart I picked up in Paris. Attractive, amusing and dull-witted."

"More sharp-witted than you know, *monsieur*. You have been used."

So that was it. For once Trace blessed the ISS for the strength and depth of his cover. "You're mistaken." There was a low edge of fury to his voice.

"No, I regret it is you who are mistaken. The woman purposely sought you out, hoping you would bring her closer to us and her brother. I assume she played her part well."

"Very well. If you're correct."

"Quite correct. A short time ago she was in Mexico, where she sought out and enlisted the help of a certain ISS agent. We can assume it was he who instructed her on what course to take. Do you know the name Il Gatto, Cabot?"

Trace drew out a cigarette, making sure his hand didn't appear quite steady. "I know it."

"He seeks revenge on the general, and uses you and the woman to gain it."

"Who is he?"

"I regret I do not yet have that information." Anger broke through the sophisticated calm briefly. "The general was unfortunately hasty in executing three men who might have been able to identify him. But the woman knows, and will tell us. In time."

"Where is she?" Trace blew out a stream of smoke. "I do not tolerate being a woman's pawn."

"On her way here, if not here already. You are welcome to speak with her when you return. Once we have her notes, and she has identified Il Gatto, I may consider it a gesture of goodwill to give her to you."

"Bastard." Flynn raised his fist and would have struck if Trace hadn't moved more quickly. Grabbing Flynn's arm, he twisted it up behind his back and held him close, their faces an inch apart.

"Your whore of a sister owes me." Flynn bared his teeth but was helpless to strike back. "I'll take my payment from her, and from you, Doctor." He shoved him aside. "I've seen enough," Trace said curtly, and strode toward the door.

"Let me see Caitlin. Let me see my daughter, you son of a bitch," Flynn cried.

"Perhaps tomorrow, Doctor," Kendesa said calmly. "Perhaps then I shall reunite your family." In the same unhurried manner, he opened the door and locked it behind him. It gave him some pleasure to see the smooth, sleek André Cabot with his feathers ruffled.

"There is no need for embarrassment, my friend. The woman, under the guidance of Il Gatto, was a formidable enemy."

Trace turned on him. In an instant he had Kendesa against the wall. Even as the guards' guns clicked into place he had the key from Kendesa's pocket palmed in his hand. "I will not be made a fool. The woman is unharmed?"

Kendesa waved the guards aside as Trace's grip relaxed. "We did not want her damaged."

"Good." A muscle twitched in his cheek. "Very good. When I return in three days, I want her. Get the information you need, Kendesa. Get the information and then turn the woman over to me. The price of the shipment can be reduced another quarter of a million francs, between us."

Kendesa lifted a brow. "The price of your pride is high."

"Before I am through, she will wish, with a full heart, that you had killed her." Trace straightened his jacket and seemed to bring himself under control. "I assume the child is still alive."

"She is kept on the second level. Mild tranquilizers keep her quiet. They are full of passion, these Irish."

"Indeed." Trace saw the car and driver waiting where he'd left them. "I will report to my associates. If the papers are in order, we will finish our current business."

"Cabot." Kendesa rested a hand on the door of the car. "Does Il Gatto disturb you?"

Trace looked directly into Kendesa's eyes. "I feel he would have little interest in me, and a great deal more in you. I should watch my back, *mon ami*. Cats strike quickly."

Trace settled in the back seat and for the first time in years began to pray.

He would waste precious time traveling back to Sefrou, contacting Breintz and gathering the weapons. As the driver started down the mountain, Trace considered putting him out of commission and going back. But how far would he get alone, with a miserable peashooter of a .45?

Straining against his own impotence, he looked at his watch. Automatically he reactivated the homing device, but he was more interested in the time. He could be back, fully armed, by dark.

She'd be all right. She was strong. She was braver than she should be. He would come back for her and get her out, no matter what had to be done, no matter what had to be sacrificed.

But the cold sweat he was in reminded him what it was to fear for more than your own life.

When the tire blew out, he was thrown against the side of the car. Swearing, he straightened. Instinct had him reaching in his pocket as he stepped from the car. The driver got out, turned toward the damaged wheel, then dropped like a stone.

Trace drew out his pistol. Smelling ambush. Even as he whirled, Breintz rose from a rock. "Your mind's elsewhere, old friend. If I'd wanted you dead, you'd be dead."

Trace pocketed the pistol. "They've got Gillian."

"I know. One of her guards lived long enough to contact me." Breintz dropped agilely from the rock. "My orders are to give you twelve hours to get the Fitzpatricks out. If you're unsuccessful, Hammer's headquarters is to be destroyed."

"Give me your weapon."

"One rifle?" Breintz lifted a brow. "Such conceit."

"Twelve hours doesn't give me a hell of a lot of time. Give me the rifle."

"For once Il Gatto is not using his head." Breintz bent down to examine the driver's clothes. "Could it be the woman is more than an assignment?" Breintz drew off the driver's braided headdress and settled it over his hair. "An adequate fit."

Trace schooled his breathing until his head cleared. "You drive. We can take out the guards at the gate and use their weapons. The layout's simple enough. We get Fitzpatrick, I find Gillian and the kid."

"Agreed." Breintz gestured for him to follow. With the ease of a goat, he climbed over the rocks. Trace saw the case he'd purchased from Bakir. Breintz only smiled. "I have worked with you before." Breintz handed Trace a grenade launcher. "And this is my country. I say modestly that my contacts here are excellent."

Trace yanked off Cabot's raw-silk jacket and threw it in the dirt. He slipped the strap of the weapon over his shoulder and reached for another. "I'd forgotten how good you were."

"Old friend—" Breintz was quietly taping clips together "—I am even better now."

Trace strapped on an ammo belt. "We have to wait until dark."

Breintz sat cross-legged. "It will come soon enough."

"You don't have orders to go in with me."

"No." Breintz closed his eyes and began to drift into meditation. "Charles Forrester was a good man."

"Thanks."

Wishing he could find the same kind of serenity, Trace sat beside him. And waited for sundown.

Gillian awoke slowly, with her head throbbing and her mind fuzzy. Once or twice she nearly found consciousness, only to go into the grayness again. She heard weeping, quiet and heartfelt, and wondered if it was her.

She felt warmth against her side, then again warmth stroking along her arm. Instinctively she reached out for it.

"Aunt Gillian, please wake up. Please, Aunt Gillian, I'm so scared."

It was like the nightmare. Gillian felt her skin go clammy and fought it off. Just a dream, she told herself, but Caitlin's pleas were coming clearer and clearer. Opening her eyes, she saw her.

"I thought you were dead." Caitlin, eyes puffy and red, buried her face in Gillian's hair. "They dropped you on the bed and you lay so still I thought you were dead."

"Baby." She pushed herself up and nearly passed out again. The drug had been strong and had left her with a raging headache and traces of nausea. Unsure what was real, she reached out and touched Caitlin's face. "Oh, baby. It's you. It's really you." Gathering the child close, she rocked her. "Oh, Caitlin, little darling, go ahead and cry. Poor little lamb, how frightened you must have been, all alone like this. I'm here now."

"Are you going to take us home?"

Where was home? And where were they? As she looked around the dim room, Gillian remembered the waiter, the prick of the hypodermic. Closing her eyes, she cursed herself for her stupidity. Did they have Trace, too? Oh, God, did they have him, too?

"Can we go home now? Please, I want to go home."

"Soon," Gillian murmured. "As soon as I can. Caitlin, can you dry your eyes and talk to me?"

With sniffles and nods, Caitlin burrowed closer. "You won't go away?"

"No. No, I won't leave you." They'd have to kill her

first, she promised herself as she kept Caitlin close. "Where's your da?"

"They keep him downstairs, in a laboratory."

"Is he all right? Be brave now, darling. Is your da all right?"

"He looks kind of sick. I can't remember when they let me see him last." She swiped her hand over her wet cheeks. "He cried once."

"It's all right. It's going to be all right. There's a—" She cut herself off as she remembered how carefully Trace had searched their hotel rooms for microphones. Someone could be listening to them even now. She couldn't mention his name or give her niece the comfort of knowing they had help. "There's sure to be a way out," she said instead. "We just have to be patient. We're together now." Then she lifted a finger to her lips, signaling to the child to be silent. As quietly as she could, she searched the room.

She knew it was more luck than skill that led her to it. When she found the mike, her first instinct was to smash it. Even that small sign of defiance would have been satisfying. But she made herself think coolly. Leaving the mike in place, she climbed back onto the narrow bed.

"I met a man in Mexico," she began, knowing whoever was listening would already be aware of that. "He said he'd help. He has a funny name, Caitlin. Il Gatto. It means 'cat.'"

"Does he look like a cat?"

"No." Gillian smiled to herself. "But he thinks like one. When I don't contact him tomorrow," she said, "he'll come after us."

"And take us home?"

"Yes, darling. Do you know where we are?"

"It's like a big cave with lots of tunnels."

"I see." Gillian lifted Caitlin's eyelids and examined her pupils. Drugs. The fury rose and nearly overpowered her. "Do you ever go outside?"

"No. There aren't any windows."

Caitlin cringed as the door opened and a man with a rifle over his shoulder carried in a tray. He set it on the edge of the bed, gestured to it, then walked out again.

"I bit him once," Caitlin said, with some of her old spirit.

"Good for you."

"He smacked me."

"He won't smack you again." Gillian looked at the tray. There was rice and some cubed meat with two glasses of milk. She sniffed at it. "Have you been eating well?"

"The food doesn't taste good, but I get hungry. Whenever I eat, I get sleepy."

"You need to eat, darling." But she shook her head as she lifted the tray. "It helps keep up your strength." Gillian dumped the contents of both plates under the bed. "And you need to sleep, as well." Looking around for a likely place, she poured the milk on a pile of dirty linen in the corner. Caitlin watched her with wide eyes. "Come on, baby, try to eat a little more."

When Caitlin pressed a hand to her mouth and giggled, Gillian nearly wept from the sight of it.

"That's it. Now drink your milk." Grinning with her, Gillian climbed into bed again.

A trace of mischief lit Caitlin's eyes. "I don't like milk."

"It's good for your bones. You wouldn't want soft

bones, would you?" Gillian cuddled with her. Putting her mouth against the child's ear, she whispered, "They put something in the food to make you sleep. You have to pretend to sleep so they don't find out we didn't eat it. Do just what I say. If one of the men comes back, lie very still so they don't know we've fooled them."

Caitlin nodded. "Don't go away, Aunt Gillian."

"No, I won't go away."

Gillian cradled the child in her arms. In the dark, she stared at the ceiling and planned.

Sunset came with brilliance. The mountains went pink with it, and the sand gold. In the last of the light, Breintz changed into the driver's clothes after fixing the tire while Trace loaded weapons on the floor of the car.

They worked in silence now. Everything had been said. As the sun dipped below the high peaks, Trace stretched out on the floor in the back and Breintz climbed behind the wheel. They headed east for the last time.

Breintz began to whistle tunelessly as they approached. As Trace had, he noted the sentries on the ridges above the building. Following Trace's directions, he punched out the code and waited for the door to lift up.

As he stopped the car inside, he lowered his head to conceal as much of his face as possible. A guard approached as the door closed behind him.

"You made good time," he said, just before Breintz brought an elbow to his throat. Trace was out of the car and leading the way to the lab.

They pulled up short some twenty feet later. Two more guards were dealt with in utter silence. Trace knew they would have to move quickly once they broke into the lab. There the cameras would give them away. Trace shrank back out of sight as Breintz moved forward, weaving slightly.

"A cigarette," he demanded in Arabic, keeping his voice a bit slurred. "What good is wine without tobacco?"

As one of the guards broke into a grin, Trace and Breintz moved quickly. Not a shot was fired.

"You still have a light touch," Breintz commented as Trace slipped the key into the lock.

"And yours has improved." Taking a deep breath, Trace opened the door. "Keep working," he said in a low voice to Flynn the moment he spotted him. "Keep as much of your back as possible to the cameras."

Despite the order, Flynn set down his tongs and test tube. "You." There was a look in his eyes that told Trace he'd been pushed almost to his limit.

"For God's sake, if you want to get your daughter out, keep working. I don't want surveillance to see anything unusual until the last minute."

"Push it along," Breintz said mildly as he kept a lookout.

"Pick up the damn test tube, do something scientific. I'm ISS."

Flynn picked up the tube, but in a grip that threatened to shatter it. "You're a pig."

"Maybe, but I'm here to get you and the kid—and your idiot sister—out of here. Keep working. Do you want to see a goddamn badge?" Trace cast a look at the first camera. "Just do what I say, do it slow, and do it right."

Something in his tone made Flynn obey, but the strain was still evident. "I thought you were French."

"I'm as Irish as you are, Fitzpatrick," Trace said reassuringly, and grinned. "And, by the saints," he said, dropping into the easy brogue of his alter ego, Colin, "we'll be gettin' out and blowin' this place to hell."

Maybe it was simple desperation, but Flynn responded. "When we do, the first bottle's on me."

"You're on. Now move as far as you can to the left, the edge of camera range. Go after those papers."

Flynn set down the tube and obeyed. With his back to the cameras, he looked over the papers as if he were checking his equations. "How did you find us?"

"Your sister had a lot to do with it. If you've got half the guts she does, we're going to make it. Now keep reading. Something doesn't check out. Take out your pencil like you're going to make notes. I'm going to blow the camera out. When I do, you run. Breintz'll take you out while I go up for the kid and Gillian. Now!"

Trace blew the camera out with a single blast. When Flynn passed through the door, both agents had their weapons ready. "Give me twenty minutes," Trace said to Breintz.

"I'm not going without Caitlin."

"I'll get her." Trace shoved Flynn in Breintz's direction. "You're the key. If they get their hands on you again, none of us is going to make it."

"She's my child." Weariness and despair had frozen into icy determination. "I won't leave her behind."

"You're her brother, all right," Trace muttered. And time was running out. He shoved a rifle into Flynn's hands. "Can you use it?"

Flynn felt a ray of hope bloom like a sunrise. "With pleasure."

"Say a prayer to whatever gods work best," Trace told Breintz.

"I already have."

Gillian heard the door open and lay as silent and still as Caitlin. The child had truly fallen asleep, a natural sleep. Gillian gripped the pitiful weapon in her hand. During the hour she'd lain in the dark, she'd tried to accept that Trace was gone. They'd discovered the deception, killed him and kidnapped her.

She wanted to mourn for him, to grieve, to rage. But first she would have her revenge, and her family's freedom.

With her eyes half open, she saw the man bend over her. Gillian held her breath and swung. The edge of the plate caught him full force on the bridge of the nose. She heard the grinding break, saw the spurt of blood. While he was blinded by it, she lifted the other plate and struck again. He staggered but grabbed at her arm as he went. Though her arm twisted painfully, she remembered what her neighbor in New York had told her.

Go for the eyes.

This time he yelped. The butt of his gun slammed into her side as he tried to bring it into place. And then she was fighting for her life.

It was through a red wave of fear and fury that she heard Caitlin begin to whimper. As she had in the nightmare. At the sound of it, Gillian fought like a madwoman. She gripped the rifle. So did he. It exploded with the most terrible sound she'd ever heard.

Then she was standing, holding it, and the man, whose face she had never seen, was at her feet.

"Aunt Gillian!" Caitlin climbed out of bed to grasp Gillian's legs. "Is he dead? The bad man, is he dead?"

"I think—I don't know." She swayed, as though the drug had taken over again. "I don't know. We have to go. We have to go now."

Then she heard the gunfire, close and coming closer. Shoving the child behind her, Gillian lifted the rifle again. Her hands were slick with sweat as she prepared to protect her own.

They'd found the first guard faster than Trace had counted on. The alarm was out, and if it hadn't been for luck and a brutal frontal attack they would have been cornered. They'd reached the second level.

"I'll hold them here." Breintz took his position behind a column at the top of the stairs. "Find the woman and the child."

Trace switched to the grenade launcher and sent three over the rail. "Keep down," he ordered Flynn, and began to move. He broke open a half-dozen doors, then saw the one that was already open. With his back pressed against the wall, he gripped the gun in both hands and took two deep breaths before swinging into the opening, prepared to fire. Gillian's bullet grazed his left shoulder. He was too shocked to feel the sting.

"Good God, woman."

"Trace!" With the gun lowered, she sprang forward. "Oh, Trace, I thought you were dead."

"Damn near." He brushed his fingers over his sleeve, disgusted when they came away red.

"Flynn." With a sob, she fell against him.

"Da!" Caitlin flew across the room and was scooped up by her father.

"Family reunions later," Trace told them. "Let's move. Breintz!" Trace sent another few rounds into the first level to cover the agent. "Get them out. I'll keep everyone busy." He unhooked the Uzi he'd taken off one of the guards. "Fifteen minutes," he said between his teeth. "Send it up in fifteen minutes."

"I would prefer to see you again."

"Yeah." Trace swiped sweat from under his eyes. He dashed back toward the stairs, sending bullets flying, before Gillian realized what he was doing.

"No! No, he can't!"

But he could. Gillian knew that he had to face his destiny, just as she did. "I'm sorry, Flynn." She kissed him quickly. "I have to stay with him. Go quickly." Then she was racing behind Trace.

He set off a series of explosions that not only cleared the stairs but nearly obliterated them. He was halfway down when he heard the noise at his back. For the second time, he turned on Gillian.

"What in the name of God—?"

"You know they have a better chance if we separate. I'm staying with you. That was the deal."

It was too late to send her back. If he'd had even seconds to spare, he would have shouted at her. Instead, he grabbed her arm and hauled her along with him.

They'd caused considerable damage, Trace saw with satisfaction. And more confusion. The general was out, waving and firing the TS-35. As he furthered the damage to his headquarters and added to the casualty toll among his own men, he ordered them to stand and fight the army of invaders. The unexpected attack appeared to have cut the bonds on his last hold on sanity. Trace lifted his gun. The general fell before he pressed the trigger.

"Fool." Kendesa stood over the gold-cloaked body. "Your time has passed." Bending, he retrieved the American-made weapon. "What you have cost us." He whirled to shout at the scattering soldiers. "To the front entrance, idiots!" he ordered. "Bar the front entrance!"

Too late, Trace thought grimly as he stepped out from cover. "You've lost, Kendesa. And the fool is you for believing that the woman duped me when it was I who duped you."

"Cabot."

"When it suits me."

Kendesa's expression changed. "Il Gatto, at last."

"Definitely at last. Our business is finished, Kendesa, and this is personal."

Perhaps he would have killed him where he stood. He'd been prepared to. But before it could be put to the test, the general raised his handgun. "Traitor." He wheezed as he fired. Kendesa staggered back, but didn't fall. Again Trace aimed.

This time, heaven interfered.

The ground shook, violently. Trace's first thought was that Breintz had set the charges early. He grabbed Gillian's hand and started to run. Another tremor had them both ramming into the rock wall.

"Earthquake," Trace said as he fought for breath. "A real one. The whole place is going to go."

"They got out, didn't they?"

"They had time." It was all the hope he could give her.

They raced down one passage, only to have it cave

in in front of them. Gillian heard screams as the dust blinded her. Without pausing for breath, Trace pulled her down another. "There's got to be more than one way out. We won't make it to the front." Again he went with instinct and headed for the general's quarters. "He'd have an escape route," he said as he blasted the lock off the door. Pulling Gillian inside, he went for the obvious. "Look for a button, a mechanism," he shouted as he searched the bookcase. He could hear stone falling from great heights. Something was burning, and the fire was close. With both hands, he shoved aside books. Then he found it. The panel slid out.

The corridor beyond was narrow and vibrated from the tremors underground. But it was unguarded. Praying his luck was still holding, he shoved her through. In seconds they were out in the night.

Men ran and shouted, scattering. Behind them the building was splitting apart, huge chucks of rock tumbling down with a noise that seemed impossible. Then the noise grew greater with the first explosion. Without bothering with cover, Trace ran. No one came after them.

It seemed to Gillian that they ran for miles. He never let her stop to rest, and she didn't ask to. Then, like a shadow, Breintz rose from a rock.

"So we do meet again."

"Looks like." Trace dragged Gillian over the rocks to the makeshift camp.

"The gods made it unnecessary for me to complete our plan." With his usual calm, Breintz handed Trace night-vision glasses. Lifting them, Trace focused in the direction they had come from.

"Not much left."

"And Kendesa?"

"The general took care of him." Trace lowered the glasses again. "If not, your gods did. Hammer's smashed." He handed the glasses back. "Looks like a promotion for you."

"And you."

"I'm finished." He sat with his back to a rock and watched Gillian gather her family to her.

"I owe you." Flynn sat with his daughter curled on his lap and his sister close against his side.

"Just doing a job."

"In any case, I owe you. You have a name?"

Trace accepted the bottle Breintz handed him. The long swig he took had a kick he could have lived on for a week. "O'Hurley."

"Thank you, O'Hurley, for my daughter."

Caitlin reached up to whisper in her father's ear. Then, at his murmur, she rose and walked to Trace. "My da says you saved us."

"Sort of." She was thinner than in the snapshot, and her eyes were too big in her pale face. Unable to resist, Trace reached up and tugged on one of her tangled red locks. "It's all done now."

"Can I hug you?"

Nonplussed, he shifted his shoulders. "Yeah, sure."

She cuddled against him and, with the resilience of childhood, giggled. "You smell," she said, not unkindly. "I guess I smell, too."

"Some."

As she pressed a wet kiss to his cheek, he held her, and his eyes drifted to Gillian.

"Just little pieces," she murmured to him. "All we can change are little pieces. But it's worth it." Because she was afraid she would weep, she rose to walk a little way into the shadows. She heard him come up behind her.

"I know you want to know how I got there and what happened, but I can't talk about it now."

"All right. It's all right." He started to reach for her hair, then dropped his hand again. "We have to get going. There'll be a plane in Sefrou to fly us to Madrid. The ISS will take care of you."

"I thought they'd killed you." It was anger, rather than tears, that sparkled her eyes as she turned. "I thought you were dead, and all you can talk about is planes and the ISS?"

Trace touched the blood drying on his shoulder. "The only hit I took was from you."

"Oh, God, I'd forgotten." She came to him quickly. "I might have killed you."

"Not with that aim."

"You're wrong." She wiped the back of her hand over her mouth. "I killed a man. With my own hands." She looked down at them now and shuddered. "I didn't even see his face, but I killed him."

"And you think you can't live with that." He cupped her chin in his hand so that she would look at him. Her face was filthy, and there was blood on it from a scrape along her cheekbone. "You can, Gillian. You can live with a lot of things. Believe me, I know."

"Trace, would you do something for me? One more thing?"

"Maybe."

Still cautious, she thought, and almost laughed. "If it wouldn't put you out too much, would you hold me? I don't want to cry, and if you hold me I won't."

"Come here," he murmured, and wrapped his arms

around her. It was over, he thought, and she was safe. Maybe, just maybe, they had some time. "Cry if you want. It doesn't hurt anything."

He was warm and hard against her, and the night was quiet again. "I don't need to now."

Chapter 12

"After everything we've been through, I don't understand how you can be nervous over this."

"Don't be ridiculous. I'm not nervous." Trace yanked at the knot of his tie again. As far as he was concerned, Cabot was dead, and the ties should have gone with him. "I don't know why in the hell I let you talk me into this."

Enormously pleased with herself, Gillian sat in the rented car as they drove away from the Los Angeles airport. "You gave me your word we could go anywhere I wanted after things were settled again. And where I wanted to go was your sister's wedding."

"A shabby trick, Doc, after I saved your life."

It was precisely because of that that she was determined to save his, or at least a small part of it. "A man's word is his bond," she said solemnly, then laughed when he swore at her. "Oh, Trace, don't be cranky. It's a beautiful day, and I don't think I've ever been happier in my life. Did you see how wonderful Flynn and Caitlin looked when we left them? I can hardly believe it's all over, really over."

He relented enough to put a hand over hers. "It's over. Your brother and the kid can go back to Ireland and put all this behind them. With Husad and Kendesa gone and Hammer's headquarters destroyed, they've got nothing to worry about."

"Addison wasn't pleased about the Horizon project being destroyed, or Flynn's refusal to try to duplicate it."

Trace gave a short laugh. Maybe he'd been wrong about scientists—or at least some of them. Fitzpatrick had stood toe-to-toe with Addison, turning aside offers, pleas, bribes and threats. Gillian had taken the same stand, saying nothing about her memory and leaving Addison and the ISS with a handful of doctored notes. For better or worse, Horizon was finished.

"Addison wasn't pleased about much. He grumbled for an hour over losing a crate of weapons, including a TS-35."

"I think he was more displeased to be losing one of his best agents."

Trace lifted a brow. "I don't think he'd put it that way."

"But he did, to me." She ran a hand down the skirt of her dress. She'd fallen in love with the rich green silk. It was a bit more elaborate than her usual style, but, after all, this was Chantel O'Hurley's wedding. "He was hoping I could convince you to stay 'on board,' as he put it."

It was hard not to feel a nasty little streak of satisfaction at that. "What did you tell him?"

"That he was mad as a hatter. Oh, look how tall the palms are. In New York it's probably cold and sleeting."

"I guess you miss it?"

"Miss what?" She turned to look at him. "New York? Oh, I haven't really thought about it. I suppose everyone at Random-Frye thinks I've dropped off the edge of the earth." She sighed, content. "In some ways I think I have."

"I guess Arthur Steward wonders."

"Dear old Arthur," Gillian said with a smile. "I suppose he might, at the odd moment." It didn't surprise or even annoy her that he knew about Arthur. After all, she knew about his squashed beetle. "I'll have to send him a postcard."

"You'll be back in a couple of days."

"I don't know. I haven't decided." She wasn't going back to New York, or anywhere else, without him. He just didn't know it yet. "What about you? Are you winging straight off to the islands?"

Why was it she could make him so uncomfortable when she smiled that way? It was as if she could see what he was thinking. Or trying not to think. "I've got some business to take care of in Chicago first." He paused for a moment, because he hadn't taken it all in yet. "For some reason, Charlie left me his house."

"I see." She smiled again, brilliantly. "So it seems you have a home after all."

"I don't know anything about real estate," he mumbled. They were in Beverly Hills now with its mansions and trimmed hedges. This was the kind of place his father had always dreamed of. The O'Hurleys had come up in the world, he thought. Or some of them had. He yanked at his tie again. "Listen, Doc, this is a dumb

idea. We can head back to the airport, take a flight to
New Zealand. It's beautiful there."

And at the other end of the world. Gillian resisted
the urge to lecture or comfort. "A promise is a promise," she said simply.

"I don't want to spoil this for Chantel, or the rest of
them."

"Of course you don't. That's why you're going."

"You don't understand, Gillian." And he'd never been
able to bring himself to explain it before. "My father's
never forgiven me for leaving. He never understood
why I had to. He wanted—I guess he needed for me to
be a part of the dream he had. The O'Hurley Family,
in big, bold lights. Broadway, Vegas, Carnegie Hall."

She was silent for a long moment. Then she spoke
quietly, without looking at him. "My father never forgave me, never understood me. He wanted me to be
one thing, and I was always another. Did your father
love you, Trace?"

"Sure he did, it was just—"

"My father never loved me."

"Gillian—"

"No, listen to me. There's a difference between love
and obligation, between true affection and expectation.
He didn't love me, and I can accept that. But what I can't
accept is that I never made peace with him. Now it's
too late." She looked at him now, and though her eyes
were dry they shone with emotion. "Don't make that
same mistake, Trace. I promise you, you'll regret it."

He could think of nothing to say, no argument to
give. He was here because he'd promised, but more,
because he'd wanted to come. The ideas, or maybe
he should call them dreams, that had begun to form

couldn't be brought to fruition until he'd resolved his life. He couldn't do that until he'd closed the rift with his family. With his father.

"This could be the biggest mistake you've ever made," he said as he pulled up to the gates guarding Chantel's estate.

"I'll risk it."

"You're a stubborn woman, Doc."

"I know." She touched his face. "I've got as much on the line as you do."

He wanted to ask her to explain, but a guard knocked smartly on his window. "You're early, sir," he said when Trace rolled down the window. "May I see your invitation?"

She hadn't thought of that, Gillian realized with a start. Before she could speak, Trace pulled out a badge. "McAllister, Special Security."

The ID looked official, because it was. The guard studied it, compared the laminated photo to Trace, then nodded. "Go right in, sir," he said, nearly snapping a salute.

Trace tooled through the gates and started up the long drive.

"McAllister?"

Trace slipped the ID back in his pocket. "Old habits die hard. Good God, what a place." The house was huge and white and elegant. The grounds were trimmed and rolling. He thought of the crowded hotel rooms they'd shared, the meals his father had cooked on hot plates, the airless dressing rooms, the audiences that snarled as often as they applauded. And the laughter. And the music.

"It's beautiful," Gillian murmured. "Like a picture."

"She always said she'd do it." The pride came through, deeper than he'd expected. "The little brat pulled it off."

"Spoken like a true brother," Gillian said with a laugh. She was helped from the car by a man in uniform, and was suddenly every bit as nervous as Trace. Maybe she should have made him come alone. She was hardly prepared to meet royalty, even the Hollywood variety. And his family might resent... As he came to her, she reached out a hand. "Trace, maybe I shouldn't."

The front door burst open and nearly cracked on its hinges. A woman with a wild mop of red curls and an exquisite dress of sapphire blue raced down the stairs. With something close to a war cry, she launched herself into Trace's arms.

"You're here! You're really here!" With her arms in a stranglehold around his neck and her mouth smothering his, Trace could do little more than absorb the scent and feel. "I knew you'd come. I didn't believe it, but I knew. And here you are."

"Maddy." Because he needed to catch his breath as much as he wanted to look at her, Trace drew her back by the shoulders. There were tears streaming down her face, but she was grinning. And the grin was exactly as he remembered. "Hi."

"Hi yourself." She pulled the handkerchief out of his pocket, blew her nose hard, then laughed. "Chantel will kill me if my nose is red." She blew again. "How do I look?"

"Terrible, but there's so little you can do with that face." With the laughter, they were close again. He held her and wished he could believe it would be so easy with everyone. "Maddy, I love you."

"I know, you jerk." Her breath hitched on a sob. "Stay this time?"

"Yeah." He brushed his cheek against her hair. "I'll stay this time." Looking over her head, he watched Gillian.

"I can't wait to show you off." Maddy drew back beaming, then glanced at Gillian. "Hi."

"Maddy, this is Gillian Fitzpatrick."

Still sniffling, Maddy turned. "I'm so glad to meet you." Gillian found herself enclosed in the same exuberant hug. "In fact, I'm thrilled." She drew away far enough to wink, then squeezed Gillian again. "You look wonderful, both of you, just wonderful." She slipped an arm around each of them and started up the stairs. "I can't wait for you to meet Reed. Oh, here he is now."

Coming down the hall was a leanly built man with hair shades darker than Trace's and more conservatively cut. He looked as if he'd been born in the tux. So this was Reed Valentine of Valentine Records. Rich, well-bred and straight-line. Thinking of his free-spirited, unconventional sister, Trace decided he could have come up with no one less suited to her.

"Reed, it's Trace." Maddy gave Trace another quick kiss, then dashed to her husband. "I told you he'd be here."

"So you did." Reed slipped a protective arm around Maddy and sized up the brother even as the brother sized up the husband. "Maddy's been looking forward to seeing you again." With his arm still around Maddy, he offered a hand. Trace took it. It wasn't as smooth as he'd expected.

"Congratulations."

"Thank you."

"Oh, don't be stuffy, Reed. We have to kill the fat-ted calf, at least."

Reed saw the expression on Trace's face and smiled. "I have a feeling Trace might prefer a drink." He turned a smile of considerable charm on Gillian. "Hello."

"Oh, I'm sorry," Maddy began. "This is Gillian. She's with Trace. We should go in and sit down, and I'll find everyone. Things are a little confused."

To prove it, two boys raced down the hall, one in oblivious and desperate pursuit of the other. "I'm going to tell Mom."

"I'm going to tell her first."

"Whoa!" Maddy grabbed an arm each before they could come to blows. "Slow down. You'll have those cute little tuxedos filthy before we can start the wedding."

"He said I looked like a geek," the smaller of the two said.

"He kicked me," the older said righteously.

"I *tried* to kick him, only I missed." He looked across at his brother, hoping he'd have another chance.

"Kicking's not allowed. And, Chris, you do not look like a geek. In fact, you look very handsome. Now, can you behave long enough to meet your uncle?"

"What uncle?" Ben, the oldest, looked up suspi-ciously.

"The only one you haven't met. Trace, this is Ben, and this is Chris. Abby's boys."

He wasn't sure whether he should shake hands, crouch down or wave from a distance. Before he could make up his mind, Chris stepped forward to give him a good study.

"You're the one who went away. Mom said you've been to Japan."

So crouching down seemed natural. "Yeah, I've been there."

"We studied about it in school. They eat raw fish there."

"Sometimes." Good God, he thought, he could see himself in the boy, just as he saw Abby's solemn eyes in the brother.

"Did *you*?" Chris wanted to know.

"Sure I did."

Chris made a face. He couldn't have been more pleased. "That's gross. Dad—that's Dylan—took us fishing, but I wouldn't clean them."

"I did," Ben said, tired of being left out. He shouldered Chris out of the way to get a good look for himself. "I liked the spaceship model you sent me. It was neat."

"I'm glad you liked it." Trace wanted to ruffle the boy's hair, but figured it was too soon.

"He only lets me play with it if I beg and beg," Chris put in.

"That's because you're a geek."

"Am not!"

Ben started to launch into a full-scale exchange of insults, then clammed up when he recognized the sound of footsteps.

"Trouble?" Dylan said mildly as he stepped into the hall.

"Dad, we've got another uncle, and he's here." Delighted to be in charge, Chris grabbed Trace's hand and dragged him forward. "This is Uncle Trace. This is my dad. We changed our name to Crosby and everything."

So this was the brother no one knew very much about. Dylan's writer's instincts were humming. "Glad you could make it. Abby's always showing the boys where you've been on Ben's globe. You get around."

"Some." Trace was pleased enough to meet the brother-in-law, but he was wary of the journalist.

"He eats raw fish," Chris supplied. "Hey, Mom, guess who's here?"

Abby came from the direction of the kitchen, her dancer's legs still graceful beneath the deep rose dress that draped over the child she carried. Her dark blond hair swung loosely at her shoulders. "The caterers want me to tell certain greedy little fingers to keep out of the canapés. I wonder who they might mean." Her brow was lifted as she smiled at her husband. Then, looking past him, she saw Trace.

"Oh." Her eyes, always expressive, filled as she opened her arms. "Oh, Trace."

"Mom's crying," Ben murmured as he watched his mother being held by this man he'd only heard about.

"Because she's happy," Dylan told him, placing a hand on his shoulder. "Imagine if you didn't see Chris for a long, long time." Ben considered it, and a gleam came into his eyes. "Monster." With a laugh, Dylan ruffled his hair.

"It's such a surprise. Such a terrific surprise."

Trace brushed a tear from her cheek. "Maddy already stole my handkerchief."

"It doesn't matter. How did you get here? Where did you come from? I've so many questions. Give me another hug."

"This is Gillian," Maddy announced, though Gillian had done her best to stay in the background. "She brought him." At Trace's lifted brow, Maddy grinned. "I mean, he brought her."

"Whichever way, hello." Though she sensed some intrigue, it could wait. Abby kissed both of Gillian's cheeks. "I'm glad you're here, both of you. And I can't wait to see Chantel's face."

"Why wait?" With a laugh, Maddy hooked an arm through Trace's. "She's upstairs making herself more beautiful."

"Nothing changes," Trace commented.

"Not much. Come on. Gillian, you, too. Chantel will want to meet you."

"Maybe I should—"

"Don't be silly." Abby cut off her protest and took her hand. "This is a once-in-a-lifetime."

"Dylan and I will...check on Quinn," Reed said.

"Thanks." Maddy threw him a smile as she climbed the stairs.

"I wonder how Pop's going to react," Dylan murmured.

"That's something I don't want to miss. Come on, boys, let's see how the bridegroom is holding up."

With her usual flair for the dramatic, Maddy rapped on Chantel's door.

"I don't want to see anyone unless they have a bottle of champagne."

"This is better." Maddy opened the door and stuck her head inside. "Abby and I brought you a wedding present."

"At the moment, I'd prefer the champagne. I'm a nervous wreck."

"This'll take your mind off it." With a flourish, Maddy pushed the door wide.

Chantel sat at her dressing table in a long white robe,

her crown of pale-blond hair done up in intricate coils.
She saw Trace in the mirror and turned very slowly.

"Well, well," she said in her dark, alluring voice.
"Look what the cat dragged in." She rose to look at him.

She was every bit as beautiful as he remembered.
Perhaps more. And was undoubtedly every bit as hard
a nut to crack. "You look pretty good, kid."

"I know." She tilted her head. "You don't look too
bad. A little rough around the edges, maybe."

He stuck his hands in his pockets. "Nice house."

"We like it." Then she let out a long breath. "Bastard. There goes my makeup." He met her halfway and
swung her in one long circle. "I'm so glad you're here,
and I hate you for making me cry so I look like a hag
for my wedding."

"A hag?" He drew her away. "Fat chance."

"Trace." She brushed the hair from his forehead.
"We always knew the day would come, but you couldn't
have picked a better one. God, don't you even have a
handkerchief?"

"Maddy took it."

"Figures." She used the heel of her hand.

"This is Gillian." Maddy all but shoved her into the
room.

"Oh?" Always cautious, Chantel lifted a brow. "How
do you do?"

"I don't want to disturb you." Chantel's brow lifted
a little higher at the accent, and a smile came into her
eyes. "I think I should go down or—"

"She's with Trace," Abby put in.

"Is she really?" In the way of triplets, the sisters
communicated the rest. "Well, isn't that nice? Excellent
taste, Trace." She took both of Gillian's hands. "Sorry

I can't say as much for yours, but champagne is definitely in order."

"I'll get it."

"For heaven's sake, Maddy, I'll have one of the servants bring it. You can't go traipsing up and down the stairs in your condition. Take everyone into the sitting room down the hall. Quinn's barred from this wing, so I'm not risking any bad luck. I'll be there as soon as I fix my face again." She put a hand on Trace's arm. "Stay, please."

"Sure." He shot a look at Gillian, but she was already being washed away in the wave of his sisters.

"We missed you," she said when they were alone. "Is everything all right?"

"Yeah, why?"

With her hands in his, Chantel sat with him on the bed. "I guess I always figured you'd come home in absolute triumph or absolute destitution."

He had to laugh. "Sorry, it's neither."

"I won't ask what you've been doing, but I have to ask if you're staying."

"I don't know." He thought of Gillian. "I wish I did."

"All right. You're here today. I hate to be sloppy, but I can't tell you how much it means to me."

"You start crying again, you will look like a hag."

"I know. You always were a pain in the—"

"Chantel, Reed said you needed me. I've been trying to keep your father from fighting with the—" Molly paused halfway into the room.

He'd thought he'd prepared himself to see her again. She looked older, but not old. Changed, but somehow constant. She'd scolded him and comforted him, walloped him and soothed him. Whatever was needed. He felt twelve years old as he stood and looked at her.

"Mom."

She didn't want to burst into tears. That would be a foolish thing before she'd said so much as a word. With the strength that had gotten her through years on the road, she took a deep breath. "Let me look at you." He was thin, but he always had been. Like his father. So like his father. "It's good to have you back." She took the next step and folded him in her arms. "Oh, Tracey, how good it is to have you back."

She smelled the same. She seemed smaller now, more delicate, but she smelled the same. He buried his face in her hair and let himself feel. "I missed you. Mom, I'm sorry."

"No regrets." She said it almost fiercely as she held on. "There's to be no regrets. And no questions." She drew away to smile at him. "At least not now. I'm going to dance with my son at my daughter's wedding." She held out a hand for Chantel. Some prayers *were* answered.

"Molly! In the name of all that's holy, where did you run off to? Those so-called musicians don't know a single Irish tune."

Molly felt Trace stiffen. "Don't repeat mistakes," she said with a sternness he remembered well.

"What's the matter with that girl, hiring a bunch of idiots? Molly, where the devil are you?"

He bounced into the room the way he bounced through life. Sure of himself and on the edge of a dance. It was rare for Frank O'Hurley's feet to falter, but they did when he saw his son.

"I have to see about champagne," Chantel said

quickly. "Mom, there's someone I want you to meet. Come let me introduce you."

Molly stopped at the door and looked into her husband's eyes. "I've loved you all my life," she said quietly. "And will no matter what foolish thing you do. Don't disappoint me, Frank."

Frank cleared his throat as the door shut behind him. A man shouldn't feel awkward with his own son. But he couldn't help it. "We didn't know you were coming."

"I didn't know myself."

"Still footloose and fancy-free, are you, Trace?"

His spine stiffened. "So it seems."

"That's what you always wanted." It wasn't what he wanted to say, but the words came out before he could stop them.

"You never knew what I wanted." Damn, why did it have to be a repeat performance? "You never wanted to know. What you wanted was for me to be you, and I couldn't be."

"That's not true. I never wanted you to be anyone but yourself."

"As long as it fit your standards." Trace started to walk out, but then he remembered what Gillian had said. He had to make peace, or at least try. He stopped, still feet away from his father, and dragged a hand through his hair. "I can't apologize, I won't apologize, for being who I am, or for doing anything I've done. But I am sorry I've disappointed you."

"Wait a minute." Frank held up a hand. A moment before he'd been afraid he would lose Trace again, and he hadn't been sure he would be able to get him back. He'd had years to regret. "Who said I was disappointed? I never said I was disappointed. What I was was angry, and hurt, but you never disappointed me. I won't have you saying it."

"What do you want me to say?"

"You had your say once, twelve years ago. Now I'll have mine." His chin was jutted out. He, too, wore a tux, but on him it looked like a stage costume. Trace would have bet his last nickel there were taps on the bottoms of his shoes. He hoped there were.

"All right, but before you do, I want you to know I didn't come to spoil Chantel's wedding. If we can't do anything else, I'd like to call a truce for one day."

The calm strength surprised Frank. His boy had grown up. Pride and regret pulled him in opposite directions. "It's not a war I want with you, Tracey. It never was." Frank pushed a hand through his hair in a gesture that surprised Trace because it mirrored one of his own habits "I—I needed you." He stumbled on the words, then cleared his throat. "You were my first, and I needed you to be proud of me, to look up to me like I had all the answers. And when you wanted to find your own, I didn't want to listen. Knowing I was a failure to you—"

"No." Appalled, Trace took the first step forward. "You never were, you couldn't be."

"You sent your mother money."

"Because I wasn't around to give anything else."

The old wound remained, gnawing. "I never gave you—any of you—the things I promised."

"We never needed things, Pop."

But Frank shook his head. "A man's meant to provide for his family, to pass some legacy on to his son. God knows I never gave your mother half of what she deserved. The promises were too big. When you left, saying what you said, I had to be bitter. Because if I stopped being bitter, I couldn't have stood knowing I wasn't the father you wanted, or being without you."

"You've always been the father I wanted. I didn't think…" Trace let out a long breath, but it didn't steady his voice. "I didn't think you wanted me back."

"There's not a day that's gone by I haven't wanted you back, but I didn't know how to tell you. Hell, didn't know where you were most of the time. I drove you away, Tracey, I know that. Now you've come back a man and I've lost all those years."

"There are plenty more. For both of us."

Frank put his hands on his son's broad shoulders. "When you leave, I don't want it to be in anger. And I want you to know that just by looking at you here, I'm proud of what you've made yourself."

"I love you, Pop." For the first time in twelve years, he embraced his father. "I want to stay." He closed his eyes because the words brought such tremendous relief. "I need you. I need all of you. It's taken me too long to figure that out." He drew away. "I want my father back."

"Ah, Tracey, I've missed having you." Frank reached for his own handkerchief and blew smartly. "Damn girl ought to keep a bottle in here."

"We'll find one, Pop." Trace looked into his father's damp blue eyes. "I've always been proud of you. What you gave me was the best. I just had to see what I could do with it on my own."

"This time, my boy, we kill the fatted calf." He put his arm around Trace's shoulder. "And we'll have that drink, you and me. When this hoopla of your sister's is over, I might even risk your mother's temper and get a little drunk. A man's entitled to celebrate when he's given a son."

"I'm buying."

Frank's damp eyes sparkled. "That's my boy. Made a bundle, did you? And you saw all those places you wanted to see?"

"More than I wanted to see," Trace said and smiled. "I even sang for my supper a time or two."

"Of course you did." Fresh pride burst through him. "You're an O'Hurley, aren't you?" He gave Trace a slap on the back. "Always had a better voice than you had feet, but that's no matter. I expect you've got stories to tell." He winked as they started out. "Start with the women."

That hadn't changed, either. Though he hadn't expected it, it made him glad. "It might take a while."

"We've got time." He had his son back. "Plenty of it."

They were halfway down the stairs when Trace saw another tuxedoed figure. "I'll check it out," the man said into a phone with his back to the stairs.

"Quinn, my boy." Frank's call could have brought down the roof. "I want you to meet my son, Trace."

Quinn turned. He and Trace stared at each other. The shock of recognition came, but it didn't show. "Nice to meet you." Quinn held out a hand. "I'm sure Chantel's thrilled you're here."

"It's interesting meeting all my in-laws in one fell swoop."

"We need a drink," Frank announced. "Guests'll be trooping in before we know it." And he was going to show off his family. All his family.

"Pour me a double." Trace patted his father's shoulder. "I'll be right with you."

"We'll make it a quick one for now. I still have to straighten out those musicians."

"Small world," Quinn commented when they were alone.

Trace shook his head, studying the man who had once, in his early days with the ISS, been his partner. "It's been a while."

"Afghanistan was what—eight, ten years ago?"

"That's the ballpark. So you're going to marry Chantel."

"Come hell or high water."

"Does she know what you do?"

"I don't do it anymore." Quinn pulled out his cigarettes and offered one. "I've got my own security business. You?"

"Recently retired." Trace pulled out matches. "I'll be damned."

"You know, I'm amazed I didn't put it together, O'Hurley."

"We weren't using names in that operation, not real ones."

"Yeah, but the thing is, you look more like her than either of her sisters."

Trace blew out a long stream of smoke and laughed. "If you don't want to sleep on the couch for the next six months, I wouldn't mention that to her."

The O'Hurleys overwhelmed her. Gillian had never met anyone like them. She found herself sitting with the family as Chantel was married in the warm California winter under a white silk canopy while some five hundred guests looked on. There was champagne by the bucket, flowers by the truckload, and tears enough to swim in.

For hours she was caught up in the whirlwind they created until, head spinning, she sought out a quiet spot to let it all settle. She wasn't sure it was quite proper for her to slip into the parlor, but the music was muted here. And she could put her feet up.

"Sneaking out?"

With a gasp, she pressed a hand to her heart. "You scared the life out of me." She relaxed again as Trace came to sit beside her. "You shouldn't creep up behind a person."

"I've been doing it for years." He stretched his own legs out. "Feet hurt?" he asked as he looked at her discarded shoes.

"I feel like I've danced my toes off. Doesn't your father ever slow down?"

"Not that I've ever noticed." God, it was good to be back.

Gillian snuggled back against the pillows. "He likes me."

"Of course he does. You're Irish. Then there's the fact that you can do a fairly adequate jig."

"Fairly adequate?" She sat up straight again. "I'll have you know, O'Hurley, your father said I could go on the road with him and your mother anytime I wanted."

"Packing your trunk?"

She sat back again with a sigh. "I don't think I could keep up with either of them. They're all wonderful. Every one of them. Thank you for bringing me."

"I think I've figured out who brought whom." He lifted her hand and kissed her palm, leaving her speechless. "Thank you, Gillian."

"I love you. I just wanted you to be happy."

When he let her hand go again, she curled her fingers into the palm he'd kissed. "You said that before." Rising, he walked to the window. From there he could see the tables ladened with food and wine and hundreds of people milling around and dancing.

"That I wanted you to be happy?"

"That you loved me."

"Did I?" Very casual, she studied her nails. "Isn't that interesting? As I recall, you didn't have much of a reaction then, either."

"I had things on my mind."

"Oh, yes, saving my brother and Caitlin. We haven't quite finished there." She reached in her purse and drew out a piece of paper. Standing, she offered it to him. "The hundred thousand we agreed on. I had my lawyers send the check." When he didn't move, she walked over and pushed it into his hand. "It's certified. I promise it won't bounce."

He wanted to jam the check down her pretty throat. "Fine."

"Our business is over, then. You've got your retirement fund, a house, your family." She turned away, knowing she was very close to murder. "So where do you go from here, Trace? Straight to the islands?"

"Maybe." He crumpled the check and jammed it in his pocket. "I've been thinking."

"Now *there's* good news."

"Watch your mouth. Better yet, just shut up." He took her by the shoulders and kissed her hard. As he hadn't, Gillian thought, in much too long.

The door opened. Abby took one step in and stopped.

"Oh, excuse me. Sorry." Just as quickly, she was gone again.

Trace swore lightly. "Maybe you *are* in love with me. And maybe you're plain stupid."

"Maybe." This time she swore, too, and made his brow lift. "Maybe I'd like to know how you feel."

"We're not talking about how I feel."

"Oh, I see."

Before she could move away he had her close again. It was amazing how quickly panic could come to someone who'd lived his life one step ahead of danger. "Don't turn away from me."

She gave him a straight, level look. "I'm not the one who's doing the turning, Trace."

She had him there. And, damn it, his palms were damp again. "Listen, I don't know how attached you are to New York, to that place you work. I could sell the house in Chicago if it didn't suit."

She felt the gurgle of laughter—or triumph—but swallowed it cautiously. "Didn't suit what?"

"Didn't suit, damn it. Gillian, I want—"

This time Maddy burst through the door and halfway into the room. "Oh, hi." At the expression on Trace's face, she rolled her eyes. "You didn't see me," she said as she began to back out. "I never came in. I was never here. Now I'm gone." And she was.

"Some things never change," Trace muttered. "I never in my life had a minute's privacy with those three around."

"Trace." Gillian put a hand on his cheek and shifted his face back toward hers. "Are you asking me to marry you?"

"I'd like to muddle through this in my own way, if you don't mind."

"Of course." Very solemn, she sat on the window seat. "Please go on."

Did she think one of her long, quiet looks was going to make it easy for him? He could write down how he felt, he could put it to music. The words would come then. But now, just now, he was fresh out.

"Gillian, I think you're making a big mistake, but if you're set on it, we could try it. I've got some ideas about what to do with myself now that the ISS is history." His hands were in his pockets again, because he didn't know what else to do with them. "Maybe I could pitch some of my songs—but that's not really the point," he went on before she could speak. "The point is whether or not you could handle—that you'd be willing to— You know, you really have no business getting tangled up with me."

"This time you shut up."

"Wait a minute—"

"Just shut up and come over here." He scowled, but crossed over to her. "Sit," she said, then gestured to the seat beside her. She waited until he sat down, then took his hands. "Now, I'll tell you exactly what the point is. I love you, Trace, with all my heart, and I want nothing more than to spend my life with you. It doesn't matter where. The house in Chicago is special, I know, and there are laboratories in the Midwest. What I have to know is that you'd be content. I won't start the rest of my life by holding you down."

There was no one else like her. And there would never be anyone else for him. He wished he had the right words just now, something soft and sweet. One day, he thought, they might come easily.

"I told you when we first met that I was tired. That's the truth. I don't need to climb mountains anymore, Gillian. I already know what's at the top. I'll probably be a lousy husband, but I'll give you the best I've got."

"I know that." She took his face in her hands and kissed him lightly. "Why do you want to marry me, Trace?"

"I love you." It was a great deal easier to say than he had thought. "I love you, Gillian, and I've waited a hell of a long time to make a home."

She rested her head on his shoulder. "We'll make one together."

* * * * *

HARLEQUIN
PLUS

Try the best multimedia
subscription service for romance
readers like you!

Read, Watch and Play.

Experience the easiest way to get
the romance content you crave.

Start your **FREE TRIAL** at
<u>www.harlequinplus.com/freetrial</u>.